Please turn to the back of the book
for an interview with Alice
Borchardt.

519 - 389 - 3935

"A VERY VIVIDLY WRITTEN STORY. I REALLY GOT INTO IT."
—MARION ZIMMER BRADLEY
Author of the *New York Times* bestseller *The Mists of Avalon*

*Please turn the page
for more reviews....*

"SENSUAL, HAUNTING, VIVID, EROTIC, HYPNOTIC . . . DARK, LYRICAL, AND PASSIONATE . . .

Every single Anne Rice fan in the world is going to want to read this book . . . A huge novel packed full of decadently intriguing characters, heart-wrenching romance, and sublime sensuality the likes of which I haven't read since A. N. Roquelaure's *Beauty* trilogy. I was crying like a baby when I finished this book. Great ending! I loved it!"

—*Explorations*

"Borchardt has written a winner . . . This is fantasy at its best . . . Vivid and engaging . . . *The Silver Wolf* is a richly textured, lush epic of history, romance, and fantasy, all interwoven like a beautiful tapestry. This is a novel not to be missed . . . Like *The Vampire Lestat* . . . [*The Silver Wolf*] is ripe and delicious in its panoramic view of history and the fantastic beings who inhabit it . . . I loved this book, and for those who relish a swashbuckling story of the supernatural, Alice Borchardt delivers. Her history is colorful and lively, and her supernatural love story is enchanting. Highly recommended."

—Douglas Clegg
barnesandnoble.com

By Alice Borchardt

DEVOTED
BEGUILED
THE SILVER WOLF*

*Published by The Ballantine Publishing Group

THE
SILVER
WOLF

Alice Borchardt

BALLANTINE BOOKS • NEW YORK

A Ballantine Book
Published by The Ballantine Publishing Group
Copyright © 1998 by Alice Borchardt

www.randomhouse.com/BB/

Library of Congress Catalog Card Number: 98-93999

ISBN 0-345-42361-5

Printed in Canada

First Hardcover Edition: July 1998
First Mass Market Edition: June 1999

10 9 8 7 6 5 4 3 2 1

TO
MY BELOVED HUSBAND
CLIFFORD BORCHARDT
"See those fireflies dancing? That's what I want to do:
dance in the moonlight, sing
to the stars, jump straight up at the moon."
I did with you.

I

THE SUN WAS GOING DOWN. THE FIERY CIRCLE shone past the acanthus-crowned columns of a ruined temple. They cut the incandescent ball into slices of red radiance. *Almost night,* the girl thought, then shivered in the chill autumn air blowing through the unglazed casement.

The window was barred—heavily barred. One set running horizontally, the other vertically. The bars were bolted into the stone walls of the tiny room.

She knew she could close the window. Reach out through the bars. Pull the heavy shutters shut, and seal them with the iron bolt. But she pushed the idea out of her mind with a sort of blind obstinacy. The sight of freedom, even an unattainable freedom, was too sweet to give up.

Not yet, she told herself, *only a little longer. Not yet.*

The air that raised gooseflesh on her arms was sweet to her nostrils. Oh no, more than sweet. A speaking thing. Each vagrant increase in flow, each slight change in direction, each passing movement sent images to the deepest part of her mind.

Somewhere a patch of thyme bloomed. The tiny blue flowers let down their fragrance into the chill evening air. This delicate scent was mixed with the heavy smell of wet marble and granite. These and many others stood out against the tapestry of odors given off by the flowers and greenery that cloaked the ruined palaces and temples of the ancient imperium.

The vast restless spirit of this, the greatest of all empires, seemed at last brought to rest at the soft hand of the great green mother herself.

Regeane didn't know what she'd expected of the once-proud

mistress of the world when she'd come to Rome. Certainly not what she found.

The inhabitants, descendants of a race of conquerors, lived like rats squabbling and polluting the ruins of an abandoned palace. Oblivious to the evidence of grandeur all around them, they fought viciously among themselves for what wealth remained. Indeed, little was left of the once-vast river of gold that flowed into the eternal city. The gold that could be found gilded the palms of papal officials and the altars of the many churches.

Regeane's mother, desperate to save—as she saw it—her daughter's soul, pawned what few jewels she had left. The money was sufficient to pay the bribes necessary to obtain a papal audience and finance the equally expensive papal blessing.

Regeane had gone into the awesome presence, her body drenched in a sweat of terror. If her ailing mother said the wrong thing to the church's leading prelate, she might find herself being burned or stoned as a witch. But as she approached the supreme pontiff, she realized just how foolish her fears had been.

The man before her was a ruin. Ready to be taken by age and sorrow. She doubted if he understood much of anything said to him. Weeping, her mother implored the intercession of God's chief minister on earth with the Almighty. As the ever-dutiful Regeane knelt, kissed the silken slipper, and felt the withered hands pressed against her hair she caught a whiff of a scent other than the thick smell of incense and Greek perfume that pervaded the room: the musty, dry smell of aging flesh and human decay.

God, it was powerful. *He is ready to die,* she thought. *He will go speak on Mother's behalf to God in person very soon.* She knew this blessing, as all other blessings her mother, Gisela, had traveled so far and squandered so much of her wealth to gain, would do no good.

This was the end. Regeane knew it. She was frightened. If the pope himself could not lift this strange gesa from her and let her live as a woman, to what earthly power could she turn? More to the point, to what power could her mother turn?

Gisela was fading as quickly as the only-too-human man on

the chair of Peter. Though a comparatively young woman, she was worn down by the string of fruitless journeys she had taken with Regeane and by some secret sorrow that seemed to fill her mind and heart with a bottomless wellspring of grief.

Regeane lied. Her mother believed. And for the first time in many years, Regeane felt the tiny woman who had traveled so far and borne so many burdens was at peace. Regeane's lie carried Gisela through till the end.

Three days after the papal audience she had gone to awaken her mother and found Gisela would never wake again. Not in this world.

Regeane was alone.

She watched with greedy eyes as the sun became a half circle, faded into a glow silhouetting the tall cypresses of the Appian Way, followed by the deep blue autumn twilight. Then, and only then, did she turn from the window and wrap herself in an old woolen mantle and return to her pallet bed. With the exception of the low bed and a small, covered, brown terra-cotta pot in the corner, the room was bare.

Regeane sat on her bed, her shoulders against the stone wall, her legs dangling, head thrown back, eyes closed. She waited silently for moonrise. The silver disc would be lifting itself above the seven hills now. Soon, very soon, its journey across the sky would bring it to her window where it would throw a pool of silver light on the floor. Ignoring the crosshatched black lines of bars, she could drink at that pool. Allowed once more to breathe, if not to glory, in the air of freedom.

The door to the outer room slammed shut. *Damnation.* The girl on the bed scoured her mind for oaths. *No . . . curses.* Young girl that she was, she was never allowed to speak them, but she could think the words. And she often did. Oh, how she did when those two were present. There were worse things than loneliness. Overall, Regeane felt she preferred silence and emptiness to the presence of either her Uncle Gundabald or Hugo, his son.

"I pissed blood again this morning," Hugo whined. "Are all the whores in this city diseased?"

Gundabald laughed uproariously. "All the ones you pick up seem to be. It's as I told you. Pay a little extra. Get yourself something young and clean. Or at least young, so all the itching and burning a few days later are worth it. That last you bought was so old, she had to ply her trade by starlight. What you save in cunt rent goes out in medicines for crotch rot."

"True enough," Hugo said irritably. "You always seem to do better."

Gundabald sighed. "I'm sick of trying to instruct you. Next time, retain at least a modicum of sobriety and get a look at her in a good light."

"Christ, it's cold in here," Hugo said angrily. A second later Regeane heard him shouting down the stairs for the landlord to bring a brazier to warm the room.

"It's no use, my boy," Gundabald told him. "She's left the window open again."

"I can't see how you stand it," Hugo grumbled. "She makes my skin crawl."

Gundabald laughed again. "There's nothing to worry about. Those planks are an inch thick. She can't get out."

"Has she ever . . . gotten out, I mean?" Hugo asked with fear in his voice.

"Oh, once or twice, I believe, when she was younger. Much younger. Before I took matters in hand. Gisela was too soft. That sister of mine was a fine woman—she always did as she was told—but weak, my boy, weak. Consider the way she wept over that first husband of hers when the marriage was so abruptly . . . terminated."

"She divorced him?" Hugo asked.

"Ah, yes," Gundabald sounded uneasy. "To be sure, she divorced him because we told her to. She had no choice in the matter. Even then, everyone could see Charles' mother was becoming a power at court. There were many well-endowed suitors for Gisela's hand. The second was a much better marriage and made us all wealthy."

"Now all that's gone," Hugo said bitterly. "Between you and Gisela, if our coffers have a miserable copper in them we're lucky. You wanted to rub shoulders with all the great magnates of the Frankish realm. To do that, you found out your shoulders had to be covered with velvet and brocade. And, oh yes, they wanted to be feasted. Worse than a horde of vultures, they swarmed over your household devouring everything in sight.

And like vultures when the carcass was picked clean, they departed in a cloud of stink and were never seen again.

"Whatever they missed, Gisela laid hands on, squandering it on relics, shrines, blessings, and pilgrimages, trying to lift the curse from that wretched brat of hers. You told me to get myself something younger. I've a good mind to pay that cousin of mine a visit . . . by day of course and—" Hugo screamed. "Father, you're hurting me!"

Gundabald's reply was a snarl of fury. "You so much as touch that girl and I'll save us both a lot of trouble and expense. I'll slice off your prick and balls. You'll be the smoothest eunuch between here and Constantinople. I swear it. She's the one and only asset we have left and she—*must*—marry. Hear me!"

Hugo howled again. "Yes, yes, yes. You're breaking my arm. Oh, God. Stop!"

Gundabald must have released him because Hugo's shouting ceased. When he did speak, he sniveled, "Who would marry that . . . thing?"

Gundabald laughed. "I can name a dozen right now, who would kill to marry her. The most royal blood of Franca flows through her veins. Her father and mother both were cousins of the great king himself."

"And those same ones who'd kill to marry her will run a sword through both you and the girl the moment they find out what she is."

"I cannot think how I got such a son as you as the fruit of my loins," Gundabald snarled. "But then your mother was a brainless little twit. Perhaps you take after her."

Despite the sadistic nastiness of Gundabald's voice, Hugo didn't rise to the bait. Most of the people around Gundabald quickly learned to fear him. Hugo was no exception.

"You liked the way we lived well enough when we were in funds. Vultures, eh! That's the pot calling the kettle black. You fucked all night, fed all day, and drank with the best of them. Now, you leave things you don't understand to your elders and betters. Shut up! And send for some food and wine—a lot of wine. I want my supper, and I want to forget what's behind that door in the next room."

"It was a mistake to bring her here," Hugo said. His voice was high and nervous. "She's worse than ever."

"Christ Jesus! God!" Gundabald roared. "Even a dumb animal has the sense to do what it's told. Dolt with the brains of a cobblestone! Shut up and at least get the wine. My God! I'm dying of thirst."

Marry, she thought listlessly. How could she marry? She didn't believe even a snake like Gundabald would connive at something so dangerous. Or succeed if he tried. Her mother still had a little land left in Franca, a few rundown villas. They generated only just enough money to feed and clothe the three of them. But nothing she was heir to would be enough to attract the attention of any of the great magnates of the Frankish realm.

As for her relationship to Charles—a king beginning already to be called the great—it was a rather distant connection to his mother. The dear lady, Bertrada, had never even for one moment acknowledged Regeane's existence. In fact, one of the things that endeared Bertrada to King Pepin the Short was that she was followed by a whole tribe of relations. They approached the court ready to swing their swords for church and king, not to mention their odd wagonload of loot that somehow didn't manage to fall into the king's treasury.

Regeane was very much lost in the crowd. She had nothing to offer. She was poor, a woman, and not beautiful. She didn't think there would be many takers for her hand in marriage. Yet if Gundabald could find some poor mope to swindle, she had no doubt he would auction her off without the slightest compunction and then leave her to her fate. She just didn't think he would find anyone. Besides, Gundabald had, as they said, a hot throat and a cold prick. He wanted to cool the one and heat the other as frequently as possible. To indulge himself he needed what little money came in from her estates. He would certainly sell her, but not cheaply. It remained to be seen if he could get his price. At the moment, she couldn't bring herself to care much one way or the other.

When the papal blessing proved fruitless, the thread of hope that had drawn her across the Alps and sustained her in the difficult journey to Rome . . . failed.

Gisela's death had been the final blow. She had been

Regeane's only protection against a world that would destroy her in an instant if it so much as guessed her secret—and against the worst excesses of Gundabald's greed. She had been Regeane's only confidante and companion. Regeane had no other friends, no other loves. She was now abandoned and utterly alone.

Dry-eyed, Regeane followed her mother's body to the grave. She was overcome by a despair so black, it seemed to turn that bright day into bitter night.

Now a faint silver shadow appeared against the blackness of the floor.

There is nothing left but moonlight, Regeane thought. *Drink it, drown in it. She will never reproach me. I will never see her tears again or suffer because of them. Whatever may become of me, I am alone.*

She stood, stripped off her dress and shift, and turned toward the silver haze.

The gust from the window was icy, but pleasure wouldn't exist without the sharp bite of pain. Even the brief flash of orgasm is too intense to be absolutely pleasurable. The cold caress was seduction, the quick cruel touch that precedes pleasure.

Regeane went forward boldly, knowing that in a moment she would be warm. Naked, she stepped into the silver haze.

The wolf stood there.

Regeane was, as wolves go, a large wolf. She had the same weight as the girl, over a hundred pounds. She was much stronger than in her human state—lean, quick, and powerful. Her coat was smooth and thick. The pelt glowed silver as it caught the moonlight on its long guard hairs.

The wolf's heart overflowed with joy and gratitude. Regeane would never have admitted it in her human state, but she loved the wolf and, papal blessing or not, she would never let the wolf go.

From the bottom of her heart, she reveled in the change. Sometimes, while in her human state, she wondered who was wiser, she or the wolf. The wolf knew. Growing more beautiful and stronger year after year, the wolf waited for Regeane to be ready to receive her teaching and understand it.

The silver wolf lifted herself on her hind legs and, placing her forepaws on the window sill, peered out. She saw not just with eyes as these maimed humans did, but with sensitive ears and nose.

The world humans saw was like a fresco—dimensionless as a picture painted on a wall. To be believed in by the wolf, a thing had to have not only image, but smell, texture, and taste.

Ah God . . . how beautiful. The world was filled with wonder.

The rain must have come in the evening. The wolf could smell the damp, black earth under the green verdure as well as mud churned up by horses' hooves in a nearby lane.

The woman hadn't noticed it. She'd spent the day in grief-stricken reverie. For this she earned a brief flash of contempt from the wolf. But the wolf was too much a creature of the present to dwell on what was past. She was grateful for each moment. And this was a fine one.

Usually in Rome, the scent of man overpowered everything else. That effluvia of stale perspiration, raw sewage floating in the Tiber, the stench of human excrement which, even by comparison to that of other animals, is utterly vile. All these filled the air and pressed in around her. Overlaying them were the musty omnipresent evidence of human dwellings: stale woodsmoke, damp timber, and stone.

But not tonight. The sharp wind blew from the open fields beyond the city, redolent of dry grass and the sweetness of wild herbs growing on the hillsides near the sea.

Sometimes the fragrant breath from the Campagna carried the clean barnyard smells of pig and cattle, and faintly, the enticing musk of deer.

The night below was alive with movement. The cats that made their homes among the ruins sang their ancient songs of anger and passion among forgotten monuments. Here and there the slinking shape of a stray dog met her eye; occasionally, even furtive human movement. Thieves and footpads haunted the district, ready to prey on the unwary.

Her ears pricked forward and netted what her eyes could not see—the suade thump of a barn owl's wings in flight, the high, thin cries of bats swooping, darting, foraging for insects in the chill night air.

The rush and whisper of the hunters and the hunted, silent until the end. The agonized death cry of a bird, taken in sleep on the nest by a marauding cat, rent the air. The chopped-off shriek of a rabbit dying in the talons of an owl followed.

Those and many others were woven together by her wolf senses into a rich fabric that was unending variety and everlasting delight.

The silver wolf dropped her forepaws to the floor with a soft, nearly inaudible cry of longing. Then her lips drew back from her teeth in a snarl at the sound of voices in the other room.

Hugo and Gundabald were eating. The wolf's belly rumbled with hunger at the smell of roast meat. She was hungry and thirsty, longing for clean water and food.

The woman warned her night side to rein in her desires. She would get nothing.

The wolf replied. They were both gone—the woman from her prison, the wolf from her cage. The wolf stood beside a clear mountain lake. The full moon glowed silver in the water. All around the lake, black trees were silhouetted against mountains glittering white with unending snow.

The memory faded. The wolf and woman found themselves staring at the locked door.

The wolf and woman both understood imprisonment. Regeane had spent most of her life behind locked doors. She'd long ago learned the punishing futility of assaults on oak and iron. She ignored what she couldn't change and bided her time.

They were speaking of her.

"Did you hear that?" Hugo asked fearfully. Hugo's ears were better than Gundabald's. He must have heard her soft cry of protest.

"No," Gundabald mumbled through a mouthful of food. "I didn't and you didn't either. You only imagined you did. She seldom makes any noise. That's one thing we can be grateful for. At least she doesn't spend her nights howling as a real wolf would."

"We shouldn't have brought her here," Hugo moaned.

"Must you start that again?" Gundabald sighed wearily.

"It's true," Hugo replied with drunken insistence. "The founders of this city were suckled at the tits of a mother wolf.

Once they called themselves sons of the wolf. Ever since I found out about her I've often thought of that story. A real wolf couldn't raise human children, but a creature like her . . ."

Gundabald laughed raucously. "A fairy tale made up by some strumpet to explain a clutch of bastard brats. She wouldn't be the first or won't be the last to spin a wild story to cover her own . . . debauchery."

"You won't listen to anything," Hugo said petulantly. "She's gotten worse since we came here. Even while her own mother was dying she . . ."

The silver wolf's lips drew back. Her teeth gleamed in the moonlight like ivory knives. Even in the wolf's heart, Hugo's words rankled.

Pointless the smoldering anger. Pointless the brief, sad rebellion. The door stood between her and her tormentors. The barred window between the magnificent creature and freedom.

She began to pace as any caged beast will, obeying the wordless command: Stay strong. Stay healthy. Stay alert. Fear not, your time will come.

II

MAENIEL WAS A WORRIER. TODAY HE HAD A LOT OF worries as he stood on the half-ruined gallery once intended for the delight of a Roman governor.

He envied the man, who had probably stood here once, taking the air and complacently surveying his broad domains. Today, among other things, Maeniel worried about the hay. It didn't seem to be ripening as fast as it should. And they needed that hay to carry them through the long, cold winter. Still, he sighed; the man had been too powerful to worry about hay. He'd probably had other concerns, possibly even more troubling than Maeniel's. Say, for instance, politics in Rome.

"Politics in Rome," he muttered.

Gavin, the captain of his guard, sat dozing on a bench, his back against a mural of Perseus slaying Medusa. The gorgon's head in the hero's hand glared at him. This didn't worry Gavin. Nothing worried Gavin. He opened one eye and repeated, "What about politics in Rome?"

"I was just thinking that even though the Roman governor didn't worry about the hay as I do, he probably worried about politics in Rome."

Gavin opened both eyes. "Let me get this straight. You left off worrying about the hay to worry about what a long-dead Roman worried about?"

"Yes," Maeniel said.

"Thank you for clarifying that." Gavin closed his eyes. "Now if you don't mind, I'll go back to sleep."

"It doesn't seem to be ripening as quickly as usual," Maeniel persisted.

"The hay, or politics in Rome?" Gavin asked.

"The hay." Maeniel bit his lip.

Gavin sighed deeply, opened both eyes, and looked out over the surrounding countryside.

The land lay drowsing in the warm gold of the afternoon sun, a picture of tranquil, bucolic beauty. Three prosperous villages lay scattered along the mountainside surrounded by tilled fields, their deep green just beginning to bear the first tinge of autumn's rich red, brown, and gold.

Higher up against the face of the mountains were scattered flocks of sheep, goats, and cattle, fattening in the high summer pasture. Beyond them, snowcapped peaks floated in delicate ethereal beauty against the sky.

"The hay," Gavin said, "seems to me to be ripening much as it always has ever since we came here."

"Do you really think so?" Maeniel asked hopefully.

"Yes," Gavin replied, closing his eyes again.

Maeniel shook his head. "Still, I hear from Clotilde that it's going to be a bad winter. She says the fleeces of the sheep have grown twice as thick as is usual and—"

"No," Gavin said firmly. "I won't listen anymore. Every year at this time it's the hay. Then, when that's in, the question will be, is it enough to carry us through the winter? Or should you send to the lowlands to buy more, to ensure the survival of our stock? Then, you will fret yourself about wood. Have we enough? Suppose a really bad storm comes and the snow is too deep for us to venture out to cut more? So we must cut more now, stacking it ever higher and higher until we must sleep in the snow because the wood fills all of the houses.

"In between, you will be venturing out in blizzards to visit every cow, sow, ewe, and nanny goat with a pain. To hold her hoof until she delivers. If one sneezes, you hear it in your sleep and come wake me up to commiserate with you. Hold the lantern up, Gavin. Ply your axe with a will, Gavin. Pull, Gavin. Push, Gavin. Take your men and fall on those brigands, Gavin. I know they are not on my land, but I like it not that they raided so close, Gavin.

"Now it is the worries of deceased Romans, and politics that concern us not at all in our mountains. At first I wondered when Rieulf, old and ill, placed his demesne in your hands. But after the first winter I understood the wisdom of the old man's choice. He definitely knew how to pick the right man for the job."

Maeniel listened meekly to Gavin's tirade. They were old friends. He heard it several times a year when Gavin grew frustrated with him.

"I wish," Gavin wound down, "that you would find something else to worry about besides hay or the sheep, goats, wood, and snowstorms. At least it would be a change for me to listen to." His voice trailed off as he sniffed the air. "Fresh baked bread," he whispered. "I forgot it's Matrona's baking day." His body floated from the bench. He seemed pulled along by the enticing odor, his nose sniffing the air.

Maeniel placed one big hand on Gavin's shoulder and pushed him back down on the bench. "Matrona has a lot of work to do on baking day. She becomes very irritable. Remember the time I had to rescue you? She was trying to push you feet first into one of the ovens. You had both feet braced against the wall on either side of the door. You were screaming at the top of your lungs, and if I hadn't—"

"You didn't have to rescue me," Gavin denied hotly. "It's just that I'm a gentleman and didn't want to hurt her."

"To be sure," Maeniel soothed, "to be sure. Besides you were right . . . I mean about the worry business."

"You're giving it up?" Gavin asked.

"No," Maeniel said. "I have a new one." He handed Gavin a letter.

Gavin gave it a cursory glance; then realizing its importance, he began to read more slowly.

"Not politics in Rome," Maeniel said. "Politics in Franca. The woman comes recommended by Charles, the great Charlemagne himself. I had better marry her."

"I wouldn't," Gavin said handing him back the letter. "I'd tell the *great* Charles to go fly his hawks or chase Saxons, whatever the hell a king does. Forget marrying. When some royal cousin comes here, lock your gates, sharpen your sword, and wish them Godspeed over the pass into the valley. I'm betting you'll never hear any more about her."

"I can't take that bet," Maeniel said quietly. "The stakes are too high."

"No, they aren't," Gavin insisted. "You're sitting in an impregnable fortress. This rock has never fallen to assault, not even in the time of the Romans."

"And if Charles ever seriously decides to dig me out," Maeniel said flatly, "he can. Why do you think I send Charles' court a hefty sum of silver? Every year a nice present of gold and jewels is sent to the court in time for Christmas. I keep the roads clear of thieves and bandits, don't overcharge the merchants traveling through the pass. In between I keep my fingers crossed. So far he's left me alone.

"But no more. The reckoning has come, and in a form I can't really quarrel with. He's offering me a marriage with a woman of the royal house. I dare not refuse. The letter says she is young, comely, and—"

"The letter," Gavin broke in, "does give every pertinent fact about the lady: her birth, her lineage, yes, every fact, but one. What's wrong with her?"

"What could be wrong with her?" Maeniel asked.

Gavin stared out glumly over the village. "Now who's the optimist? Aside from dire poverty, I can think of a few things. Promiscuity, drunkenness, insanity, dishonesty, stupidity, leprosy, cruelty, and greed. Any and all of the above. In addition, she'll probably turn out to be a humpbacked dwarf with only one tooth remaining in her head and halfwitted in the bargain."

"Sometimes I think it was a mistake for your father to send you to school. It stimulated your imagination no end," Maeniel said.

"I know," Gavin agreed. "I told him that every day until it was a question of what would wear out first—his arm, his belt, or my backside. As it was, you and I both ended up trying to run away to seek our fortune. Well, we found it, and now you must marry this . . . creature to keep it."

"It's a small sacrifice," Maeniel answered.

"Let's hope," Gavin said.

"If she's a humpbacked dwarf, she may have a pleasant personality. If she's insane, I'll see she's cared for. Drunken, dried out at intervals; promiscuous, persuaded to be discreet. Cruelty and greed can both be restrained. And even leprosy, God help me, can be treated. At this altitude the sick either recover quickly or die."

"That's it," Gavin said. "Look on the bright side. She may not survive the first winter."

"Or she may be as the letter says: young, comely, and amiable. Poverty might be her only real fault."

"No," Gavin said. "If that were the only problem, they'd never be offering her to such as you. A down-at-the-heels Irish mercenary. If it hadn't been for Rieulf, we'd still be earning our bread selling our swords hither and yon. As it was, you did him a service and he began to love you. You were lucky . . ."

"That's true." Maeniel looked out over the valley again, still somewhat preoccupied by the hay. "What do you think, Gavin? Should we get some of it now and—"

A loud yell erupted from the direction of the kitchen.

Maeniel turned. Gavin was gone. The lure of fresh-baked bread had proved too much for his captain to resist.

Gavin on a horse, sword in hand, might be the terror of every brigand in the mountains, but when he fought Matrona, he invariably lost.

Maeniel decided to go rescue him. Leaving the hay and the future to take care of themselves, he started off in the direction of the commotion in the kitchen.

III

REGEANE WOKE NAKED ON THE BED THE NEXT morning. The wolf had paced the floor until moonset. Until the two in the next room were deep in sodden slumber and snoring loudly. Then, she climbed into the bed, rested her muzzle on the pillow and slept. She didn't remember turning human. The bed smelled of warm animal, human and otherwise.

Her old, blue dress lay across the foot of the bed. Though she thought it blue, it had been faded by a thousand washings into a muddy gray.

As she stepped into it, she realized the dress, only months ago very loose, was becoming tight across the shoulders and breast. Once, she had been able to wear it only if she held the hem off the floor. Now, it barely covered her ankles.

The dress, when it was new, had broad bands of embroidery at the neck and sleeves. The thread was gold. A thing Hugo and Gundabald scrounged assiduously for among her mother's possessions. One of them had long ago picked out the rich strands.

Outside, the light was bright. *They should feel safe,* she thought.

They must have. The heavy door opened at a touch.

Gundabald was sitting at the table. His eyeballs looked as if they were bleeding. Drool was dried in the stubble of his bristly black beard, but he gobbled the dark bread, whey cheese, and sour wine with a good appetite.

Hugo knelt on the floor, retching into a chamber pot.

The large round loaf was in the center of the table. Regeane twisted off a big hunk. The bread was thick and smelled of olive oil and onions in the dough. Regeane's strong teeth ripped into it. She had good teeth.

Little was left of the cheese but rind. She ate that along with the bread, biting her fingers twice in the process.

A brown terra-cotta bowl of figs rested next to the bread. She reached for a fig. The flat of Gundabald's knife came down across the back of her hand. It made a slapping sound. It hurt.

She flinched and snatched her hand back. Her eyes met Gundabald's.

He chuckled, spraying crumbs from his mouth.

Her hand was still on the table near the bowl. The fingers were long and tapered finely, so it was not noticeable that the nails were dense, narrowing to blunt points at the tips.

Gundabald hit her again; this time raising a weal on the backs of Regeane's fingers. She didn't flinch or pull away. Gundabald loved hurting people. To show pain only encouraged him.

He glared at the red marks his knife made, then back at Regeane's face. He seemed baffled by her stoicism.

"Eat some more of the bread," he said. "It'll put meat on your bones. You need some."

Hugo had finished vomiting. He was sitting in one of the chairs by the table. His face beaded with sweat. But he managed to turn an appreciative eye toward Regeane. "She's not bad now," he said. "That hair. Those eyes." Then he applied himself to a cup of red wine. The first swallow gagged him. He hawked and spat on the floor, then very quickly gulped a few mouthfuls.

Gundabald eyed him, then Regeane. *She does have her points,* he thought. Her hair was long and dark, almost black at her scalp and neck, shading toward silver and, finally, white at the tips. It never tangled. He had himself seen it rise and fall back into position when the wind blew it too far out of place.

Her eyes were truly beautiful, large, warm, and dark—until they caught the light. Then they flared into gold, as water does in the setting sun.

Aside from that, she wasn't much. Skinny, pale, and colorless. Gundabald favored women who allowed him to get a good grip—those who would squeal, moan, and give him a hard ride. He had a feeling she wouldn't do any of the three. And God help the man who woke in bed with her by moonlight.

Still, she was nearly as helpless as any other woman by day and he needed to take measures to protect her. Charlemagne's star was on the rise, and she was a potentially valuable property.

Hugo gulped more wine, presumably trying to keep his mutinous stomach from reacting to the insult. The wine was of strange substance. It stank. Between swallows of wine, he gnawed on some of the bread. He had less success at eating than Regeane and Gundabald did. Hugo had a few rotten teeth.

Gundabald drew his foot back slowly and carefully. Then slammed his heel into the unsuspecting Hugo's groin.

Hugo didn't scream. Regeane doubted that he could scream. He clutched at the spot between his legs. His eyes rolled back in their sockets until only the whites showed. His chair tipped over backward. His skull hit the wooden floor with an audible crack.

Gundabald stuffed the last of his food into his mouth, sighed, and rose to his feet. He stood over Hugo and turned the gasping man on his side so he wouldn't strangle.

Hugo spewed a fan of vomit on the floor: bread, wine, then fragments of meat and turnips as his violated innards reached for last night's supper.

Regeane rose to her feet in horror, one hand on her breast. She knew they were a violent pair, but this exceeded the usual measure of savagery.

Gundabald snorted in derision at the fallen Hugo, then dropped a few silver coins in front of him. "Get her a maid," he said.

Hugo made a gurgling sound that somehow seemed to indicate puzzlement.

"Hire a maid," Gundabald said in a louder voice. "Get your cousin Regeane a maid."

An old woman came into the room. She was small, bent, and twisted with the disease Regeane had observed lingered among the narrow dark streets of cities. Her face was pockmarked. She had a bent nose and a cauliflower ear. Gray hair straggled down from under her veil.

She cursed Hugo for making a vile mess on the floor. She also cursed Gundabald, apparently for the crime of existing. She ignored Regeane. She spoke the rough argot of the Roman streets, a language Regeane found obscene, fascinating, expressive and, at times, almost beautiful, but definitely not Latin any longer.

Gundabald didn't understand her, but he got the message. "What are you yammering about, you old hag?" he roared.

To Regeane's surprise, the woman's speech slowed. She spat out a very imaginative description of some of Gundabald's probable ancestors.

He took a step toward the tiny woman, his fist raised.

In an eye blink, a dagger appeared in her hand. The blade was black and pitted with rust, but the edges were honed fine and glittered wickedly.

Gundabald stepped back quickly. "Everyone's in bad humor today," he grumbled. Glancing down at the fallen Hugo, he dropped a few more pieces of silver beside him. "Are you listening?" he shouted.

Hugo nodded vigorously. He was in no position to defend himself against his father's wrath.

"You will hire a maid for Regeane. You may rape the maid if she will let you. You may not touch your cousin. You may not put your hand under her skirt or on her leg. If you lay one finger on her, I will cut that finger off. Show any further signs of 'affection' for your cousin, and I'll put you out of action painfully and permanently. Understood?"

Hugo nodded vigorously again.

Gundabald wrapped a ratty velvet mantle around himself and strode toward the door.

The old woman was mopping the floor. As he passed, Gundabald with deliberate malice drove the toe of his boot into the side of the bucket. Dirty water flew everywhere.

The old woman's knife appeared again. She described a sexual perversion Regeane didn't know existed and attributed it to Gundabald. He laughed and left, slamming the door behind him.

Hugo began moaning and crying for help. Regeane ignored him and sat down.

The old woman glanced at her, then left. In a few moments,

she returned with a sausage and gave it to the girl. The wolf visited Regeane briefly when she bit into the sausage, but even the beast's hyperacute senses couldn't identify what type of meat filled the thing. For all she could tell, it might have been a previous visitor to the lodging house—one who attempted to leave without paying his bill. Thyme, fennel, and garlic overpowered all other odors, but she was ravenous. She wrapped the malodorous thing in bread and gobbled it. When she was finished, she felt better. The old woman continued to clean with surprising efficiency.

Hugo pulled himself up from the floor and sat on the chair, holding his head in his hands. Regeane was finishing the last piece of bread. He dropped his hands, glared at her and said, "Bitch! You've eaten everything."

Regeane's chin lifted. The wolf paced slowly out of darkness, head lowered, lips wrinkled back from her teeth in a smile of killing rage. She, not Regeane, met Hugo's eyes. He bore her stare for a few seconds, then turned away.

Between one thing and another, Gundabald had dropped a good bit of silver on him. He gathered it up quickly from his clothing and the floor. Then he rose and, giving the old woman a wide berth, was gone.

The old woman muttered several obscenities at the closing door, then chuckled, saying something else in the local dialect.

"Don't do that," Regeane said. "I speak the Roman—" She broke off, not knowing what to call the local idiom.

The old woman chuckled. "I don't care what you know. He fears you. I can't say why, but he does. The old devil needn't worry. The little puddle of puke wouldn't dare lay a hand on you."

"Gundabald likes hitting people," Regeane said dully.

The old woman nodded assent as if this were a given. "Best hope, he tries it again with me. I'll slice off the hand that touches me."

"Do you have any water?" Regeane asked hesitantly. "I'm so thirsty and the wine . . ."

"Is hog piss." The woman finished the sentence for her. She dropped the mop with a clatter and shambled out. She returned a few minutes later with a large brown earthenware cup. "Most often," she said, "I would say don't touch the water in Rome. Even the lowest grade of wine sold at the tavernas is safer. But last night torrents of rain fell. They flushed and cleansed the cistern."

When Regeane's lips touched the water, she and the wolf drank. It was cold with a faint undertaste of lime plaster and smelled of the winter sky: chilly gray, hung with rain or mist filling the hollows among the hills before sunrise, bearing an icy dew thick enough to drench the garments of early risers on winter mornings. Somewhere on a hilltop, long grass swirled, danced, and bowed to the storm winds while above transparent gray clouds fleeted across the sun.

When the cup was empty, Regeane closed her eyes. She and the wolf communed in the darkness of her soul. The wolf snarled. She was ready to tell Regeane how much she hated Hugo, Gundabald, and the life she was leading. She was ready to fight back, escape the trap she was in. Better death than the world they inhabited.

Regeane felt, for the first time by day, the faint dislocation brought by the wolf as she approached by moonlight. The woman jerked back in terror. She feared the consequences of rebellion. She didn't want to know how much she hated Gundabald, how deeply she feared him. Vile as her family was, she clung to them. They were better than the alternative.

The punishments visited on witches sickened and horrified her. Her mother had whispered into Regeane's ears tales of the last agonies of those women doomed for practicing unnatural arts. Naked in a barrel studded with nails, the barrel rolled until the screams stopped. Fire and the stake; sewn into a sack with a rat, a dog, and a snake and thrown into the river. Punishments worse than those designed by fiends from hell to torture the damned were devised by men of God to confront what they saw as evil.

"No, no," Regeane said to the wolf. "I'm too afraid. I can't. Go away. Please, please go away."

The wolf gazed at Regeane solemnly, then she made a soft sound of regret and vanished into the darkness.

"What's wrong?" the old woman asked. "Are you sick?"

"No," Regeane said. "Only tired. Thank you," she said to the woman. Then she went into her room and barred the door.

The narrow stone cell was icy, but brightly lit by the sun on the walls. Regeane lay down on the bed, wrapped the mantle around herself, and slept.

HUGO HIRED THE MAID. HE BROUGHT HER HOME IN the early hours of the morning.

Regeane was awakened by the commotion.

Gundabald was up late. He was entertaining a guest. Whether boy or woman, Regeane couldn't tell. She might have summoned the wolf. No one could fool *her* nose, but the wolf was a virgin and a fastidious one. Regeane couldn't face dealing with her disapproval and downright disgust. The night creature believed humans were oversexed and felt her human partner was too preoccupied with prurient curiosity.

The air drifting under the door reeked of raw sex. Regeane fell asleep to the grunts and snorts of passion.

She was awakened not by sound, but by scent. The wolf was present. Something, no not something, a snake was hunting among the vines near her window. If the reptile musk disturbed the wolf, it gagged the woman. Regeane rose to her feet in the darkened room.

Even this slight sound was enough to frighten the slender predator sliding among the vines. The scent weakened. She heard a thump and a swish below her window as the interloper departed.

Hugo crashed through the door in the next room.

Someone shrieked.

Hugo screamed, "Sodomite!"

Evidently, the visitor *had* been a boy.

This was followed by the sound of running feet.

"God damn him!" Gundabald roared. "Now, see what you've done. The little ass fucker took my purse with him."

The sound of a blow followed.

Hugo howled.

A feminine screech followed, then four screams, in rapid succession.

Boom. Boom. Boom. Boom.

Regeane gasped and backed away from the door. She

recognized this sound. The landlord below was pounding on his ceiling.

A volley of curses followed, along with threats to throw them out into the streets *now* if the noise didn't stop.

The voices in the other room dropped.

Hugo cursed Gundabald.

Gundabald cursed Hugo.

The girl's voice sobbed.

"Shut up, you stupid little cunt," Gundabald whispered hoarsely. "I'll twist your other tit if you don't stop caterwauling. Strike a light, damn it. It's black as a mole's ass in here."

Regeane heard the snap of flint and steel.

"Merciful God, who is this?" Gundabald asked.

"Regeane's maid," Hugo answered. "I found her in a tavern."

"Where in a tavern? Down the cloaca? In the shithole? She makes most nanny goats look bewitchingly beautiful."

REGEANE REALLY DIDN'T CARE TO SIDE WITH GUN-dabald, but in this she had to agree with him when she met the girl the next morning.

Her name was Silve. She was bowlegged, skinny, buck-toothed, walleyed, and sallow-skinned, which might not have been too bad if she'd been intelligent, kind, or even hard-working and well-intentioned. She was none of those. When she was not sleeping in her alcove off the main room or being violently and noisily ridden by Hugo, she joined with him in harassing Regeane.

As her mother had done, Regeane tried to bring some measure of order into their lives. She took over the chores Gisela had once performed. She did her best to stretch the little money they had. She cooked simple one-pot meals for the four of them, saw to the washing when she could persuade Gundabald to pay the washerwoman, and helped the old woman—Regeane never knew her name and always thought of her as "the old woman"—clean up after the other three.

The old woman was the only one who could get any work out of Silve. She accused her of such vile obscenities that Silve, afraid to attack her, would be so galvanized by rage that she scrubbed and washed with a will.

In her spare time, Regeane would retreat to her narrow room and, with cold, numb fingers, try to put her scanty wardrobe in order. She had no decent sewing needles. The few she had were made of bone and their points blunted quickly. She had no thread so she unraveled rags to get enough thread to alter her dresses.

Her mother had been buried in her one good mantle and gown. Regeane had seen to that, even though Gundabald and Hugo cursed her for a fool, saying Gisela wouldn't need warm clothes where she was going, only a winding sheet. What remained of both her mother's and her wardrobes was shabby beyond belief.

Regeane accepted the situation. Most women had the same problem. Cloth was expensive. With a loom, she could have woven her own, but a loom was a large, costly piece of equipment. Few families had access to one, so women spent their time often as not resewing what few clothes they had, trying to decently cover their nakedness.

As autumn slowly wore into winter, Regeane's despair deepened. The lodging house was part of an old ruin. Even the proprietor had no idea of the purpose it once served. The icy winter wind sobbed and moaned through the stone rooms by day and by night. A charcoal brazier heated the air for only a few inches around the coals. The walls and floors remained bitterly cold to the touch.

Gundabald and Hugo were more than happy to eat the food Regeane prepared, though they denigrated it as coarse peasant fare. They scattered bones under the table, spat gristle on the floor. When they pissed, they missed the pot and left reeking yellow puddles everywhere. After eating, Gundabald wandered off to a tavern in search of further entertainment.

Hugo and Silve went to bed and exercised the webbing under the mattress. They fucked each other blind, drank themselves incapable, then into a sodden coma.

Gundabald usually returned in the small hours and—depending on his luck with the dice box, boys, or women—he might or might not wake Silve and Hugo and chase them 'round and 'round the room, flogging their screaming, naked bodies with his leather belt. The landlord's fury usually put an end to these entertainments, whereupon they all retired.

In the morning, someone would wake early, usually Silve—she was most easily ejected from a warm bed—would open Regeane's door so she could come out and clean up the mess.

To compound Regeane's problems, the rain moved in.

The wolf loved it. The winds moving through the city blew the human stench away. Freshets swelled the Tiber, flushing out the raw sewage seeping into the river. Downpours cleansed cobblestones and walls. Briefly, in the watery winter sun, the city became a place of light and color. Marble gleamed. Orange stucco walls glowed. Long wands of red valerian grew in brickwork, and crumbling pediments waved red and pink banners against the cloudy gray sky.

The Romans loved flowers. Window boxes and pots on balconies flamed with late blooming blue sage, golden yarrow, fragrant dusty white chamomile, and yellow autumn daisies.

A few sellers of iris, lavender, and late blooming roses clustered in the city's squares and piazzas. Usually, the vendors huddled around fires or charcoal braziers, warming their hands, the flowers looking incongruous against the cold black and gray cobbles, their petals nipped and tossed by the icy wind.

On days like this, Regeane managed to drag Hugo and Silve outside, ostensibly to visit churches. Actually, Regeane hated churches. She had some compelling reasons. First, because after her mother's death and the failure of the papal blessing, she believed God had abandoned her. Secondly, because she could see ghosts.

These visitations weren't frequent, but they were always unsettling. Most often the materializations happened near churches. Usually not inside, but near the door as she was entering or leaving.

The wolf didn't care. The brute was the most logical of creatures. What, after all, can the living do for the dead? To the woman, the dead were a source of pain.

The worst had been a shadow-faced cadaver wearing rich velvet and brocade garments. They were moldering, falling to pieces, and stank of damp, rotting rags and decay. She followed

Regeane, weeping and wringing hands that seemed at first to be flesh, then bony claws. The sobs and moans came from a face that wavered, as the hands did, between beautiful, pale, aristocratic features—but with only holes where the eyes had been—and the foggy shape of a naked skull.

The ghost terrorized Regeane for three days and only departed when Gisela, at Regeane's repeated urgings, left the shrine they had been visiting. Regeane had been sixteen at the time. She'd tried to ascertain the source of the shade's grief, but the ghost's rotting brocade and the horror of the empty-eyed face inspired an overwhelming terror. Besides, she and her prominent tomb in the church were clothed in a sense of evil. Her outcries were not those of sorrow and repentance, but outrage at a well-deserved damnation—a fate she was unhappy at facing alone.

Regeane's other encounters had been brief and less frightening, but she couldn't remember any of them without a shudder of revulsion. She had learned to be wary of churches.

This day began with something a little bit like happiness. Regeane managed to persuade Gundabald to part with a few coins. Not a lot, but enough to buy a stewing hen, some fennel, tarragon, parsnips, and a nameless bunch of greens. The old woman contributed garlic and a rather withered onion. Regeane put them together in a pot to cook slowly over the low fire.

The morning had been foggy, but near noon the weather cleared. The sun came out. The air was mild, almost warm. The old woman ladled up bowls of stew for Regeane, Hugo, Silve, and herself; on the strength of her contributed onion, she was due her share. For once, Silve and Hugo weren't too hung over to eat. They all chewed the tasty chicken meat, ate parsnips, and dunked their tough gray-brown bread in the broth.

When they were all replete, Regeane, Silve, and Hugo left to visit churches. The old woman remained behind. She placed the leftover stew in a covered dish for Gundabald and went on with her cleaning.

The church Regeane chose was a very ancient one, said to go back to the time of the apostles. A few steps down led to the door. The church itself was located in the atrium amid the magnificent reception rooms of an ancient Roman villa. The building was so old, the walls were sunk three feet below street level.

Just inside the door, the roof was open to the sky. Below the opening in the roof was a small pond. Some green reeds and a few purple iris still bloomed in the pale light.

Regeane knelt. The floor was covered by a thin layer of clean straw. She found this a kindness to her knees. Away from the small, ancient atrium, the villa had extended into a long room colonnaded on either side. Tall, slender, white Corinthian columns led the eye toward the sanctuary.

The acanthus leaves at the top still bore faded traces of green paint. The walls and roof were stark white stucco. Here and there, a flaking bit of plaster showed a trace of color. Regeane knew the plaster must have been placed to obliterate frescos either too explicit or too pagan for the nascent church.

The altar was—after the custom of time—an unadorned clean square white marble table. Four small grainless pure white marble columns supported a simple blue silken awning over the altar.

A sanctuary lamp burned near a basin of blessed water, alerting a visitor to the fact that the real presence in the form of consecrated hosts must be nearby.

The place, she knew, must always have been sacred.

Long ago, when Rome was a small village on the Tiber, a family lived here. The eldest male in the family, together with the women, children, and even slaves, gathered at the altar to sacrifice to the fructifying spirits of earth and sky. And also to care for their own dead, most of whom were buried in the fields and orchards surrounding the villa.

They honored all of those things without which no one can live, things still present here: earth, air, fire, and water.

The bread of consecration rises from the burgeoning wheat field. The wine from the cold, bracing air of the mountains. Vines hold the soil to rock with roots like claws clinging to steep slopes where nothing else will grow. Red and white grapes ripen while the sun warms their hearts and cool breezes caress their skins. The fire flickering near the altar remembered the woman-tended hearth, and water in the basin commemorated the source of all life.

Around the small atrium the city grew. The family's wealth increased. The villa was extended, but the ancient sacred heart of the house was preserved.

Where the altar now stood, the owner of the villa must have sat in state to receive his clients and tenants. His tenants would have knelt before him, presenting him with the money due in rents and fees. His clients would have kissed his hands, solicited favors. In return, they followed him through the streets, bully boys, increasing his importance in the eyes of the Roman mob, ready to intimidate any of his enemies.

Time passed. The family dwindled. Its power faded. More and more parts of the villa were sold off until only these quarters remained. When they became Christian, the great family slipped into the family of man. Still, the little atrium was sacred and always would be.

Regeane saluted Christ, but not as a friend. She did not think He would ever be her friend. Still, she showed Him due respect and did not court His enmity.

When she rose to her feet, she noticed Silve stood alone by the door. "Where is Hugo?" Regeane asked.

"He sneaked off," the girl said resentfully. "He's probably in some wine bar with his hand up the barmaid's skirt. You want me to go find him?"

"No," Regeane said shortly. Send Silve after Hugo? Ha! In a few hours they would be sleeping in the sawdust on a taverna floor.

She spotted a bench along the back wall of the church, no doubt once intended for the villa owner's clients and petitioners. It seemed a perfect spot to take her ease. She and Silve walked over and sat down.

The church was a peaceful place. The present watched over the past without enmity. The air was cool, but without the bite of the wind outside. Mottled sun shone in around the white marble altar and from the opening in the roof above the atrium pond.

She could see now as her eyes adjusted to the dimness that under the straw the church boasted a sumptuous mosaic floor gardened with a pattern of bright spring flowers.

Silve took a jug from under her robe, jerked out the cork with her teeth, and took a long pull. She offered it to Regeane.

Regeane declined. Silve and Hugo both favored tavernas where the host adulterated the wine with substances designed to increase its potency. The occasional patron of these establishments went permanently mad or dropped dead after a heavy drinking bout. Regeane didn't wish to join their number.

Silve got a bit glassy-eyed as the wine hit her. She discussed Hugo's ancestry, then laughed. "He'll have to peddle his ass in the back room to get a drink," she said. "I have the money. Oh, look!"

Regeane looked. Silve was pointing to the atrium pool. Regeane's eyes picked up movement in the water. "It's a carp," Silve said. She began pulling off her veil. "Let's see if we can net it. I'll hold the veil. You chase the fish into it. He'll make a wonderful supper." She started to rise, but Regeane caught her arm and pulled her back.

"I'm not sure that's a fish," Regeane said.

The thing in the pool lifted its head above the water. A snake.

Silve made a sound reminiscent, to Regeane, of an ungreased axle being overstressed. Then bolted. She ran in the wrong direction toward the altar where there was no exit. She leaned against one of the columns and applied the jug for a bit more restorative.

The serpent moved out of the pool easily to the straw-covered floor and glided toward Regeane. The woman was afraid, but the wolf was indifferent, queenly even. She knew the snake wasn't poisonous or even angry, only curious.

Put to it, Regeane scorned to show fear in front of Silve. She was, after all, the daughter of Wolfstan the Saxon prince, called by his people a talisman, and Gisela, blood kin to Charles Martel, the hammer of God. She would not be shamed by the creature before her.

The thing did not move very quickly, thus it allowed her to prepare for its arrival. She noticed on closer examination the snake wasn't ugly. The scales were a tightly fitted mosaic similar to the colors of water sparkling in the sunlight—white, blue, and green. They formed a pattern down his back overlying darker bands at each side.

The wolf eyed him with a bow of appreciation for such good camouflage. He must be nearly invisible when swimming in the muddy sun-struck Tiber.

The snake reached Regeane's shirt and investigated the hem with a brief flicker of his forked tongue. The wolf was aloof, yet the woman stretched out her hand as to a courtier.

The serpent's head rose. She felt the flickering, timid caress of the tongue on her fingertips. He, or perhaps she, made an amazing U-turn and hurried back toward the water.

"Aha! Ahaa! Ahaaaaa!" Silve commented. "It paid you homage."

"Like hell," Regeane said. "It decided I was too big to eat. Now, shut up. If there's any attendant or a priest about, you'll have him bolting in her to find out what's wrong."

Silve shut up probably because she couldn't scream while finishing off the contents of the clay flask.

Regeane rose and walked toward the pool. She watched as the serpent—with the air of one who knows where he is going—swam down toward the drainage pipe that probably emptied into the river. As he entered, she saw the woman.

There was a small marble bench near the pool. She was sitting there, staring contentedly into the still water. A child sat on her lap—a little boy. He was sleeping, small, curly head resting on his mother's breast.

For a second, Regeane wondered when she had come in. Then realized the woman could not have entered without her noticing, and that she could see the far wall of the church through their bodies. She understood what she was looking at. The wolf yawned, bored.

Regeane felt a bit envious: the expression on the spirit's face was serene and filled with love and peace.

Above the opening in the roof, the sky brightened. Regeane looked up. When she turned her eyes back to the bench, the woman was gone. *Yes,* Regeane thought. *This place has always been holy.*

Silve wailed. She sounded like an unhappy hound dog.

"Oh, for Christ's sake!" Regeane shouted. "What is it now? The snake is gone."

"You were looking at someone on the bench. There couldn't have been anyone on the bench. But I saw something on the bench—" Again the stressed axle sound.

Regeane had enough. "Silence!" The building's acoustics were excellent. Regeane's voice reverberated loudly under the roof.

Silve made a snorting noise and shut up.

Regeane marched past the colonnade until she reached Silve. Took her by the ear, led her to the door.

"Hugo says—" Silve screeched.

Regeane cut her off. "You might give some thought to the fact that you and Hugo drink at the same wineshops."

They passed through the door and up the small flight of steps into the square. Regeane looked up. She saw the sky had grown even darker than when they had entered the church. Light rain sprinkled her upturned face.

Silve sniveled. Regeane let go of her ear. "I'll die," she wailed. "The cold and damp will be the death of me. You don't care if I do die. You don't care about anything. You just sit in that little stone room of yours with your face all stiff. Judging us. I'll get siiiick." She wailed. "My lungs will fill up with stinky pus and when I cough, I'll cough up bloooood! I won't be able to walk or climb stairs. I'll get the flux. IIII'llll dieeeee."

If there was anything on earth more disgusting than Silve, Regeane thought, it would be Silve coughing up blood and stinking up their cramped lodging by getting diarrhea. Advertently or inadvertently, Silve had hit on the one thing that would open Regeane's purse. Regeane fished quickly in the leather scrip tied on her belt and pulled out a copper coin. She handed it to Silve. "Oh God, oh Christ! In the name of His Holy Mother and all the saints, go ahead and get yourself some more wine."

"Yukkee," Silve burbled happily, then leaped to her feet and ran around the corner to the wine bar of her choice. Regeane remained near the church.

The sky grew darker, and Regeane felt someone watching her. This didn't surprise her. The Romans, especially Roman men, watched everything. Women were important targets and young women were at the top of their list. The undressing stare was one of their favorites. Regeane thought wryly, *If so, in this case the starer has his work cut out for him.* She wore long, linen drawers attached to long, linen stockings. Strophium around her breasts. Her mother always made her wear it, accompanied by dark warnings that she would sag later in life if she neglected the binder too often. One long, sleeveless linen shift, and another long, linen shift with sleeves at the wrist. Overdress with wide sleeves to the elbow. Dark, woolen mantle wrapped around her head and body. Covering a veil which in turn hid most of her face.

Her eyes searched the square for the watcher, and did not find anyone. The rain increased slightly. The only other person abroad was a beggar. He or she was a filthy pile of rags sleeping on the porch of an insula nearby.

She could still feel the stare. *I am imagining things,* the woman thought. The wolf demurred. She didn't use words, but she knew how to say "no." Her hackles rose. Regeane felt as if a trickle of cold rain ran down her spine.

The stare was malignant, icy, and somehow not . . . living.

She pulled the mantle down further over her face and hurried off in the same direction Silve had taken. She found Silve sitting in a mud puddle near a wineshop. She was cursing. In one hand, she held a large clay bottle, in the other her drawers and strophium. Her stockings were down around her ankles.

"Cool your ass in that, bitch," the wineshop owner shouted.

"You faggot cocksucker," Silve screamed. "What makes you think you ever warmed it?"

Regeane grabbed Silve by the arm. The tavern keeper seemed to be searching for a weapon. Regeane hustled the servant down the street. She found an empty alleyway and served as lookout while Silve put her underwear back on.

"What happened?" She peered down the empty street.

"I gave him the copper," Silve answered, "and he told me if I gave him a little extra, he'd sell me something special—wine with syrup of opium and hemlock."

Regeane was horrified. She had a very good education. She knew how Socrates died. "Hemlock?" she asked.

"It's very good." Silve had her dress up over her head and was tying her strophium. "It gives you a nice tingly feeling."

"To be sure," Regeane answered. *And if you get tingly enough, you die.*

"Anyway, we went in the shit room. We did it on the floor and then when he rolled off, he tried to take the wine jug back." Silve's voice was a yell of sheer outrage.

"So?" Regeane asked.

"I smeared shit on the bastard's head."

"Ah," Regeane said.

Silve washed her hands in a rain puddle, then drank some of the wine. She thrust the jug at Regeane.

"No," Regeane said. "What now?"

Neither of them wanted to return to the lodging house. Silve knew that if Gundabald had returned and was in a bad humor, he'd beat her. So might Hugo if—as she said—he'd had to sell himself to a sodomite for drink money.

At present, no one would lay a hand on Regeane. Hugo never would and Gundabald wouldn't want to risk disfiguring her. She suspected a lot of beatings would come her way if she did not prove as saleable as Gundabald thought. This was only in the nature of a temporary respite. No, she wouldn't be beaten, but she would be locked up and sent supperless to bed. Gundabald would be angry that she didn't return when Hugo sneaked away.

The air was misty with rain. She could see it in the afternoon light sifting past the second-story windows of the houses. She felt the stare again. This time, it seemed closer. She scanned the street. The windows above were tightly shuttered. There were no doors, only blank walls made of the narrow terra-cotta brick the Romans favored. Ahead, the street curved away into the foggy distance.

"Let's see if we can find a bread seller. Have you any more money?" Silve asked.

"A few coppers," Regeane said. She and Silve both loved the flatbreads the Romans made, stuffed with olives, onions, garlic, and savory bits of pork. Regeane's stomach was griping.

They wandered off together in search of a bread seller. In due time, they found one and got lost in the narrow twisting streets near the ruined Colosseum. Regeane spotted the tall cypresses lining the Appian Way and they found themselves walking along the most famous of all roads to Rome.

They were looking down on the city. It was covered by low-ering rain clouds. Swags of mist stretched like gauze curtains between earth and sky. The afternoon was wearing on toward night, the wind getting colder and colder.

"Let's stop and finish the breads here," Silve said. They'd each eaten one when they got it. Each had one left.

"There's no place to sit," Regeane said.

"Don't be silly. If we take the bread home, Gundabald and Hugo will eat it." Silve pointed to a ruined tomb down the road. "We can go in there."

At the height of the Roman order and power, people had buried their dead here. Now, all the tombs were desecrated; robbed long ago.

This one must once have belonged to a great man, but now the building was empty. The sarcophagus rested at the roadside. Shepherds driving their flocks to market used it as a watering trough.

The tomb once looked like a small house with a pitched roof, but one wall was broken and the side of the structure opened to the elements. However, the overhanging roof and the low plat-form that once held the sarcophagus created a dry spot where they could sit, look out on the road, and finish their stuffed bread.

Regeane was ravenous. She felt a mild despair as she de-voured the food. She could have eaten several more. Silve drank the wine with her loaf. She was soon replete and slightly glassy-eyed. She itched and started scratching herself everywhere.

Regeane finished the bread, licked her greasy fingers, and wondered if there was enough food in the world. She also understood why Silve and Hugo drank the noxious mixture of wine and drugs—they stilled the pangs of hunger. She was tempted by what remained in Silve's jug, but resolutely resisted the temptation. The stuff was poison and, sooner or later—probably sooner—it would kill them.

Silve continued scratching vigorously.

"Silve," Regeane snapped. "Are you taken with a plague of bugs?"

"No," Silve said. "It's the poppy gum. The stuff takes you that way sometimes."

Regeane glanced around uneasily. The sky seemed to have grown even darker.

"Shit," Silve said thickly. "It will rain all night. I've a good mind to find a warm taverna and spread my legs in the back room. Come one! Come all! A copper apiece! At least I'll get to sleep half the night. The tavern keeper will want part of my take, but he'll give me plenty of wine, and I won't have that damn Hugo rubbing me raw while he sweats the drink out of his carcass. The bastard can get it up while he's drunk, but the nasty little cocksucker can't get it down."

"Why don't you leave him then?" Regeane asked.

Silve laughed. "Because, of the nearest two, I owe money to the owner of the first. The barmaid of the second told me if I took away any late night business from her, she'd cut my face."

"Awkward," Regeane said commiseratingly.

"Whatever," Silve replied.

The Appian Way gleamed in the fading light like a narrow black ribbon. As Regeane watched, a few lights appeared in farmhouse windows along the road.

"We have to go," Regeane said, some alarm in her voice. "It won't be safe here after dark. As it is, I'll be locked up and you'll probably get a beating."

"Noooooo," Silve moaned. "It's dry here. Waaaaarm. I want to stay," she sniveled.

Again, Regeane felt the sensation of being watched. She glanced at Silve and saw a wasp crawling over her face. The insect was black, an iridescent blue-black. The tiny carapace shone like a dark rainbow. She looked more closely and saw the whole right side of Silve's body was covered with them crawling everywhere. Dark antennae quivered on their heads; feet feeling, exploring. Their bulbous abdomens armed with the vicious stingers wavered above Silve's skin.

Regeane reached out, snatched Silve's dress at the shoulder, and pulled her out of the tomb. Silve saw the wasps. She screamed and began waving her arms, beating at them with her hands.

To Regeane's momentary surprise, the wasps didn't sting

Silve. They drew away and hovered near the entrance to the tomb like an evil black cloud. Silve, still half drunk, staggered. She was searching her face and body for possible lumps.

Regeane looked down the Appian Way and saw it coming.

"No," she whispered. Then screamed, "Run, Silve! Run!"

"Run?" Silve said looking around. "Run where?"

The thing was approaching faster and faster, moving like the first rocks of an avalanche, but headed up the road toward Regeane. It gabbled and gibbered with a thousand voices, somehow one in madness and agony. It stank of burning cloth, burning wood, burning bone, burning flesh. Then, as it drew closer, of decomposition and death.

She could hear its voice, howling and shouting at her. "Where is she? You saw her. You can bring me to her."

Then it was all around Regeane, and the anguish in the voice was almost beyond endurance. "They said I killed her—her and the child. I never—I never—" The thing moaned.

Regeane threw her mantle over her face, trying to escape the stinking cloud surrounding the apparition. She found herself alone in the dark with it. Its existence flowed with sorrow.

"I couldn't feed them." The desolation in the voice was pain compassed by the hoop of eternity. "I couldn't stand to see their faces as they starved." Sorrow, so heartwrenching it seemed to drown the whole world in grief. "I was mad with pain."

"No," Regeane heard herself shouting. "You were mad with pride." She remembered the woman and the child in the church. "They had wanted to live," she yelled at the damned and damnable thing around her. "They wanted to live! You killed them and you paid the forfeit."

The air around her stank of putrescence. "They hanged me in chains!"

Regeane saw and smelled it. The rotting body swaying at the gallows. Leg only, bones trailing rags of flesh, dancing almost as if alive in the night wind. Falling and scattering in the grass. The torso coming apart at the belly; the hips falling to splatter against the earth dragging the lungs and the skin from the ribs. Last of all, the head and shoulders coming down; the fleshless skull striking the cobbles and bursting with an appalling stench.

The almost-liquid brain mass that had once been the man running off in puddles, congealing to be trampled in the road.

The wasps struck, sinking their stingers into her face through the mantle into her cheeks and tongue, through her dress into her arms and breast, and, worst of all, through her eyelids into her eyeballs.

She didn't hear the wolf roar. Her own screams deafened her. She only knew she had four legs, not two. Her jaws opened with a shout of outrage and fire filled the air around her.

When she woke, she was lying on her side. One shoulder rested in a clean rain puddle. She opened her eyes and slowly got to her feet. One side of her dress was soaked. She explored her face and neck with trembling fingers. No swelling. No pain. Had the whole thing all been a dream?

She glanced down. Near the puddle a big patch of mud showed canine footprints. She remembered the wolf coming to her aid. Had she really been here? Somehow fought off the terror? Regeane was too stupefied by shock to consider the implications of this.

She looked around. Silve was gone. She had evidently found somewhere to run. Then she realized the tomb where they stopped to eat had vanished. It simply didn't exist any longer.

Regeane picked up her skirts and ran.

She stopped running near the city. Not because she was winded. Her stamina was usually greater than most humans'. But because she passed some laborers working near the city. And was frightened by their stares. Respectable women alone were an uncommon sight. Prostitutes advertised their wares. So she wouldn't be taken for one of them, but she might be mistaken for a married woman sneaking out to see her lover. As such, she left herself open to being accosted by some lecherous opportunist. She stopped, wrapped herself tightly in her mantle, pulled the veil down over her face, bowed her head, and walked on.

She didn't dare pass through the ruined Forum so late. She started home through the narrow streets surrounding the Pantheon. These alleys were impassable except on foot. Flights of stone stairs surrounded the terra-cotta brick walls. Among them, it might as well have been night.

The sky above was a dim blue-gray pall. What little light remained showed only rain misting past high shuttered windows.

She was making her way home as quickly as possible when she met the funeral cortege. It was a poor one—the corpse wrapped in a winding sheet carried on an open bier. Torches flared in the hands of a few relatives and friends following the dead man. The flames sputtered in the wind, funnelled down the street, and burned blue from the damp.

Regeane flattened herself against the wall to let them pass.

Silve appeared from the darkness like a bat flying out of the mouth of a cave. "Witch!" she screamed as she pointed at Regeane. "Demoness! She is here to steal his soul. Kill her! Kill her! She will drag his soul to hell and sell it to the devil in place of her own!"

Regeane stood for a few seconds transfixed by both fear and sheer astonishment. Then she saw the dead man's relatives believed Silve. The pain and sheer terror in her voice carried a dreadful certainty with them. Even Regeane could tell that whatever the truth or falsity of the servant's outcries, Silve herself believed them—absolutely. Suddenly, the bier rested in the street and the burial party were groping for missiles in the shadows.

Regeane ran again. The only thing that saved her was the relative scarcity of stoning material. Yet even as she fled, she felt something hit her hard in the small of the back. A broken roof tile slashed past her arm, leaving a burning sensation behind. Then she was clear of the enclosing walls, running along a thoroughfare intended for more than foot traffic. The lodging house was just ahead.

She slowed, not wanting anyone to see how frightened she was. The sky was indigo blue twilight, not quite night. An outside stair on the side of the house led to their quarters.

She was climbing the stairs when she saw her arm was cut and her hand bloody. She wiped it on her dark mantle. The thick woolen mantle was almost black; she hoped the blood wouldn't show. She flexed her arm, and the cut closed.

She was thinking only of warmth and safety when she entered the door. She knew she would be locked in for the night, but even the narrow room seemed a secure haven after what she'd been through today. She had no idea what awaited her.

IV

FOR THE FIRST TIME IN MONTHS, THE ROOM WAS warm. Braziers glowed in each corner. A roaring fire burned on the hearth.

Regeane sank into a chair by the fire.

Hugo and Gundabald sat together at the table, feasting.

The wolf's nose wandered among perfumes, saffron, cinnamon, cloves, and pepper—spices that didn't find their way into the food ordinary people ate.

Gundabald was disjointing a capon stuffed with a forcemeat of preserved figs, seasoned with butter, cinnamon, and the excruciatingly expensive pepper. His cheeks gleamed with grease. He popped some of the moist, delicious meat into his mouth, then glared angrily at Regeane. "Where the hell have you been?"

She realized his anger concealed some anxiety. Since he had never before shown any concern for her welfare, she couldn't help but believe his worry must be rooted in some change in her status.

"You've found a match for me, and it's a wealthy one," she said.

"Clever girl! Now, where the hell have you been?" He was rising from the table.

The wolf warned her. She didn't listen or react quickly enough, but she was on her feet when he reached her. He backhanded her across the face as hard as he could. Her head flipped loose on her neck like a broken doll's. She lost consciousness for a second. Her ankle caught on one leg of the chair. She fell, striking her head hard against the floor. This was the first time she felt the full power of a man's fist directed at her. The sheer force and destructive ability was shocking.

She sat up, then. Using the arm of the chair, she pulled herself to a standing position. Blood was streaming from her nose and trickling from one corner of her mouth.

Gundabald stood in front of the fire, warming himself at the flames.

She reached for a napkin, one of the ones on the table.

"Damn! Don't stain the linen," Gundabald said.

Regeane used her mantle to wipe off the blood on her face.

"Now, where have you been?"

"Hugo deserted us," she said.

Hugo—his mouth full—made a gabbling noise.

"Shut up!" Gundabald said, then clouted him hard on the side of the head.

Hugo strangled, and began coughing on what he was trying to swallow.

"I'm surrounded by fools!" Gundabald mused. "Don't you ever dare leave your cousin alone in the streets again! Hear me!" he roared. "Or that's only a taste of what you'll get."

"God! God! God! Yes," Hugo moaned. "Christ Jesus Savior, what's gotten into you! First, you try to spoil what little looks she has . . . then you're . . . clubbing at me . . . what . . ."

"Shut up!" Gundabald roared.

Hugo shut up.

"You," Gundabald said, "are a fool who never can see beyond the end of your nose. And she," he pointed at Regeane, "is a hateful little snob who no doubt wishes both you and I are in hell! But she is now very valuable property! She is sold! And a damned generous price I got for her in the bargain. No! It's not a great match. That's not to be expected. She's too damned poor, but it's a wealthy one. The fellow is sitting on a pile of gold. The king wants to bring him to heel. A marriage is cheaper and a whole lot less trouble than throwing an army against his stronghold. The king will expect him," Gundabald chuckled, "to be deeply and tangibly grateful for a match among the royal kin, and so will I. In fact, the moneylenders had only to hear his name and their purses opened. Did you think all of this luxury fell like manna from heaven?"

Regeane's nose had stopped bleeding though she could taste salt in her mouth from an oozing cut on the inside of her cheek. But the terror she felt outweighed the pain. "What about the full moon?" she whispered.

Gundabald stepped toward her. She shrank back, cringing away from his fist.

"Wolf," Gundabald said softly. "More like a dog, and a whipped dog at that."

Regeane hated herself for being grateful that he didn't hit her again. Somewhere in the darkness deep down, the wolf was enraged beyond reason, but the woman wouldn't let her near consciousness.

"You are a fool," he continued. "Do you know that? This man loves you about as well as you love him—that is to say, not at all. What were you thinking he'd do—welcome you to his bosom? A penniless woman fobbed on him by a king. A mighty king. A king he dare not disobey."

Gundabald backed up and warmed his rear end at the fire. He laughed harshly. "God, my sister was a mawkish sentimentalist. The idea of bringing up a thing like you to be a proper lady? But then considering what has to be done, perhaps you're better off as you are. No, trust me, bitch creature. Your secret is the least of your worries. From the day you arrive, you'll probably have to be careful of everything you eat or drink. As soon as he dares, he'll be rid of you."

Regeane stared at him, eyes wide, her guts turning to water, sick with terror.

"Wake up, you lackwit," Gundabald said gleefully. "Nothing protects you. How many wives have been dismissed in disgrace, labeled barren by their husbands because they were never bedded?" Gundabald smiled. His big, blunt teeth gleamed yellow against his black beard.

"Barren," Gundabald mused. "Barrenness is a kindly, even compassionate excuse. Are you aware of how easy it is for a great lord to arrange the pollution of his marriage bed? He waits until nightfall, then sends a strong servant to her room. They are caught. The man—already paid—flees. But the next morning, she is led out into the wilderness with a halter around her neck. Unless she has a family to uphold her protestations of innocence, the woman is doomed. There, near a lake or swamp, the erstwhile wife is strangled or drowned. She is forgotten, the mud is her tomb.

"I've only mentioned two ways husbands have of ridding themselves of inconvenient spouses. There are others, many others. One wrong move—one moment's silly arrogance—and he'll be done with you." Gundabald shrugged and smiled his terrible smile again. "Perhaps your foot won't even have to slip. Perhaps he prefers his concubines already. In fact, the more I think about it, the less I doubt my own judgement. And, as for you, whey-faced brat, you have nothing to recommend you. Not wealth. Not strong kinfolk. No, not even a hint of beauty. You pale, flat-chested, stupid little twat . . ."

"Father," Hugo shouted. "Stop! Look at her. I've seen dead men with more color in their faces. You don't want her to hang herself before she even sees him. We need the money!"

Gundabald snorted. "What do you want me to do? Let her go into this marriage with her head stuffed with moonbeams? Most men are like me, even the good ones. They have the morals of bulls or stags.

"This one now. This one likely has the morals of a jackal." He spoke thoughtfully, at least as much to himself as to Regeane. "Else, how did he rise from paid hireling to his present position of eminence?

"God, but Gisela spoiled you. It is time you found out how the world goes and what drives it. I see it's up to me to teach you and, if you don't learn, your husband will likely kill you, if the church doesn't burn you first."

Regeane could feel herself trembling. Her stomach muscles fluttered. Not so much because of the threats Gundabald held over her head. She had confronted them all her life. But because she knew she was in the presence of evil. Gundabald was cruel, but when he was sober, his outbursts were almost always calculated to serve his interests. He wanted something from her and it couldn't be good.

Regeane wiped blood from her mouth with her hand and looked at it.

Gundabald walked up to her and slapped her again. Not as hard as before. This time only enough to make her ears ring and her nose bleed a little. "Pay attention," he said smiling. "Pain is a great attention-getter. At least I've found it so. Now, don't be downcast," he said gently. "And don't be afraid. We won't abandon you."

She wondered if he was egotistical enough to believe she found this promise comforting.

His face was close to her. His breath laden with the scent of the elaborately spiced food was hot on her skin. She sat down to escape the sickening smell.

"This man's demesne straddles one of the passes through the Alps. Every merchant and traveler crossing the mountains makes him richer. But this rascal is an upstart, lord of a band of mercenaries. Their loyalty can, no doubt, be bought once his strongboxes are in our hands. But it will be up to you to make the killing look like an accident!

"Now." He lifted her out of her chair by the loose fabric on the front of her dress. She could feel his knuckles pressing into her sternum. His lips were near her ear. "Now, little girl," he said softly, "tell me you understand me and will do as I say. Sweet, now," he shook her lightly. "Repeat after me. 'I will do as my wise uncle tells me.' Say it!" he commanded.

Regeane's hands rose from the chair arms. The nails were sharp at the tips. She dragged them down both of Gundabald's cheeks to the chin. Blood and skin peeled in long strips from his cheeks.

He screamed. He lifted her upright with one hand. With the other, he drove his fist directly into her face.

She flew backward. The chair went over. Her body hit the floor and rolled. In the darkness, she fought the wolf for control. The creature was madly trying to come to her aid, but she had the woman's more rational terror on her side—the fear that if the creature appeared in her present weakened condition, Gundabald would be able to kill it.

The wolf was hesitant—retreated into savage silence. Regeane came to full consciousness on her knees.

Gundabald was holding her body up by her hair and flogging her with his belt. She was in so much pain, fighting back was instinctive.

One of the braziers was within reach. She snatched at it, got one leg, and flung the coals at Gundabald.

He ran across the room, drawing his sword. Hugo jumped behind him.

Regeane realized the reason for their terror. The brazier was solid iron. No normal woman or even most men would have been able to lift it and scatter the contents as she just had.

"The building will burn," Hugo squeaked.

No, Regeane thought. *I might hope so, but it won't.*

She was right. Damp had invaded every piece of wood in the holy city during the last few weeks of rain. The floor was slimy with it. The coals smoked, stank, and hissed viciously, but began going out one by one.

"It's dark outside." Hugo gave a hiccuping wail.

"Yes, I know," Gundabald said, flourishing the sword. "Jesus Christ," he continued in a soft, astounded voice. "She's just like her father."

Regeane was on her feet—swaying a bit, but standing.

"Twice," Gundabald said. "I hit her as hard as I could with my fist. A normal woman would be dead or at least unconscious."

"Tell me about my father?" Regeane asked.

Gundabald shrugged.

"You want this man to die very suddenly. The same way my father did. He was hard to kill, wasn't he?" Regeane asked.

"Nearly impossible. In fact, we wouldn't have succeeded with him if your mother hadn't taken a hand."

"No!" Regeane shouted. "Not my mother!"

"Oh, yes," Gundabald said cynically, "the saintly Gisela."

"It's not true," Regeane said, shaking her head from side to side like a tormented beast. "I don't believe you. I won't believe you. I can't believe you. She loved him."

Gundabald sheathed his sword, sat down, and poured himself a cup of wine. Gundabald was smiling again. He loved inflicting pain and he was succeeding beyond his wildest dreams with Regeane. "Oh, yes, we tried twice. His constitution defied poison. He had the wolf's ability to vomit immediately anything that disturbed him. We sent paid assassins. They didn't return. I can't think of what he did with them."

Gundabald looked baffled for a moment. "We never found

any trace. Not clothing, weapons, bones, not even skulls or—damnation on it—teeth. They simply vanished. It wasn't until we convinced your mother that his powers were demonic, and he would carry her off with him, that she took a hand. She was difficult to persuade. I believe they may have had that sexual intensity between them that passes for love. At any rate, he fell victim to her wiles.

"They had a place near his stronghold—a love nest where they crept away alone to engage in private dalliance. We all rode out on a hunt party—you must understand ordinary hunts bored him—she enticed him to their special bower and I—" Gundabald paused for effect and simply beamed upon Regeane. "I put a crossbow bolt through his heart. He died instantly before his alter ego had time to heal him."

Regeane bowed her head and rested her forehead against the back of the chair. She wondered for how long she had refused to see, refused to understand.

She'd spent her life burdened with her mother's sorrow, long nights of weeping, self-accusation. Her mother's despair had been their constant companion as Gisela dragged Regeane from church to church, shrine to shrine. Gisela spent the remainder of her life on her knees, begging God's forgiveness for the one sin she didn't dare admit, even to Regeane: the murder of the man she loved.

"Those Saxons," Gundabald continued. "I was afraid of them, but there again, your mother was invaluable. Her grief was so terrible we had to set a watch over her lest she do herself some harm. So his people were convinced we couldn't have had any part in his death. When they understood his line failed—their sorrow was nearly as great as your mother's. They departed for their northern forests. Unfortunately, as I found out later, they also took the greater part of his wealth with them. Your mother retained only what was bestowed on her on the morning after the wedding. A very generous sum. A handsome endowment for a woman, but not nearly enough for a family's needs. Now you have a chance to repair our fortunes. And you're playing the fool!"

"I'm sorry," Regeane said quietly. The wolf gritted her teeth, but the woman really tried to sound penitent. "You had not heretofore fully explained the situation. My mother understood her duty to her family. I'm sure I will understand mine."

A crossbow bolt through the heart. She'd never seen a human shot with a crossbow, but they were common weapons. Mostly used on large animals, wild cattle, boar, or bear. She had once seen a stag brought down by one. Though not hit in a vital spot, the deer fell, its shoulder crushed. It died of shock and blood loss a few seconds later. Her mind turned from the memory. Wolfstan had known himself betrayed by the woman he loved, even as he fell.

They planned to use her in the same way they'd used her mother. Even if she refused to help them, she knew that wouldn't stop their plotting. They had turned to her mother only when other methods failed with Wolfstan.

Gundabald eyed her suspiciously. Her capitulation had been too rapid. "My, we are mealy-mouthed all of a sudden," he said.

"Yes," Regeane replied, "but I don't really have a choice, do I?"

Gundabald uncovered another one of the dishes. This one a highly spiced fish stew, thick with onions, leeks, and blazing hot cracked peppercorns. "Want some?" Gundabald asked, spooning it out on a trencher and falling to with his fingers.

The dish assaulted the wolf's nose across the room. "No. I have no appetite. My head is spinning." She looked around. The air in the room was a smoky haze, left by the brazier's embers as they burnt themselves out.

The blazing hearth fire was dying down, the remaining braziers darkening. Cold began creeping in.

Regeane walked over to the table. Gundabald was occupied by his greed and a jug of good red wine. Hugo, when he saw her walking toward him, scuttled to the other side of the table. Gundabald rolled his eyes at him, annoyed. "Where is your sword?" he mumbled, his mouth full.

Hugo looked shamefaced. "I pawned it to buy drink a few days ago."

Regeane stopped in front of the table.

"Have some food," Gundabald invited her.

Regeane shook her head. "Only a cup of wine."

Hugo poured it and offered it to her, keeping his arm extended, well away from her.

She took the wine—sipped it. *Very good*, she thought—finished the cup and placed it on the table. Exhaustion was on her like a leaden cope, weighing her down.

"Remember," Gundabald said.

"Yes," Regeane answered.

"You don't really have any choice." His face was red, smeared with grease, flushed with all the wine he'd taken. The marks scored by her nails on his cheeks were still visible. He probably couldn't feel them now, but in the morning he would, along with his hangover.

She felt she'd gained at least a small advantage. She'd better press that now. "I'll need some money," she said.

"For what?" he asked, then ate a large prawn yellowed with saffron. "Wonderful!" he exclaimed, then gulped a mouthful of some pale vintage.

"Clothes!" Regeane said. "Look at me. This is the best dress I have. I'll need at least one new mantle and two respectable gowns. Not to mention something to attend the marriage feast in."

"Don't worry," Gundabald said. "He won't be in Rome for months."

"I'll still need to get a start," Regeane said.

Gundabald was almost drunk. He was happy, things were going his way. He knew the girl was going to be a problem, but he had months to break her, crush her spirit.

Outside the wind buffeted the building. A particularly loud blast rattled the shutters, making it sound as if a giant hammer was being flung at the walls. He shivered. Next time, he wouldn't tackle her after dark. True, her face was swollen and mottled with bruises, the gown she wore stiff with bloodstains, but she still looked entirely too good to have taken the full force of his arm.

Next time, he would face off with her by day and he could learn to judge more exactly how much punishment she could take without being maimed or killed. Physical suffering inflicted on a regular basis would soon sap her will to resist him. So much the better if it didn't leave scars behind.

He fished in his scrip for some money. Regeane saw the glint of gold among the coins. She didn't think she'd get any. She was right. Twenty or so copper coins and four silver dinars landed on the table. Thankful for that much, she quickly scooped them up and went into her room.

The imprisoning bolts rattled shut as soon as the door closed behind her. She had one bolt on her side, and she drove it home. She stripped off her dress and shift. Then the wolf smelled food!

She burrowed under the blankets with her hands and found the pot. The old woman must have put it there. Protected by earthenware and the blankets, it was still just warm. The room was freezing. The shutters over the barred window did nothing to stop the wind.

Unimpeded and welcome, the wolf visited. She was starving. It took her less time to finish the stew than it would the woman. Her fur sealed out the cold. The rough tongue made one last circuit of the bowl.

Then, the woman jumped up naked and climbed quietly into the bed. Regeane crouched down under the covers and blessed the old woman: she'd double blanketed the bed and put on clean linen sheets. They were patched, worn, and threadbare, but smooth and comfortable to the touch.

When the wolf left, she took most of Regeane's injuries with her. Her body no longer ached, though she remained exhausted almost to the point of unconsciousness. Still, her mind would not stop working.

Gundabald! The devil! They were one and the same. She knew she'd only begun to taste the misery he planned to deal her.

How could they have persuaded her mother to connive at the death of one who had loved and protected her? What kind of exchange had Wolfstan been for Firminius, her mother's second husband? She remembered him as notable only for corpulence, indolence, and monumental greed.

No, she had nothing to hope for from Gundabald and everything to fear. Somehow she must escape, but she had no idea how. The little money he had given her would not carry her far.

The she-wolf, bold creature that she was, was simply angered by the usurpation of her freedom. She was physically mature, but her sexual maturity didn't match the woman's. She was yet the lean hunter—meat provider of the pack—able to outrace even the fleetest deer. Vestal virgin of the moonglow—

unchosen, untouched. She might rise to defend the woman on the marriage bed.

Ye gods! the woman thought. *A true disaster.* She must escape. How? Where?

Something plucked at the edges of her memory the way an importunate beggar plucks at one's sleeves. Wolfstan! His people believed his line had failed. Gundabald let that slip. But it hadn't failed. She was here, carrying the same powers he had. They called him the Talisman. Who told her his story? She couldn't remember and was too tired to try.

Her decision was made. It left her at peace. Could she find her father's people? She would face pursuit and treachery by Gundabald and Hugo. So be it. The female hunter of the dark stared at her from the edge of sleep with glowing eyes, beckoning her into beyond.

She would succeed or die trying. She and herself were in accord. Regeane followed the wolf drifting into darkness where, in the shadowland of sleep, she and her companion could run free . . . through the endless forests of her dreams.

SHE WOKE EARLY. ONLY A FAINT BLUE LIGHT SHONE in around the shutters. She ruffled through the basket under her bed, searching for a few clean things to wear. Again, the old woman had not failed her. She had freshly washed a clean gray linen gown and a worn, but redyed, brown mantle. Underwear and a very threadbare veil of her mother's—it had large, translucent patches—completed the ensemble.

She was afraid the door might be locked, but the old woman was there, involved in her endless cleaning, and she had undone the bolts.

Regeane collected Hugo—he protested weakly, but mindful of Gundabald's orders, he came. She passed the old woman sweeping the hall with a twig broom.

Hugo was already out and going down the steps. Regeane paused next to her and pressed one of the silver coins into her hand.

The old woman could tell by the touch it was more than a copper. Her eyes widened as she secreted it. "Good fortune," she whispered. "May the Virgin watch over you. Take care. They are both pigs . . ." she muttered. "Pigs!"

Regeane hurried down the stair following Hugo. The sky was gray, as was the light around them.

"It's before dawn," Hugo whimpered. "Where are we going?"

"The thieves' market," Regeane said.

"I'll kill that little cunt, Silve, for leaving me with this problem," Hugo muttered. "What did you do to her? I went looking for her last night."

Gundabald probably made him, Regeane thought.

"I couldn't find her in any of the usual tavernas. She's disappeared. Oh, my head," he sniffed. "My tongue tastes like the floor of an outhouse. My eyeballs are fried. The food, it burnt doing down, but it was worse going out. It feels like somebody poured hot grease up my ass."

"It's the pepper. Would a jug of wine quiet your nether regions?" Regeane asked.

"A jug of wine would quiet a lot of regions," Hugo replied.

Regeane gave him some copper coins. "Please don't buy the same stuff Silve did yesterday."

"What was it?" Hugo asked.

"She said it had poppy gum and hemlock in it."

"No wonder I couldn't find her," Hugo commented glumly. "She's lying dead somewhere and nobody noticed her because she hasn't started to stink yet."

Regeane's stomach rumbled with hunger. "Go get your wine," she said irritably.

Hugo returned with a wineskin. He dosed himself liberally on their way to the market. He brightened a bit, but continued complaining as they walked. "It's dangerous," he said, "even for a man. You might be subjected to insults not proper for a lady to hear."

Regeane stopped so quickly Hugo ran into her.

They were turning into a piazza by then. "Go away," she whispered between her teeth to Hugo. "Amuse yourself. I don't care how, but don't bother me while I'm trying to shop. Now, go away."

He did, drifting off after giving her an apprehensive look.

The little market square was filled with merchants whose mules were still harnessed to their carts. All in all, a highly mobile group. Ready to vanish quickly when the papal guard, the only effective law in the city, made one of its periodic sweeps through Rome. They were close to the river. The insulas surrounding the square were run down. In many cases, the first floors were abandoned to the Tiber's periodic floods and the omnipresent damp.

The cloth seller's cart was sandwiched between a slave dealer's wretched stock and a load of broken furniture. To Regeane it looked like kindling. Irredeemable junk. The man hawking it was aggressive. On seeing Regeane, he tried selling her a "beautiful" chair—a perfect chair if only she had the enterprise to add one leg. And, he burbled cheerfully, he had several ones that would do. And he would offer them to her at a very nominal price.

"Firewood," Regeane said.

The cloth seller cackled gleefully as Regeane pushed past and began examining the dresses hanging from the staves of his two-wheeled cart.

She glanced at the slaves, then quickly away. She shuddered. They were a painful sight. All women, too young, old, or ugly to interest the dealers in more attractive human merchandise at the bigger markets.

By and large, the dresses were equally hopeless. Most were worn. All were too small. Regeane was considered tall. The condition of the cloth discouraged her more than anything else. Silve had told her there were bargains to be had here, but nothing she'd seen was worth flint and steel to turn it into fire and smoke. If she could find good cloth, she was willing to rip out the seams, bleach, dye, and resew. But cloth so rotten it tore while being handled was hopeless.

"Cleaning rags," she whispered.

The furniture seller looked angry. "Firewood!" he said in the Roman gutter argot. "Cleaning rags! Barbarian hellcat. She needs a lesson."

The cloth seller laughed again, then dragged something from under the debris in the cart. The thing, though stained at the hem, was beautiful: an overdress of blue brocade trimmed in white fur. The cloth seller dangled it before her.

"How much?" Regeane asked suspiciously.

"Six coppers only," the cloth seller said, placing it in her hands.

Yes, it was in good condition. Her knowing fingers explored the fabric. Not pure silk, but that wasn't to be expected, not here. If the stains didn't wash out she . . .

The world vanished. She could feel the garrotte around her throat and even before it closed, she knew herself a dead woman. The man's hands tightening the wire and twisting the wooden dowels at the back of her neck were too strong for her to challenge. Even though she ripped into them with her nails, felt the skin peel, and her fingertips slick with blood. She knew the hands would not release the wire and even probably took some satisfaction from the proof of her agony.

The steel thread crushed her windpipe. Sight was gone. Air was gone. Life was gone. The only thing remaining was the scream . . . silent . . . only in her brain and it went on and on and on and . . .

Regeane threw the dress away from her.

"What? Are you sick?" the cloth seller shouted. "Are you pregnant?"

"Why is it?" Regeane replied acidly. She was leaning on the cart, trying to get her stomach under control. "Why is it when a woman turns pale or seems ill—if she's below seventy years—the nearest man asks her if she's pregnant?"

"Because she often is," a musical voice answered. "But in your case, I believe you to be unusually perceptive."

Regeane turned and looked at the speaker. She was dangling the luxurious robe by one finger as if it were some filthy discard. "Take this . . . thing," she said to the cloth seller, "and dump it into the unmarked grave where she lies. I'll pay you."

"Oh, God!" Regeane said. "That's foul." She was wiping her hands on her mantle. She felt contaminated.

The cloth seller tucked the robe deep into the rags on his cart.

The woman continued lazily. "Its previous owner betrayed her lover to a man named Paul Afartha. He pulled the strings on our late Lombard pope. Her lover belonged to the present pope's party. Paul had him tortured but—unfortunately for her—not to death. He was released when Hadrian became pope. He's blind in one eye and lacks some fingers, but he still has one good eye and two hands. He strangled her. She was wearing that dress at the time."

"It's a good piece of cloth," the man grumbled.

This time the imposing woman spoke sharply. "Bring the thing to my house. Apply to my maid, Susanna. She will pay you and burn it. Sacred blood, man! Stains from her last natural functions discolor the hem. Do as I say."

"Yes, my lady," the man replied meekly.

Regeane felt disheveled. She was. Mantle at her feet, veil on her shoulders. The speaker, a tall woman, was fingering her hair.

Regeane had an impression of rich clothing and silky exquisite perfume. Two large men who flanked the lady prevented forward progress. Regeane tried to ease backward. Impossible. She was caught between the cloth seller's cart and the furniture man's. They were pushed together at the back. She was wedged between them.

"What's a beautiful creature like you doing fumbling through trash like this? I could easily find you a . . . protector who would buy you better gowns," the lady said.

"I wouldn't . . . I don't think . . . I don't know . . ." Regeane stammered, trying to push past the lady and her escort. The two men planted themselves like boulders and refused to let her by. The lady blocked the passage between them. They all looked amused.

Regeane had never been so close to anyone as well dressed or as clean and sweet-smelling as this woman. The wolf was charmed and half in love already.

"Cluck, cluck, cluck." The furniture seller mimicked Regeane. "Stand up and speak to Lucilla like a proper woman. She's as nervous as a pullet in a yard full of roosters," he told Lucilla.

Regeane was stung.

The wolf was stung.

Regeane drew herself up and studied the woman called Lucilla.

At first sight, she seemed young, but then Regeane realized this was an illusion created by a number of deftly applied decorations. Her shift was Egyptian linen, a fine weave embroidered with white silk. The overdress she wore was a woolen silk damask, dyed two shades of green and of such a fresh, bright color that it reminded Regeane of the first flush of new leaves in the spring. Some very clever painting. Powdering had been done to her face. She was still beautiful, but carried the telltale marks of age in the lines around the eyes and mouth, and the faint, as yet so very faint, webbing of wrinkles on the brow and cheeks.

"How do you do this to your hair? By what art?" Lucilla asked. "Teach me. I'll pay you well. I'd like to learn it."

"No art," Regeane said. "I know no arts. My hair has been so since I can remember." Her hair was as the silver wolf's fur, dark shading to white at the tips. Each tress appeared dipped in moonlight.

"No art," Lucilla said. "Of course not. I was foolish even to ask. You are obviously as nature made you. Not even a strophium." Regeane's hair fell from her fingers.

Regeane gasped. Her hands came up to search her breasts. Her cheeks glowed. "Oh, my God," she gasped. "I forgot."

Lucilla's escorts and the two merchants doubled whooping with laughter.

Lucilla stretched out her hand and cupped one of Regeane's breasts. "May the angels bless my soul," she said quietly. "A ripe peach. My poor dear, you don't need a binder."

Regeane knew she should be angry at the liberties taken with her person, but she found the lady's touch stimulated a stab of pleasure in a part of her body far from her breast. She caught Lucilla's wrist, but didn't push her away. Lucilla withdrew her hand at her own pace, slipping her wrist slowly through Regeane's fingers.

"Are you a free woman?" the lady asked abruptly.

"Free and freeborn," Regeane replied proudly and a little angrily. This woman was frightening her. She wondered if she should shout for Hugo, but then abandoned the idea immediately. The two mercenaries accompanying Lucilla were well armed, well dressed, well paid, and—doubtless—well practiced servants of a noble house. Either one of them could pulverize Hugo with one hand.

"Married or betrothed?" Lucilla asked.

"Betrothed," Regeane answered doubtfully.

Lucilla pounced on the uncertainty in her voice. "Then you don't like him?"

"I don't know." Regeane felt at a loss. "I've never met or even seen him."

"Aah," Lucilla said. She smiled, lowered her eyelids. Regeane was amazed to see the eyelashes were outlined in black and the lids themselves were stained pale blue, shading away at her brows.

"Why not come home with me," Lucilla said. "I'll give you a good dinner, then you can share my couch. In the morning, my maids will fit you with a better dress than any you could buy here. And if I find you especially pleasing, as I believe I will, you shall have a little gold in the bargain."

Regeane didn't say anything at first because she didn't understand. When she did, the proposition was so foreign to her experience, she was confused by it. She blushed, then became very annoyed with herself for blushing and made a determined effort to get out of her corner.

Lucilla and the two mercenaries stepped aside laughing. Regeane was ready to flee, not out of displeasure, but embarrassment. She was brought to a halt immediately.

The cloth seller, perched on his wagon seat, had a good grip on the back of her dress. He shook her gently. "Fluffy little hatchling. Don't pay any attention to her, Lucilla. Her feathers are still damp. She doesn't understand what a fine offer you've made her. Listen to the barbarous turn of her Latin speech. She's a Frank."

"He's right, lovely one," Lucilla said. "Don't run away until you're sure you want to. Girls have gone from my arms to the beds of kings, cardinals, and popes." She lifted one beautiful long-fingered hand in a graceful gesture. "I, and I alone, have made the fortunes of several noble families."

The cloth seller let go of her dress and tapped Regeane on the shoulder. "You see before you," he said indicating Lucilla, "the richest and most successful courtesan in Rome. Her interest in you is an honor. Ah, these stern, virtuous barbarians. They keep their women so closely guarded. She looks still a virgin. She must be." He lifted Regeane's arm. "Such skin she has, white as the finest grainless marble. Touched with only the faintest blush of rose," he rhapsodized. "Certainly she's still a virgin."

"I don't know," Lucilla said, tapping her teeth with a fingernail. "Like all barbarians, she's been out in the weather too much. She's a bit tanned. It isn't fashionable at present."

"Tanned!" the cloth seller cried. He sounded mortally wounded. "She isn't tanned. A touch of the sun brings out the warmer flesh tones." He lifted Regeane's arm, exhibiting it like a trophy. "Look at that golden down, softer than the fur on a newborn kitten. Look how it glows in the sunlight." He must have had a good imagination. The sky was gray. The sun hadn't been seen for weeks. "Think how it would glow by lamplight as she undressed herself in your chamber. Think how delightful it will be to instruct this young foam-born Venus in the first arts . . ."

Regeane had heard enough. More than enough. She snatched her arm away from the cloth seller, shouting, "What? Are you getting a commission?"

All the men laughed.

"Yes," Lucilla said. "He began waving his arms at me the moment you reached his cart, but don't worry, he's already earned his pay. The man admires you. He has a good eye. Tell me, do you still want to run away?"

Regeane knew what her mother would say. "Pick up your veil, snatch your mantle from the stone street. Flee! This woman is painted vice. The very embodiment of sin." *Yes,* Regeane thought, *and you murdered my father. You murdered a man who loved and trusted you.* In a twinkling, her mother was gone and the wolf looked out at Lucilla.

The woman's brows drew together slightly as if she sensed someone else was present.

A thousand cues flooded Regeane's human-wolf senses. The deceiver smells of anxiety, fear, and decaying body chemicals drench the skin and make the truly unscrupulous stink. Nothing like that here. Only clean soap, warm flesh, woman at the

armpits and groin. She didn't trail the nauseating effluvia of
sorrow or pain . . . only peace, silence, but somewhere, grief.

The wolf left. She knew something she hadn't or couldn't tell
Regeane, but she registered no disapproval, only a wish for Lucilla's touch. *My,* Regeane thought, *and what have I to look forward to? Only the narrow stone room and an unknown spouse
who might be both repulsive and cruel.*

"Well," Lucilla prompted. "Still want to run away?"

"No!" Regeane said. "I will never return home."

"My," Lucilla said. "Such grim resolve. And in one so
young. Tell me—"

Hugo, on the other side of the cart, screamed. "The little bitch
bit me."

Regeane peered past the mules' rumps at the group of slaves.

Lucilla chuckled. "It appears one of the slaves just bit a
customer."

"I know," Regeane said. "My cousin, Hugo."

Lucilla clucked her tongue in polite sympathy. "Too bad."

"Not at all," Regeane said. "I hope she drew blood."

They all peered past the carts at Hugo and the slave dealer.

"Cocksucker!" the slave dealer screamed at Hugo. "Why
were you pawing the merchandise if you hadn't the coin to
buy."

"You painted, dung-eating pimp!" Hugo shouted as he drew
his dagger.

"Oh, no!" Regeane cried, trying to push past Lucilla and her
men-at-arms.

"What!" Lucilla snapped, catching Regeane's arm in an iron
grip. "Are you mad! Getting involved in a quarrel in a place like
this? Whatever my people may have become, little barbarian,
they have not quite forgotten they once ruled the world." She
shoved Regeane between the two carts and ordered the soldier
to stay by her side. The cloth seller and the furniture man immediately jumped down, forming a barrier in front of her.

Regeane held her peace. Lucilla was right. Regeane's inter-
ference could do no good. It might rather get her beaten or
killed along with Hugo.

Lucilla elbowed the mercenary not occupied with Regeane.

"Hurry," she said. "Go hit that idiot over the head and content the slave dealer with some silver—if it's not too late."

Luckily, Hugo, not the bravest of men, and the slave dealer, who really didn't have the stomach for any fight involving more than words, were still standing about ten feet apart, hurling insults at each other.

Between the two of them, they had a lot of material. Hugo, who could barely carry on a polite conversation in broken Latin, had fluent command of all the vilest obscenities current among the Roman mob. The slave dealer had a hair-raisingly well-furnished vocabulary also.

A crowd was gathering to watch the show and urge the combatants on; each no doubt hoping some particularly exotic insult would be sufficient to prod one or the other of the antagonists into an attack. The situation could turn ugly at any moment.

But Lucilla's man reached Hugo. He smacked him hard on the side of the head with his sword hilt. Hugo staggered. A glassy stare entered his eyes, then they slowly closed. The big mercenary caught him by the back of the shirt and eased him slowly to the ground.

"By the horned one's balls," Lucilla whispered, "thank heaven for small mercies." She strode toward the slave dealer. He was still waving his arms and shouting in a fine Roman fury. Giving him a contemptuous look, Lucilla quelled him with a sentence in street argot too rapid for Regeane to follow, then placed some silver in his hand.

"Which one bit my cousin?" Regeane asked.

The slave dealer looked around at the wretched huddle of women and children that constituted his stock, then immediately began screaming again.

"What's wrong now?" Regeane asked, frightened.

Lucilla sighed. "The little girl's run away." She spat one word at the distraught slave dealer, one Regeane didn't catch, but it brought him up as short as if she'd flung a shovel full of hot coals at his face.

The slave dealer fell to his knees on the cobbles. "I'm ruined," he moaned. "My wife will starve, my children—"

Lucilla made several statements concerning the slave dealer's relations with his wife, added a short discussion about the paternity of his children that made Regeane gasp and blush, then organized a search for the child.

"Why not let her get away?" Regeane whispered to Lucilla.

Lucilla shook her head. "No. Think. Sooner or later she'll be caught by someone. What will happen to her will be worse than what might happen here. It can't be better."

Regeane nodded. She understood the voice of reason. Even the cruelest protector might be better than to struggle starving and begging at church doors.

The wolf visited Regeane's eyes and ears. The girl staggered slightly with the shock. The light in the square became intense. Smells an overwhelming experience: wet stone, damp air, musty clothing, perspirations shading from ancient sticky filth to fresh acrid adrenal alarm. A veritable flood of sound changes, but one—the most important one—close by. Rapid, frightened breathing near the cloth seller's cart.

Somewhere, the silver wolf stood. She lowered her head to touch noses with a cub, one yet unsteady on its tiny legs. Trust passed between them. The wolf was satisfied, then gone.

Regeane found her eyes were closed. She open them and pried the three remaining silver coins from her scrip.

The slave dealer was still shouting and tearing his hair.

"I'll buy the girl," Regeane said. "How much do you want for her?"

The slave dealer broke off in mid-screech.

Lucilla said, "What!"

"I said, I'll buy the child," Regeane repeated. "Name a price!" She clutched the silver tightly.

The man's eyes fixed on Regeane, a look of hard calculation in them.

"Wait a minute," Lucilla said. "You're going to buy a runaway slave you've never seen. Are you ill? Let me feel your forehead. You must have a fever."

"No!" the slave dealer shouted. "She must know where the child went. It's a put-up job between you."

Finding the search for the slave girl fruitless, the crowd

was beginning to collect around them to watch this new entertainment.

"Where is she, you robber?" the slave dealer screamed at Regeane.

Passion seemed the order of the day. Regeane drew herself up. "Do you want my money or not?" She watched avarice and fury war in the man's face. She gave avarice a little encouragement. "Three silver dinars."

"Done," the slave dealer said.

Regeane slapped the coins into his outstretched palm.

"Where is she, then?" Lucilla asked, hands on hips.

"She's mine," Regeane said. "You're my witness."

"Yes, I'll support you. You're the child's owner. Now, tell us where your property is hidden."

Regeane turned to the cloth seller's wagon. "Come out," she commanded. "Come out now."

The crowd pressed closer. The wagon had been searched, its contents prodded with arms and poles. No one believed the runaway could be there. Laughter could be heard among some of the onlookers.

"Come out," Regeane repeated. "You're safe with me. I'll only like you better for biting Hugo." She glanced over at Hugo. He was sitting up, muttering unintelligibly to himself, and holding his head. Regeane continued. "I have often wished for a . . . similar—yes, similar is the word—opportunity myself."

The little girl dropped from under one of the dresses hanging from the sides of the cart. She was small enough and strong enough to cling like a small monkey to the inside of the dress and so not be found by the hands poking and prodding the cart's contents. Only Regeane and the wolf heard the rapid breathing.

The child was an unattractive specimen. Her blond hair was matted with filth. Little could be told about her features because the small nose was swollen and two steams of blood ran down, smearing her mouth and chin. She was barefoot. The one garment covering her body was a single torn rag. Her expression was one of mutinous bad temper. Obstinate resistance. Regeane approved.

The little girl muttered, "Hyrrokkin wicca."

Hyrrokkin's witch.

A picture flashed from the wolf's mind to the woman's: a face of unearthly loveliness but so white it seemed fashioned of snow. Eyes of terror flashing with the myriad pale blues, greens, and blacks of glacier ice. She of the snowy wastes where the foot of springtime never falls. The "never born," older than the gods, witch queen of mountaintops and glaciers locked in eternal winter. She for whom the only proper sacrifice is human, always ready to choose her own victims: unwary wayfarers, travelers among the high passes deceived by fine days, blinded in the whiteout, wandering in circles, mad with terror. At length when they sink exhausted to the snow, her servants, the wolves, claim them. Men say, or perhaps only whisper, "They looked into her eyes."

The little girl was a Saxon. Regeane spoke the language. Even after her father had died, she had a Saxon nurse for many years. "No," Regeane replied in the child's native tongue. "She never leaves her snows."

Regeane pulled off her veil and handed it to the child. "Go wash your face. Come with me. We will be companions."

The child rose slowly. She studied Regeane's face closely. Then ran toward the fountain carrying the veil.

Lucilla stood next to Regeane. She looked puzzled and a bit disapproving. "I don't deal in children, and I have no truck with those who do," she said. One look at Regeane's horrified expression was enough. "Forget I said anything, please," she pleaded.

Regeane and Lucilla followed the child to the fountain. The child had managed to clean off the blood, but the top layer of grime was intact. Regeane washed the child's face vigorously, grumbling, "You're filthy. Have you been looked after at all? My God, the hair is a rat's nest. I can't do anything with it here."

The little girl closed her eyes and accepted the scrubbing with dignity. "I have but one face. Don't wash it off."

"I want to see what you look like under the filth," Regeane said and smiled. "There, little one. That's better. Are you hungry?"

"But of course she's hungry," Lucilla said. "Children are always hungry."

"It doesn't trouble me," the child said stubbornly.

"She's Saxon," Regeane said proudly. "Most of them would die rather than complain."

Lucilla lifted the child's chin, gave her a quick professional appraisal. "Not bad, better than at first sight. A bud, and a green one at that, but she may yet grow into a beauty."

The child jerked away from Lucilla. "I don't want to be beautiful! I want to be a man. Then I could be revenged on that!" The child stared at Hugo. He was on his feet. The very soldier who'd knocked him out was sympathetically helping him stagger toward the fountain.

"Don't feel too bad about being a woman," Lucilla said, patting the child's head kindly. "Women get their opportunities for revenge, also. Ugh, such hair. She's probably lousey."

"Yes," the child said. "My head crawls and my clothes, too. At home I kept myself clean. I hate this." She shifted her gaze from Regeane's face back to Hugo. "At home," she whispered, "my father would have taught him what it means to lay hands on the daughter of a thane."

Then the child's eyes filled with tears. "I'm crying. I don't want to cry. It's weak to cry, but I want to go home." The soft wail of grief reached into Regeane's heart past all the layers of caution and indifference into the deepest part of her being.

"It's too far away," the child sobbed. "The ship must have sailed thousands of miles. I'll never see home again."

Home, Regeane thought. *Yes, I, too, would like to go home. At least she knows where hers is. All I have is a name, Wolfstan, and a people who vanished into the forest.*

Disregarding dirt and lice, Regeane held the child against her body and let her cry her grief out. Feeling for the first time since her own mother died, a gentle warmth as the slender arms wound around her and, for a time, clung as if they would never let go.

Lucilla shook her head. "You're kindhearted, I see that already. It's sad, but there are thousands like her. You can't help them all."

"No," Regeane said, "but I can help this one." She moved the child protectively away from Hugo. He was dunking his head in the water and muttering imprecations directed at the general state of the universe. Regeane flicked a contemptuous look at him.

"Coming with me?" Lucilla asked.

"Yes," Regeane replied as she used her wet veil to dry the child's tears.

Lucilla sighed and produced a square of clean linen. Regeane dropped the veil on the edge of the fountain. It landed with a wet plop. She took the clean linen and continued wiping the child's face, whispering, "There, there, little one. It's not so far. Perhaps if your father is a thane we can find—"

Suddenly the square filled with the thunder of hooves.

Lucilla shouted in alarm. Her men-at-arms joined her quickly.

"The militia!" someone cried.

The Roman Militia, the papal guard controlled by Pope Hadrian, was the arm of civil order in the city. It was both respected and feared by the citizens.

"No," Lucilla said softly. "It can't be the militia. I would know. Besides, they never bother with this place." She whispered something to one of her men-at-arms. He promptly vanished into an alleyway. As did several merchants. Others began to gather their stock hurriedly and beat a quick retreat into nearby houses.

Regeane pressed back against the fountain. She felt naked. Her mantle was lying near the cloth seller's cart, her veil sopping wet.

The armed men fanned out and began to search among the carts and tables.

"A curse of piles on the lot of them," Lucilla snarled. "May they itch, burn, and bleed. The bastards are blocking the only exit from the square. Hold the child's hand," she commanded Regeane. "They will think you her mother and a married woman. They seldom bother—"

One of the armed men shouted, "Stop running, fools. We don't want you or your trash."

"Christ!" Lucilla's remaining man whispered. "Basil the Lombard."

Lucilla said, "Don't—"

This was as far as she got. He clapped his hand over her mouth and carried her bodily into the nearest vacant house.

Regeane gasped. The child jerked her arm. "Don't look," she said. "Eyes front. If they see you looking, they'll know where she went." Regeane was terrified and, at the same time, utterly bewildered.

What could men like these want here? They were mercenaries. Their arms and armor proclaimed them the most competent of the violent breed. They sported heavy dark linen tunics under new leather armor. Each man wore heavy cross-gartered leggings. They were chasing the merchants with drawn swords. Top quality hand-forged, hand-filed steel glimmered in the gray light. Dark, oxhide cross-braced shields hung on each man's arm.

The leader—he wore a rich black velvet mantle over his armor and his sword hilt was more ornate than the rest, so Regeane surmised he must be the leader—had reined in at the cloth seller's wagon. He began browbeating the man who crouched near the feet of his horse.

The answers he was getting seemed to satisfy him because he backed his horse and allowed the cloth seller to rise. The man stood trembling, visibly relieved that the powerful warrior ceased threatening him.

He backed his horse again. *God,* Regeane thought, *the creature is beautiful.* It was a Barb of the kind parts of Greece and North Africa were still famous for. White, but with gray at the hooves, tail, and muzzle. A magnificent arched neck, deep chested, muscular but high at the shoulder with long, slender, graceful legs. The slightly darker mane and tail curled magnificently. A stallion. The long member hung in its sheath at the loins.

The horse was restive. Regeane knew why. The wolf was with her as much as she could be by day. The horse knew.

The square had fallen silent as both the people and the mercenaries waited for the leader's commands. The horse stomped and snorted. The man on his back curbed him firmly, pulling his head down. At the same time, his gaze made a circuit of the square.

Regeane caught a good look at his face: superficially handsome. Large, dark eyes, Roman eagle profile, broad strong nose, mouth, and chin. *Oh, no!* she thought. She'd never seen this particular man before, but she'd met the type often enough. They were without mercy or love, existing in absolute selfishness—the very sort she was afraid her future husband might be. The endless wars threw them up the same way a breaking wave foams as it falls.

She had learned in her travels to be utterly wary of them. They didn't reject kindness, caring for another, the sweet gestures of human intimacy; most of them simply didn't know these good things existed. To them, the world was one big, gray passage of human images like the faceless figures on a worn frieze circling some forgotten monument—except that, at times, those faceless figures bled.

A change of expression too brief for reading flickered across his features when he saw Regeane. He turned toward the cloth seller.

Regeane snatched the child's head around and buried it in her skirt so she wouldn't see.

The man spoke negligently, quickly to the soldier at his side. A spear went through the cloth seller's chest. He died, folding into a heap like one of his worn garments. His face showing no fear or pain, only mild surprise.

On the other cart, the furniture seller began screaming and pointing directly at Regeane.

Regeane shoved the child away. "Run!" she shouted. Groping hands pulled the child into the crowd.

The leader of the mercenaries drew his sword, wheeled his horse, and charged straight for Regeane.

The wolf was with Regeane, pouring into her blood, muscles, bones, lending her the beast's strength, the cunning, the absolute concentration of the self-disregarding killer. Pandemonium exploded in the square. Some tried to flee, others to attack with improvised weapons: firewood clubs, axes, hammers, and paving stones.

Regeane stood her ground. Instinctively knowing that if she ran, she would be cut down in a few steps.

Horse and man swept past her in a cloud of leather and sweat smell. His knee slammed into the side of her head, even as he realized he'd thwarted himself. She was on his left, protected by the fountain. He couldn't get a clear swing at her with his sword.

God, what a blow. Regeane staggered, her vision cleared.

The stallion turned with an almost catlike grace and reared, his fore hooves striking down, driving her into the open, away from the fountain.

Regeane leaped to one side into the center of the square. The mercenary laughed, lighter teeth flashing in his weatherbeaten face. Giving him a look of almost childlike delight. He had her now. He was sure.

There was one chance. As the stallion's fore hooves descended, she and the wolf both saw an opening. She darted in toward the horse's head and snatched the bridle at the bit. She pulled her right arm, turning the horse's head too quickly for him to follow. The beast's legs skidded out from under him.

She saw the sword rising from the corner of her eye—then disappear as man and horse fell, landing with a crash beside her. She leaped clear of the thrashing hooves and caught one last look at the expression of stunned disbelief on the man's face.

Mouth like velvet, she thought as she bolted into one of the narrow alleys surrounding the square. It sloped upward like a ramp. From the square came the furious shout, "After her. By Christ's bones, I'll have the bitch's blood."

Hoofbeats clattered echoing on the stone. Regeane went like the wind. The ramp ended in a blank wall.

The entrances of the few houses leading into the alley were barred by heavy wooden doors, as were the shuttered windows looking down into the gloom.

To her right, the street continued as a flight of stone steps. They were slimed with the eternal Tiber damp and raw sewage from the overlooking houses. The stench choked the wolf, but the woman plunged headlong up and up. Scrambling, her feet slipping on the filth, Regeane made the top of the steps on all fours.

A shout rang out. Regeane turned. The little Saxon girl was taking the steps two at a time. "Keep running," she cried. "One of them is right behind me."

Regeane did. The child paced her. "Why didn't you run to Lucilla?" Regeane gasped reproachfully.

"Argumentative now?" the child asked. "Punish me later." She passed Regeane and drew ahead.

Shouts and curses rang out as the horseman encountered the steps. Hoofbeats become booted footsteps.

Regeane's heart hammered with terror. The alley was narrowing, no longer wide enough for two to walk abreast. The walls pressed in closer and closer. The street turned—a hairpin turn and ended in—a blank wall.

She spun around, her back against the wall, and looked around desperately. The insulas surrounding the alley were three stories tall . . . Three stories straight up. Smooth surfaces of narrow terracotta brick up to the cold, gray sky.

The wolf tried to come, tried to draw Regeane into the change and—couldn't. She was too weak. She subsided when she seemed to realize in her dark heart that she was only draining the woman's strength.

The footsteps sounded closer now. Hurrying

"Hisst!" The voice called from close to her feet. The opening was so clogged with debris, she'd missed seeing it.

"Hurry!" the child's voice called. "If you keep dithering, he'll have you."

"I'm not dithering," Regeane snapped in a hissing whisper. "Is it big enough?"

"Yes . . . maybe . . . well, I don't know." This a wail. "I went down so fast, I don't know. But, please—"

The mercenary appeared at the entrance of the cul de sac. Her panicked brain estimated he was approximately three times her size. Another part of her brain presented her with a really gruesome picture of her upper body stuck in the drain while the soldier hacked at her lower body and legs with his sword.

Regeane's hands cleared dead leaves and twigs aside. The wolf, a burrower, made a lightning calculation. Regeane dove for the hole.

With a shout of fury, the warrior leaped after her.

The tunnel was downhill, the walls slippery with slime. The man's hand closed on her ankle. Regeane screeched and clawed desperately at the inside of the clay drain. It was too slick for a handhold.

Something gripped her hair and yanked. She shot out of the other end of the tunnel like a greased pig, landing right at the feet of the child, leaving one shoe in the soldier's hand.

Shouts, evidence of the man's frustrated rage, echoed in the pipe.

"Let go of my hair!" Regeane ordered as she got shakily to her feet.

The child looked offended. "You are lucky I got as good a grip on it as I did. You're too fussy. You should have jumped in when I told you to." The child tried to look up the drain, still reverberating with the soldier's fury. "Don't worry," she said. "He can't get through until he gets more of his armor off."

"And it won't take him long to do that," Regeane said emphatically as she pulled the child away.

The courtyard was surrounded with two-story insula. Every door and window was closed and barred. Regeane could see no escape.

"Up," the child said pointing to a row of stone balconies that ringed the second story of the houses. The balconies were tiny and shallow, but even in this poor quarter, each sported at least one pot of herbs and flowers. The nearest one held quite a few more. It offered at least a possibility of concealment.

Regeane snatched up the child and boosted her over the rail, then pulled herself up behind her. She tried the shutters with her fingers. Solid planks. She saw bolts at the bottom, middle, and top. No escape there.

The warrior slid out of the drain.

Regeane and the child crouched down behind the flowerpots and tried to make themselves as small as possible. The warrior down below turned in circles, scanning the empty courtyard. He may have discarded his armor, but he carried a large, lethal-looking sword. She remembered the cloth seller and shivered.

"It's no good," she said softly. "He will find us."

She felt the little girl's clutch tighten on her arm. She shook herself free and stood up. He was standing almost under the balcony.

She seized a pot of gray sage sporting long spikes of blue

flowers and dropped it on his head. She scored a direct hit, but it didn't do much good. He was wearing his helmet.

He gave a roar of fury and turned, leaping for the balcony rail. He pulled himself up with one hand, sweeping the sword ahead of him to keep her off.

Regeane's fingers closed on the lug handles of a big rosemary jar. She parried the sword's backswing with it. The man's wrist and sword hilt crashed into the jar. The warrior yelled again, this time in pain, and started to drop down.

Regeane was too quick for him. With all her strength, she smashed the bottom edge of the pot into his forehead.

Both man and pot went down, landing with a ringing crash on the flagstones. He rolled over amidst the dirt and broken crockery, getting to his hands and knees.

"Oh, God," Regeane whispered. "No."

"Yes," the little girl said, her mouth set in a tight line. "He's very obstinate." She selected a clay pan of chamomile. This time when the soldier went down, he lay still.

Regeane stood leaning against the rail, gasping for breath and trembling.

"Why do they want to kill you?" the child asked. "What have you done?"

Regeane shook her head. "Nothing," she answered, completely bewildered.

The little girl looked up at her, disbelief written in every line of her features. "You won't tell me then," she said, sounding deeply offended.

"I don't know what to tell you," Regeane said. "Truly I don't."

"Maybe you're right," the child said pensively. "The way I cried in the square, that was shameful and you think me weak." She looked up at Regeane with an expression of almost adult belligerence marred only by a slight protrusion of the lower lip. "But I'm not weak." She climbed over the rail, dropped to the ground, and drew the fallen man's knife.

Regeane scrambled down quickly to join her.

The little girl's fingers were twined in the soldier's hair.

Regeane cried, "No! It's wrong. It's dangerous. You are

not yet a free person and I'm a foreign woman. We might be punished."

Crouching beside the man's head, the little girl looked up at Regeane, an expression of disgust on her face. "You are making excuses. A fine protector you'll be. Not even the courage to cut a man's throat. I'd do better on my own."

Regeane reflected that, for a number of reasons, this might be true, but she was determined not to let the child take the risk. The consequences were unacceptable. She had seen the grisly punishments visited on slaves.

She snatched up the child's hand and pulled her away from the unconscious man. "No, you will not cut his throat. Come. We'll try to find a way out of—"

Regeane broke off because the child's expression changed suddenly from one of disapproval to one of terror.

"WHAT?" REGEANE ASKED.

The little girl reached inside her dress. She wore something around her neck—a piece of stone on a thong. She clutched it and whispered a low prayer in her own tongue and began to back away quickly.

Regeane heard footsteps. She spun around. A soft whimper of terror rose in her own throat.

The thing half limped, half shuffled toward her. Most of its body was covered by a heavy black cloak and hood, but what Regeane could see was bad enough. It held the hood over the lower part of its face with the stumps of fingers.

Bone protruded from dangling shreds of pale, rotten flesh. Inside the black cloth of the hood, the nose was half eaten away by disease, the septum clearly visible. All around, the silver wolf smelled the stench of death, yet above the horror of the nose, two living eyes stared at Regeane. Eyes that were almost beautiful: large hazel eyes fringed with dark lashes.

"My garden," it whispered. "You've ruined my little garden."

It stopped, dropped to a crouch beside the broken pot of sage, the blue flowers blooming proudly amidst the dirt and shattered clay. It stroked the petals softly with one pale, bony index finger.

"My garden," it keened softly to itself, "my poor little garden. It was all I had left."

"I'm sorry," Regeane stammered, "but the soldier was chasing us."

"You still had no right to ruin Antonius' garden," someone screamed accusingly at Regeane.

The doors to the little piazza were opening. A young woman stood in one of them. Her long hair was hennaed bright red, showing black at the roots. She might have been pretty, but for the big hole in one cheek through which two rows of her teeth could clearly be seen.

A hand lifted Regeane's skirt. Something giggled. She looked down.

It hopped along on the stumps of its legs. The arm attached to the hand was long and simian. The face was dished as if it had been bashed and flattened by a giant club. Mucus flowed from the nose, and drool spilled from a grinning mouth filled with the stubs of yellow teeth.

Regeane gave a stifled shriek and backed away.

The thing followed, reaching, chanting, "Pretty lady. Pretty lady."

She backed into another, but this one only stared at her solemnly, a boy so deformed by his humped back that he scuttled on all fours. His eyes had a vacant stare. She realized as she twisted away from the thing's hands that this one was blind.

They were everywhere, all around her. Every doorway and balcony held one or another twisted obscenity. Some bore the marks of torture and mutilation—noseless, eyeless, ears cropped, hands or feet stumps. Were they alive? Had she fled somehow into a quarter peopled only by the dead?

Regeane felt something clutching at the other side of her skirt. Her body jerked violently; then she realized it was the child clinging to her desperately, face buried in the folds of her gown. She put her arm around the little girl.

"She doesn't like us," the red-haired woman shouted with a shrill laugh. "Who asked you to bring your pretty face here and remind us of what we've lost? Get out." She picked up a piece of broken flowerpot and threw it at Regeane.

They clustered around Regeane, hemming her in, their voices a cacophony of idiot babbling, giggling, and here and there, most frightening, a cry of hatred or rage.

Regeane felt a strange weakness. The wolf was trying to claim her. She sensed the quivering readiness to change, a frisson between the day-to-day world and the drifting wraiths of moonglow.

"For shame." The voice was hoarse, yet commanding. It came from the first one Regeane had seen, the one who had bemoaned the ruin of his garden. He came forward, leaning on a long staff. The lower part of the hood was held up more tightly over the ruined face and now all she could see were those two oddly beautiful eyes gazing at her over the black cloth.

"For shame," he repeated angrily. When he reached Regeane's side, he swung the staff in a wide circle, driving back those who had crowded most closely around Regeane and the child.

"Here is a stranger come among us, seeking courtesy and protection." The hooded head turned and looked at the soldier still lying in a heap on the stones of the street. "Whatever we are," he said quietly, "we cannot be dead to all compassion or humanity. If that passes from among us, what will we become?"

The crowd fell silent. The gentle rebuke of the hooded one seemed to carry great weight among them.

"You, Drusis," he spoke to the legless man, the one who had been trying to lift Regeane's skirt. "Go fetch my brother." He went on sternly. "Wash the rheum from your face. You're not fit for the eyes of a gentle lady."

To Regeane's surprise Drusis looked abashed, hung his head, and hopped away quickly.

Then Antonius turned to Regeane. The clear, calm eyes

looked into her own. "Drusis will bring my brother," he assured her, "and he'll be able to lead you out of here. You must pardon the bad manners of my friends. It's not often that an outsider strays into . . . the house of the dead."

The little Saxon girl peered past the folds of Regeane's skirt up at the hooded figure. "Are you then a dead man?" she asked fearfully.

The eyes shifted from Regeane's face to the child's. "Not quite," he answered, "but the next thing to it. I am a leper."

Regeane felt her knees grow weak, not with terror, but relief. The fear that she'd strayed into a precinct populated by those dim shapes she saw clustered at church porches or near cemeteries was dispelled. Compared with those, the poor deformed outcasts were not terrible, but pitiful.

"Oh," she sighed, "thank God. I . . . I feared you might be . . . something else."

The hazel eyes shifted back to her face and, if she wasn't mistaken, the expression in them was one of mild perplexity.

"I believed you a ghost," she explained.

"No," he said calmly. "Soon enough, but not yet. Do you often see such things?"

"Yes," Regeane admitted reluctantly, then qualified her statement. "Well, not so often. Only two or three times a year, but when it happens . . ."

There was a stir in the crowd. A man pushed his way through.

"What in the world . . ." he said, then stopped, looking in astonishment at Regeane.

The hooded leper turned to him. "Stephen, my brother, this lady and—" He indicated the child with a quick gesture of his hand. "—her little friend came here pursued by that one over there." He pointed to the soldier, still lying amidst the dirt and shattered pots. "Please, if you would, conduct her to a place of safety."

Stephen was a tall man, lean-faced, with a thatch of gray hair and an equally gray clipped beard which curled crisply at his chin. His dress was as simple as that of the Latin farmers Regeane saw every day driving their cattle and flocks to market, just a brown woolen tunic and sandals. He didn't wear the mantle most of the freeborn men used as an overgarment, but the ancient cloak of the people of the earth, a simple square of cloth with a hole cut out for the head and gathered in at the waist with a belt. Yet aside from his simple garb, there was something about him in the set of his shoulders and the firmness of the mouth under the strong jut of the nose that bespoke one used to authority, used to giving commands and having them obeyed.

"Crysta." He spoke to the woman with the hole in her cheek. "Who does that belong to?"

The woman walked over and looked down at the warrior. "He's one of Basil the Lombard's followers. I can't call his name, but Basil is his master."

"Basil, eh?" A small wrinkle appeared between his brows. "What's he doing here? You, Sixtus, Numerus." He pointed to two men, one who had iron hooks for hands, the other lacking nose, ears, and part of his scalp. "Take that offal and dump it somewhere. I don't want him to wake here." Then he turned to Regeane. "You, my lady, follow me," he said.

"I'll come," Antonius said diffidently to Regeane, "if my presence doesn't offend you?"

"Oh, no," Regeane shook her head. She was still deeply grateful for his rescue.

Then she remembered the few pieces of copper in her scrip. She pulled them out quickly and extended her hand to Antonius with the coins in her palm.

"Here, please take this," she said. "It's for your garden, your flowers. I'm so sorry that we broke the pots, but you'll see. The flowers will grow again."

Antonius didn't move or stretch out his hand to take the money. Instead, his eyes sought his brother Stephen. "The widow's mite," he said. He turned again to Regeane. "I'm well looked after. My brother sees to all my needs. I, in turn, must apologize for being so childish about a few pots."

When Regeane looked at Stephen, she realized that the sternness in his expression had softened into a look of kindness.

Regeane glanced anxiously at the soldier. Stephen's men were dragging him off by the heels. *Rather callous procedure,* Regeane thought. His injured skull bounced along the stones. "Is there any chance I could be called up before the magistrate and accused of . . . I'm not so worried about myself, but the child . . . is . . . she's not yet a free person."

"No," Stephen snapped. "He shouldn't be here at all. Were I not in the service of Christ, I would order his summary execution. The present pope Hadrian had ordered the Lombard faction out of Rome and—"

Antonius broke in with a soft chuckle. "It seems Hadrian hasn't had as much success as he hoped in controlling their activities."

Stephen looked annoyed. "No," he growled. "But I think once Hadrian is aware of the problem, he will be able to take measures."

"Never think it," Antonius broke in, more seriously this time. "The Roman families are still hedging their bets, and likely so are the clergy. Believe it, brother, and be careful," he cautioned.

"What's 'hedging a bed'?" the child asked.

"Hedging a bet," Regeane corrected her and, since she didn't know the answer herself, she shushed the little girl and told her not to ask so many questions.

The child's lip shot all the way out. The small eyes flashed fire. She and Regeane glared at each other. "I only asked one. And besides, my father says the only way to find out anything is to ask questions. So there!"

"She's right," Antonius said. "Questions, answerable or not, are always a necessity. In this instance, 'hedging a bet' refers to the last pope who was dominated by the Lombard party in Rome. The present pope, Hadrian, has declared his independence from the Lombard duke Desiderius and expelled his man, Paul Afartha, from the city. Basil was Paul Afartha's captain. Many of the poor wretches you see here were afflicted by nature, but others suffered at the hands of Paul and Basil. Their sin was belonging to the wrong party. So far as hedging bets is concerned, the Romans are still not sure if Hadrian's policies will be successful. In other words, they fear the present pope may fall under the influence of the Lombards, also. So they are trying to be very careful not to offend anyone."

"But what has this to do with me?" Regeane asked, distressed.

"Brother," Antonius whispered. "If we could go inside and sit down, I would be deeply grateful. These days I find heat and cold both difficult to bear. And even walking a few steps tires me." The words were spoken serenely without any touch of whining or self-pity. Regeane realized they were the simple truth.

"I'm sorry," Stephen said penitently. "And I'm forgetting my duties as a host."

Regeane would have scorned to beg for herself, but she knew the child must be hungry. The girl looked very much as if the slave dealer probably starved her in an attempt to break the independent little spirit. "Please, sir, if you could find a bit to eat for the child."

"I think we might find something for both of you," Stephen said. "Come this way."

Stephen led the way, Antonius shuffling after them across the piazza.

She followed him into a church, a small place, rather bare like most of the chapels serving the poor people of Rome.

The blank whitewashed stucco walls had only a few narrow windows that let in long shafts of light. Its only adornment was a fresco wrapped around the sanctuary, framing the altar with its worn canopy and bare marble surface.

The painting depicted a meadow at dawn. The green grass was bejeweled with spring flowers. The ruby cups of poppy, bluebells, delicate violet, wild basil, and over them all, glowing amethyst and gold, the first magical light of sunrise.

Illuminated by an opening in the top of the cupola above the altar, the scene filled the simple little church with the fragrance of a spring morning and the freedom of wide vistas under the open sky.

"It's dawn," Regeane said.

"No," Antonius said behind her. "Sunset. I know. I painted it. It's easy to mistake sunset for dawn. The light is almost the same."

"How wonderful to be able to make something so beautiful," the little girl said.

"Hush," Regeane said, remembering the condition of Antonius' hands, the white stubs of bone protruding from the flesh.

"It's all right," Antonius said. "She doesn't understand."

Regeane was leading the little girl through the church. The child stopped and pulled back against her.

"What don't I understand? If I don't understand something, I want it explained to me so I do understand it." Her small face had a mulish expression and the lower lip was protruding again.

"Come along," Regeane said, embarrassed, "and stop being a nuisance."

The child tested her strength against Regeane's firm grip on her arm and decided that dignified progress was better than being dragged.

"It is one of those things that I'm supposed to wait till I'm older to know. People are always telling me that! If they'd only explain, I'd understand now!"

Regeane heard a chuckle behind her and realized that Antonius wasn't offended.

"She can't be yours," he said. "You're too young."

"Of course I'm not hers," the little girl said indignantly. "I'm a Saxon. She's a Frank. Can't you tell the difference?"

"Whatever you are," Stephen said, "you're a handful."

They were near the altar by now. Stephen pushed open a door in the wall and ushered Regeane into what she knew must be his living quarters.

She was suddenly conscious of her own disheveled state. Her mantle was gone. She remembered with a shiver the cloth seller lay bleeding to death on it. She didn't think she'd want it back. She'd used the worn veil as a wash rag. She'd dropped her shoes—one pulled off by her pursuer, the other falling as she climbed into the balcony. She looked down and wiggled her toes. The dress she wore, threadbare to begin with, was stained and spattered with the filth of the streets and the slime of the tunnel. Her hair clung to her scalp, matted by sweat and dirt.

The room was immaculately clean, and though sparsely furnished, its appointments might have come from one of the beautiful patrician villas that guarded the city.

An alcove at one end of the room held a curtained bed. It was, as most Frankish beds were, a wooden box that served as container for the feather tick and quilt. But the coverlet had the sheen of silk and the simple design that bordered it was picked out in golden thread. The linen of the bedsheets and curtains was bleached to snowy whiteness and edged as simply as the coverlet, but with cut lace, the eyelets embroidered in silk.

A table stretched the length of the room. Regeane's first impression was that it was very old and her second that it must have once graced a palace. Oak and iron-hard with a satiny gleam, the surface inlaid with curving ivory acanthus leaves.

The benches that stretched the length of it were of equal quality, and decorated with ivory in the same pattern.

At one end of the table near a fireplace set into the stone wall stood a high-backed carven chair before a bookstand. The book on it was a big one, and Regeane's eye caught the gleam of bright gold and blue illumination on the parchment.

One piece of furniture in the room stood out by virtue of the fact that it didn't match the quality of the rest. A simple wooden bench with a straw cushion at the end of the table opposite the high-backed chair.

Antonius limped into the room behind Regeane and shuffled toward it, explaining, "That's mine, so that when . . ." He paused for a poignant second, poignant because Regeane understood what he did not say. "When I no longer need it, it may be burned."

He moved with difficulty as if in pain. Regeane sensed that the time to burn the bench might come soon.

His Latin speech was clear and beautiful, closer to the language of the Caesars than the argot spoken in the streets of Rome. Clean, precise, the accent that of a wellborn and well-educated man, though strangely slurred. Regeane didn't like to think of the condition of the lips from which the words issued.

The voice may have been young, but his movements were slow, painful, and unsteady as if he dragged himself along by an effort of will. His brother's eyes rested on him with so much love and resigned sadness. They spoke more clearly than any words the certainty of Antonius' doom.

Regeane and the child hesitated in the doorway.

Antonius paused beside the bench. "Please come in. You need not fear any contagion. While in this room I sit only on my bench and handle nothing that is my brother's. He is not infected and never has been, though I and the other unfortunates who dwell here are in his care."

"Oh, no," Regeane cried. "It's not that." She looked down at her tattered dress and the child's matted hair. "Our own state is . . ."

"We are dirty," the little girl said flatly, "and we're sorry, but we had no time to be particular. We were running for our lives. The slave dealer who had me wouldn't let me wash. He kept me chained up. He was afraid I'd run away. He was a bad man, though he was right. I would have run away if I'd gotten a chance. And," she said, looking up at Stephen, her dark blue eyes defiant, "I am not a handful. My father always said I was a good, obedient child. And I am."

Antonius chuckled again, the sound muffled by the heavy mantle.

Stephen suppressed a smile and showed them to a small scullery where Regeane and the child did their best to repair some of the damage wrought by their flight. They had clean hands and faces when they returned to the other room.

Stephen set wine, bread, and yellow cheese before them, then sat down in his big chair at the head of the table, taking only a little watered wine for himself.

At the sight and smell of the food Regeane realized she was ravenously hungry. It was all she could do to keep from bolting it down. Only when she'd taken the worst edge from her hunger and relaxed, sipping the wine, did Stephen begin to question her.

"Now, why was Basil the Lombard chasing you?" he asked.

"She wouldn't tell me," the little girl said. "Maybe she'll tell you."

Regeane was annoyed. "I can understand your skepticism, but don't carry it too far. I am truthful in most matters. We both know what is generally said of liars."

The child shot her a glance. "I stand corrected," she said stiffly. She sniffed and applied herself to the food.

"Brother," Antonius said, "I don't think you need to look any further than her lovely face. Basil saw her and—"

"No," Regeane broke in. "He tried to kill me, charged at me sword in hand to strike me down."

"How did you escape?" Antonius asked.

"That was wonderful," the little girl said. "She caught the

horse at the bit and pulled him down. I've heard of that warrior's move," she said enthusiastically, "heard my father's men talk of such things, but never before seen it done."

"Who are you?" Stephen asked. "The child said you were a Frank. What is your name?"

Regeane turned toward him. "Regeane, daughter of Gisela and," she hesitated, then said proudly, "Wolfstan."

"Gisela the Pepined?" he asked.

"Yes," Regeane answered.

"You are betrothed to Maeniel, the outlander. No wonder Basil wanted to kill you." Stephen sat back on the chair. He looked horrified. "What is a lady of *your rank* doing wandering around the streets of Rome unescorted and in the thieves' market of all places!" He looked outraged.

"I was trying to buy a dress," Regeane stammered. "You see, we're very poor and . . . his name is Maeniel, then? Gundabald didn't tell me his name. He only said he was a mountain lord."

"Yes," Stephen answered. "Something of a man of mystery, this Maeniel, but he holds a fortress that commands a pass through the Alps."

"A very powerful position," Antonius said. "The king of the Franks has bestowed an important match on you."

"I don't understand," Regeane said. "What has that to do with Basil?"

Stephen pushed his chair back from the table. "You need not concern yourself with such things, girl. Tell me where your uncle lodges. I'll call two of my men. They'll see you return there safely. Don't stick a hand or foot out of doors until I have a chance to drop a word in the ears of a few of my friends and see to it that Basil is driven out of the city."

"No!" Regeane shouted, jumping up so quickly she almost overset the bench. "I'm not going home. As for this Maeniel, he can find some other woman to marry. Today in the square I met a woman named Lucilla. She—"

"What is this nonsense!" Stephen shouted, slamming his fist down on the table. "Lucilla! Are you so foolish, so naive as not to know what Lucilla wants of you?"

Regeane faced him, chin lifted defiantly. She groped for the Saxon girl's hand, caught hold of it, and said, "I'm neither foolish nor naive. I know exactly what Lucilla wants of me, but it's better than being sold to some man who'll hate me. Living my life in fear, afraid to eat and drink . . ."

Stephen stared up at her in astonishment. "What fancies are these? Who's been stuffing your heard with foolishness? How can you despise an honorable match and turn to a courtesan like Lucilla?"

"Regeane," Antonius said, half rising from his bench. "Stop shouting and sit down. No one here will force you to do anything."

Regeane turned toward him. He still held the mantle up over his face, but the dark eyes above it looked up calmly and compassionately into hers. "And," he said turning to his brother, "I do not find her evident terror at this match to be unfounded. Consider the situation of Desiderius' daughter. That marriage was also hailed as a brilliant one, securing peace and amity between two great kingdoms. How did it end? The girl was sent home, driven from her husband's bed disgraced, her reputation ruined. She was the daughter of a Lombard duke. There are other frightening stories. At times the women fared even worse. Regeane's not a child. No child successfully escaped Basil and—"

The Saxon girl piped up proudly. "She dumped him to the ground. The horse kicked like mad. The warrior cursed and shouted. Everyone began fighting. I crawled through people's legs and escaped."

Stephen sat back in the chair and shaded his face with a hand cupped at his forehead, but Regeane could see he was smiling.

"Very well," he said, dropping his hand to the table and looking back at Regeane. "As usual my brother is right. He nearly always leads me back to the path of wisdom when I stray from it. These things should be discussed calmly, rationally, so sit down. No one will force you into anything."

Regeane sat; her knees still trembling.

Stephen leaned forward and folded his fingers together. "What do you know of politics, girl?"

Regeane shook her head. "Almost nothing."

"Good," he said. "Then I won't have any silly misconceptions to clear up. So listen; this is how it stands. Rome, the once-proud mistress of the world, is now fallen on evil times."

"So I noticed," Regeane said.

"Yes," Stephen said, the dark eyebrows rising. "It doesn't take a genius. The city is two-thirds ruined, its inhabitants struggling with poverty and intermittent food supplies. The magnificent aqueducts my ancestors built are cut off. Even fountains which until recently ran pure water are dry. We are nearly powerless, placed as we are between two great powers—the duchy of Spoleto and the kingdom of the Lombards. Either one of which, I might add, would be happy to gobble us up, sit in the rubble, and pick their teeth with our bones. What prevents them, girl?"

Regeane looked at the shrewd face with a feeling of surprise. She wasn't used to being talked to in this way by distinguished gentlemen. "Respect for the Holy Church," she hazarded.

Stephen gave a hollow laugh. "No, my dear. The Franks do."

Regeane was bewildered. "How can the Franks keep them from conquering you? They are far away."

"But very powerful," Stephen said, "and both Desiderius and the duke of Spoleto fear them. And its very much in the Frankish king's best interest to secure the Alpine passes. If he doesn't, he could wake up some fine spring morning to find himself with a Lombard army at his back. So you can see why Desiderius would like to prevent a marriage between a woman of the royal house and this mountain lord, Maeniel. Basil is, as his name implies, a confidant, servant, and friend of Desiderius, king of the Lombards."

"I still can't understand why I'm so important," Regeane said. "Couldn't the king simply find another lady to wed this Maeniel?"

"Yes," Stephen said, "but these are matters of some delicacy and, in the meantime, Desiderius, seeing this Maeniel uncommitted, might begin other maneuvers to bring him into the power of the Lombard kingdom. Besides, in some ways you're ideal for Charles' purposes."

Regeane looked away from Stephen and down at the bread in her hand. She crumbled a little of it with her fingers. "My family is poor, you mean, and I have no proud kinfolk to object to such a match. And I am no great beauty, so . . ."

"On the contrary," Stephen said, "it was of your youth and beauty that I was thinking when I said you were ideal."

" 'Whey-faced' and 'flat-chested' were the terms my Uncle Gundabald used."

"Indeed," Stephen said. His eyes hardened and his mouth drew into a tight line. "Did he? Why, pray tell, did he say such a thing to a maiden who is so soon to be married?"

Regeane looked up at his face. Something in it and the way he asked the question frightened her. She thought, *This man has power.* She didn't know what kind of power or how much, but there was in his expression the absolute self-assurance of a ruler.

"He would like me . . ." She faltered, realizing she didn't dare communicate Gundabald's plans to these men. "To help him . . . He feels this lord should be grateful for the marriage . . ."

Stephen's eyes narrowed. "I begin to like this Gundabald less and less, and I haven't even met him."

"What a cruel insult," Antonius spoke up softly, "and not true."

Regeane turned toward him. His beautiful eyes were fixed on her. The shadow of an almost forgotten hunger shone in them.

"You have not the matron's blossom, but the maiden's pliant grace. The air of springtime hangs about you. You are a bud, velvet petals as yet unfolding, the golden fruitfulness of its heart untouched by the sun of love."

The compliment was so beautifully spoken, so gently turned, that Regeane's palms flew to her cheeks.

"In other words," Stephen said, "there are many things about you that would tend to endear you to a husband—beauty, youth, and the ability to cement his relations with the royal house and legitimize his position."

"Besides," Antonius said softly, "you are not as unprotected as you may believe."

"How so?" Regeane asked.

"Charles is a very powerful king. He personally arranged this marriage. If word were to reach his ears that you were badly treated by your husband, he might see such behavior as an affront to his honor. And, my dear, Charles is not a man I would care to insult."

Regeane shook her head. "But Charles doesn't know me and besides, Gundabald said he—my husband—likely had the morals of a jackal and he probably has other women he'll prefer to me. And I'll be poisoned . . ." To her own horror, Regeane felt tears start in her eyes. "I'm sorry, but don't you see? I can't live on fruit and spring water . . ."

"Stop yammering," the child snapped. "You are making a fool of yourself and convincing these men you are a coward when really you're *dauntless*, like me. Besides you can't get married."

Antonius cocked his head to one side. "Why not?"

"She has no breasts, and you can't get married without breasts, because you can't catch a man."

Regeane made distance from misery to mortification in one leap. "What!" she shouted.

Stephen turned his face away and Antonius pulled the cowl down over his eyes.

"Are you bent on embarrassing me?" Regeane asked furiously to the child. "How dare you . . ."

"Wait!" Stephen said. "Don't be angry. She is a child and has a child's frankness. We understand." He grinned wickedly. "I would like to know more of this matter of breasts."

Antonius had himself under control and cautioned, "Brother . . ."

Regeane turned her face away.

The child spoke animatedly to Stephen. "My cousin, Matilda, came to visit us. She was to be married. My aunt stood her up next to me and I was taller."

"Mmmm," Stephen said. "So?"

"Well, they said it was a disgrace I was so big and flat-chested and ran around and played like a boy and if I didn't stop growing soon and get some breasts, I would never marry." The child stopped and took a deep breath. "I asked them what I needed breasts for and they said I couldn't get married without them. I said I hoped I would never have any there, but later on I cried. But my father said I should not worry about breasts yet.

He said they were not important. What was important, he said, was to be truthful in all matters of consequence."

"Yes," Antonius said. "We are allowed tact, kindness, and excuses, are we not?"

"You mean like saying you're busy when you're on the pot?" Antonius nodded.

"And, he said to give one's word sparingly, but once given to always keep it, for good or ill."

"True," Stephen said.

"And," the child sighed, "to be dauntless in battle. She is," the child indicated Regeane, "and so am I." She ended proudly, "You know, though, I still don't understand about breasts."

"Well, don't ask these men about the matter," Regeane said acidly. "Wait until we're alone and I'll explain it to you." The child subsided. "She's still innocent," Regeane said. "I can't bring her home with me. She bit Hugo and he hit her in the face. God knows what he'd do to her. No, I know what he'd do to her and the fact that she's a child wouldn't make a bit of difference to him. I won't bring her back and let him get his hands on her."

"Very bad," Antonius said. "Brother, can't you see how much damage is being done here? Her relations are terrorizing this girl. And Regeane, I believe you understand why."

"Yes," Regeane said bitterly. "They are very poor and want my help in extorting money from my husband."

Stephen nodded his head. "What will they do with the money if they get it?"

Regeane shrugged. "What they do now—spend it drinking and wenching in every taverna and brothel in Rome. They boast of my future husband's wealth, saying the mere mention of his name opened the moneylenders' purses immediately."

Regeane bit her lip. She'd made her decision last night. Her fear was that this Stephen, whoever he was, might have the authority to return her by force. If so, she wasn't going to place herself in the position of having them tell Gundabald to take measures against her running away. Still, she was more afraid for the child than herself. A night with Hugo and the little girl would wake up far less sure of the ultimate goodness of the world than she was now. First, Regeane had to secure her safety.

"Please," she continued, "place the child in the Saxon colony in Rome and I will return peaceably to my uncle if you wish."

"No," Antonius exclaimed decidedly. "No. Brother, look at this lady. She arrived hungry and the dress she's wearing would not do credit to the lowest maid in an honorable house, much less to a lady of rank. And, Regeane, whatever my brother decides about you, the child may remain here among us. Many here are not infected with disease. They are the victims of Paul Afartha's cruelty. That woman, Crysta, has a bitter tongue, but a kind heart. She will look after her."

Regeane felt a wave of relief wash over her. She was sure, and oddly the wolf was also certain, that with Antonius' protection, the little one would be safe, even here.

"I don't know," Stephen said slowly. "The men in her family are her legal and traditional guardians."

The sigh Antonius gave rippled the covering over his mouth. "All my life, your face and only one other have been the fairest I have ever looked upon. When I wander among the shades I will ask the gods to remember only you two. But, Brother, there are times when, dealing with you, I feel I'm facing a talking law book.

"If this mountain lord comes to Rome and finds his bride in her present neglected condition, he is more than likely to believe she has been discarded by her royal kin and the marriage was intended not as an honor, but a cruel jest. He may rebuff her and turn to the Lombards. Brother, I beg you, don't allow your scruples to override your common sense. Send the girl to Lucilla."

Stephen stared thoughtfully at Antonius. "Lucilla is an old friend. She'll do as I ask."

Regeane looked quickly from one to the other. "I don't understand you. Only a few moments ago you spoke as if Lucilla were a woman of . . . the streets; her home a house of . . . ill repute."

Stephen waved a hand at Regeane in a gesture of negation. "No. No, not at all. Lucilla's ladies aren't streetwalkers and never become so. They usually go to her as virgins and, after some training, she places them discreetly in the arms of one protector or another where often they remain for many years. Not a few eventually marry quite respectably."

"That sounds heavenly," Regeane said. "I wish I were so free."

"Well, you aren't," Stephen said harshly. "Your marriage is in a minor way dynastic and the king of the Franks must understand that we—"

"Brother!" Antonius exclaimed sharply.

Regeane glanced from one man to the other again. Stephen had been about to reveal a secret, and Antonius had prevented him.

"Ah," Stephen continued, "my brother and I are of a noble house. We are well connected. I'll write a letter to Lucilla explaining the situation. She's a woman of intelligence and, as I said, a friend of mine. She'd be the first to understand the importance of this match to both you and the city. Lucilla is a staunch supporter of the Holy See." Stephen smiled a quick, rather strange smile and gave Antonius a meaningful look. "As I am, my dear."

"Now, as for the child, tell me your name, little one, and your father's. There are many Saxons living here in Rome. I can inquire among them. It's possible that someone here knows your family."

The child gave Regeane a reproachful look.

"Oh, God, yes," Regeane cried. "I knew I was a fool when I bought her from the slave dealer, but, you see, she bit Hugo and I—"

"Wished to bite him yourself," the little girl finished the sentence for her.

Regeane's cheeks began to burn again. She glanced down angrily at the child. "I did not say that," she exclaimed, then added equivocally, "well, not exactly . . ." Her whole face flamed. She was sure her cheeks were scarlet. "Must you repeat everything you hear?"

The small face looked up at her. The blue eyes were pools of reproach. The lower lip was extended again. "Why not, if you're going to abandon me like a pregnant cat?"

"A what?" Regeane snapped.

"My father says that the three most annoying things in the

world are a drunken man, a shrewish woman, and a pregnant cat. He says everyone wants to be rid of them. He told me when he tied a strip of leather around our tomcat's things. You know," she said, "the little furry things they have in the back."

Regeane's face felt incandescent. "Oh, God," she said, "for heaven's sake, hush." She was afraid to look at the two men.

"Why should I hush?" the child protested. "Everyone knows about cats. They are very lecherous beasts. He was right, though. There were no litters for a while, but then they started back and my father said she must have found another friend. I asked him why our tomcat didn't defend his honor, but he said—Ouch!" Regeane kicked her hard in the ankle.

"What did I do now?" the child asked in an aggrieved voice, clutching her bare foot.

Regeane glanced quickly and covertly at Stephen and Antonius.

Antonius was looking down. The black mantle covered most of his face, but his shoulders were shaking. Stephen's hand was up, hiding a smile.

Regeane glared down at the child. "Stop going on about cats and breasts and all manner of foolishness. Tell us your name," she said between her teeth, "and tell us now! Do you hear me?"

"Oh, all right. I was just getting to that. Elfgifa."

"Elfgifa," Stephen said.

"And your father?" Regeane asked.

"Eanwolf. He's one of the king's thanes," she said proudly.

"Thank you, Elfgifa," Stephen said. "If your father is an important man, it's likely that one of the Saxons living here in Rome will know of him and we can return you to your kin. Your lady doesn't mean to abandon you, but she has responsibilities of her own and must consider them." He spoke gravely, graciously as if to an adult.

The child nodded.

Stephen rose. "Now," he said to Regeane, "I'll see about sending you to Lucilla. And," he said gently to Elfgifa, "when you see Lucilla, be sure to ask her about breasts. She will explain their function and importance." A shadow of the wicked smile returned to his face. "You may tell her I told you to apply to her for the information."

VI

A FEW HOURS LATER, REGEANE SOAKED IN A POOL in the tepedarium at Lucilla's villa. Lucilla sat on the side of the pool, studying her with open admiration. "What a pity. I had the perfect man in mind for you. He's a little old. In fact, he's very old, but a realist, my dear. He knows you wouldn't share his bed for the joy of it. You'd be showered with presents and, if you're as discreet as you are lovely, you could easily end by being a wealthy and influential woman."

Regeane rolled over on her back and floated in the warm water, looking up at the ceiling of the bath. Plugs of thick glass set in the domed ceiling let in a soft, diffuse, yet brilliant light. She felt perfectly relaxed and happy. A half hour ago when she'd arrived, she'd been weeping and half hysterical with relief to find Lucilla not only alive, but well, and in fine fettle.

"We truly settled those devils! The temerity of it, that rat Basil coming to Rome in despite of the pope. The Papal Guard arrived. I sent men after you and the child, but they couldn't find any trace of where you'd gone.

"I'm sorry I seemed to desert you. Evoie, the captain of my guard, became frightened when he saw Basil. He was convinced it was an assassination attempt by the Lombards. He was right, but he had the wrong woman in mind."

A delegation of Lucilla's maids arrived and collected Elfgifa. They oohed and aahed over her. The most knowledgable of them, Susanna, pronounced her beautiful, which Regeane was sure secretly pleased Elfgifa. Then they all agreed she needed a thorough scrubbing and new clothes.

Elfgifa asked the question Stephen had told her to ask.

Everyone, including Lucilla, found it hysterically funny. They departed, whooping with laughter, taking Elfgifa with them to be bathed, fed, dressed, and cosseted.

To Regeane, it seemed as if she were now caught in the matrix of some glowing jewel. The pool was of gray polished marble, the floor surrounding it peach, the walls of alabaster marble inlaid with green porphyry, each inlay shaped into fantastic trees and tall ferns.

The water swirled around her, cradled her, soothing away her fears and relaxing the tension in her muscles. She floated in delightful, languorous peace.

"I think it's the most beautiful place I've ever seen," she told Lucilla. "I didn't know people lived in such surroundings, enjoyed such luxury. I thought only churches were decked in glowing stone, cut and polished with such exquisite care."

Lucilla smiled at Regeane's artless admiration. "Oh, yes. Some did and a few still do. It's said that this villa was built by the Emperor Hadrian for a favorite of his—whether boy or woman, I can't say. But he intended a quiet retreat, small, where he could come and relax without being surrounded by the hordes of courtiers, hangers-on, supplicants, and other nuisances."

"He made a wonderful thing," Regeane said muzzily, closing her eyes and drifting in the blood-warm water.

"Did he?" Lucilla scanned the room with a slightly cynical expression.

The change in her tone made Regeane open her eyes and look inquiringly up at her face. "Didn't he?"

"What if I told you that once the hypocaust that heated these baths was fired by slaves who never saw the sun from one end of the year to the other. Men, and perhaps women, to whom even the simplest of human joys were denied. Since the water must always be kept warm to await their master's pleasure, those slaves had no rest from their labors."

Regeane rolled over with a splash and stood.

"I'm sorry." Lucilla smiled with gentle malice. "Did I spoil your fun?"

"Yes."

The water was shallow, coming up to Regeane's shoulders.

She paddled over to where Lucilla sat. The beautiful room seemed suddenly darkened by horror.

Regeane rested her arms on the edge of the pool. Lucilla reached down and gathered Regeane's long hair together and coiled it into a knot at the neck.

"My pleasure isn't worth such suffering," Regeane said.

Lucilla laughed. "Don't worry, little one. That was long ago. Now, my men are paid extra to fire the hypocaust and they're always happy to do so. They spend the money in the wineshops and bordellos of Rome. This world is better than that of the ancients. I only wanted to make the point that all this beauty and luxury aren't conjured up by magic. There's always a price to be paid."

Lucilla, naked as Regeane was, slid into the water behind her and began washing her hair, scrubbing Regeane's scalp with her fingers and then smoothing out the tangles with a steel comb.

Regeane rested her cheek against the cool marble at the edge of the pool and submitted to Lucilla's ministrations. She shifted when Lucilla's fingers fell from her head and began gently to caress her breasts.

"I see—the price," Regeane said.

"No," Lucilla said with a soft laugh. "Not at all. You come highly recommended. Stephen is . . ." Lucilla paused. "A powerful man. A powerful protector. You need not love me or even allow me to make love to you."

She finished with Regeane's hair and draped the long coil of it over her shoulder. She was behind her, breasts pressing against Regeane's back, her belly against the soft curve of her buttocks. Lucilla's head drooped forward, lips near Regeane's ear.

"You needn't accept my love, little one, but do accept it. For know my love can't hurt you. I can't make you pregnant, can't enslave you into a marriage you hate. I can't even take that oh-so-marketable virginity of yours." Lucilla laughed softly. "I haven't the equipment."

Deep in Regeane's brain, the silver wolf stirred, and woke, rising from the abyss of primal darkness to welcome the pleasure brought by Lucilla's touch. The beast, aflame with life's sweetest happiness, is innocent of man's fall from grace. Desire burned in the wolf. Desire without conscience, memory, or regret.

Regeane yielded to the wolf as she had to Lucilla's touch. They were one and the same. Her head slipped back to rest, eyes closed, against Lucilla's shoulder while the long fingers explored her body.

"Come," Lucilla whispered, guiding Regeane toward the flight of steps at the end of the pool. "Come out of the water where my kisses can delight you."

They lay together on linen towels beside the pool. True, Lucilla was no longer young, but she was beautiful, skin soft, muscles firm and taut, belly flat and tight, her big breasts upright, ripe, and full.

Only her hands and face showed her age—the soft pleating of the skin of her wrists and the sadness of her eyes as she bent over Regeane's young body.

"Ah, what torment. Why do I torment myself so?" she whispered.

"What torment?" Regeane asked as she reached up with her own hands, trying to give back some of the exquisite pleasure wrought by Lucilla's gentle, sure fingers.

"Hush," Lucilla murmured, lowering her mouth to Regeane's breast. "Be still. Love me. Let me love you."

Regeane felt the wolf, strong in her, whimpering deep in her throat as her body seemed to ignite into a quivering fire of pleasure.

The moisture flowed between her legs, rich, warm and sweet, as Lucilla's mouth reached down, lips parted, tongue red between her teeth for that final, most intimate kiss of all.

Later, they dressed in Lucilla's chamber. Lucilla handed Regeane a transparent silken tunic, then began slipping her own arms into another just like it.

"What happened to my clothes?" Regeane asked.

"Phew. Those rags. I burned them." Lucilla covered her own tunic with a stola of soft, white linen, embroidered with gold at the neck and hem.

Regeane donned the tunic, then looked down at herself. "I can't walk around like this. It's . . . indecent."

Lucilla smiled. "No. I have a stola for you, too, but first I want to show you something."

Lucilla's room was as most Roman bedrooms, very simple, unadorned, the walls whitewashed. Her large bed of cedar inlaid with gold was the only departure from the norm. It was comfortably appointed with a goose-down tick, lush pillows, and bleached linen sheets and hangings.

She noticed the direction of Regeane's gaze and said, "Yes. You northern barbarians have taught us Romans a few things. Bless you for it. You sleep more comfortably than we do."

Then she turned to Regeane, the appeal in her eyes wistful, almost sad. She touched Regeane's cheek gently. "Share that bed with me tonight, my pretty one."

Regeane took the soft hand between her palms and kissed it. Unaccountably, there were tears in her eyes. "I thought I'd never know love, but today you showed me what it is. I'm glad you still want me, glad I wasn't too . . . clumsy."

"Clumsy?" Lucilla freed her hand from Regeane's grasp and, taking her face between her palms, kissed her softly on the lips. "Inexperienced, perhaps. Experience comes with time. But clumsy? No. No. Never clumsy, my sweet one, but come."

There were two crowns of flowers on the bed resting on the coverlet. White lilies and roses were woven together with rosemary and thyme.

Lucilla placed one on Regeane's head, then led her to one end of the room where a strip of tapestry covered the wall. She pulled a cord and the tapestry leaped aside.

Regeane looked at herself. She had never seen herself, not all of herself. The figure that looked back was beyond her reckoning of beauty, beyond her wildest dreams.

The face, crowned with flowers, was a soft oval; the eyes of melting tenderness, their depths both gold and luminous black; lips brushed with the blush of rose petals; her skin reflected the pallor of the lilies with its fresh velvety softness.

Her body was as Antonius had said, slender, but with the tightly furled slenderness of the bud almost ready to burst into bloom; small breasts tipped in pink, high and pressing against the silken gown; the dark pubic triangle below a mystery of desire and fruitfulness.

Regeane stretched out her hand until it almost touched the silver mirror; surely the girl-woman standing before her must be a painting, could not be real, could not be herself.

But the fingers of that outstretched hand mimicked the movement of her own arm and her reaching fingers brushed the polished silver surface of the mirror.

Lucilla stood nearby, her smile like the serpent offering the apple to Eve.

"Gundabald lied," Regeane said.

"Your uncle?"

"Yes. He told me I was ugly."

"Pimp!" Lucilla spat the word and stroked the long spill of hair on Regeane's shoulders. "That's what pimps do—lie to the girls they sell. Degrading them for losing their honor. Saying 'Only I could love you,' so that they despise themselves and so are easier to buy and sell. But I don't pimp. My women know their worth.

"Ah, I should love to lead you forth to a banquet. I would invite the sons of Rome's best families to amuse myself by watching them vie for the honor of being the first to possess you, the first to embrace you. None knowing that I have come before all the rest. But enough." Lucilla drew back. She jerked on the cord and the tapestry covered the mirror again.

"What we experienced today is but the gustato, the appetizer before the banquet. This is to teach you how to be delighted. I will train you in the arts of pleasing him and yourself. And, last of all, in the most delicate task—that of teaching him to be your enduring source of boundless pleasure. But come, this is the time of day I love most. We'll sit together in the atrium, take the air, and watch the sun set. It's best not to gaze too long into a mirror. In your case it might lead to an excess of vanity; in mine, my dear, despair."

"You're beautiful," Regeane said as they strolled together along the gravel path that edged the atrium pool.

"Yes," Lucilla said. "I believe there's something left of what I was when I was your age. And doubtless I could still ensnare a lover or two, but I've reached the time of life when I value my leisure, my quiet evenings in the garden alone or in the company of a good friend. I'm rich enough to indulge myself."

She paused beside the fountain that fed the pond. A bronze nymph, green with age, poured clear water across a fall of stone, crusted with emerald moss, into the long, still pool. The water reflected the changing hues of the evening sky, now a sheet of gold as the sun-struck clouds drifted across the surface, shading into the turquoise and violet at the approach of darkness.

The villa garden was a dream of beauty. Iris, purple and yellow, bloomed at the edge of the water, clumps of lavender, and, here and there, the arching stems of the rose of paestum still bore large pink flowers.

The beds, arranged against the back of the house, held sun-loving herbs—yellow-crested yarrow, small-flowered fragrant chamomile, large-leafed basil, and tall scarlet-flowered sage. Climbing the pillars of the porch were the tall thorny stems of the Eglantine rose, heavy with the scarlet roseships of autumn.

The gentle fragrance of each herb bathed them as they passed. Here and there, Lucilla stopped to brush a leaf gently with her fingers and drink in the perfume. She remarked that it was a pity that the rosa gallica had faded for the season. Regeane followed her, wrapped in a dream, until they reached a marble bench. Resting on it were a pitcher and two cups. Both goblets were miracles of the glassmaker's art.

Regeane lifted hers to catch the last light. A cameo of white on blue showed a procession of youths and maidens turning garlands to escort the chariot of the bride. "How beautiful," she whispered.

"And how apropos," Lucilla said as she raised the silver pitcher to pour the wine. The silver spout was the head of a wolf.

Knowledge fisted Regeane in the belly. She was in a trap.

The cup fell from her hands into a patch of thyme growing at her feet. The wine stained the white flowers like a splash of blood.

She was in a trap, a beautiful, dangerous trap.

Truly, she could abandon herself to the loveliness of this heavenly garden, to the pleasure of Lucilla's caresses. But this idyll could have but one ending. The mountain lord would come to claim her and one of them would die!

"My God! What's wrong?" Lucilla exclaimed, setting down her own cup to stretch out her hands to Regeane.

Regeane bent over, clutching her stomach for a moment. She felt again that blurring of the world and the first shadows that took her before she changed.

Desperately, she fought it off. The shadows around her in the evening garden reached toward her, but then drew back as she felt Lucilla's hands on her arms.

"What is it, girl?" Lucilla asked.

Regeane realized that for a little while she'd allowed herself to think like a normal woman . . . To look at her approaching marriage and her bridegroom the way any other young girl would. She couldn't. She didn't dare.

Regeane reached down, fumbled for the cup lying among the thyme, afraid she'd broken it. "I'm sorry," she whispered. "Your wonderful cup,"

"The devil with my cup," Lucilla said, hands gripping Regeane's arms. "Are you all right? Never have I seen such an expression of terror on a human's face. What happened? What frightened you so?"

"There," Regeane lifted the cup out of the bed of thyme. "Thank heaven it's not broken."

Lucilla took the cup from her hands, filled it with wine, and held it to Regeane's lips. "That's better. The color's coming back into your cheeks. Now, tell me what's wrong."

Regeane knew she could not. No one would understand the silver wolf, not even a woman as worldly-wise and clever as Lucilla. Regeane forced her whirling mind into a semblance of coherence. She'd lived with the wolf for most of her life, and deception had become second nature. She parried Lucilla's question with another. "What would happen if I defied the king and became a courtesan like you?"

Lucilla looked away from her abruptly, out across the dark garden. "I couldn't be a party to that."

"Why?" Regeane asked desperately. "Is Charles so powerful?"

"Yes," Lucilla said, turning to stare back at Regeane. "He is. It would cost my life to cross him."

Regeane again felt the terror of her flight from Basil and

the despair that filled her heart the night after her talk with Gundabald.

When she first spoke to Lucilla in the square it seemed somehow miraculously a way of escape lay open before her. The demands made on a courtesan, the sale of her body for money, was repulsive. Yet, she could have borne such a life if it offered freedom to the beautiful, silent creature she was by moonlight.

A courtesan lives alone. She could contrive excuses for her lover or lovers on those nights when the mistress of heaven commanded her heart.

But apparently her encounter with Stephen and Antonius had slammed that door in her face. She was again trapped, with Gundabald and Hugo her only refuge. She had no assurance she could trust them once she had become their accomplice. Either one of them might betray her out of greed or simply spite.

Lucilla stared at Regeane's face, shadowed by the blue dusk that now lay over the garden, her brow furrowed and troubled. "Little one, tell me what it is you fear so terribly. Maybe it's nothing so awful that it can't be taken care of. Eh? Tell me. Is it the touch of a man, a man's love? Believe me, that can be dealt with. I'll show you what happens. Most women are afraid at first, but that turns quickly to tedium or, if the woman's blood is warm enough and the man is reasonably skilled, joy."

She leaned closer to Regeane and placed an arm around her shoulders. "I'll tell you a secret. Men love to please their wives and the most clumsy and stupid of them can be trained to pleasure even the most difficult women."

The look of desolation on Regeane's face didn't change.

"Is it childbirth, then?"

Regeane shook her head.

Lucilla drew back. "I am at a loss."

"Suppose there are other women."

Lucilla laughed, a high silvery sound. "Is that all?" She patted Regeane's hand, then kissed her cheek. "Oh, my little one, with your assets—beauty, grace, and a great name—it won't be necessary for you even to acknowledge other women exist." Lucilla sniggered. "Set out to enslave him and you will. I guarantee it. If you but learn a little of what I can teach you, he will worship at your feet."

Regeane pretended to be reassured. She sipped her wine. The light was gone from the sky, but it was not quite dark. The white flowers of the garden still glowed faintly against the darker masses of vegetation. The reflecting pool was beginning to fill with stars.

Behind her in the open rooms of the villa she could hear the clatter of dishes and cutlery. Lights shone through the open doors and the voices of Lucilla's servants called back and forth as they set the table for supper.

It was beginning to be chilly. Lucilla's arm embracing Regeane's shoulders was warm, and somehow, in spite of the fact that Regeane couldn't fully confess her fears, comforting.

"Now, my dear," Lucilla said, giving her shoulders a squeeze, "are you feeling better?"

"Yes," Regeane said softly, lifting the cup to her lips. She added hesitantly, "But there is one more art you could teach me."

"What's that?"

"The art to which one appeals when all other arts fail."

Lucilla looked down at her, puzzled for a moment. Then she understood and stiffened. Her arms dropped from around Regeane's shoulders and she drew away. "I see," she said coldly. "You're not as guileless as you appear. Is this your idea or was it planted in your head by that uncle of yours?"

Regeane set the cup on the bench and rose to her feet. She stood facing Lucilla, a slender figure in the white stola, the older woman's face just faintly visible in the light of the lamps in the room behind her.

Regeane felt tears running down her cheeks, tears of rage and sorrow. "All right," she sobbed out. "I am afraid, but not of men or of children or of my future husband's wandering eye. The truth is . . . Oh, my God," she faltered, "the truth is I can't tell you the truth. How can you know what my life has been? These hours, these few hours I've spent with you, are the first happy ones in years. Since I first bled, since my womanhood came upon me, since . . ." Regeane clenched her fists and stared up at the moonless sky. "Oh, my God, how can I ever explain?" She cried out, covered her face with her hands and tried to run.

But Lucilla stood up and clasped the girl's trembling body to her, quieting her as she might a panicked child, stroking her hair and patting her back gently.

"There, there. Don't torment yourself so. I do believe you are as afraid as you say you are. I don't know why you won't tell me this dark secret, but I believe that it exists if only in your mind. And yes, if you so desperately wish it, I'll teach you that final art. God knows it's not difficult—a half dozen plants grow in this garden alone. Some in moderation help nature. Increase the amount and they harm it. Physicians steep the poppy capsule in wine. The one who drinks it enjoys a better sleep and freedom from pain; but too much of this potion renders that sleep eternal."

"I don't want it for him," Regeane said, "but for myself."

"What!" Lucilla stepped back. "Yourself?"

"Some kinds of death are better than others," Regeane said miserably.

Lucilla's eyes probed Regeane's tear-stained face relentlessly. Finally she murmured, "I wish you could bring yourself to trust me with this terrible secret. I get the feeling there's much more wrong here than . . ." She broke off as one of the maidservants left the lighted triclinium and approached them.

"My lady, we await you at the table. Shall I bring the child?"

"Oh, Elfgifa. I'd forgotten her, but no matter. There's more than enough. Yes, yes, get her. She must be tired of waiting for us to join her."

The maid dimpled. "No, my lady. Right after her bath she fell asleep and awakened only a few minutes ago."

Another one of the maids approached, leading a yawning Elfgifa by the hand.

"Come," Lucilla spoke quietly, taking a still distraught Regeane by the hand. "I'm forgetting my duties as a hostess. Don't upset yourself anymore. We'll talk tomorrow. For tonight, enjoy yourself. Only light conversation at dinner. After all, we met only today. Why should you trust me with the secrets of your heart?"

Regeane was quiet during the meal, her fears pushed into the background by the problems of dealing with the unfamiliar Roman style of dining.

They ate reclining, the food brought to the couches and set before them by the serving girls. There was a separate table for each course. While this might have been a quiet, informal little supper to Lucilla, it was a grand affair to Regeane.

The tables set before her were decked in embroidered white linen. The dishes and cups were of silver. Above her head, lamps in the shape of alabaster doves had flames leaping from their mouths. Painted on the walls of the chamber, songbirds played out their gentle rite of spring lovemaking amidst the flowers of a garden.

Elfgifa, wide-eyed and on her best behavior, watched Lucilla's every movement like a hawk and copied her carefully, as did Regeane herself.

Lucilla treated them both with amused indulgence and, as promised, she kept the conversation light. Still, Regeane felt she was being instructed, since most of Lucilla's talk concerned the multifold factions of the holy city.

The food was simple, but beautifully prepared. Spiced olives and a white cream cheese covered with pepper were the gustato. The appetizers were followed by roast pork with a stuffing of bread, honey, red wine, and bay, served with a miraculous red wine.

The taste astonished Regeane. "It's wonderful," she told Lucilla, awed by its smoothness and silken freshness.

Lucilla laughed. "Oh, you Franks reckon wine ready to drink when enough of it will knock a man down, but we age our best, sealing it in clay jars. It mellows the flavor and softens and smoothes it. This is only ten years old, but I have tasted rare vintages upwards of forty and fifty years."

"Doesn't it spoil?" Regeane asked.

"Sometimes," Lucilla admitted, "but those amphoras that survive make it worth the trouble. The worst that happens is that it becomes vinegar, and that may be used in cooking. This wine is from my own estate. Very few people bother to age wine these days," she explained. "Fine vintages command a correspondingly high price. It's much more lucrative simply to sell the young wine as soon as it's drinkable." She looked sad. "So these civilized arts vanish, but I set aside a few jars for my own table."

When the pork was gone, the tables were taken away and they relaxed over a chilled, sweet white wine served with honey cakes. It was late now, and Lucilla's villa, set away from the bustling heart of Rome, partook of the quiet of a country farm. The only sounds Regeane could hear now were the faint night songs of insects in the garden outside and the whisper of the breeze that drifted cool and refreshing through the open door of the triclinium.

A long day, a full stomach, and the half cup of watered wine Lucilla allowed her were all too much for Elfgifa and she fell asleep on the couch. She awakened only briefly when Lucilla signaled a servant to carry her off to bed. Elfgifa protested, but it transpired that the child only wanted a goodnight kiss from Regeane before she would allow herself to be settled in for the night.

Regeane obliged, and Elfgifa went peaceably. When she was gone, there was a brief, awkward silence between the two women. Then they spoke almost simultaneously.

"I'm sorry," Regeane started to say.

"I do apologize, Regeane . . ."

They both laughed.

Then Regeane said, "I'm the one who should apologize. I feel I made a fool of myself. I suppose I've allowed my fears to prey too much on my mind."

"Not at all, my dear. I shouldn't have pressed you."

Suddenly one of the maids ran into the room from the garden. "My lady, there's a party of men at the gates!"

Regeane heard shouts and a crash. A woman screamed.

Lucilla jumped up from her couch and ran past the girl into the garden.

A half-dozen armed men stood in the atrium. The light of their torches reflected in the dark water of the pool. One of them stepped forward, and Regeane saw the face she remembered from the square earlier in the day.

He pointed to her and shouted, "There she is. Take her."

Regeane cringed and turned, not knowing where to run, but Lucilla strode toward him. "Basil, are you mad?" she shouted. "We are under the protection of the Holy Father himself!"

The men with Basil hesitated.

Lucilla's tall form, her chin lifted fearlessly, stood between Regeane and Basil. "I'll have your heads for this! All of you!" she threatened.

The men with Basil drew back, looking at each other.

Seeing she had the upper hand for the moment, Lucilla stepped forward to press her advantage. "Leave my house this instant, and I'll forget this unsavory incident ever occurred."

Basil laughed, his white teeth gleaming in his dark, bearded face. "My, what airs we give ourselves now, threatening us with the power of the church and the pope. This from the greatest whore in Rome. Whore and panderer."

Lucilla stiffened with rage, her face a frozen, beautiful mask of fury. Her reply to Basil was low, hoarse, and deadly. "One more step toward me, Basil. I won't bother about your head. I'll see you die in torment."

Basil returned her stare with a heavy-lidded look of contempt and turned toward his men. "What are you, children, that you fear the anger of a woman? I said, take the girl! And as for you, bitch," he said to Lucilla, "interfere with me again and I'll send you to ply your trade in hell."

Basil and the men with him advanced on Regeane and Lucilla.

Lucilla caught Regeane by the wrist and whispered urgently, "It's no good. I can't hold them. Where in God's name are my men? Run!" She darted toward the back of the garden, pulling Regeane along with her through a door.

The abrupt change from the light of the torches to the darkness of the passage blinded Regeane. When she could see again they were stumbling across the furrows of a kitchen garden. Ahead, she could see the tree limbs, an orchard, and then a wall.

Basil and his men erupted from the passage in a blaze of torchlight.

Regeane's foot kicked against something. Lucilla bent down and snatched it up—a hoe.

The nearest of Basil's men was less than six feet behind them. Lucilla turned and drove the handle of the hoe with a straight thrust into his groin. The man doubled over, howling.

"Run, girl, run!" Lucilla called to Regeane.

The rest of Basil's soldiers hung back, perhaps a little intimidated by the fate of the first. Then another leaped forward and snatched at the hoe in Lucilla's hand: a mistake. She fetched him a crack across the side of the head with the handle that sent him to his knees, clutching his skull. Then she chopped viciously at his face with the blade.

Regeane couldn't bring herself to leave Lucilla. She was sure Basil would kill Lucilla.

Basil drew his sword, leaped past Lucilla, ignoring another swing of the hoe. He grabbed Regeane by the arm. She screeched and tore free, staggering, and fell on her face in the soft earth of the garden. Basil's sword chopped into the furrow near her face, showering her head with mud.

Regeane came to her knees, clutching a handful of soil. Basil caught her hair with one hand, stretching out her throat, positioning his sword up and back to cut off her head.

Regeane let fly with the mud. Wet filth caught Basil full in the face. He gave a shout of fury and let go of her hair to clear his eyes.

The darkness of the moon flooded Regeane's brain. She was wolf. Shocked and terrified, she staggered. The light of the torches dazzled the wolf's eyes more than it had the woman's.

In the wake of her shock and terror rushed a triumphant fury.

Basil was still pawing at his eyes with one hand while hacking at Regeane's discarded dress with his sword. He believed she was still in her clothes.

The silver wolf lunged for him clumsily. He kicked her in the ribs.

The woman's will, still alive in the wolf, was overwhelmed by rage. The wolf made an eel-like turn around the legs in front of her, teeth slashing for a hamstring. Her fangs laid open the calf of his leg.

Basil shrieked and chopped down at her with his sword. But the silver wolf leaped clear.

Three men struggled with Lucilla, one holding her around the body, two grappling with her for her quarterstaff hoe. For the moment they had their hands full. A fourth stood back, torch in hand.

"You damned fool," Basil shouted. "Drive off that mad dog."

The fire flared in the silver wolf's eyes, blotting out everything as the torch was thrust down toward her face.

"Jesu mercy!" the man screamed. "That isn't a dog!"

She went back on her haunches. The woman commanded the wolf. *The torches! Get the torches! In the darkness you are the stronger.*

The wolf backed, twisted away from the flames. The man holding the torch was trying desperately to draw his sword.

The wolf, maddened by rage and fire, thought only of two things—throat and groin. With the merciless logic of a killer, she went for the groin. The throat was too far. She wasn't sure enough of her powers.

She uncoiled, driven upward like a striking snake. She missed the groin, but her teeth snapped shut in the soft tissue of the upper thigh. Blood, salt, and thick stinking of raw meat flooded the wolf's mouth and nose.

The man gave a piercing scream of pure agony, tore free, and bashed at the wolf's back with the torch.

The wolf dropped off, rolling.

The man staggered backward, crashed into Lucilla and the other men struggling. They all went down in a heap. The torches fell clear and lay flickering, half extinguished by the damp soil.

The garden was suddenly in darkness.

The wolf lunged with a roar of fury at the men on top of Lucilla. They scattered, scrambling, crawling in all directions.

Basil dived for a torch as Lucilla came up fighting, the hoe still in her hands. She slammed one man across the chest; a few of his ribs snapped. She caught another across the back, driving his face down into the mud.

Screams and cries rang out from behind the wolf. More torches appeared. "The pope's militia!" someone shouted. "They're coming!"

The garden blazed. Lucilla's servants mustered to defend their mistress.

Basil and his men ran. The wolf barrelled along behind them. She broke through a low screen of pomegranate bushes and raced among the tree trunks of the orchard toward a low wall. Basil and his men were up and over it in seconds.

The wolf hesitated, then gathered herself. She had never

really run free. One easy leap took her over the barrier. Basil and his men were already mounted and galloping away.

For a second she stood still in the darkness; flanks heaving with exertion until a thunder of hoofbeats sounded from behind and sent her diving for cover.

A company of the Roman civil militia swept past, riding hard after Basil and his men.

Silence fell. The silver wolf slipped out of the brush and stood, paws in the dust of the road, dread and terror churning inside her.

Beyond the walls of the villa she could hear voices. She moved off down the road quickly, instinctively, seeking the comfort of darkness, the obscurity of the night.

There was no moon, only the dazzling streamer of the Milky Way arching above her. A road of light. She didn't know what Lucilla or Basil had seen. Basil had a face full of mud. Lucilla was fighting for her life.

One thing the silver wolf did know. She didn't want to go back. The silver wolf was free, bewildered, frightened, and yet aquiver with frantic joy.

She was free.

She trotted on, dropping into the mile-eating lope of a creature that makes nothing of a fifty-mile hunt.

The wolf's heart sang. Old memories called out of the ebb and flow of the blood in her veins. Memories not her own. Oh, there were forests the wolf's heart remembered: tall forests that clothed mountainsides, trees of pine, fir, and spruce, a landscape bejeweled by the blue lakes filled with fish. Lowland forests of oak, ash, beech, and elm, swarming with the dark antlered shapes of deer. They fed in clearings drenched by moonlight.

She hunted them, age upon age long gone. She was the swift-footed, sharp-fanged mistress of the night, taking her blood tribute in the silver glow. She fled across sun-drenched plains where the smoke of grass fires hung sharp in her nostrils. She ate her fill of beasts fallen in panicked flight from the flames.

She tracked her prey across frozen, lifeless wastes. Her belly rumbled with hunger. Her paws, frost-crusted with splinters of ice forming between her pads, left bloody footprints in the snow. Her heart yearned for the warm, blood heat of the kill, a full belly, and sleep.

She was all these things and more—strength, courage, and a defiant beauty. *Am I wolf or woman?* she wondered, then stopped on the crest of a low hill to feel the stillness, the aliveness, the perfect solitude of the night. It enfolded her as a mother's arms enfold a child and protect it from harm.

The wind was cool, refreshed by the scent of dew just beginning to settle on green growing things. It ruffled the fur of her neck and face pleasantly. The woman would have been cold, but the wolf, protected by her pelt, was warm.

The legion of stars shed a faint light on the landscape. On one side, the dark hills rolled away, sloping gently into the plain of Campagna; on the other lay the city of Rome, its lights a cluster of fireflies flickering around the smooth, black snake of the Tiber. The breeze from that direction carried the stench of an open sewer.

Am I wolf or woman? she wondered again. Both the wolf and the woman were in accord with each other; each would be incomplete without the other. Yet the open spaces of the hills and even the desolation of the war-shattered Campagna called out to the wolf's heart. She wanted to turn her face into the clean wind, to vanish into the tall grass and remain a beast among beasts forever.

But the woman knew better. The woman knew morning would come and she would find herself naked and defenseless and alone. For better or worse, her destiny was forever linked with sleepers whose lights flickered like dying embers in the valley below.

Neither wolf nor woman, she thought, *but something more than either one, or less, different and so, perhaps, damned.* Would she end hated and accursed, dying in flames at a stake, condemned by the church? Or perhaps stoned by humans fearful of her powers? She remembered with icy fear the funeral party's quick acceptance of Silve's accusation. Others might be as precipitous as they.

That she had lived this long was a challenge to the accepted order of her world—a challenge to death. And live she would until life was torn from her. Live and never yield the woman to save the wolf, or the wolf to save the woman. She would live to be herself, to be free or be dead.

She trotted to the center of the road and sniffed the air. Amidst the smell of horse and sweat, animal and human, there was the scent of blood.

The wolf dropped her nose to the ground. She'd wounded one of Basil's men. He was still bleeding. She set off in pursuit.

Basil and his men hadn't returned to the city. They'd circled its outskirts, traveling out across the Campagna toward the sea.

On the rich plain of the Campagna, nature had once smiled beneficently on man. Blessed with the fertile soil of volcanic peaks, mild summers, and gentle winters, it once overflowed with milk and honey. Now, no more. Four centuries of warfare over that pearl of prizes, the imperial city, had turned it into a wasteland of swamps and ruins.

Unlike most of rocky Italy, it was not locally defensible and no power remained strong enough to protect it. The fortress of Casino, towering alone above the plain, offered refuge to those few travelers who braved its fear-haunted darkness. Only armed parties of men traveled here alone at night. They, and the silver wolf, drawn by she knew not what.

She moved with the easy lope of a hunting wolf, following the trail of blood, the scent of horses and men clear in her nostrils now.

Her nose caught the tang of woodsmoke, even before she saw the fire. She increased her pace.

It had once been a temple of Apollo, a sanctuary of the god of light. Now, the tall columns were fallen and the cella was an empty shell. Even the statue of the god was gone. Only the face of the dread monster brooded from the pediment—her hair snakes, her tongue protruding from her mouth as if to lap up the blood of sacrifices.

Basil and his men were camped in the ruins. They were gathered around their fire blazing on the broken porch of the temple.

The wolf stole up through the black poplar trunks of what once had been the gods' sacred grove. She stopped, face screened by the tall grass, listening and watching. The wolf was disappointed. Basil had many more men with him than he'd had at Lucilla's villa.

Far too many for a lone wolf to challenge.

Basil stood on the stained marble steps to the temple, speaking to someone hidden by the firelight. "There's no rescue for you, and none for that brother of yours. Not now that I have him. Whatever path he takes leads to his destruction."

"Do you hate him so much then?" a voice asked from the doorway into the ruined cella.

The wolf knew the voice. *Antonius*. She eased to one side, where her eyes weren't blinded by the flames, and saw him, robed in black, the mantle, as always, covering his face.

"Hate him?" Basil asked. "Christ, no. I don't give a damn about him. When I take the city, he can stay pope as long as he does as he's told."

Pope! That rocked even the wolf's mind. Regeane had known "Stephen" had power. But she hadn't guessed quite what kind or how much. That Stephen might be Pope Hadrian himself hadn't entered her mind.

She drew closer. She peered through a leafy screen of low bushes and tall grass at the men gathered before the porch of the temple.

"I can't think I'll be of much use to you," Antonius said with angry bitterness. "I'm a dying man, and I hope my brother has more sense then to let you blackmail him with threats against my rotting carcass."

"A very apt description, my friend. The stench of the charnel house does hang about you," Basil said. "But you were a young man when you were taken with the disease, and I'll lay odds you'd last a long time tied to a cross."

The two eyes, all that Antonius ever showed the world, closed slowly. The shoulders under the black mantle slumped in resignation. He got to his feet, went to the fire, and fished out one of the flaming branches.

"I assume," he said to Basil with quiet dignity, "that you wouldn't begrudge even a captive a fire against the cold."

Basil drew away as if afraid of contagion. "No, I wouldn't, and you'll have food if you want it."

"I don't."

"As you wish," Basil said indifferently. "Now crawl into your hole and give the rest of us some relief from the sight and stink of you."

Whack! An arrow quivered in the trunk of a sapling near the silver wolf's shoulder. In seconds she was twenty feet away, deep in the darkness. It took all the woman's strength to master the wolf's reflexes.

She heard Basil shout, "What the devil!"

"Eyes!" one of the men shouted. "The eyes of some animal, watching us from the darkness beyond the fire."

The silver wolf stood trembling among the tree trunks.

"Build up the fire then, and stop shooting at shadows," Basil snarled.

The silver wolf crouched and then moved farther away as men with torches approached the spot where she'd been hiding.

Some laughed. "Look, Drusis. You killed a tree."

"I saw eyes," Drusis insisted stubbornly. "I missed, that's all."

"Whatever it was, it's miles away by now."

"The eyes were big and high up off the ground. It was a wolf. I've hunted wolves."

"Not on the Campagna, you haven't," Basil said. "It was likely an owl."

Still arguing, they returned to the camp and began to bed down for the night.

The silver wolf waited until the camp quieted. They left only one man on guard to tend the fire. He sat dozing on the temple steps, secure in the knowledge that no large party of men could take them by surprise in the open country.

During the commotion, Antonius had withdrawn into the interior of the temple to sleep.

The wolf whined and snapped at the air as Regeane took control of her. Antonius was in deadly danger and the woman's sharper human mind comprehended it at once.

She grasped that neither Hadrian nor Antonius would alter state policy under threat of Basil's blackmail. In fact, he was a suicidal fool to attempt such a ploy. Antonius would die a horrible death.

An enraged Hadrian would, no doubt, avenge him by killing Basil. Everyone would suffer and nothing would be changed.

The wolf didn't comprehend the convolutions of human cruelty. To her, Antonius was simply a friend. A pack brother, stricken and in need of protection. The woman stepped back and loosed her reins on the wolf. She acted on instinct.

She drifted slowly and silently around to the back of the temple and found what she sought.

Although it had been faced in marble, the fabric of the structure was clay brick. One of the trees of the grove had fallen and taken down part of the wall of the cella with it. A hole gaped wide. The entrance, choked with weeds and brambles, was only a few feet above the ground.

The wolf forced her way through without difficulty and stood looking out at Antonius.

He sat before his small fire, head bowed, his back against the wall near the door.

She walked toward him and stopped on the other side of the fire. Even alone, he kept most of the mantle wound around the lower part of his face, but the wolf could see enough of that face to understand why.

On one side, his lips were gone and she could see the teeth. The lesion extended up into the nose. The area spared by the disease was haunted by the shadow of a great beauty.

The human ruin reminded Regeane of one of those statues of ancient gods, abandoned, broken, part of the face eroded by wind and rain, but still bearing traces of the glory of its prime. As Basil said, Antonius was very young.

His eyes were closed.

The silver wolf stood there, baffled.

When she entered the building she hadn't had any clear plan in mind, only a hope of somehow helping him to escape Basil. Escape. The idea was ridiculous. She couldn't even make him understand what she wanted. How could she talk to him? How could she persuade him to talk to her?

The woman would have laughed. The wolf was only frustrated. She whined softly, expressing her aggravation.

He blinked, looking surprised, but not frightened.

At first he must have thought she was a dog because he made

as if to stretch out his hand. Then his eyes took in the long, vulpine muzzle, the erect ears, and the magnificent silver-black ruff that framed the face. He drew the hand back.

"My poor friend," he said. "Have we usurped your den? Your eyes must have been the ones Basil's archer shot at."

Since the wolf simply stood, staring at him, he continued. "What is it? Do you want something from me? Something to eat? I almost wish you had me in mind. Your teeth and jaws would be more merciful than Basil's cross."

He turned to one side. A half-loaf of bread, some olives, and goat cheese lay on a wooden trencher near the doorway. He lifted it and set it in front of the silver wolf.

"Here, take this. I have no appetite for Basil's food. The less I eat, the sooner I'll be free of Basil and no longer a trouble to my brother."

The silver wolf dropped her nose to the trencher, then, ignoring it, trotted to the door, skirting the glow cast by Antonius' small fire.

The man on guard was slumped against the base of one of the ruined columns. He'd piled some fresh fuel on his fire. It burned high, the flames wavering and crackling in the night breeze. The guard snored softly.

The wolf returned and stood by Antonius' fire, looking over it into his eyes.

"Wolf, you are beginning to puzzle me very much. You don't behave like any wild beast I've ever met."

Deliberately she reached out, set her teeth in the edge of his mantle, and pulled.

"What?" he asked in surprise. "You want the mantle?"

Desperate to make him understand, she lunged, caught him by the wrist, gently, and pulled. Regeane was a small woman, but she was a big wolf.

Antonius slid a foot or so away from the fire.

She released his arm and stepped back.

He stared at her, then at his wrist in astonishment. "If you wanted to kill me," Antonius said softly, "you could kill me easily."

The wolf made a low sound in her throat, an urgent sound. She ran to the hole in the temple cella, then back toward Antonius.

"This is madness," Antonius said. "What are you? Who are you?"

She caught the corner of his mantle again and tugged.

"Don't you see? They have horses. I'd be ridden down," he whispered.

This time she snarled softly, her lips lifting clear of her teeth.

Antonius got up. "I'm standing here now, explaining myself to a wolf."

She tugged again at the mantle.

"Maybe you're right. Anything seems better than the fate Basil has planned for me."

HE HAD TO SADDLE THE HORSE ALONE. SHE FOUND the saddles in the darkness for him, the scent of leather loud as a shout in her nose. She stood in the shadows at the edge of the camp keeping carefully downwind of the horses, waiting impatiently and watching the guard who still snored on the temple steps.

The horses were picketed on one long rope tied between two trees. Her teeth severed the rope with one bite. The nearest horse to her reared, a black shape against the sky. She leaped aside, dodging the slash of a forehoof.

The horses tore free. Still tied together, they didn't run, but circled and milled.

The silver wolf would have loved to have been able to curse. As it was, she leaped back from the milling animals with a vicious snarl of fury. It was too dangerous. She couldn't get close enough to cut them free of each other.

Antonius' horse reared. The wolf saw he'd lost control of it.

He stayed in the saddle by a miracle.

The guard on the temple steps gave a shout.

The wolf was frantic.

Basil and his men awakened, reaching for weapons and torches.

The wolf flattened her ears and lunged, nipping at the hocks of the nearest of the horses. The animal lashed out at her with its heels and bolted at Basil and his men.

They thundered in a tight group across the bedground of Basil's camp, Antonius' horse following.

In blind panic, Basil's men scattered to avoid being trampled. Basil himself ran to the top of the temple porch as the horses flew past, followed by Antonius on the last of them, clinging desperately to the pommel of the saddle. "Stop him!" Basil screamed.

The men around him were too stupefied to react. Basil snatched a crossbow and fired.

The wolf saw Antonius' horse swerve and stagger as the bolt thudded into its side.

Basil grabbed another bow and the wolf went for him, taking the path cleared by the stampeding horses.

"Deus meus," someone screamed. "It's the dog. The dog from the villa."

"Dog, nothing," another voice shouted. "It's Lupa herself, the wolf of Rome."

Basil spun around, taking aim at the flying silver shape.

The fire blazed ahead of the running wolf, between herself and Basil. She saw the rage in his eyes above the bow and the glitter of a sharp-ridged bolt aimed at her. She cleared the fire on one bound and crouched, gathering herself as the bow thrummed.

The head of the bolt seared her back as it grazed past, plunging into the fire. She leaped upward, fangs gleaming, for Basil's throat.

Basil aimed a clubbing blow at her with the spent bow. It took the wolf in the ribs, sending her rolling down the temple steps.

"Kill the damned thing. Kill it," Basil screamed to his men.

The wolf got her legs under her and ran.

She followed the horses. The woman strove to control the wolf. Part of her was terrified, yet, she was exultant and delighted. She'd deprived Basil of his prey and nearly gotten him. She slowed her pace and looked up at the stars, realizing for the first time the horse Antonius was riding was running the wrong way—away from Rome, out across the wilderness of the Campagna toward the coast.

She stopped, sides heaving, and became aware for the first time that she was injured. The scratch seared her back, out of reach of her healing tongue. It itched and burned. She shook herself. Her fur rose, then fell back into place. Not mortal, she decided. Not even serious.

In the silence far away, Basil's voice came to her ears. "After them," he was telling his men. "The horse is wounded. I put a bolt through its ribs. Antonius is crippled and won't get far on foot."

The men's reply was unintelligible, even to the wolf's preternaturally sharp ears, but it was evidently a demur because she heard Basil shout, "In the name of God, why am I afflicted by such fools? Take the torches. The thing's just a wild animal. What are you, women, to be afraid of such a thing?"

She had to find Antonius before Basil did. She lowered her muzzle and began circling. In a few moments she picked up the trail of the horses, including the blood scent of the injured one. It had dropped back, trailing the rest. Crossbow bolts were deadly things. Shock and hemorrhage kill quickly.

It was not long before she caught up to Antonius. He was on his feet beside the wounded animal. It stood, legs spread, head lowered, breathing in harsh, roaring gasps.

She knew he'd seen her silver-tinged shadow come up beside him, for he spoke. "What now, my friend?" He stared back the way he had come. The torches of Basil's men bobbed across the flat countryside toward them.

She edged her body between him and the horse, pushing him away. As the horse scented her, it stamped its feet. The head came up and she saw the pale gleam of one rolling eye.

With a roar, she launched herself at the animal, her teeth meeting with a snap just inches from the equine neck.

With a cry of terror, the horse lurched forward at a staggering run.

The wolf stood quietly, listening as the drumming of hoofbeats faded into silence.

"I see," Antonius said, looking back at the bright knot of torches behind them. "They'll follow the horse."

The wolf whined softly, then made a grunting sound in her throat.

"Mother of God," Antonius whispered. "You can think."

The wolf didn't venture any kind of a reply. She was unhappy about what she'd just done. The animal was dying. She felt detached from herself. There had been more compassion in the wolf's heart for the horse than for the human. "To use" was a purely human concept. The wolf didn't understand it. The wolf's actions were dictated by need.

She turned her face into the clean wind and led Antonius away from the torches. She had to find a place to put him because, in the morning, the wolf would forsake her. Sunrise signaled the end of the silver one's power. She must find shelter before she became woman again. The thought hung over her head like a sword.

To the wolf's ears the night sang with a thousand voices.

Regeane felt as she had when, as a child at her mother's knee, she'd first been confronted with a book. The tiny letters fascinated her and she was sure there were wonderful secrets contained within them, if only she knew how to interpret them.

So were the voices of the night: a book opened before a caged beast's eyes. A book she couldn't read. As wolf or woman she had been confined so long.

She left Antonius behind for a moment and ran in a wide circle, her head up, sniffing the wind. She could smell water far away, and the musky scent of deer.

She had to keep reminding the beast that when dawn came, the joyous creature would fade and she would be abandoned to God knew what fearful fate, naked on the Campagna alone.

Besides, Antonius was in pain. He couldn't walk very well and the rag bindings on his feet were already tattered. She whined softly.

"Yes, Lupa," Antonius said, "and I hope you know what to do because I don't. I don't have any idea."

She ran down the slope of a low hill, then up another to the very top. She stopped, a lean dark shape under the stars.

The breeze was cool. Even from far away, she could smell the city. A cleaner smell of wood smoke came to her nostrils. The torches of Basil's men? No, high above the plain she saw the distant light of Monte Casino. Could she find shelter for Antonius there? Reluctantly she decided against it. Basil would look there first. She didn't know if the monks could prevent him from taking away someone under their protection.

She realized the scents mapped out the Campagna for her,

the city so far away. Casino on the horizon, and a damp, vertiginous odor. What? It was coming from a heap of ruins nearby.

She returned to Antonius and guided him in that direction.

Hidden in a fold of ground near a clean stream were a few chimneys almost covered by the lush vegetation that flourished near water on the dry plains.

The woman's mind remembered something like them once near Paris on the Seine. A glassworks.

She dipped her muzzle into a clear pool and lapped. The water was fresh and sweet.

Antonius hunkered down beside her. "Where have you brought me, Lupa?"

The wolf made a low sound in her throat.

Antonius waited. Then she trotted off and began to circle. After a few minutes she found the flue. The glass furnaces had to be vented from below to get the fire hot enough to render the sand molten for the blowers.

There were two furnaces. The first tunnel was choked with dirt and debris, but the second was open. She led Antonius to the tunnel.

He stared at the hole in dismay. "Lupa, are you sure?"

The wolf was growing afraid. She wasn't sure how long she'd been out. It was late. She *must* return to Rome before morning. She whined urgently.

Antonius crawled into the hole. The flue led to the bottom of the turnip-shaped oven. When Antonius reached it, he said quietly, "I see."

Part of the chimney above had fallen away and thick bushes and small trees had grown up around it. The entrance was overgrown by tall weeds. The only reason the wolf had been able to find it was because at some time in the past, another wolf had used it for a den. She'd picked up the scent.

She hoped that if Basil's men searched the area they wouldn't think to look down into the ruined ovens. They might not even know what they were.

When Antonius was safely inside, she hurried out and began to run toward the city.

She was terrified. During her race, her terror grew. She hadn't realized she'd come this far. When she reached the tombs along the Via Appia, she realized she was caught. She wouldn't be able to reach Lucilla's villa before dawn. When the sun topped the horizon and the gray light around her turned to gold, she would be woman again.

The lodging house where Hugo and Gundabald had their rooms wasn't far off. She had no choice.

As she was going up the outside stair to their apartments, she met Hugo coming down. All the desperate, exhausted wolf wanted to do was dodge past him, but Hugo didn't know that.

He gaped at her. Despite the faint light of early dawn, she saw his jaw drop and his face turn green with terror. He lunged back up the stair, opening the door, and trying to slam it in her face.

The silver wolf dropped back on her haunches and sprang for his throat. Her flying body crashed into his chest, and he went down on his back.

She found herself, paws on his chest, staring down into his horrified face.

Hugo's mouth opened. He looked as if he wanted to scream, but was too paralyzed by terror to make a sound.

He gazed up into a wrinkled muzzle filled with long, white teeth. Her hot breath fanned his cheek. Her snarl was loud as a thunderclap.

She had Hugo where she'd always wanted him She knew an instant's regret that she could not prolong the moment. Hugo looked as though, if she were able to remain in her present position, he would shortly die of fright.

How delightful.

Too bad she was going to be human in a second. If she bit him, he would leave a very nasty taste in her mouth.

She felt mildly grateful for at least this momentary satisfaction. She knew Gundabald would make her pay dearly for it.

Hugo pissed on himself and fainted. Warm light flowed through the doorway. Regeane snatched away his mantle, anything to cover herself. It was dawn outside and she was naked.

VII

SHE AWOKE IN HER CELL IN THE AFTERNOON. SHE crouched next to the wall. She had never felt more of the beast. Her body was human female, but the wolf prowled in her brain. The wolf might be the only reason she lived.

She was naked. The narrow stone room was empty. She was chained to the wall by an iron collar around her neck. Her skin was blue with cold, her fingers and toes numb.

She was on her knees, one shoulder pressed against the stones. Her hair offered a little warmth, so she kept her head bowed. It hung around her breasts and shoulders like a cape.

In any case, she couldn't stand. The chain running from the collar around her neck to the staple in the wall was too short, only about three feet long. The iron collar was heavy. The edges were rough. Every so often, when she moved, she saw a rivulet of blood run down her breasts and stomach.

There were many more blood stains on her skin, some particles dried, dark; others red, only beginning to stiffen. The beast said, *Sleep, withdraw from the pain and the cold,* but the woman couldn't. She'd reached the point where cold and pain were so intense, they wouldn't let her.

Her stomach cramped viciously. Her back throbbed with a dull ache where Gundabald had flogged her.

She ended by being almost as terrified of him as Hugo had been of her. Gundabald seemed at first to have lost all control. He grabbed her by the hair, pinned her to the floor facedown with his boot on her shoulder. He flogged her with his belt until Hugo's mantle was bloody and her screams roused the keeper of the lodging house.

Gundabald wouldn't open the door to him. But the man and his wife stood outside and cursed them both so savagely—Regeane for screaming and disturbing the other tenants, Gundabald for causing the screams—that Gundabald finally stopped hitting Regeane.

"Think you're getting away with something, don't you?" he'd asked as he stripped off Hugo's mantle. "That thing from hell will come to you and heal you."

Regeane, thinking he meant to rape her, fought desperately with the only weapons she had left—voice, teeth, and nails.

The landlord began shouting and pounding again.

Gundabald had Regeane cornered near the fireplace. Regeane appealed for help, screaming Gundabald meant to kill her. Gundabald promised the landlord and his wife a gold piece if they would go away and leave them alone.

The landlord and his wife left.

Gundabald clubbed Regeane down with a chunk of firewood. It took three blows. She still wasn't completely unconscious when he dragged her into the cell and snapped the collar shut on her neck.

Her head throbbed. The left side of her face was swollen. She moved her neck against the rough edge of the iron collar, this time deliberately.

Blood flowed—scarlet, warm, even hot, against her blue-tinged skin.

When Gundabald slammed the door shut, she'd begun to awaken. She'd fought the chain, screaming, pulling at the staple in the wall with more than human strength, thrashing and jerking at the collar. Nothing helped. The iron, forged and hammered, was beyond her strength.

In her wildest nightmare, she hadn't believed Gundabald would go this far. After she fought, she begged. Sobbing and pleading for at least some water. Something, even if only rags, to cover herself.

She received no reply—nothing—and finally realized Hugo and Gundabald had probably gone with the landlord to the nearest taverna. They were likely all drunk by now, sodden and sleeping off the morning's exertions.

Her stomach cramped. Her gorge rose. She gagged. Then

leaned to one side and vomited a puddle of light green liquid on the floor. It began slowly trickling across the uneven floor toward the wall.

Another puddle of yellow liquid rested near it. She'd stood the torment of needing to empty her bladder most of the morning. When it became unbearable, she'd let go.

She closed her eyes. The cell stank to both the wolf and the woman's nose. But an icy wind blew and the room filled with the clean delicate smell of the Rosa Canina—the dog rose.

She saw a woman's face, then a man's. He wasn't much. Sandy fair hair, cropped short, wide cheekbones, a wickedly humorous grin. You might pass him in the street and not notice him. The woman was small with the same fragile, pink-and-white beauty as the abundantly blooming rose sheltering their bower.

They lay naked together, limbs entwined. The velvety rose petals drifting down to rest on skin warmed, blushing with the heat of an inexhaustible erotic fire. He cradled her in his arms. He had loved her. The languorous relaxation of her body was clear evidence. And, if the position of his hands was also evidence, he was gently preparing her to be loved again.

Until he saw the tears on her cheeks.

He turned. He was naked. Helpless. His weapons weren't far. But he would never reach them.

Regeane and the wolf awoke with a start. The collar bruised her neck. A few drops of blood dripped down her arm.

The bit of sky she could see through the barred window was dark gray. The wolf, whose internal clock was netted with the wheeling stars, knew afternoon. Another dark rainy day labored toward its close. When night fell, the wolf would come, trying to heal her, to protect her. But how long could that last?

The wolf looked at Regeane through a scree of blowing snow. Not the southern snow with big, soft flakes melting on the fur or even the nose. But snow like icy sand, blistering exposed skin like a rubbing with pumice stone and then freezing the blood oozing from the raw wound.

The wolf's eyes were clouded, her ribs showed. Her spine ridged like a broken stone down her back. She, too, needed

food, water, sleep, and warmth. In the end, she would perish as
the woman would without them.

Regeane knew what Gundabald wanted: a pale puppet of a
woman. A creature so terrified of his displeasure that she would
yield to any command and pretend to be pleased to obey him
rather than risk his anger—and his punishment.

How many times would she have to be dragged to the cell
and chained by the neck? How much starvation, thirst? How
many beatings—beatings the wolf would heal over and over
again—before she became a witless, broken thing? Living like
Hugo and Silve between a flagon and a fuck. Willing to do anything she was told rather than risk this horror one more time.

Suddenly, she and her nightmare sister were one. The wolf's
eyes looked at her from the land where the sun only rolled on
the horizon, casting a purple, scarlet, violet, and gold fire. Its
rays painting a dead, white, frozen plain. When the sun was
gone, the wolf died. Long ago, and only one of her deaths. She
lay down in the snow and there wasn't enough flesh on her
bones to keep her warm through the subzero night. She still lay
there entombed in ice forever. Her spirit ranged the stars.

There was a chance—one chance. Lucilla. Regeane might be
rescued, but after having seen Antonius in Basil's grip, she
wasn't sure if Hadrian was still pope. Or if Lucilla had the
power to release her.

But if Lucilla had no power, Regeane did. Release was
within her power. She reached up and touched the jagged edge
of the collar and felt how sharp it was. She remembered the
wolf's teaching about rivers of blood, dark and bright, pulsing
below the skin.

Her eyes closed as a sick beast's will. She waited, at peace,
her decision made, resting, conserving her strength for what
would come.

THE SOUND OF LUCILLA'S VOICE IN THE NEXT
room woke her.

"Damnation!" Lucilla shouted. "Build up the fire. I have
been in warmer and more cozy catacombs. No! You stingy
fool—put on more than that. I want a roaring blaze."

Regeane heard the landlord's voice. An obsequious murmur as he verbally bowed and scraped to a very testy Lucilla.

"We will want food. No! I do not want your leavings. I saw a taverna down the street. It had a cook shop."

The landlord's voice murmured objections.

"What!" Lucilla said. "Don't tell me what they won't do! You see this? It's gold. Not copper, not silver, gold. You and Euric go to the cook shop. I want the best they have—wine, food, bread. The best. And I will expect change. A gold piece that size is enough to feed a family for a year."

The bolts on the door rattled.

Regeane tried to call out. All she could manage was a husky whisper. "Lucilla."

"Well, I hear her, so she must be all right. They were beating her, you say?"

"Yes, my gracious lady. The girl screamed pitifully. My wife and I came up to try to help, but her uncle barred the door against us and we couldn't . . ."

The rest of his reply was lost in the rattle and clash of the sliding bolts.

Lying pig, Regeane thought. He had been only too happy to be bribed by Gundabald.

Lucilla stepped into the room. Regeane saw the color drain from Lucilla's face. She gasped and swayed where she stood.

"Don't faint," Regeane croaked. "Don't let the men see me like this."

The door was slightly ajar. Lucilla pulled it shut, tightly shut. She closed her eyes and turned away from Regeane, her forehead resting on the closed door. "Is your uncle mad?" she asked faintly.

"No," Regeane replied. "I don't think so. He wants to rule my mind. He doesn't care if there's anything to rule when he's finished."

"My lady," Euric asked from outside the door. "Do you need help?"

"Go away, all of you," Lucilla screeched.

"My lady," Euric queried again. "What's wrong?" He sounded alarmed.

"Nothing," Lucilla stammered. "I mean, nothing I can't handle.

You and the landlord go and purchase the food. I adjure you, go at once and leave two men at the door with orders to admit no one. If her uncle returns unexpectedly, I don't want to have to fend him off with my dagger. Now, go!" she shouted and stamped her foot.

A few moments later, Regeane was sitting in a chair in front of the fire, her feet in a bucket of warm water, eating a bowl of chicken and leeks in heavy cream. She wore a threadbare dress intended for a woman far gone in pregnancy. It hung in heavy folds around her body.

Lucilla stooped over her to examine her face. "God," she whispered, "I thought that looked worse a few moments ago."

Regeane knew the wolf was present.

"What happened to you last night?" Lucilla asked abruptly. She was rummaging through a chest in the corner. It contained a few of Gisela's gowns. "My God," she said, lifting a tattered garment of indeterminate color and holding it up. "Hadn't your mother any sense of what was due to her from her kin? She was a noblewoman. They should have dressed her better than this even if they had to go hungry."

Regeane was up. Her body was warm now. She'd finished the chicken dish and was raiding another on the table: spinach cooked with slices of rich, sweet bacon. "My mother had a nice dress," Regeane gabbled between mouthfuls. "I buried her in it." She tried to sound pathetic.

Lucilla dropped the dress. The look she gave Regeane could have etched glass. "Don't . . . you . . . dare . . . try . . . to . . . make . . . sport . . . of . . . me, my girl! What happened last night? I want to know and I want to know now!" Lucilla commanded.

Regeane had a story ready. "I . . . I got frightened. I ran away in the dark. I got lost . . ." Regeane looked up from the food and gave Lucilla a quick glance to see how she was taking this.

Lucilla nodded gravely.

"I was afraid . . . I found the lodging house . . . near dawn. My uncle thought I had been with a man . . . He went crazy. Thank God you came. I was dying," Regeane said faintly.

"My . . . my . . . my," Lucilla said, every word dripping sarcasm. "And all without your clothing."

Regeane finished the soup. Lucilla's gaze was fastened on her like a death grip. Regeane couldn't think of any convincing lie at all. She was naturally more or less truthful, but telling the truth in this case was impossible.

Regeane slurped the juice left in the dish and snatched up a loaf of bread. One of the kind stuffed with rich, black olives. She dunked it in the juice. Then she said a word. The nastiest one the old woman ever taught her.

"Ha!" Lucilla said. "That's better." She returned to her task at the chest. "There was blood on the ground, in the garden, a lot of it, *and* on the wall, *and* in the road. Someone—something— did a remarkable job of slicing up Basil and his friends. But you wouldn't know about that, would you? You were too busy running away, naked, without your clothes, into the cold, wet winter night."

"It's not necessary to belabor the point," Regeane said. This time she tried for dignity.

"Also," Lucilla said, shooting a probing glance at her features. "You heal very quickly. When I first saw you, I was afraid you might be disfigured. But now they are only minor patches of purple and yellow. However, when we return to the villa, I'll have my own physician look at you."

Regeane went limp with a relief so profound it was dizzying. "Are we returning to the villa?"

"Oh, yes," Lucilla said. "I, we, you have no choice. Your mountain lord will need to be impressed. I can't think he'd be impressed in this . . . squalor. The pope handed me the task of persuading Maeniel he is being honored by this match. Men don't value what comes to them too cheaply. So, you must be taught how to dress, learn at least some semblance of proper behavior in polite society. Be introduced to the problems of running a large household. And, lastly, be brought out. Fortunately, your future husband is no doubt a filthy barbarian, so he won't expect too much."

"I know you're angry with me," Regeane commented darkly. "But there's no need to insult my betrothed because of it. And what is brought out?"

"Brought out is being introduced to the right people by the

right people," Lucilla replied haughtily. "And, as for this Maeniel, I'm beginning to think—even though you played on my sympathy last night like a viol—I now know you will probably be more than a match for him. Whatever he may be.

"This marriage, though you don't know, grows more important by the day. I will apply to the moneylenders again in your name. If they can't produce enough coin to dress and bejewel you properly, the state coffers may crack open a bit. Come, finish eating. We must leave soon. I don't want a brawl between your relations and my men. I don't want any loose talk about you—whatever you may be. That monstrous uncle of yours can't be allowed to cripple or kill you before your marriage. When I hand you over to Maeniel, my responsibility will be discharged. I don't have much time. Your eager barbarian will soon be in Rome."

"Rome!" Regeane gasped.

"Yes," Lucilla said. "The pope sent for him. He feels there's no time to waste."

Regeane said another word the old woman taught her.

"Regeane," Lucilla said sternly. "There are various ways of purifying a young woman's speech. I warn you, I know most of them."

"I was carried away by strong emotion," Regeane said sweetly.

"Regeane," Lucilla began, but then was distracted by a commotion at the door. "What's wrong?" she asked. "Is it her uncle?"

"No," one of the soldiers outside answered. "A . . . woman?"

"Maybe it's the old one. She may want to clean. Let her in," Regeane said.

The door opened a crack. Silve scuttled in on all fours. She saw Regeane. She made twelve hiccuping sounds, six horse snorts, followed this with an undetermined number of sheep bleats as she gained the space under the table. Silve was so wet she left a trail of water from the door to the table.

"What are you doing here?" Regeane snapped. "The last time I saw you, you were trying to get me killed by that funeral party. Now, you have the nerve to come back—"

"You wanted to steal the man's soooooul! You did! You did!

Pleeeaaasse," Silve gurgled. "I'm cold! I'm starving! Hugo beat me and stole the money I worked alllll night to get—" Silve made a sound like a drain backing up. "—enough. I was going away. I was! I really waaas. I won't tell, won't tell. I promise! I vow. I swear. On my father's head, my mother's head, my sister's—"

"Silence!" Lucilla said. She peered down under the table. "Who is she?"

"My maid," Regeane said.

"Your maid!" Lucilla replied, horrified. "She's a—" The word she used was one not even the old woman ever taught Regeane.

"I am not!" Silve screeched. "I always charge at least a copper."

"At most a copper, I should say," Lucilla replied disdainfully.

Silve made some sounds reminiscent of an inadequately strangled chicken. One that escaped the hands of the executioner before its neck was quite broken. Regeane snatched up some bread, a bowl of soup, and passed them hurriedly to Silve.

"Sllluuuurrrrpppp!" from under the table, then rapid crunching.

"What is this nonsense about you stealing someone's soul?" Lucilla asked, outraged. "Do you *do* things like that?"

"No!" Regeane shouted back, scarlet with indignation. "Besides, what would I want with someone's soul? Whatever I may be, I have no truck with the evil one. I was born the way I am. I can't help it. You blame me for it. She, my mother, blamed me for it. Hugo and Gundabald don't think I'm human."

"You aren't!" Silve screeched. "You made a place that wasn't there, be there. You had teeth, big teeth. Fire was all around you. The wasps died in it . . . the ghost thing stank . . . burnt black and flew away."

"You!" Regeane screamed. "You! You . . ." She couldn't think of a word sufficiently unpleasant. "I protected you against that nightmare, you ungrateful little wench. If you don't shut your mouth, get out from under that table, and behave yourself right now I'll . . . I'll . . . turn you into a toad and you can spend the rest of your life sitting in the Forum ruins catching flies with your tongue. So there!"

Lucilla threw up her hands.

Regeane had never seen anyone actually throw up her hands. She found it an interesting sight.

"I'll never get things sorted out here," Lucilla said.

Silve slithered from under the table and sat on one of the chairs, still gobbling the bread.

Lucilla looked at her and said, "Yeech! God! Turning her into a toad would be an improvement."

Silve began to cry, slobbering onto the bread.

"Don't make her cry," Regeane said. "It's worse."

"So I see," Lucilla replied. Then to Silve, "Stop caterwauling!" Her tone did not admit the possibility of disobedience.

Silve stopped caterwauling.

"You are warm?" Lucilla asked.

"Yes," Silve replied.

"You are fed?"

"Yes," Silve replied.

"Very well," she said to both Regeane and Silve. "We are leaving now. My carriage is waiting downstairs."

"Silve, you are going with us. She can rest on my side of the carriage," Regeane added hurriedly. She was used to Silve's aroma. Actually, this was one place where she and the wolf took separate paths. The wolf found it interesting. Regeane would rather have been spared the experience.

Lucilla shared her feelings. "Not in my carriage she won't!" Lucilla said firmly. "I have no doubt the crabs that cluster around her source of income are sufficiently large and numerous to march on a walled city. I have no doubt a few moments' work with a comb would be sufficient to capture enough from her head to defend the battlements. And, in addition, I believe she may not have ever had a bath in her life. A pile of rotting garbage in the summer sunshine is far more pleasant company than she is."

Silve opened her mouth.

"Shut it," Lucilla said.

Silve shut it, but managed to whisper, "I could leave."

"Oh, no, you couldn't. I'm not giving you a choice. You *will* do as you are told. Or . . . I'll have you strangled, attached to an anvil, and thrown in the Tiber."

Silve's lips parted.

"Or . . . perhaps . . ." Lucilla continued, "if I find myself sufficiently annoyed, I might not have you strangled, instead thrown into the Tiber attached to an anvil—and let you breathe water—all the way down."

Silve's mouth opened, but nothing emerged.

Regeane snatched up an old mantle of her mother's and handed it to Silve. It was faded, ragged, torn, and patched, but ample and warm.

"Now!" Lucilla said. "Downstairs! Take your place behind my litter and say nothing to anyone and wait. *Quietly.* Understood?"

Silve said nothing, but she nodded vigorously.

"March!" Lucilla said loudly clapping her hands.

Silve fled.

"You do just leave them strewn about, don't you?" Lucilla said.

"What do you mean?" Regeane asked.

Lucilla smiled for the first time. It showed all her teeth. "People who know far too much about you."

"Is that why we're taking her?" Regeane asked anxiously.

"Yes," Lucilla answered shortly. She was still going through the clothing looking for something decent for Regeane to wear. The dress she had on covered her well, but came up rather high on her legs. Giving up on finding anything, Lucilla lifted the hem and looked at it. "Maybe I can let it down quickly . . . It's cut off!" she exclaimed. "Well?" she asked Regeane.

"Hugo and Gundabald," Regeane sighed. "The hem must have been embroidered in gold or silver thread."

Lucilla gave an angry, exasperated snort.

"Did you really mean to drown Silve?" Regeane asked.

"Yes," Lucilla said, peeling off her mantle and wrapping it around Regeane. "And I still might if she doesn't do as she's told. I don't want her roaming the streets, carrying tales to your future husband, the Lombards, Basil, those wastrel relatives of yours, or even the pope. God knows, he has enough on his mind right now.

"Your marriage is important, very important. Securing the Alpine passes is vital to King Charles' interest and . . . the pope's. Desiderius, the Lombard king, has given Basil a free hand here, promising him lordship of the city if he succeeds in unseating Pope Hadrian or bringing him under his domination.

"Hadrian wouldn't dare flout the grandson of Charles the Hammer. I can't afford loose talk about you in every bordello and dive in the city. She will not drag your name through the mud. And neither will those relatives of yours. If they give me trouble, I'll have them all silenced! Understood? Understood?"

"Yes," Regeane answered hurriedly.

The mantle was beautiful, she saw, even as she used it to conceal most of her face and body. An autumn brown, Regeane felt it must have been the natural color of the very soft, silken wool used to weave it. Embroidered with a pattern of long willow leaves in mixed gold and silver thread.

"Woe the willow," Regeane whispered. "It weeps for the dying. Where is the cypress?"

Lucilla's lips tightened, a bleak hard expression froze on her features. She looked, for a second, her age or even older. A matron standing before a tomb.

"It's not time for cypresses, yet," Lucilla replied. "They guard the dead. But I do think you might be better off with a new maid and as an orphan."

"Why an anvil?" Regeane asked.

"Simply the best choice," Lucilla said. "It holds the corpse to the bottom until decomposition is far advanced. No identification can be made. Though in the case of those three, I can't imagine anyone caring. It's still safer."

"What do you do when you run out of anvils?" Regeane asked.

"Don't be pert," Lucilla said. "You are warm and fed?"

"Yes."

"Very well, downstairs into the litter immediately. Now! March!"

LUCILLA'S CARRIAGE WAS LIKE THOSE USED BY ROmans in the past: curtained and cushioned with silk and velvet within. But the Romans of earlier days had been borne in comfort, high above the throng on the muscular arms and shoulders of sweating slaves. A smooth ride was probably guaranteed by the presence of a driver with a large whip.

Lucilla's carriage rode anything but smoothly. It was drawn down the Corso by four stout gray mules. Steel wheel rims pounded the cobbles. Silk and velvet the interior appointments might be, but they were not enough to make the ride comfortable.

Lucilla sat at one end of the litter, her back against the cushions. Regeane rested on the other. Cushion or no cushion, Regeane was flung into the air at every bump and pothole. She came down sometimes painfully on her backside, sometimes off balance. She had to grab for the heavy canvas curtains to keep from falling out.

One wheel went into a deep hole. Regeane skidded sideways, arms flailing in desperation, sure in a second she'd be lying in the street. Lucilla caught her wrist just in time and pulled her back. She gave Regeane a nasty smile. "Relax, it's just like riding a horse. You must go with the movement. Faster," she shouted to the driver.

Regeane gripped the pad covering the bottom and dug in with her fingers. But, inexplicably, the litter didn't speed up. Instead it rolled to a stop.

Something thumped against one of the heavy canvas curtains surrounding them. Lucilla whispered something ugly in gutter Latin, then pushed aside the curtain and peered out.

A small crowd gathered around the litter. They eyed the magnificent vehicle with a mixture of awe, curiosity, and veiled hostility.

A voice in the back of the crowd shouted, "Throw aside the curtains, Lucilla, and let the people get a good look at the pope's whore."

Lucilla snatched at the curtains and shoved them back with a loud clatter of rings. "Very well," she shouted. "Here I sit. Now, you, sir, step forward so that I can get a good look at your face . . . and remember it."

The man who had shouted the taunt at Lucilla ducked down and vanished into an alleyway.

"How very brave," Lucilla commented in a loud voice, then asked the crowd, "Are any of the rest of you of his opinion? Is he a friend of yours? Can any of you give me his name?"

A nervous titter of laughter swept through the idlers around the litter, and they melted away with magical speed.

Lucilla shouted a command and flung the curtains shut. The litter started forward again. "The pope's whore, eh?" she said between clenched teeth. "I wish I'd gotten a better look at him." She gave Regeane a rapid, hard glance. "You don't seem surprised to hear me called the pope's whore."

"I'm not," Regeane found herself saying. She remembered that last night Basil had called Antonius the pope's brother. Stephen, she thought, as Lucilla studied her from the corner of her eye. He is the pope himself. And Lucilla . . . When Stephen realized what sort of rascals Gundabald and Hugo were, he hadn't shown the slightest hesitation in sending her to Lucilla, about placing her under Lucilla's protection. "I imagine," Regeane said, "that you've been the pope's mistress for a very long time."

Lucilla went slack-jawed with astonishment for a second.

A flurry of missiles thudded against the curtains.

Lucilla's teeth caught at her lower lip. Her fists clenched, but she didn't open the curtains again. Regeane heard the crash of galloping hooves and a loud cry of pain. She surmised the stone thrower had been punished by one of the men in Lucilla's personal guard.

"Hydra-headed monster," Lucilla whispered bitterly.

"What?" Regeane asked.

"The Roman mob," Lucilla answered.

"What's happened?"

"No one wants a strong pope, Regeane," Lucilla said, "least of all the Lombards. Basil's minions in the churches have been giving sermons accusing Hadrian of being tainted with a vile disease, one that makes him unfit to be supreme pontiff."

"They wish everyone to believe him a leper, as Antonius is?" Regeane asked.

At that moment the covered litter lurched to a stop before Lucilla's door. Without waiting for help, Regeane swung herself down. Lucilla followed more slowly.

When Regeane entered the atrium, a small body launched itself at her like a missile thrown from a catapult. Elfgifa hung around Regeane's neck and threw her long legs around her waist.

"You're back! I knew she'd get you! I was the one who

found you. Did she tell you?" The small face stared up at her expectantly.

"Did she?" Regeane asked, untangling herself from Elfgifa and turning to Lucilla.

"That terrible, terrible child," Lucilla said fondly. "Yes, she did. The moment she heard you were missing, she climbed over the wall. She reappeared a short time later with the filthiest little boy I've ever seen. He demanded a silver coin and a bath."

"A bath?" Regeane asked.

Elfgifa glanced coquettishly up through her eyelashes at Regeane.

"Yes," Lucilla said waspishly, "a bath. He got his bath and his silver and," she continued, placing her hands on her hips and glaring down at Elfgifa, "a big, wet kiss."

Elfgifa pursed her lips and lowered her eyes modestly. "I promised him a kiss, but I told him I wouldn't kiss anyone as dirty as he was." She tossed her head. "My father says a man who doesn't wash himself before he goes to a woman and after doesn't respect himself or the woman. I can understand 'before,' but why 'after'? I told him I thought once would be enough, but he said after, too. Why is that?"

"Why didn't you ask him?" Lucilla's lips twitched.

Elfgifa frowned. Her lower lip began to creep forward. "He smiled the way you're smiling now, and told me I'd understand better when I grew up."

"Don't start going on about how you want to understand now," Regeane said haughtily. "You embarrassed me in front of Stephen and Antonius."

Elfgifa stared up at them mutinously.

"You must remember you're only a child," Lucilla said. "There are some things you'll have to wait to understand."

Elfgifa sighed. "Thank you for calling it to my attention. That's what my father says when I tell him things he doesn't want to hear. I know I'm a child, but I understand . . ." She broke off as another train of thought struck her. "Besides, my Uncle Thungbrand and Aunt Huldigun visited and neither one of them washes ever. I asked my father about it. He says they are both strangers to any kind of water. I couldn't understand that either except that they both got as drunk as some of my father's men and rolled up under the table with them and . . ."

"I think possibly that may have been what your father meant." Lucilla said.

"They don't put any water in their wine either?" Elfgifa asked.

"Yes," Lucilla said. "Now run along. I've called my personal physician to see Regeane."

"Did he beat you?" Elfgifa asked. "Postumous—he's the boy who told me where you were—he said three Franks, one called Hugo, lived near the Forum. He said you were screaming this morning."

Lucilla began hurrying Regeane along the peristyle walkway toward the back of the house. "Yes, he beat her."

"Oh," Elfgifa said. "May I see?"

"No, you may not," Lucilla said sternly.

Elfgifa clasped Regeane's hand firmly. "If I'm going to be her lady's maid, I'm going to need to—"

"Who in the world said you were going to be her lady's maid?" Lucilla asked.

"Your maid, Susanna, told me," Elfgifa said. "And I want to be one. She says it's wonderful to be a lady's maid. You get to order the menservants about, and all the tradesmen give you expensive gifts so you'll bring them your lady's custom. You can take all the lovers you want and you don't even have to marry some dirty old man for his money and . . . though why you should marry a dirty old man for his money is another thing I don't understand. Don't young men have any money?"

"I can see," Lucilla said ominously, "that I must have a word with Susanna."

"Oh, no," Regeane said. "I'm sure the woman meant no harm." The feel of the small, warm hand in hers was very comforting. "Please don't send Elfgifa away."

Lucilla stared down her nose sternly at Elfgifa. "Very well, I won't if . . . if you promise to sit in the corner and be absolutely quiet while the physician examines your mistress. If you're going to be a lady's maid, the first thing you'll need to learn is when to speak and when to be silent."

"Susanna didn't tell me that was part of it," Elfgifa said.

"Didn't she?" Lucilla said. "Expensive gifts from the tradesmen, eh? Apparently it's something she hasn't learned herself."

The physician, Pappolus, arrived. He was a tall, well-dressed young man who assumed an air of dignity beyond his years.

Regeane balked at undressing in front of a man, but with Lucilla standing over her like a female dragon and Elfgifa watching curiously from one corner of the room, she was at length prevailed upon to show the physician her back.

He sniffed and studied her, then gave his opinion in long, complicated phrases well-larded with very impressive Greek words, took his pay, provided an ointment for Regeane's back, and left.

Lucilla sniffed the ointment suspiciously, then threw it away, saying, "He once prescribed an eye ointment for one of my girls. Her problem got worse, not better. I investigated and learned he believed hippopotamus dung, which he imports from Egypt in powder form, is a sovereign remedy for everything. I was hard put to save the girl's sight. But much as I hate to admit it, he has greater expertise than I have in preventing scars from forming. That's why I asked him to see you."

Lucilla pressed a sleeping draught on her. Again, Regeane resisted, but finally drank. Lucilla conducted her to a cubiculum. The small room was dark, even by day. The only light was the lamp in Lucilla's hand and the glow from the sun shining beyond the pillared portico into the atrium. She made Regeane stretch out on the bed.

Lying down, Regeane could feel the sleeping potion clouding her mind, dulling her senses.

Lucilla stood over her, holding the dove-shaped lamp. By its flame she seemed only a disembodied face, a void in the cool, pleasant gloom. "Rest," she said quietly in a soothing tone. "Sleep." Then, even more softly, "Sleep."

Though Lucilla was as quiet as possible, the snick of the bolt on the heavy door going home was loud to both Regeane and the wolf.

She was half paralyzed by the sleeping draught and absolute exhaustion. The wolf's powers weren't infinite. All her reserves were completely drained. She'd been warmed and fed. Now, she *must* sleep.

Antonius? He was alone on the Campagna. Without her help, he would die. She reflected that Lucilla might not starve or torture her, but she was capable of imprisoning her just as efficiently as Gundabald could. More so, in fact, as she had the greater resources.

Regeane's eyelids lifted. She saw the window of the bedroom was as well-barred as that of the one in the lodging house.

The daylight was brighter outside than it had been earlier. The rain must have passed. It was early afternoon. The wolf yawned. *Sleep now. Do now what now demands. Night must fall.*

VIII

REGEANE WAS AWAKENED BY THE WOLF AT DUSK. Her eyes opened slightly. Through her lashes, she could see the stars, each tiny light pricking through the deep, blue velvet twilight. She lay still. Two voices were speaking nearby.

"Well, I'm sorry. I simply won't give her any more. It might kill her." She recognized the voice. It belonged to the physician, Pappolus.

"I doubt it," Lucilla replied skeptically. "She has the constitution of a lioness. You wouldn't believe the condition she was in when I found her. Now, she's nearly healed. She's not completely human."

"Bha!" Pappolus snapped. "Good God, woman, I had thought you superior to your sex in trusting reason above the spider's web of superstitions that bind most women hand and foot. Besides, I told you: sometimes it doesn't work."

"Yes, but in this particular case, why not? The rest babbled of everything—loves, friends, plots, lust, greed, and a simply un-believable amount of envy, jealousy, and downright hatred."

"Yes," Pappolus replied. "Some of it real and a lot of it imaginary."

"But all *she* did was talk nonsense," Lucilla snapped.

"Nonsense that made my skin crawl," Pappolus said. "Rose petals, pink and white like a fair woman's skin, steeping in pools of blood. I understand she's to be married. Well, marry her off. You'll be rid of her."

"Now, who's being superstitious?" Lucilla asked.

"She could be a thing of nature. Many strange and dangerous things are thrown up by the real world. I have, after all, seen the giraffe while I studied on the banks of the Nile. Few more pecu-liar things exist than the giraffe. I was greatly impressed by it.

"Besides, she may talk nonsense because her thoughts are nonsense. I've told you in the past, you judge other women by your own nobility of mind. Most are really very stupid. Some philosophers, as you know, saw them only as animals, like a cat or a cow that somehow acquired the power of speech. A fine horse or hound exceeds them in an ability to think ab-stractly and in the virtue of loyalty. A horse or hound will, as you know, serve or defend its master's interest to its last breath. Whereas women, all too often, fail to show any appreciation for the benefits conferred on them by men. They defy their fa-thers, deceive their husbands, and demand completely unrea-sonable loyalty from their sons! Most unsatisfactory. Most," he clucked. "Now, dear lady, if I may be so bold, I have another patron of distinction to wait upon. He has gout. I pray you give me leave to depart."

"By all means, go," Lucilla said darkly.

When Regeane heard the door close, she sat up and opened her eyes.

"Ah," Lucilla said, "I thought you were awake. I heard your breathing change when it became dark outside."

"You drugged me to learn my secrets," Regeane said.

"Not expertly enough, I fear," Lucilla said. She directed an incandescent glare at the door through which the physician had departed. "Idiot. Did I not know that that imbecile develops a palsy of shivering at the mere thought of my displeasure, I would have him followed from my house by assassins. Probably do his 'noble patron' more good than his medicines."

"What did you want to know?" Regeane asked.

"Where is Antonius?" Lucilla lifted the lamp she was holding higher so she could see Regeane's face.

"Hidden on the Campagna," Regeane said. "I'll tell you where, but I can't be sure even *you* could find it." She managed to meet Lucilla's stare with a look of limpid innocence. From somewhere warm and bright, the wolf gave Regeane a stare of pure disgust.

"Well," Lucilla said. "Basil's men certainly can't. My sources tell me something—or someone—got him away from Basil last night and hid him so well that even all of Basil's men combing the area close to the old shrine of Apollo couldn't find him."

"Yes, well *I* can," Regeane said.

Lucilla walked to the door. She opened it to be sure no one was in the corridor. The hall was empty. In the distance, Regeane could hear the clatter of pots and pans and the sound of feminine laughter. Lucilla closed the door. This time, she bolted it from within.

The only light in the room was cast by the alabaster dove lamp in Lucilla's hand. The flame burned deep in the lamp, seen only through the translucent sides of the bird. It flickered and danced over the wick and oil, casting kaleidoscope shadows that fluttered against the walls.

Lucilla placed the lamp on a low table near the bed. This left her face in shadow, her expression unreadable.

Regeane could smell Lucilla's body fear, an acrid smell so strong it almost made the wolf's eyes tear. The odor was so powerful, Regeane could only remember smelling it being so overpowering once before—on a brigand captured on the Via Julia when she and her mother were entering Rome. He was being conducted out of the city by soldiers. They were going to execute him. Lucilla had to be desperate.

"What do you want?" Regeane asked.

"It's time for Antonius to die," Lucilla whispered out of the darkness.

"I'm not a murderer," Regeane said.

"You don't have to be," Lucilla said.

Regeane realized the reason Lucilla was whispering was because she was panting. She sounded as if she couldn't get her breath.

"What do you want me to do, then?" Regeane asked.

"Take him the poison. And . . . and." Lucilla's breaths increased in rapidity. She sounded almost like a spent animal.

"And?" Regeane prompted.

"And tell him I sent it. He will know what to do and how to do it." Lucilla gave one last gasp.

"The choice of life or death is his," Regeane said.

Lucilla didn't answer. She sank down next to Regeane on the bed.

"Very well," Regeane replied. "I will do as you ask. I will wish a reward."

Lucilla said, "Naturally," with a negligent wave of her hand. Her head was bowed.

"I will need help with the marriage contract," Regeane said. "I want it written to give me a separate residence, my own servants."

"And bodyguard—men-at-arms you can pay and who are correspondingly loyal," Lucilla added.

"You are clever," Regeane commented.

Lucilla smiled. *A dreadful smile*, Regeane thought. *A smile the ghastly-faced woman must use in place of tears or madness.*

"Is that what I am?" Lucilla asked.

The wolf turned away, afraid, her hackles up.

"God knows what happened last night. I certainly don't," Lucilla whispered. "You vanished. You simply vanished. One minute Basil was after you with his sword, the next . . . nothing. But Basil's men were screaming and, by the amount of blood, wounded when they ran."

When Regeane made no response, Lucilla gave her an appraising glance. "How I would love to get that fool Charles here. We'd hear no more of mountain lords. He'd want to plunder your blossom himself. At least for the first time. I could plant you at the Frankish court as a friend of Hadrian's. You

would be a wealthy woman, powerful, able to engage in any nefarious activities you . . ."

The wolf didn't listen. She was far away. She'd found the
morning. The sun was hot on her face. She was walking at the
top of a hill. The countryside was open, a parkland. The grass at
her feet was low, not lush, but still rich, though tufted and
coarse.

Many small trees were scattered across the hills. They had
thick, deeply ridged bark, and small, feathery green leaves.
They, and the grass, still flashed with the scattered diamonds of
morning dew. Birdsong rang out all around her. The wind's
voice rose and fell in her ears. Now a ragged fluttering followed
by a rasp as it visited undergrowth and the tree trunks, then
fading away into a sigh.

The wolf lifted her head. The hills rolled away into the distance. Green at first, the closest ones, then hazy pale blue until
they reached the edge of the world at the horizon's rim.

"Now go and bathe," Lucilla's voice intruded. "We will dine
together and take the poison to Antonius."

Regeane rose and went in search of the baths. She bathed,
and when she stepped out of the pool, she found two of Lucilla's maids waiting for her. They dressed her in a chiton. A
Greek garment of great beauty that draped over her slender
form. It hung straight down to the floor in soft folds.

Lucilla's maids offered her jewels. This required more thought.
At length, Regeane selected an antique necklace of silver and
pearls. The links were large, the metal very soft. She could dent
it with her fingernail. Gold sandals were laced to her feet and a
gold fillet bound her hair.

She realized she was being dressed for Lucilla's pleasure
when she looked at herself in the mirror. The soft, tightly woven
linen was almost transparent. Not quite, but almost. It showed
the pink breast tips and the dark pubic triangle.

One of the maids showed her how to undo the girdle at the
waist and the two clasps at the shoulders. This would allow the
chiton to fall around her feet.

Regeane asked to see Elfgifa, and was conducted to a small,
comfortable chamber. Elfgifa was sleeping curled in a tangle of

knees and elbows. She looked like a grimy little ball. It appeared as if she might have spent the afternoon playing in the garden. A few tendrils of soft, blond hair curled on her forehead. Regeane brushed them aside and kissed her gently.

The maid who shared Elfgifa's chamber was a stout, motherly woman with graying hair. "I was Antonius' nurse once," she told Regeane. "We haven't had a child in the house for some time. I miss them."

"What do you think? Did she take any great harm from her captivity?" Regeane asked.

"No," the woman said. "I don't think so. She is, as she claims, gently bred. Despite her sometimes hoydenish ways, she is very mannerly and obedient. Always has a 'please' and 'thank you' for everyone waiting on her. She has been a bit indulged. She says her mother died before she can remember her. Her father did not care to marry again. I believed he cherished the child. She worships him. He must be wild with grief. I hope he can be reunited with her as soon as possible. Theirs is a cruel separation."

Regeane nodded.

"So tender, and she is not even your own." Lucilla was a dark shape in the doorway. "Imagine how you would love her if she were your own."

Regeane didn't answer. The maidservant made as if to squeeze past Lucilla.

"Fausta!" Lucilla said to the woman. "You loved him as much as I did. Don't abandon me to my grief."

"My lady," Fausta said softly, "years ago my family took me to the slave dealer. My mother wept while my father bargained for the best price. I was but thirteen years old. They saw my sister as the beauty who would ensnare a husband. My brother as a strong back to work the land. In me, the purchase of a new bullock. You took me from the slave dealer because you said I had a kind face. I helped you bring up your son. Everything good in my life has come from you. I have loved him. I have loved you. But no one in the world loves Antonius as you do. If he finds his death tonight, so will you. Don't ask me to betray either of my loves. You are not the only one in mourning."

After so speaking, she slipped away softly, taking the lamp and leaving only darkness behind her.

Once the light distracting her eyes was gone, Regeane found she could see quite well. The wolf was present.

Lucilla's face was blank with shock. She was trembling.

The wind was flowing into the casement, blowing Lucilla's scent away from Regeane. She was glad. Even the wolf didn't find the atmosphere Lucilla walked in interesting.

"Your son, Lucilla?" Regeane asked. "Your son?"

Lucilla didn't answer. "I'll go bathe now. I will meet you in the dining room. And . . . I cannot bear any more discussion of the matter. My decision is made. Did I not love Fausta, I would put her out on the street tomorrow to beg her bread on church steps and spend her old age sheltering in doorways from the rain."

Before Regeane could reply, Lucilla turned and hurried away. The night air coming through the window was cold. Regeane closed the shutters, bolted them, and covered Elfgifa. The child stirred. Regeane kissed one soft, still-grimy cheek. Elfgifa heaved a deep sigh and stretched out a bit under the warm coverlet.

Regeane was uncertain. Was the child safe here?

The wolf was satisfied. Something about Fausta. Her quiet speech. Her ripe apple smell reassured the wolf. A fine pack member, not bold, but always to be relied upon. One of the steady ones.

Regeane hurried toward the dining room.

THEY DINED IN PRIVACY AS LUCILLA HAD PROM-ised. The two couches faced each other over a low table containing what to Lucilla was obviously her usual fare—and, to Regeane, a sumptuous meal.

A perfumed breeze drifted into the room from the dark garden.

The dinner was spread out on the table before them: venison done over an open fire, covered by a sauce made with the drippings; a larded capon cooked with honey and almonds; black olives; bread; and a few boiled eggs.

A silver tray with red glass cups and a jug sat on the table.

Lucilla lifted one of the red goblets and poured Regeane a cup of wine. "This is my very oldest vintage. I preserved it for my son's wedding feast, but it will do as well for his funeral, because he must die tonight. Tell me where he is."

Regeane shrugged. "I wouldn't know how. I found a secret place."

Lucilla stared at her. "You're lying."

"No." Regeane denied the accusation. "I'm not a huntsman. I don't travel the same way Basil and his clumsy henchmen stumble around. I'm . . . different."

Lucilla sobbed deep in her throat. Then she lowered her head, resting her brow against the high-raised cushion at the end of the dining couch.

Regeane stretched out her hand to the food. Her fingers swirled a chunk of venison in the sauce and carried it to her lips. The wolf was hungry, half starved, and she set Regeane to work as quickly as possible.

The wolf's feelings were too strong for the woman's verbal mind. The wolf knew only that somewhere in the depths of her being, she had come to a decision.

She had come to it without argument or analysis, almost without thought of the ramifications or consequences. She was going to save Antonius. Regeane was in accord.

With the clarity born of the almost hysterical tension within her, Regeane looked around the room at the beautiful frescoes on the walls that gave the illusion of light and space, at the alabaster lamps, the purplish-red velvet cushions on the dining couches.

Lucilla didn't eat, though she took a goblet of the dark wine.

The dining room that had seemed so splendid the night before now seemed tawdry and cheap. The frescos were stained and darkened by time and the sooty smoke of a thousand contaminated dinners. Here and there bits and pieces of paint were flaking away, showing the bare walls.

The dove-shaped lamps were the overstated touch of a procuress, a brothel keeper. But that was what Lucilla was, wasn't she? Whatever pretty words she put on it—a pander.

Regeane finished the venison. She snapped a wing and a

breast from the capon and her teeth tore at the soft-scented white meat.

Even if Lucilla served the first families of Rome, her goddess was still lust. Aphrodite with golden fingers. Noble lords took the girls as Maeniel would take Regeane. Lucilla took her pay. And her son's blood.

For what seemed like a long time, Regeane ate without speaking. She felt caught in a maze. A journey that began when Gundabald told her she was going to be married and what he wanted her to do to Maeniel after she wedded him. He wanted her to be a compliant wife and lure Maeniel into a false sense of security.

But come the night of the full moon or even, she thought joyfully, any darkness, she could change. Change and tear her inconvenient husband's throat out. The men in the garden last night hadn't stood much chance against her. She was not only much bigger than a normal wolf, she was much more intelligent. She could wait and pick her time.

She glanced around again at the luxurious room's shabby grandeur. She felt sickened, disgusted by Lucilla's readiness to murder her own son because he was politically inconvenient.

Lucilla's voice broke in on her thoughts. "Where is he?" she asked again.

"Why do you want to kill him?" Regeane asked.

Lucilla reached across the table and snatched Regeane's hair. She shook her head viciously. "Why do you torment me with this nonsense?" she screamed. "What's Antonius to you? Why should you care if he lives or dies? Tell me where he is and be done with it."

It took everything Regeane had to keep the wolf from coming into being, but the beast spoke, and the voice echoed in Regeane's throat. At the same time, the woman's arm swept out. Her palm landed with a loud crack on Lucilla's cheek.

The growl and the slap cut through Lucilla's rage. She drew back with a shudder and whispered, "Christ, what was that sound? God, what are you?"

"Keep your hands off me," Regeane spat. "I'm . . . not . . . taking . . . any . . . poison . . . to . . . Antonius."

"You said—" Lucilla began.

"No," Regeane shouted as she jumped off the couch to her left.

"You promised." Lucilla's voice was shrill and murderous as a bird of prey's.

"I lied!" Regeane shrieked. "I had to get out of that room with a bolt on the door. I had to . . . I don't know if I can help Antonius, but I'm going to try." Regeane's head snapped back as the wolf tried to seize her. Then the night creature fled, snarling as the woman slapped her away . . . hard. Regeane stopped. She was gasping, partly with the effort of keeping the wolf down, partly with purely human fury.

Lucilla stared at her, shocked into silence. "Regeane, Regeane. Do you think I want to kill my own son?"

"No," she answered. "I think you feel you must."

Lucilla nodded. "I do. You saw that mob today, saw how quickly they surrounded my litter, heard the insults they hurled at me?"

"Yes."

"Well," Lucilla said, "if that mob really comes to believe Hadrian's family is tainted as Antonius is, they will destroy him. Factional politics, my dear, aren't simply a problem in this city, they are a disease.

"All that has restrained him so far is that Hadrian is deeply respected by the old senatorial families and wildly loved by the people. But if Antonius is found and publicly shown to be a leper, it may be all Basil needs to unseat Hadrian."

Lucilla turned, swung her legs over the side of the couch, and got to her feet. She turned to Regeane with outstretched arms. "Since the disease began to show itself three years ago, we've hidden him. Now . . . now I can't save him. And even if I could, dear sweet merciful God, for what? For what, I ask you, girl? Until the rot reaches some vital organ and he dies, slowly and in misery?"

Lucilla's arms dropped to her sides. Then she raised one hand and thrust it into her hair, dragging at the long, blond strands as if she wanted to tear them from her scalp. "Or until Antonius takes matters into his own hands and does what he must to prevent himself from being the instrument of Hadrian's destruction."

Regeane didn't reply. She had, in truth, no answer for Lucilla. She felt the tug of the night in her flesh, in her bones. The wolf wanted to be away, to smell the clean wind, to run across the fields under the stars. Far from the humans like Lucilla who had for so many years imprisoned her in narrow stone rooms with bars on the windows. Far from the humans who created such agonizing, incomprehensible conundrums as politics and war.

The room grew dim around her. The wolf reared in the gathering darkness. Wolf and woman smelled the freshening night breezes drifting in from the atrium.

Regeane looked up at the hanging lamp festooned with alabaster doves. Some of them must have exhausted their oil. They were going out now slowly, one by one.

Lucilla staggered against the couch. "Oh, God," she whimpered. "Christ, I'm everything they say I am—whore, bitch, a sow eating her litter, and my son . . . Oh, God, Antonius!"

Her face paled to a dirty white color. A faint sheen of sweat broke out on her skin.

Regeane eased away. As the oil in the lamp was used up, the room grew darker. The wolf moved closer.

Lucilla staggered and fell to her knees. She stared up at Regeane, uncomprehending. "Where are you going?" she asked. "What are you going to do?"

Regeane backed toward the inky darkness of the atrium. The change was taking her powerfully, paralyzing her throat and tongue. She could barely form the words of her answer. "I'm going to find out what is in the night."

IX

THE PAPAL MESSENGER'S FINGERS WERE TIGHTLY wound around one of Maeniel's silver wine cups. Fast asleep, he was stretched out on the table, lying on the remnants of last night's feast.

Maeniel scratched his head and tried to remember the man's name.

Matrona eyed him from the other side of the table.

"What did he call himself?" Maeniel asked.

"Harek," Matrona answered.

"Harek," Maeniel said. "Funny, I could have sworn he was a Roman."

Matrona snickered coldly. A snicker is always cold, but Matrona's was nastier than most. "A lot of them name themselves after us barbarians. They think it makes them sound tougher." She smiled, but the smile wasn't much of an improvement over the snicker. "I can't say it helped him very much."

Maeniel nodded. The papal messenger was about an inch under five feet tall. Matrona towered over him.

"He was a bit stiff at first," Gorgo said, "but he loosened up nicely after a while."

"Too much," Matrona said.

"Oh, I don't know," Gorgo said. Gorgo was a big man whose long brown hair melted into his thick brown beard and moustache. He was still sitting upright, something of an accomplishment after a night of heavy drinking.

"How about when he chased Silvia around the hall?" Matrona said.

"Silvia?" Maeniel said. "She was afraid of him?"

"No," Matrona said, "coy."

"Maybe she wanted some privacy," Gorgo said delicately.

"I can't think why," Matrona said. "She never bothered about it before."

"That's true," Gorgo said.

"Silvia." Maeniel mulled the matter over in his mind, then asked, "Did he catch her?"

"In the kitchen," Matrona said.

"Did he achieve his objective?" Gorgo inquired.

"I can't say," Matrona answered, "but he charged in bravely, pushing things aside with his hands. He looked like he was swimming."

"Silvia has no reason to fear a high wind," Maeniel said.

"Silvia," Gorgo said, "has no reason to fear an avalanche."

"True," Maeniel said, studying the small man on the table with interest. "He's very brave for a Roman."

"At any rate," Matrona continued, "they both behaved as if they believed he had."

"Don't describe it," Maeniel said.

"It's just as well the kitchen has a stone floor," Matrona said.

"It's just as well he found Silvia attractive," Gorgo said. "I was about to see if he could fly."

"Don't do that," Maeniel said.

"Not from the parapet," Gorgo said, "just here in the hall. He called me a barbarian, a crude, stupid barbarian."

"Drink," Matrona said, "brings out the worst in him."

"I didn't chop the hole in the ceiling," Gorgo complained. "Besides, it's as I told him, if there wasn't a hole in the ceiling, how would the smoke get out? If it couldn't, when we lit the fire we'd all suffocate,"

Maeniel squinted up at the hole in the ceiling and scratched his head again.

"I can't think what they wanted so much space for anyway," Gorgo muttered.

The dining hall was what remained of a small Roman basilica. It was a long, T-shaped room with a barrel-vaulted ceiling and a high domed roof over the long table at the end. At some time in the past someone had taken a pickax to the center of the barrel vault that covered the long end of the T. A similar implement had gouged a large hole in the marble floor. The remains of a large fire smoldered in the pit under the hole in the ceiling.

A lot of Maenicl's people were sleeping heaped together around the crude hearth. Legs protruded from under the table at the end of the room.

"Where's Gavin?" he asked.

"I don't know." Matrona was busy prying the silver cup out of Harck's hands.

"You can tell he's a churchman by the tight grip he has on the silver," Gorgo said.

Maeniel glanced at the firepit. Gavin wasn't among those sleeping around it. Where was he?

Maeniel walked along the table, looking at feet. Some had their toes pointed upward, others the heels, but heel or toe, none belonged to Gavin.

He finally found him, heels up, lying between Silvia's larger feet at the end of the table.

"Gavin and the papal messenger in one night?" he asked Matrona.

"No." She was still occupied with the silver cup. "I think he just crawled on top of her so he could have a warm, comfortable place to sleep. He asked me and I said yes."

"But he was too far gone," Maeniel said.

Matrona finally freed the cup and strolled away to put it with the rest under lock and key. "I know," she shot back over her shoulder at Maeniel. "That's why I said yes."

Poor Gavin. However, poor or not, they had to get started today, and left to himself, Gavin would sleep until late afternoon. Maeniel grabbed him by the ankles and pulled him out from under the table.

Gavin screamed. "Eeeeeee! Daylight!" He went back under, powered by his fingers and toes, and tried to flop down again on top of Silvia.

Maeniel sympathized with him. She looked billowy and comfortable. She was almost as big as a bed. Silvia, however, was waking up and didn't want any part of Gavin. She straight-armed him, catching him under the chin and pushing him aside.

Gavin moaned. The cold from the icy stone floor penetrated

his clothing. He curled up on his side like an injured caterpillar
and whimpered softly.

Maeniel grabbed Gavin by the ankles and hauled him out
again. He held Gavin up like a wheelbarrow, legs in the air,
upper body free, and arms on the floor.

"Oh, God!" Gavin shrieked, both hands clutching at his
skull.

"Must I throw you in the fountain?" Maeniel asked

The fountain in the courtyard was fed by snowmelt from the
glaciers that towered over the pass. Even in the warmest
weather, the water was bitter cold.

Gavin shuddered violently, but immediately decided sobriety was the better part of valor. "I'm awake, Maeniel."

"Good." Maeniel let go of his ankles.

Gavin managed to stagger to his feet. He was pale and his
eyes were slitted against the light.

"We are going to Rome," Maeniel said. "We're leaving
today."

"No," Gavin moaned. "There's going to be something wrong
with her, I tell you, terribly, terribly wrong. You already know
part of what's wrong. You saw the letter. Her closest relatives
are such bestial scoundrels, they even managed to shock the
pope himself. And living among those dissolute and depraved
Romans, you know, it must be difficult to shock him!"

Maeniel's eyes roved around the hall. Under the table Silvia
huffed, snorted, and rolled over. "Dissolute Romans," he muttered at Gavin. "And what are we?"

Gavin staggered along the table, looking for a jug with some
beer or wine in it. Eventually he found one. He lifted it to his
lips. His Adam's apple moved up and down for perhaps half a
minute. When he set the jug down he said, "Noble, pure-
hearted, chaste barbarians. I know because that's what the
pope's messenger told me last night. Some writer named Tacitus said so."

Matrona rested her fists on her ample hips, threw back her
head, and howled. "The only time you're chaste, Gavin, is
when you chased, but could not catch her. I have seen manure
piles purer than your heart and, as for nobility, you're a by-blow
gotten on a scullery wench who was probably a slow runner."

"You notice," Gorgo said, "he had already learned better than to mention sobriety."

Gavin's face turned an unhealthy and nearly impossible shade of greenish purple. "My father," he said in a strangled tone, "is . . ."

Matrona began to roll up her sleeves. "Come on, Gorgo," she said. "He's started going on about his father. He needs to be thrown in the fountain."

Gavin backed up and jumped behind Maeniel.

Maeniel noticed Gavin had a black eye and a split lip on one side. "Who had the temerity to strike my captain?" he asked half jokingly. "Matrona?"

Matrona gave an evil chuckle. "No, I wasn't the one this time."

Joseph spoke up. He was a large man with a lugubrious face. A moustache drooped down over his upper lip. "He mistook me for Matrona."

"I didn't." Gavin's horrified denial came from behind Maeniel.

"You did," Joseph said, shaking his head. "And I feared lest you make a similar mistake with someone less patient, so I put you to sleep."

Gavin staggered away, muttering about disrespect and false friendship.

"Gorgo, Joseph," Maeniel said, "go fetch some money."

People all along the table were waking now, searching for and finding a hair of the dog.

Gorgo and Joseph returned with a large chest, "It's heavy," Joseph moaned.

"Well, dump it out on the floor," Maeniel said.

They did. A heap of gold and silver poured out. There were antique silver and gold coins, jewelry studded with precious and semiprecious stones, and the occasional showy pieces of glass, tableware, cups, plates, serving platters, and bowls.

Matrona came up with two pairs of saddlebags. She began to pack them. One pair with jewelry, the other with gold and silver coins.

Maeniel's household gathered round. Both men and women selecting jewelry for themselves and, sometimes, others.

Gavin clapped a dented diadem on his head. It was made mostly of copper, but had a ring of gold and silver birds in flight on it. "Was this a king's?" he asked.

"No," Maeniel answered. "It belonged to a priest." He looked faintly ill.

"A Christian priest?" Gavin asked mystified.

"No," Maeniel said. "A pagan one. A . . ." He groped for the word. "A druid. Now, take the damned thing off. For it *is* a damned thing, and you will find out soon if you wear it."

Gavin snatched the circlet off and threw it back into the pile.

Maeniel clapped his hands. "Listen! We are leaving this day for Rome. Those of you who want to come, scratch up some silver and gold coins. We will need to stay under a roof from time to time. And I hear living in the holy city is expensive. Matrona, who will remain here and care for the livestock?"

She had taken advantage of everyone's distraction to strip off her dress and put on a costume she found in the chest. It consisted of draped gold chains that covered her breasts and another set of smaller chains that hung from her hips and hid the pubic area. Matrona was a tall woman with a slim waist and ample hips and breasts. Her skin was dark. She had large brown eyes—they were heavy-lidded and sleepy looking—and beautiful curved, sensual lips.

Gavin stared at her. He was glassy-eyed. His mouth was hanging open.

"Matrona, the livestock! Cattle, sheep, goats, horses," Maeniel said. He snapped his fingers. "Remember."

"Three families have pregnant women among them," Matrona said. "I consulted them. They fear to risk the journey. They will remain."

Joseph looked at Gavin sadly. "Let her take him in the kitchen, my lord. His brain is mush."

Maeniel noticed that the chains didn't hide nearly enough of Matrona. "Please," he said, making a graceful gesture. "Tend to Gavin before we leave."

"I don't know why I bother," Matrona said. "His brain is always mush." She snapped her fingers at Gavin and departed. Gavin followed, looking as if he were drawn along by a ring through his nose.

"What about the papal messenger?" Joseph asked.

"Don't wake him," Maeniel said, strolling away. "Put him on Audovald. He will bring him safely down the mountain."

THE PAPAL MESSENGER DID AWAKEN WHEN THEY were better than halfway down the mountain. Gavin had fallen asleep on his horse. Matrona put a handful of snow down his neck. Gavin screamed. His scream woke the papal messenger, who screamed in turn when he realized where he was.

Maeniel, who was riding behind him, said, "Be quiet. Don't alarm Audovald. His task requires concentration. This path is steep."

"Oh, yes," the papal messenger murmured. "The horse." In truth, he had no desire to distract Audovald. The path was not only steep and marred by patches of ice. On one side the drop was straight down into a valley filled with rocks. About five thousand spruce trees clung to a slope too steep to hold snow. Insuring that if he fell, the spiny tree limbs would rip him to pieces on the way down. A boulder in the valley would reduce him to something with the consistency of fruit pulp and in addition, there appeared to be a river in the valley that would wash away what remained.

"Where are we going?" he asked in a shaky voice.

"To Rome," Maeniel replied unconcerned.

"With all your household?"

"They normally accompany me when I travel," Maeniel said. The papal envoy made as if to pick up the reins.

"Do not annoy Audovald with directions, either," Maeniel said. "He knows the way."

X

THE WOLF EXPLODED INTO THE NIGHT, THE BEAST in full control. She wanted to escape Lucilla and her dreadful grief. To flee the stifling city, the stench of its gutters, the enclosing walls. The multiple terrors of a world ruled by men like Gundabald and Hadrian. A world that would force a woman to kill her own son.

So she ran, a gliding gray shape, skimming low across the ground beyond the environs of Rome through the long grass of the Campagna. *Thank God,* she thought. *Thank God for the wolf.* The wolf had always set her free, even when she'd been imprisoned. The wolf had always allowed her to escape; given her freedom. The wolf drowned her grief for her mother, consoled her for the sense of separateness she'd felt when she'd first realized that she lived not only in this world, but in another, also.

Regeane thought. Regeane pondered. Regeane feared. Regeane struggled. But the silver wolf simply was. ·

She came to a stop in the long grass shivered by the night wind. The sweep of the countryside was faintly illuminated by the slow, unending dance of the stars.

To the wolf's eyes, it was a shimmering, dark sea of grass, an undulating satiny carpet of life.

The rhythms of the night were timeless, formed by the needs of the earth as it drifted beneath the stars. The wind rose as the parched autumn earth released its heat into the cool, night air, and the stalks of the long grasses brushed each other, rustling and whispering in the silence.

Regeane heard the hunting cries of bats as they darted and swooped above her, seeking their insect prey.

Men might have abandoned the Campagna, but all around Regeane it throbbed with life. The rattle and shift of grasses as they moved and tossed. The cry of insects as they challenged each other and made love, fighting, mating, breeding, and dying in their swift-moving miniature world. Frogs called, singing their ancient songs in the low marshy places concealed in the folds of the earth's grassy gown.

To the wolf's ears, even the velvet slap of an owl's wing was loud. She heard clearly the nervous squeak and churring of the mice foraging warily among the grass stems for food.

She scented a deer nearby; the musk vivid as a spoken word.

The scent of blood drying and fading, rising from the spot where a stoat had surprised a rabbit.

Regeane understood that the wolf knew . . . the wolf knew things she didn't.

She'd had no plan when she went flying from Lucilla's villa. She had taken the necklace with the vague idea of bringing it to Antonius in the hope that he could use the jewels to buy food and shelter for himself until she could find a way to rescue him. But what rescue could there be for Antonius or, for that matter, for her?

She had only the wolf and her dim knowledge that the world was more than the plans of men like Gundabald or follies of war and politics. But the woman had only the haziest idea of what the wolf knew.

The wolf stood perfectly still, motionless as only a wild creature can be on the hunt. She searched the Campagna with eyes, ears, and nose. Her body quivered like a harp, strung with the intensity of her desire, her need. Listening, seeing, but above all, feeling with her whole body, until far away she heard music, the distant strains borne by the night wind to her ears.

The wolf lunged forward at a run.

Regeane ran, the night wind in her face, the stars a deep cold fire above her. The act of running filled her with profound joy. She reveled in the bunching and return of the wolf's powerful shoulder muscles, the advance and retreat of the iron sinew that drove her hips and thighs.

She fled from the world of men and into the vast dark universe that stared in indifference at the follies of mankind and would, she was sure, gaze at its passing with the same indifference.

The wolf's mind joined her forebears on other runs beneath other stars. Sometimes driven by the lash of terror and starvation as she traversed barren wastes, her belly cramping with hunger. Sometimes in joy when the quarry was sighted and she bore down, closing in with the rest of the pack, tasting the warm, rich blood in her mouth.

And then there were the runs on the nights of love. For a few moments, it seemed she didn't run alone. A dark shape raced beside her. Love, brief, excruciatingly joyous love, unlike human love, without its guilt, fear, and regret.

Love, a lance of fire in her loins; its delight echoing through her whole being.

Love, the warm milk scent of the den, the life flowing from her teats into small mouths. The soft young bodies pressed against her seeking comfort and security.

Love, a circle garnering of itself, for itself, what it gives.

A love that yields and adores, that is not taken or forced.

She reveled in these memories, memories without words, images, dreamlike fragments wrenched out of time. Images of what the world had been, what it should be, and what it never would be again. Not for her. For the woman, she would be wed to a man and he would take her maidenhood by force and perhaps wreak other violence upon her unless she killed him first.

She was so deeply caught up in the wolf's memories that she was almost shocked when she realized she'd reached her objective. She saw the procession before her.

The wolf stopped so quickly it brought her down on her haunches. And when the woman realized what she was looking at, she made a soft whining sound of distress.

But the wolf ignored her. And, caught deep in the matrix of the wolf's indifference, the woman had to agree. The music was the most beautiful she had ever heard. Even played as it was by hands and lips that were dust. The instruments carried by men and women who were now only bone encased in the house of earth.

In the forefront of the procession, the priests and priestesses danced joyously to the sound of lyre, cithara, and the double flute. The low, endless throbbing pulse of the drum bound the music together.

The sacrifices led the procession: white oxen with gilded horns garlanded with flowers and greenery. They paced tamely forward, going tranquil to their fate.

Behind them, marching four abreast, came the gods' worshippers. They were crowned with gilded laurel and linked by long garlands of spring-green branches turned with daisies, clover, lilies, and roses.

Torchbearers, pacing alongside them, led the silent throng as they passed before the wolf's eyes.

The clothing they wore was that of the distant past, and reminded Regeane of the few broken monuments remaining in Rome that depicted the ruling families gathered to honor their gods. The men wore draped togas, their heads covered by one fold of the garment. They were accompanied by their wives, clad in the long stola of honorable marriage, uncut hair dressed high behind a diadem. Both sexes led and carried small children. The older children and young people walked before them, trying to emulate the dignity of their elders.

As Regeane studied this stately company, she remembered one rainy day when she paused beside a basrelief of some unknown emperor leading his family toward the capital in solemn worship. An old farmer, who'd sold his produce, paused beside her. He rested his handcart on the ground and gazed at the frieze in sorrow and asked, "Did we ever stand so . . . before our gods?"

The wolf's first impulse was to flee. They were dead. The dead had a right to the peace and joy of fond remembrance. They had no need to be reminded of the agony and struggle of the living.

Unlike so many of the shadows the wolf saw, these dead had cut their ties to the earth. To the pain and strife of those who breathe and bleed, suffer and love. They had overcome the futile grief at the terrible wrench of life's ending.

What right had she, a creature of moonlight and darkness, to bring her need to them?

But need she did.

Hunger she did. For . . . justice.

And there would never be justice among mortals for her or Antonius.

Perhaps she might find some among the dead. At least when Antonius' struggles were ended, they might welcome him and let him join them.

The glittering procession glided past her. The late night air held the biting chill of winter. The stars glittered in dense, magnificent loneliness.

But the cold breeze that stirred the wolf's fur moved not a fold of their garments. The flowers of a forgotten springtime bloomed in the crowns the frolicking dancers wore. The procession marched in the warm, still air of a summer evening. The wolf followed through the cold, winter night.

The sacred way they trod led to a high rock that towered over the surrounding countryside. A temple, bone-white, crowned the rock. Its pale columns and pediment reared against the midnight sky.

Even from where she stood, the wolf could see it was a ruin. Roofless, the columns pitted and broken, the pediment looted of the ivory and crystal-eyed statuary that once did honor to a nation and its gods.

But still it stood majestic, decked in robes of starlight, a plaything of the wind and rain, gazing with patient tranquility on the brown plain and the eternal splendor of the dark blue sea beyond.

The wolf paused at the foot of the rock and looked up.

The steep path to the summit, once paved with marble and lined by statues of kings and emperors, gods and goddesses, was now only a barren, weed-grown trace.

The marbles had been ripped out long ago to feed the lime kilns at Rome and Naples. The few standing statues were mutilated, without hands or heads. Many had fallen and were only vine-encased lumps lying on the grassy slopes leading up to the rock.

The woman inside the wolf wondered what the dead eyes of the ghosts saw. Did they behold the temple in its ancient splendor or did they see what she did—an abandoned ruin? Did it matter to them what they saw? Did they care?

The wolf sniffed the wind and scented the clean, sweet breeze from the ocean and she knew it didn't matter. They lived beyond time with no worldly trifles to diminish their ardor or tarnish their love. To them, today was as yesterday or tomorrow. Life an eternal moment.

I will come, she thought, *as a supplicant. And beg help for Antonius and . . . myself.*

Laurel bushes grew all around the approach to the high rock. A branch yielded to the wolf's jaws. A supplicant must bear a palm. The wolf began to climb the steep path to the temple crowning the summit, toward the stars.

The sacred way circled the rock, going ever upward toward the sky, until she came at last to the top overlooking the sea. The air was clear, and the breeze blew constantly.

When the wolf reached the top she found the temple empty and dark. The wind whined softly among the stark, broken columns. Before the doors to the sacred precinct the undying fire of the gods was a conical mound of pale, dead ash. The eternal sea breeze drew the ash into a veil of dust, dancing before her in the cold night air.

The wolf paused, the laurel branch still clenched tightly in her jaws. A flicker of ironic laughter danced in her mind, so softly the wolf wasn't sure if it belonged to her or another.

"You feared to trouble the dead. Now all of your fears are set at naught. See how easily they escape you when they desire." Somehow Regeane formed the words in her mind. She had only the limited resources of the wolf to draw on. And though the wolf thought well, she thought in images and patterns and not with words as humans did.

But somewhere in the recesses of the wolf's brain, she found the symbols she needed. They coalesced into words and she cried out silently. *I come as a supplicant. Hear me. Answer me. Help me.*

The night wind blew more strongly for a moment. It swirled around the fire circle, lifting a cloud of ancient ash into the air, and sobbed through the shattered columns of the temple.

Voices. Voices sang in the wind. Voices out of time. Voices whose lips were dust.

Some condemned. Some mocked. Some even laughed as if

coming from an immense distance down a long, coiling corridor of eternity where they had forgotten they were ever human.

Voices. Wordless, whispering voices. Fading and finally falling into silence around her.

Regeane gathered herself within the wolf's brain and cried out again silently. *Does no one hear the supplicant?*

The reply was the shadow of a sound. As if a vagrant breath of the ever-moving air swirled and caught at the broken pedestal where the tall statue of the god had once stood.

Be silent, the voice commanded, *for where I dwell, the supplicant is always heard.*

The sweet scent of bay seemed to grow stronger in the wolf's nostrils.

She glided from the far end of the temple toward Regeane, clothed in white, wearing the long, softly draped chiton and peplos of a woman. The peplos covered her head and arms. Not even her hands were visible.

Her form was the shape and semblance of a woman. Her face was a thing of horror. The starlight gleamed on the naked bone of a skull.

The wolf, wrapped in the beast's indifference, whined softly, deep in her throat.

The voice of the apparition resonated in the wolf's mind. "Who are you? Why do you come to Cumae to trouble the noble, the sacred dead?"

The voices in the wind leaped to a crescendo, moaning, weeping, cursing, howling. The blast plucked at the wolf's fur and rattled the leaves of the branch in her mouth.

The specter drew closer and closer.

I am wolf, Regeane thought as her consciousness strove to separate itself from the wolf's. The world seemed to recede as the woman's mind twisted and turned, trying to force the wolf's muscles to run gibbering in terror from the thing she faced.

Red fury exploded through the double consciousness as the wolf raged back at the alien creature trying to control her, to turn her from her objective.

Regeane was thrust away into blind darkness. She could no longer see or hear. Taste and touch were denied to her as she was tossed into a lightless void, screaming soundlessly. Their union was as sudden, as simultaneous as the burst of lightning and the clap of thunder when a storm breaks directly overhead.

One moment she was in darkness; the next she stood woman-wolf, naked on the broken stone before the ruined temple and its dead fire, the laurel branch in her hand.

She was woman and wolf both, and she had never known such power. She could feel the quivering tension inside her. She was taut as a wire, drawn between the two opposite poles of her nature, taut as a harp string strained to its absolute limit just before it sings its sweetest note . . . or snaps.

She confronted the unnatural horror in front of her.

The form stopped.

The night wind flowed over Regeane's naked flesh like cold water. Wind from the sea, a bath of brilliance. Regeane stretched out the arm with the cluster of laurel leaves toward the figure, their perfume still thick in her nostrils.

"I come to you," she said, "as a supplicant, and you confront me with horror."

"You summoned me," the voice answered. "What care I what you see?" The forked tongue flickered at the lipless teeth of the skull. Behind the empty eyes of the bone mask the long length of a serpent moved beyond the black stare, in the hollow of the cranium. "Who are you to come here clothed in only your flesh, naked as the goddess herself and wearing her necklace."

"I was born of darkness," Regeane said. "My father's eyes closed before mine opened. I am not of this world or the other, and I have the right to be what I am."

The death-head woman vanished into a twisted, coiling blackness, and the serpent reared before Regeane, the dark, triangular head a shadow between her and the stars shining through the broken roof.

But the woman who was not Regeane and not the wolf stood her ground. As she watched open-eyed, unblinking, the serpent faded into wispy shadow till only the stars remained. Regeane faced a twisted, wrinkled crone.

The burst of light was fire in her eyes. The temple was thrown open before her, breathtakingly beautiful as it had been on the day of its dedication. Ablaze with torchlight, lit by the twinkling fires of a thousand lamps festooned with green garlands. The festive worshippers stood arrayed in white, crowned with gilded laurel, and carried a rainbow of spring flowers in their arms.

They were still as if interrupted in their revels by this trespasser from beyond the world, gazing at Regeane with the stony distant stare of the dead.

Towering over them stood the statue of the god clothed as Regeane, in primal nakedness, and alight with the beauty of youth. He smiled down at the throng who had once and now forever adored him.

Regeane stepped around the fire and toward the doorway.

"The supplicant will be heard," the crone whispered, "but come no further for beyond this threshold is the land of the dead."

Oh, there was beauty there, Regeane thought as she met the distant eyes of the throng. *For here chaos lurks, waiting, and beauty can be a mask for horror and horror a gateway into the unimaginable.*

Regeane turned again to the old woman standing in the doorway. But was she old? Even to the creature of power Regeane had become, the apparition seemed to shift and change.

Youth and age flickered like shadows over her features. Smooth skin collapsed into wrinkles. A winsome smile turned into a gap-toothed, evil grin. Lustrous hair thinned to a few lank strands on a scabrous, balding head.

And then it all began again and again and again endlessly.

"I can't seem to see you," Regeane said.

"No," the voice answered. "No one ever has. Speak. What do you desire? For you have not much time. You said you came as a supplicant. I will hear you. Speak."

"I seek a man's life," Regeane said. "I seek to remold his flesh, to heal him."

All those crowded into the temple began to laugh. *The weeping of the dead is very terrible,* Regeane thought, for she had fled from it often. *It wrings the heart, but their laughter is worse, hideous beyond belief because there is nothing left of humanity in it. Only a cold, ringing jeer.*

Regeane almost fled from it, but the pride and power she felt wouldn't let her.

The figure standing in the doorway didn't laugh. Her face, except for the slow changes of bud, blossom, and decay, remained the same and, as Regeane watched, Regeane realized each face the twisted hag wore was a different one, yet each the same in their destruction by time. They faded into each other in unbroken sequence as perhaps they had since the very beginning of the world. And so they might until it ended. The being didn't laugh, she nodded.

"What you wish to do is very simple," the voice said. "The fire behind you still burns though its flame is no longer an earthly one. Bring him here, stretch him on the firepit, and then pass this threshold. Perhaps you will emerge, perhaps not, but what you wish will be accomplished."

Cross the threshold, Regeane thought. *Journey into the land of the dead.* With a shudder, the triumphant willpower that held her where she was collapsed and she began to run.

She didn't remember afterward when she ceased running on two feet and began to run on four, but somewhere in her precipitous flight she did, and the wolf found herself down from the rock, skimming over the Campagna, taking heaving breaths of the clean wind as she ran.

The night was growing older. The wolf could tell by the smell of the wind and the slow wheeling changes in the stars. Dew was beginning to settle in the grass over which she flew like a streak of silver light.

She ran toward Antonius.

Death. She had known death was not the end of everything, but she had not grasped the true significance of her knowledge.

The terror of endless possibility.

That was where she sinned against human thinking the way the dead did.

One of the most important things men ask of life, of the world is predictability. The sun rises. The sun sets. Serfs bow to their lords, the lords to kings and emperors.

The Romans had been oppressors, condemning whole populations to abject slavery. But their orderly rule had at least lent predictably to life. The peoples living under their heel and yoke had known what to expect.

But in this clash of nations where Lombard struggled with the pope, where Frank and Saxon merged with the ancient Gauls and all battled for supremacy and power, who knew what to expect?

She was herself to them, to mankind, a creature of restless substance . . . One with insubstantial night and the universe, an impossibility. Unknown, and therefore, uncontrollable and that was why men wanted to destroy her. Would destroy her if they caught her.

A woman they could understand, and a wolf, but the two as one? Never.

She stopped running near the glassworks. She could smell Antonius, smell his fear and the dreadful workings of the disease that slowly destroyed his flesh.

The wolf stopped, feeling the dew damping down her fur. Her flanks heaved from her long run through the night, and she was thirsty.

She drank from the rivulet that once supplied the glassmakers, lapping the crystal water with her tongue. The wolf went through the rite, its sensation unknown to man, of straightening her fur, shaking herself, forcing it to rise and fall back in a comfortable pattern.

Death. Yes, they would kill her if they caught her. She shivered, thinking of the torments visited on those convicted of black sorcery—drowning, burning.

But however agonizing the pains, death would end them and death was part of the predictable universe.

Beyond . . . who knows?

Perhaps the greatest terror the dead faced was that they could not die. That they were set adrift on the uncharted ocean beyond life. To drift forever across the sea of eternity.

XI

SHE FOUND ANTONIUS LYING WRAPPED IN HIS thick mantle. For a few seconds, she crouched against him, shivering.

"Lupa," he sighed when he felt her body pressed so tightly to his side. "So you've returned. I don't know whether to be glad or sorry. I was thinking this little oven might be my tomb. At first the thought terrified me, but after a time it became a more comfortable one.

"I could lie here, my flesh melting into the earth, my bones dissolving, watching the play of swallows above me by day," he mused. "There are swallows here, you know. They build their nests in the lip of the chimney and they must raise generation after generation of their young here."

Yes, she and the wolf thought, *and if Basil's men were not blind human fools, they would have noticed the presence of those swallows and known there must be ruins about. And they would have had you posthaste.*

"And the stars. Locked in a city as I was, you forget the stars, how beautiful they are when the Milky Way builds a bridge across the night sky. How can any artist truly hope to catch their glory?

"Perhaps if I lie here moldering for a few centuries I might learn something about them." Antonius chuckled softly as if amused by his own thoughts, by the idea of his imminent death and dissolution.

The wolf was not amused. To her it was simply defeatism. She leaped to her feet, snarling.

Antonius' beautiful eyes stared up at her from the shadow of his cowled robe. "Why, Lupa, what was that? A command or a warning?"

Both, Regeane thought, trotting toward his feet. She snapped at them, her teeth closing in the air with an ominous click.

Antonius sat up. He studied the wolf in the dim starlight. "Lupa," he said softly, "can't you see there's no way out for me? I'm as well off here as I would be anywhere else. Basil can't find me. He can't use me against my brother.

"There's water here. I can creep out and drink when I want to. I'm seldom hungry anymore. In a few days I'll cease to feel what few complaints my belly makes. And, after a few more days, a little pain won't make any difference."

More wolf than woman now, Regeane was infuriated. She was willing to dare the gates of eternity for him, and here he was talking as calmly about dying as he would about dropping into the nearest wineshop.

She crouched, sinking back on her haunches, and launched herself at him with a roar of fury that echoed back from the walls of the oven like a thunderclap. She dropped to the ground, just short of crashing into his chest.

Antonius struggled to his feet. The wolf stepped back, mollified.

Antonius studied her for a moment. "Lupa?" he asked anxiously. The wolf trotted to the little tunnel that was the entrance to the oven. "I can see I'm not allowed to die in peace."

Strangely he seemed to greet that prospect with the same equanimity and amusement he had the thought of resting in this little sanctuary forever. He had, as always, drawn the dark mantle over his mutilated lips and nose, but he smiled. The wolf felt the smile—a peaceful radiance—rather than saw it.

"Very well. I abandon myself to you. Lead me where you will."

REGEANE FOUND THE SHEPHERD A FEW HOURS later. She had been afraid of trouble from his dogs, but found when she faced the scruffy mongrels her fears had been completely unfounded.

They had encountered wolves before, but never wolves like this. The silver wolf, unlike the slinking grays of the Campagna, was a creature of dazzling power. She was a dense mass of muscle and bone clothed in the shimmer of moonlight. She was fully twice as big as any they had ever seen before.

The dogs stopped, snarls dying in their throats, their ears laid back, tails tucked firmly between their legs. They fled to crouch protectively near the white mass of sheep.

The sheep were tightly bunched against both danger and the cold night. And the silver wolf understood if she tried to attack them, the dogs, driven to desperation by a threat to their charges, would fight back. Otherwise they would do nothing. Not even warn the young shepherd the silver wolf saw beyond the massed flock. He was sleeping, curled on his side in front of a rude hut near a small fire on the hilltop.

The wolf eyed the dogs contemptuously. One of them bared its teeth at her in a silent, terror-filled snarl.

The silver wolf was shocked by a sudden awareness of her own power. She could hear the confident, steady hammer of her heart. Feel ropey muscle in chest and haunches tighten, ready to put into play the steel sinews that drove her legs.

She was not *a* wolf, but *the* wolf. A creature of matchless strength, in her prime. She knew, and the dogs knew, she could slaughter them and then tear out the throats of as many of the sheep as she cared to. The shepherd himself could easily be her first prey, a helpless victim of her newfound strength. And why not?

His hut, the clothing he wore, whatever food he had would serve to feed and protect Antonius. If the food wasn't enough, she could kill a few of the sheep.

The silver wolf loped toward the sleeping form on the hilltop. The shepherd was no more than a boy, a stripling who looked to be at most in his early teens. In repose, his face showed the placid innocence of all sleepers. The winsome and frightening vulnerability of mankind at rest. A timeless helplessness before mother night and the eternal stars.

The wolf, merciless aristocrat of killers, wasn't disposed to question expedience. The boy would be dead before he completely awakened. Regeane stopped the wolf in her tracks. The silver one shook her head in annoyance. The woman knew what the boy was, likely the youngest son of one of the small farmers whose tiny holdings clustered near one of the vast estates of the wealthy.

They lived in a poverty so absolute, it sickened Regeane. She wondered how anyone could lead a life so devoid of all pleasure, happiness, or even hope. Many had given up even trying to rear their children, selling those who did not die in infancy as slaves to the powerful as soon as they were old enough to work. Young as he was, probably even his master didn't value him much. If the boy survived the unremitting toil, the hazards of the Campagna, and was able to forage and augment his meager slave rations with enough food to grow to adulthood, he might be better treated and fed.

Right now, his survival was as precarious as the life of a runt in a litter of puppies or kittens. He might be able to struggle hard enough to win sufficient nourishment from the great world mother. Then again, he might not. If he didn't, he would go down silently, tracelessly into the dust with the world's discards. But whatever happened, Regeane would not let the wolf be the instrument of his doom.

The silver wolf stopped at the edge of the fire and lowered her head. Wood was scarce on the Campagna and the shepherd's tiny fire showed his poverty. A ring of small branches, the cull of brush and saplings, clustered at the base of one big olive log. The log supported a solitary flame.

The sheep milled and muttered softly, disturbed by the wolf's scent. Belatedly, one of the dogs barked sharply.

The shepherd awakened and saw the wolf through a veil of flame. He grabbed his staff and tried snatching up the last flaming branch from the fire. Half-consumed, it fell to pieces in his hand, burning his fingers. He tried to get to his feet, slipped, and succeeded in getting as far as his knees.

The broken ends of the branch caught and the fire flared. And, through the flames, he saw that in the place where a wolf stood only a moment before . . . a woman.

A beautiful woman, clad only in a magnificent nakedness and a necklace of silver and pearls.

The young shepherd bowed down, pressing his forehead to the earth. He choked out the words, "Oh, queen of the night, why do you come to me?"

Though woman in body, Regeane's mind was still dominated by the wolf and she was filled with the wolf's boldness. The plan had been a crude one, only half thought out. She had hoped to bribe the young man with the necklace. And if that failed, turn wolf and terrify him into submission. Finding herself worshipped was disconcerting.

But, she decided, worship was not all that bad. She had been afraid of what she might have to do to compel him to her will. Now her task seemed much easier.

She stepped toward him, keeping the low fire between them. He peered up at her through his fingers.

The wolf-woman laughed, something the wolf wouldn't have thought of and the woman wouldn't have dared to do. "Aren't you afraid that if you stare, the nakedness of a goddess will blind you?"

To her surprise, the boy raised his head and gave her a look of adoration. "They say he who looks upon the mistress of the night will be desired by all women and remain fair of face all his days. And he who touches her . . ."

Something in Regeane's expression must have changed because the boy's courage deserted him, and he threw himself into a full prostration saying, "Have mercy! Don't kill me!"

Regeane was cold. The bitter night air was hostile to her naked flesh as she became more woman by the moment. She fought the urge to desert this perilous situation, turn wolf again, and run. She gritted her teeth, tried not to shiver, and thought, *You are the goddess now. Use your power!*

"Fear not," she said, unclasping Lucilla's necklace. "I don't seek your life. I want you to protect one I love and shelter him."

The boy raised his bemused face from the ground, then took the necklace from her hand. He didn't have the courage to stare at her face again. Instead he gazed at the small, soft woman's hand that held it out to him. A hand that might be the hand of any young girl.

Regeane stepped back into the grass.

"Wait," the boy said hoarsely. "Nothing like this night will ever happen to me again."

Regeane hesitated. She hovered on the verge of change. She could almost feel the cascade of moonbeams in her flesh. "Why?"

she whispered softly. The fire was very low. She could barely see the boy's face.

"Oh, mistress of the night, only touch me once that I may never fail in love."

"Close your eyes and lift your face to me," Regeane said.

The boy's eyes closed. He was trembling. The cloud of her moon-tipped hair fell around his face, and her lips brushed his in one soft, sweet kiss.

Regeane stepped back and realized Antonius stood beside her. His face was covered by the coarse, black mantle, but his eyes stared, wide and astonished and frightened. Then the moon darkness flowed through her and she was wolf again.

The young shepherd bowed down, closing his eyes tightly, but Antonius stood staring down into her eyes.

"Why, Lupa?" he asked softly. "Why?"

But Regeane was already away, a silver shadow racing over the Campagna for home.

DETERMINED NOT TO BE CAUGHT AS SHE HAD BEEN the night before, she held herself to a punishing pace until she saw the city's lights and smelled again the usual tang of woodsmoke and garbage she associated with human habitations. She dropped to a lope and sought Lucilla's villa.

As she jumped the orchard wall, she saw a faint streak of white on the eastern horizon. She trotted to the atrium and, unable to wait any longer, lowered her muzzle to the pool.

In the growing light she saw the reflection of her face in the water—the deep, yellow eyes buried in silver-tipped fur, the thick ruff that framed her face—then abruptly a tremor of darkness flowed over her and she found herself kneeling before the pool looking down at her human face, at the dark hair flowing over her shoulders and her own strange, sad eyes.

Regeane remained kneeling among the irises and cascades of autumn daisies, transfixed by her own weariness and the beauty of the silent garden in the first light.

The pool reflected the sunrise colors, transparent blue, then rose. The flowers, heavy with the night dew, were beginning to let down their fragrance into the cool, morning air. The aromas of mint and chamomile bruised by her knees hung around her.

Regeane closed her eyes and took a long breath.

"Oh, my God," a voice gasped. "Oh, my dear, sweet, merciful God. No wonder you were afraid to marry." Lucilla sat on one of the benches beside the pool.

"You saw," Regeane whispered. "You know."

"I saw . . ." Lucilla's hand flew to her cheek and she turned her face away from Regeane. "Oh, God, I saw . . . I don't believe what I saw." She turned back to confront the younger woman.

Regeane rose slowly to her feet and walked along the flagstone path toward Lucilla, asking, "Would you lend me your mantle? The air is cold and some of the servants might come out. I'm naked."

"So you are," Lucilla said, staring at her with unbelieving eyes. "So you are, naked as a nymph. For a moment, I thought my eyes were deceiving me. They do that, you know, as you age," she babbled. "I thought, 'A wolf. How does a wolf come here? I must call my servants to drive it away,' and then in a moment it came to me. 'Old woman, that's no wolf, but only a garden statue kneeling among the flowers,' and then . . ." Lucilla drew back from Regeane, her face stiff with terror. "And then . . . and then . . . you moved."

Regeane stood only a few feet from Lucilla. She stretched out her hand. "The mantle, please. I'm cold."

Absently, still gazing open-mouthed at Regeane, Lucilla unwound the mantle from her shoulders and placed it in Regeane's hand.

Regeane wrapped herself in the heavy cloth. "Thank you."

"Don't stare at me so," Lucilla said. "Not with those eyes. I know I look a ragged hag, but I have my pride, and . . . I have passed a sleepless night."

"Are you going to denounce me?" Regeane asked.

"Denounce you?" Lucilla asked, her mouth snapping shut. "For what?"

"For being a witch, a sorceress."

Lucilla laughed. The short peal of laughter was shrill and slightly hysterical. "Of course not," the older woman said. "I never denounce anyone except those who plot against Hadrian.

Everyone knows that I've lived too long outside the law to sympathize with those superior judges, the iron-fisted soldiers who . . ."

Regeane sank down on the bench.

Lucilla took her in her arms. "Oh, dear. Oh, you poor dear." Suddenly she stared down at Regeane in horror. "Have you been out on the Campagna all night?"

Regeane sat up. "Yes, with Antonius. He's safe. I left him in the care of a shepherd."

Lucilla buried her face in her hands. She sighed deeply, then let her hands drop to her lap and stared out across the reflecting pool. Then she let out a quick, little chuckle that surprised Regeane. "You think you're a witch, eh?" she asked.

Regeane said, "I don't know what I am."

"Can you do . . . what I saw you do . . . at will?" Lucilla asked.

"No," Regeane answered. "I mean, I don't know." She began to flounder. "I never thought about it. My mother and I never talked about it."

"No, but then she wouldn't, would she?" Lucilla said. "It does explain the hold your uncle had over you. Why she let him and that dissolute son of his dress her in rags while they went out and spent her money."

"No," Regeane gasped.

"Yes," said Lucilla. "And it explains the hold they have over you, too." She sat quietly for a moment, gazing down at her lap. Her fingers played idly with the folds of the gown.

"I can just see that idiot mother of yours," Lucilla said. "A saintly woman, otherworldly. Isn't that what you told me? She locked you up, didn't she? Hid you away like some dirty little secret. And in between bars, bolts, and narrow little cells, all you got to see were the wax candles of churches and shrines decked with the decaying, wasted flesh of purported saints and holy men."

Regeane gagged and whispered, "Stop." She took a deep breath. "Stop. Don't remind me. Sometimes she got pieces of dead flesh, little splinters of bone. She pounded them to a powder and tried to make me drink them."

"Ugh," Lucilla said. "Just like that lack-wit physician with his hippopotamus dung."

Regeane gasped again. "I used to try to take her potions." She began to cry, tears coursing down her cheeks. "She suffered so much. I wanted to try to ease her pain."

Lucilla jumped to her feet. "Seems to me you were the one doing the suffering," she snarled. "All because she couldn't, and wouldn't, accept the situation and try to protect you."

"Yes," Regeane admitted uncertainly, "but who could, who would?"

"I can," Lucilla said. "I will. I just have. And so could she if she had any backbone at all."

"Lucilla," Regeane cried. "Please stop. I loved my mother."

"Child, child," Lucilla said. She strode up and down before the bench. "We all loved our mothers. I loved mine, too, but she was like yours. Whimpering and groveling before Christ and his saints, and all the while living in mortal terror of my father's fist and boot. Bearing child after child. I can't remember how many. So often they died, most before the poor little mites ever got a chance to know what life was. Perhaps they were fortunate."

Her face was set in a mask of bitterness. "The life of a farmer in the Abruzzi is cruel enough to deaden the hardest spirit. I know it nearly did mine. But no matter. It's your life and your spirit we're speaking of here. Your life and your future. First, how did this . . . change come upon you?"

"I . . ." Regeane said, "I . . . don't . . ."

Lucilla stopped pacing and stood tapping one sandaled foot. "Come, come," she prompted. "When did it first happen?"

"When I became a woman at the time of my first bleeding. I . . ." Regeane sighed. "I changed."

"So," Lucilla's eyes narrowed. "So," she repeated, "this skill of yours is like that so beautiful hair, not a thing of art, but of nature herself."

"I seem to have been born with it," Regeane said. "My father was also afflicted."

Lucilla's good-humored chuckle surprised Regeane again. "My pretty, I've known a witch or two in my time. More than two if the truth be known. A woman in my profession involves herself in all kinds of shady dealings. And let me tell you, your powers would drive any of them mad with envy. Smelly old women, dabbling in drugs, caught up in the most revolting superstition and trickery. But you. No, real power is what you have, my girl."

"Power?" Regeane asked. "Or a curse?"

"Power if you will have it, a curse if you deny it," Lucilla said. "Come. Come. I saw you read the past in a piece of cloth when we first met. You can change your shape and become a creature of the night. Tell me, what else can you do?"

Regeane stood up, clutching the mantle around herself, her mind in a whirl. "Power," she murmured.

Suddenly she staggered and Lucilla's face seemed to recede into a great distance. Her gorge rose and her throat filled with bile. She felt sweat break out all over her skin.

When she came to herself, she was seated on the bench, her head between her knees. Lucilla's arm was around her. She lifted her head and rested it on Lucilla's shoulder. "I need food," she said to Lucilla. "Food and sleep. The change . . . the moon darkness drains me."

"The moon darkness," Lucilla said. "Is that what you call it? The moon darkness?"

"Yes, because the pull is strongest at the full moon. I can seldom resist it then, and though my mother fought it with fasting and prayer, I always changed."

"I take it you did the fasting," Lucilla said dryly, "and she did the praying."

"Yes, but it didn't work."

Lucilla nodded, She embraced Regeane. Her hand pressed Regeane's face against her shoulder and she stared out over the garden.

The red and blue dawn was turning to gold as the light from the new sun reached down into the atrium. The air resounded with birdsong and jewel-like hummingbirds darted about, sipping the sun-warmed nectar from the flowers.

"Imprisonment, beatings, starvation, noxious messes forced down your throat, all in the name of purification," Lucilla mused. "All futile. Not much of a preparation for life. But come, I think I can remedy your hunger and thirst. In the evening Susanna places a tray for one in my study."

Regeane stopped and was about to pick up the dress and sandals she'd discarded last night.

"No," Lucilla said sharply. "Leave that whorish thing where it is. Follow me."

Lucilla led her through another garden. This one was stiffly formal with an ornate marble tile walkway and clipped boxwood hedges. It was dotted with numerous pedestals. No statues, just pedestals.

Regeane gaped at them.

"Yes," Lucilla said. "Once this garden was filled with beautiful bronze statues. The previous tenant, one Bishop Maxtentus, said he found them shockingly pagan and had them melted down."

"Oh," Regeane gasped. "How sad."

"Don't waste any tears on the statues, little love. Hadrian feels, and so do I, that Maxtentus found them shockingly valuable and sold them one and all for high prices to a Greek merchant who sailed away to Constantinople with them.

"He gave Hadrian the rather glib story about paganism, but when Hadrian asked him what he'd done with the bronze, Maxtentus developed a terrible stammer. When Hadrian looked into his other affairs, he found most valuable things he touched tended to stick to his fingers at least long enough for him to sell them at a profit."

"What did he do?" asked Regeane.

"Maxtentus?" Lucilla asked.

"No, Hadrian," Regeane said.

Lucilla chuckled. "Maxtentus is holding down a see in some nameless place among the Saxons. He's up to his rear end in big, hairy, beer-guzzling warriors and busty blond women who never bathe and dress their hair with butter. He speaks only Latin. His flock apparently finds him a very satisfactory shepherd. He cannot remonstrate with them about any of their bad habits. They continue to worship trees, wells, and rivers. He continues to exhort them to abandon their ancient ways in a language of which they speak not one word. And he continues to believe they could understand him if they would . . . only . . . try."

Regeane began giggling.

"What do you think of this peristyle?" Lucilla gestured at the garden. They paused near a door for Regeane to take in the view.

"Not much," Regeane said, "rather cold. I hope he doesn't steal anything from the Saxons. They'll cut off his hands."

"Not a bad idea," Lucilla replied. "The bronzes did belong to the church and they were very beautiful. Still, the pool remains." She pointed to an enormous reflecting pool in the garden. "I raise carp there." She indicated a jar near her hand.

Regeane looked down. Two large carp sulked in the bottom, fins waving gently in the still water. "Uuum." Regeane eyed then hungrily. "Breakfast?" she asked hopefully.

"My!" Lucilla looked a bit taken aback. "Raw or cooked?"

"At the moment," Regeane said impatiently, "either."

"Ah, yes," Lucilla said as she began unlocking the door. "I forgot you've been running around on all fours all night."

She opened the door. The room was small, dim, and odorous with cedar and furniture polish. It opened into a private walled garden.

The first thing Regeane noted was a napkin-covered tray resting on a circular table in the center of the room. She charged.

"Hold!" Lucilla said. "It will not fight back or even run away. Arms up."

The mantle Regeane was wearing fell to the floor. Lucilla dropped a heavy linen gown over her head.

Regeane got to the table. She found ripe pears, herbed cream cheese, bread, and a pitcher of white wine. She ignored the wine. It was the only thing on the table she ignored.

Lucilla poured herself some wine. She watered it a bit. "How is Antonius?"

Regeane stopped eating for a moment. She had to take a deep breath to talk. "He is . . . well. You know, not well, but—"

"But as healthy as he ever is," Lucilla filled in.

"Yes, even his kidnapping by Basil didn't damage his . . . composure."

Lucilla shook her head and sighed. She took her wine,

walked to the porch, and stared out into the garden. "No, of course not. Execution wouldn't damage his composure . . . as you put it. Can you help him?"

The question was asked so quietly Regeane almost didn't hear it. But when it penetrated her consciousness, she stopped eating again. "Yes," she answered.

Lucilla turned back toward her. "How?"

Regeane said, "Ummmmmm."

"Regeane, are you in danger of developing the same type of stammer Maxtentus did when talking to Hadrian?"

"My activities require a lot of explaining," Regeane said.

"Your point is well taken," Lucilla said. She bowed slightly to Regeane and turned back again to the garden.

Regeane ate. With every bite she felt better. At last, she relaxed, replete, and had the leisure to glance around the room.

Lucilla's study had a gentle dignity lacking in the over-ornate dining room. Bookshelves lined the walls. Diamond-shaped structures built into them held scrolls, flat shelves held books and, in many cases, unbound piles of papers. A slab of glass in the roof shed a clear morning light on the table where Regeane was sitting. The portico opened into the garden.

A fountain on the wall spurted water into a basin. The fountain head was an arrangement of bronze acanthus leaves combined to suggest the face of a god peering out through the leaves in a forest. The bronze glowed in the delicate gold of the new sun; water sparkled.

The rest of the garden lay in cool morning shadow. Chamomile, valerian, and poppies grew thickly clustered in beds along the garden walls. The smaller chamomile enthusiastically puffing into cushions of yellow and white presided over by drooping violet-throated poppy heads, scarlet and white, mixed with high valerian spikes.

The roof over the portico was a grape arbor shaded now by a thick growth of winter-denuded ropey vines. A few leaves remained, green at the center, crisp and brown at the edges, moving slightly in the first morning breeze.

"What is this place?" Regeane asked.

"A place where I seldom, if ever, invite even my friends,"

Lucilla said. She walked to a bookshelf and lifted a brass scroll from its place and handed it to Regeane.

Grasping the ring, Regeane unrolled it. "It's Greek," she said, disappointed. "I can't read Greek." She examined the papyrus very closely. It had been glued to a backing of a new vellum to preserve it because the papyrus was very old and already crumbling to dust at the edges.

"Neither do I," Lucilla said, "but I have a Latin translation here on the shelf beside it."

Regeane closed the scroll very carefully. "It is old and must be precious."

Lucilla nodded and replaced it on the shelf. "It is a letter written by Queen Cleopatra of Egypt to Julius Caesar on the matter of the calendar. She gives him the best opinion of the Egyptian sage, Sosthumeus, and later, her own views. Then, she makes some suggestions. It is to be noted that he took them. This is believed to be the only letter surviving written in the queen's own hand. It was salvaged when the library at Alexandria burned."

"Oh," Regeane whispered staring into Lucilla's face, "what else is there?"

"Up on this shelf," she indicated a higher one, "Arete, one of the first to write a study of natural law as it relates to women. Her fellow citizens at Cyrene are said to have amended their marriage law at her suggestion. She is called 'Lycergia' or law-giver.

"Over here are poets Myrtis, Erinna, Anyte. Those are some of the Greeks. Here, a few Romans: Sulpicia—"

Regeane burst into tears. "They are all women." The tears weren't healing. They scalded her face, burnt her eyes, and made her nose swell. When Lucilla tried to comfort her, she moved away and finally ended by washing her face in the garden fountain. "All women," she repeated as she walked back to where Lucilla stood.

"Yes, I don't banish male authors and, in fact, have many books by them, but not in here. And you may come in to read or study as you please. Only don't remove any books from this room. Not because I don't trust you, but because I have no confidence in others. I have seen men who, on finding a book was written by a woman, made haste to consign it to the flames. I protect what is here, though I cannot think it will survive me."

Regeane nodded. "I am honored. You haven't slept."

"No," Lucilla said. Her eyes were red-rimmed, her long blond hair was swept to one side and, in the growing light, Regeane could see how much gray was mixed into it.

"I have powers," Regeane said. "I will try to save Antonius."

"Yes, I know," Lucilla said. "There is one poet who is not here. I cannot find one collection of her poems still in existence. The priests have done their work well. Yet, I cannot think she won't be remembered because she reached out and touched the central chord of loneliness and longing in each human soul. I thought of her often tonight.

> *The moon has set.*
> *And the Pleiades:*
> *It is the middle of the night,*
> *And time passes,*
> *Yes passes—*
> *And I lie alone"*

Regeane's eyes burned, but no tears came. Her head hurt. "She killed him. Gundabald helped her. She helped Gundabald . . . I don't know if it matters which one of them . . . He was my father. I got the powers from him. Except she called them a curse and was sure she was cursed . . . through me."

"Yes," Lucilla replied. "That was the 'nonsense' you babbled under Pappolus' drugs. About rose petals steeping in blood. The more fool he and I for not understanding it."

"I can't promise you anything specific," Regeane said, "because I don't know where my powers will lead me."

"Yes," Lucilla said, taking her arm. "Now, come to bed. Your serious training begins this evening. You dine with the pope."

Regeane slept in Lucilla's big bed. Lucilla, beside her, passed into unconsciousness as soon as her head touched the pillow. Regeane, however, remained wakeful for one brief, beautiful moment. The wolf visited her.

She and others of her kind were walking down along a narrow beach below high cliffs. The stone was a deep bloody

black, stained faintly red and purple in places, broken along
prismatic lines into three-cornered angles like building blocks.
The sandy strand was brown stained by long darker streaks
from the mineral-rich stone. The sky above was a wrack of torn
storm clouds, dark gray where they floated on the air, reaching
higher and higher until they became crystal and white thunder-
heads, drifting between broken streaks of blue sky. Out to sea,
mist floated like smoke on the water.

The waves were quiet, rolling gray far out, becoming blue
swells as they approached shore and, at last, deep green combers arching and slapping into lacy foam at the wolves' feet.

Here and there, they had to swerve to avoid big piles of bone-
white and silver driftwood. At length, they came to a headland
stretching far out into the water.

Air blowing from the ocean was clear and cold, containing in
each breath the essence of eternity. Long shafts of light began to
break through the mist. And the wolves stood as one watching
the sun rising in splendor . . . above the rim of the world.

XII

SHE WAS ONE OF THE MOST BEAUTIFUL WOMEN RE-
geane had ever seen. She surveyed Regeane with aristocratic
disdain. "Is this the girl, Mother?"

"Regeane," Lucilla said, "May I present my daughter,
Augusta."

Regeane curtsied as deeply as she could in the robe of stiff
white and gold brocade she was wearing.

Augusta touched a lacquered finger to her lips and used it to
smooth one of her fashionably and artificially high arched
brows and then the other, as her two glorious, violet eyes

studied Regeane. "She's mannerly enough, Mother," Augusta commented and continued, "pray tell me, Regeane, what is your lineage?"

As she had been trained to do, Regeane began to recite her lineage beginning with one Luprand who had been the son of Charles Martel by a concubine and who, in spite of becoming an abbot, managed to father seven children.

Augusta broke in on her narrative before she was finished with the first generation, "Excellent, my dear girl. I see you have your ancestors at your fingertips. That's as it should be, an illustrious family, though . . . recent."

"Recent?" Regeane choked.

"My husband's family," Augusta continued with lofty condescension, "trace their ancestry back to the divine Julius himself."

"Yes, dear," Lucilla said with good-humored malice. "We know. You tell everyone sooner or later, usually sooner."

"Don't be difficult, Mother," Augusta said.

"No, dear," answered Lucilla, "but if you'll excuse us for a moment, I have a few last-minute instructions for Regeane."

Augusta managed to look both politely bored and irritated at the same time, then she turned and drifted off down the path, pausing every few moments to admire herself in the darkening waters of the atrium pool.

Regeane thought there was much to admire. Augusta's slim, curvaceous body was draped in an overgown of pale rose silk, richly embroidered with gold and Oriental pearls. Her auburn hair was piled high, held in place with emeralds and a snood of golden chains.

The face framed by the finery didn't disappoint the eye. Augusta was blessed with slender, high cheekbones with the characteristic narrow high-bridged aristocratic nose and large, heavy-lidded eyes that hinted subtly and beautifully at subdued passion.

"Oh, my," Regeane said. "The divine Julius. Is she, really?"

"Don't be silly, child," Lucilla said. "She's my daughter. She boasts of her husband's family. I must admit, though, that looking at her now, no one could ever possibly imagine that her grandmother was a peasant woman from the Abruzzi who went to bed every night on a straw tick, scratching her lice."

Regeane giggled.

"Mother," Augusta called back over her shoulder at them. "Are you saying outrageous things to that girl?"

Lucilla sighed deeply. "No, dear," she answered sweetly. "Just be patient. We'll be finished in a short time."

"Well, be quick about it. If you chatter too long, we'll be late for the feast. That's unthinkable, Mother."

Lucilla bridled for a second; then her irritation expended itself in another deep sigh. "Yes, dear," she said dutifully. She gritted her teeth. "Damn, but there's no help for it. I need Augusta to introduce you to Roman nobility. Child, you must be presented to the notables of the city in the company of someone who is eminently respectable. My daughter fits that description perfectly."

Lucilla gave a snort of fury. "I can't imagine how I did it. A line distinguished by a peasant woman and a whore, culminating in the paragon of ancient Roman virtue that is my dear daughter, Augusta. Not only has she made an impeccably illustrious marriage, but indeed, no breath of scandal has ever sullied her name."

"A family related to the divine Julius Caesar . . ." Regeane began.

"I believe," Lucilla said, "that the links between her husband's family and the first Caesar are more mythological than factual. However, one can never tell—the gens Juli was an enormous one—and I suppose it's possible they are descended from a distant relative of the great man himself.

"But," she added spitefully, "so are many other people. In any case, they rusticated in poverty and obscurity, living in a tumble-down villa in the Sabine hills, wearing coarse wool. They were only a little better off than their serfs until they were saved by the timely arrival about fifty years ago of a Lombard princess. She had high social aspirations, an iron will, and two wagonloads of gold."

To her horror, Regeane found herself giggling again. "Lucilla," she admonished, "if you want me to be respectful, you shouldn't tell me . . ."

"Yes. Yes, of course I want you to be respectful—openly, that is. I have undertaken to teach you about the world and it's imperative you learn a little fashionable hypocrisy. Besides, my little one, it's important to know the roots of social and political eminence; important that you learn they rise from the same dung heap among the poor where the rest of us come from. So that you aren't overly impressed by lofty lineages, fine clothes, and exquisite manners. And learn to look through them to the men and women beneath."

Regeane nodded soberly. "The Lombard princess?"

"Had an iron will and an equally firm grip on the purse strings. The whole family soon learned to jump to attention when she snapped her fingers. She made brilliant matches for her new husband's brothers and sisters, not to mention his numerous cousins. I understand she snatched up a few from convents and monasteries in the process and, in no long time at all, they were among the first families of Rome."

"Mother," Augusta called as she began walking back toward them, "I really must insist . . ."

"I do hate being rushed," Lucilla whispered to Regeane in a voice dripping with quiet fury, "but if we must, we must. I will introduce you to the pope, but I'll stay in the background and let Augusta present you. She will be your sponsor, not I. Try to get along with her. Luckily that isn't difficult. She's bored with everything, but talk of clothes, jewels, the servant problem," Lucilla's eyes rolled, "the high price of slaves. Encourage her along those lines and I'm sure you'll be successful.

"When you reach the pope's villa, let Augusta do the talking. Go about with downcast eyes, keep your mouth shut and your eyes and ears open. There will be a period of mingling and talk in the garden before the feast begins. Some of the men may try to draw you off on the pretext of showing you the villa. Don't let any of them get you alone. Stay close to Augusta and follow her example."

Augusta was within earshot and Regeane considered the last sentence probably was aimed at her.

"Naturally, Mother," Augusta said.

Elfgifa entered the atrium. The little girl's hair was still damp from the scrubbing she'd been given and she was dressed as

Regeane was in a linen shift covered by an overgown of heavy, embroidered silk, and a long-sleeved garment of stiff brocade.

She squirmed and stared up at Regeane with mutinous eyes. "My dress scratches."

"Show some gratitude," Regeane said. "Is this your manner to a friend who confers benefits on you? What would your father say? Lucilla had you dressed for the feast at her own expense. She's given you a fine new gown and all you can say is it scratches. Curtsey and say thank you."

Elfgifa curtsied, or rather bent her knees a little, and said, "Thank you. I don't mean to be ungrateful. My father says we should always love our friends and those who do us good, but," she fingered the heavy satin dress, "why do they put the rough part on the inside and the smooth part on the outside? The ends of the gold threads chafe my skin."

"The smooth part goes on the outside because it looks better that way," Lucilla said.

"Well, then, why can't I wear it to the party inside out, then take it off and put it on the other way?" she asked.

"Because you can't," Lucilla said, "that's why. Just think how silly you'd look in the street in front of the pope's villa taking your dress off and putting it back on."

"I'd rather look silly than itch," Elfgifa said. "Besides . . ." She suddenly broke off and sniffed at Augusta's dress. "She smells."

"You forgot to say she smells good," Lucilla said acidly.

"All right. She smells good," Elfgifa said, "but she still smells strong. Like violets."

Regeane did notice the odor of violets was almost overpowering near Augusta.

Augusta looked down her long aristocratic nose at Elfgifa. "The perfume is almost my own personal signature. My maid prepares it according to a formula of her own devising, from the petals of fresh flowers gathered every spring. I have received many compliments . . ." She broke off with an exasperated sound. "But why am I explaining myself to a child? Mother, is it absolutely necessary she accompany us?"

"Yes, it is," Lucilla said. "I believe I may have located an aunt of hers among the Saxons living in Rome. The woman, the abbess of a convent in the Saxon quarter, will be at the feast."

Elfgifa looked alarmed. She pulled her hand free of Regeane's. "I don't want to go home," she said. "I want to stay here and play with Postumous."

"She didn't leave?" Regeane asked.

"Oh, yes, she did," said Lucilla. "While you were sleeping, she went over the wall again. My servants found her a few hours later rolling around in the gutter with the dirty little urchin."

"He was teaching me how to fight," Elfgifa said proudly. "There's a trick where you can blind a man and another place where you get your fingers and squeeze." The little girl began a demonstration of how it was done by reaching down between her legs.

"Mother," Augusta gasped.

Lucilla snatched Elfgifa's hand, pulling her upright and saying, "Young woman, I don't think we want any further pearls of the wisdom imparted to you by Postumous just now, if you please."

"Why not?" Elfgifa asked. "He's teaching me words, too, and—"

"Don't say them!" Lucilla said in a voice of stone.

"Why not?" Elfgifa asked, surprised.

"Just don't," she answered, hustling Elfgifa to the entrance of the villa. "Regeane, you will travel in Augusta's litter. Elfgifa, you will come with me. We need to have a talk."

AUGUSTA'S LITTER WAS, AS LUCILLA'S, A LUXU-rious accommodation drawn by a team of white mules. Since they were away from the more crowded quarter where the poor lived, they traveled with the curtains open. Regeane found the slow pace favored by Augusta led to a much more comfortable ride than her earlier one with Lucilla.

The mules took a narrow twisting street bordered on both sides by the walled gardens belonging to the sumptuous villas of the very rich.

Regeane reclined at Augusta's side.

"A most ill-mannered and undisciplined child," Augusta

said. She was peering into a mirror, using the last light of evening to make sure none of her powder and paint was smeared and not a hair of her elaborate coiffure was out of place.

The wolf rose up out of the darkness in Regeane's brain, took a good look at Augusta, and sniffed in disgust. The overpowering scent of violets really was almost too much.

Augusta heard the sniff and said, "What?"

Regeane slapped the wolf down. Emboldened by the softening of the light, the wolf wanted to be off. She wanted to jump down from the litter to the street. Leap the high walls of the villas and investigate with her eyes and nose the green gardens beyond them. She wanted to enjoy the changes in the slowly fading evening. The soft decline of the day from gold to rose into the tranquil blue of twilight. To riot among fountains and flowers, sniffing air redolent of pine and cypress.

The wolf didn't want to think. She wanted to live and taste the pleasures of a world denied to both wolf and woman for so long.

"What?" Augusta repeated and broke in on Regeane's longings.

"Nothing," Regeane said hurriedly.

Augusta looked critically at Regeane. "You are attractive, but then, the chief charm of youth is youth. Tell me, did your mother run to fat as she aged?"

Regeane remembered her pale, quiet mother. She had seemed only a small thickening of the blankets when Regeane had gone to rouse her on that last morning. But for the face on the pillow and the hands folded under her cheek, there would have seemed nothing in the bed at all.

Regeane hadn't needed to touch Gisela to know her long struggle with an endless procession of sorrows was ended. She had touched her, though, on the cheek and the texture of the flesh had reminded her horribly and incongruously of the flesh of a fresh-killed chicken: cold and a little damp with the night dew. Dew that doesn't settle on a warm, living skin. Then she'd stood for a long moment, seeking screams or even tears in herself and not finding them.

She'd stood knowing something, she couldn't quite say what, something important had finally ended.

She stood quietly, trying to remember how much she'd once loved the shell lying in the bed before her. Trying and not finding the love anymore than she could find the tears or screams. And then, she'd gone to Gundabald and sent Hugo to fetch a priest.

"What is wrong with you?" Augusta asked.

Regeane realized her thoughts must show in her face. "My mother died only recently," she said quietly. "But no, since you ask, my mother was quite a slim woman all her life."

"I'm sorry my remarks inadvertently caused you pain," Augusta said.

She didn't sound sorry, Regeane thought. In fact, she'd picked up the mirror again and was studying her face in it.

"But doubtless you'll find consolation in your happy betrothal."

Regeane almost laughed out loud, but caught herself at the last moment.

"It isn't wise for a young girl like yourself to stay in mourning for too long, to wear a sorrowful countenance and go about veiled in black. Your chances pass you by."

"Yes," Regeane answered mechanically.

The litter creaked around a corner. For a moment Regeane could see all of Rome spread out before her. The Tiber was a ribbon of fire and the buildings were engulfed in the glowing golden haze of the setting sun.

"Your family was wise to draw you away from your grief," Augusta said. "This mountain lord, Maeniel, is, I understand, a very wealthy man."

The wolf was suddenly awake, alert, listening with every sense sharpened to the fullest. Regeane knew something was wrong. But what? "So I understand," she answered cautiously.

The mules drawing the litter turned the corner and the city lying in its pool of light was lost to view. Blue dusk hovered in the narrow street between the high walls. The torchlight of Augusta's soldiers flared against the stone.

Regeane tried frantically to think of a way to escape, to get past the soldiers guarding the carriage at the front and rear.

She realized she was sitting rigid, her back pressed against the cushions and her fists clenched. She tried to relax and

straightened her fingers slowly. Luckily, Augusta was still preoccupied with the mirror and she hadn't seen Regeane flinch.

Regeane knew she was in danger. She didn't understand why
or what kind, but danger it was because she remembered the
text of the note Lucilla sent to Augusta requesting her sponsor-
ship of Regeane. And she had been present throughout the conversation with Augusta. Even though Lucilla had mentioned
that Regeane was respectably betrothed, she had never once
spoken Maeniel's name to Augusta. As far as Regeane knew,
there was only one other person from whom Augusta could
have learned that name . . .

From Gundabald.

XIII

REGEANE SPENT THE REST OF THE RIDE TO THE LAT-
eran palace trying to tell herself not to be a fool. Telling herself
there were at least a dozen ways Augusta could have learned
Maeniel's name other than from talking to Gundabald.

Perhaps gossip about the marriage was circulating among
the Roman nobility. Perhaps Lucilla had spoken to Augusta at
some other time. Perhaps . . .

But one thing Regeane did not do was ask Augusta for an explanation of how she knew Maeniel's name. Nor did she show
by any word or expression that she'd noticed anything unusual
about the conversation.

After all, she reasoned, the explanation might be the one she
feared, and if it was, she wanted herself and not Augusta on her
guard.

It was dark when they arrived at the Lateran palace and, for a
time, all thoughts of danger fled from Regeane's mind. Nothing

in her life before had prepared her for such splendor. She was caught up in a welter of confused impressions.

The Lateran, like many other Roman houses, showed a blank forbidding facade to the street, but beyond the columned portico, luxury reigned supreme.

From a vestibule presided over by frescoes of the Three Graces and the Nine Muses, they entered a magnificent peristyle garden ablaze with lights and filled with the whole glittering panoply of Rome's first families.

The splendid dress of the men, women, and children rivaled the very torches, set among the tall cypresses, shedding their light on the paths and flower beds.

Pools and fountains were everywhere. They splashed and sparkled, reflecting the jeweled finery of the guests and the flames of the torches.

Augusta took Regeane by the hand and then, like some magnificent regal butterfly, began guiding her among the groups of people gathered in the garden.

At first, Regeane felt awkward. She knew there must be so many things she didn't know—sophisticated nuances of behavior must be required of those at home among this dazzling throng, matters of precedence and protocol simply impossible to imagine.

But she quickly learned very little was expected of her except to look demure, and allow herself to be admired.

And admired she was. Within a few short minutes of entering the garden, Regeane received more compliments than she'd ever received in her entire life. Augusta made much of her royal connections and carefully avoided mentioning her present poverty, staying with each group only long enough to allow Regeane to be seen and appreciated, carefully preventing any conversations lengthy enough for Regeane to betray any embarrassing ignorance of Roman affairs.

Besides, Regeane decided, people probably expected very little sophistication of a girl her age being presented in society for the first time.

Regeane was breathless when Augusta paused for a few moments near a moss-covered fountain in the shadows at the edge of the lighted garden.

"Is your head quite turned by all this?"

Regeane recognized the voice as Lucilla's. It came from the shadows near the fountain.

"No, not quite," Regeane said. "Addled a bit, but not turned. Though it looks like fun."

Lucilla chuckled. "It is, yet I don't really belong here. Not the way Augusta does. Most people are polite to me. They never know when they may need my influence with Hadrian. Others pretend I don't exist. But I have a few real friends here and I enjoy these affairs for the pleasure of meeting them."

"Mother, really. You're impossible," Augusta said. "Almost everyone here is at least polite to you."

"Yes," Lucilla said. "I suppose that's true. Time has taken its toll on the recalcitrants. I'm almost an institution, though, like the pretty fountain behind you—look at it closely, my girl."

"Don't!" Augusta warned. "That fountain is no sight for a maiden."

But Regeane was already looking, and her cheeks were burning.

The fountain running along the wall was a frieze of nymphs and satyrs. One of the horned and hoofed men was pissing enthusiastically into the pool. Water spurted from his engorged member. Another was embracing a nymph with one hand while his wine pitcher clutched in the other dumped its contents into the pool at his feet. The rest were coupling in lusty delight, their nude bodies arranged in every possible position of human sexual congress.

"Oh," Regeane said, and then, "Ooohahaha!"

Lucilla laughed.

Augusta flung Regeane's hand away and stalked off into the crowd gathered in the garden.

"She's angry," Regeane said. "I'm sorry. I suppose I shouldn't have looked."

"Nonsense!" Lucilla snapped. "You should examine anything you want to. Besides, I make it a point to infuriate Augusta at least once every time we meet. In any case, she's served her turn. I wanted you to be seen by the nobility of the city in her company, not mine. You have been, and so it's done. At the feast tonight, you and Elfgifa will recline beside her. Her anger or goodwill are quite beside the point. The seating arrangements aren't under her control, but the pope's. You are, after all, royal. She will probably be quite pleased to be placed so near his couch, beside you."

Regeane took another long look at the fountain and, to her surprise, found her eyes prickling as they slowly filled with tears. "They seem so happy," she said softly.

"Love is a happy thing," Lucilla said. "I have found it so, and I hope some day you will, too. But come, we haven't much time and I want you to meet Hadrian privately before the feast begins."

"Lucilla, how did Augusta learn Maeniel's name?" Regeane asked. "Did you tell her? She mentioned it on the way here in the litter."

Lucilla paused. Her eyes narrowed. "No, I didn't. I operate on the premise that the less Augusta knows about my business the better. She's a conformist, terrified she'll make even the slightest social error. She quakes at the thought of incurring even the mildest form of displeasure from her husband's incredibly snobbish family. She's my own beloved daughter, but she isn't very strong or very smart.

"I can't believe she's up to anything. She doesn't dare court my displeasure either. But I'll keep an eye on her, just in case. Someone else may have told her. Gossip rolls like the sea in Rome. What is said at the Lateran is being repeated within the hour at the Vatican. No one can keep their mouth shut—least of all Augusta."

Lucilla led Regeane away from the lighted garden, crossing the small shadowy courtyards, all dark and silent under the glow of the stars. Away from the magnificent reception rooms deep into the villa's private heart.

They found him seated on a bench in a small, quiet garden. A lamp burned on the bench by his side. He was feeding bread to the carp in a pool at his feet.

Drawn by the bread and the light, the fish were shadows moving in the water, given away only by the gleam of an eye or the flash of shiny scales catching the light.

"My dear," Lucilla said softly.

Hadrian raised his head, threw the last bread into the water, and said, "Lucilla."

And Regeane heard his heart in the word, in the way it was spoken.

Lucilla walked toward him, her hands outstretched.

He took her hands and they gazed at each other for a long moment before they embraced. She stood quietly in the circle of his arms, her head on his shoulder.

"My dear," Lucilla said, "my very dear. What are you doing hiding here alone?"

"I was visiting with some old friends," he said, indicating with a glance the fish in the pool, "and waiting to greet another friend." He let her go. They stood together, hand in hand, watching the fish moving in the water at their feet.

"Well, I've brought yet another friend to greet you," Lucilla said. She beckoned to Regeane.

Regeane stepped into the circle of light. As she drew closer, she lifted the stiff, brocade dress and tried to kneel and kiss the pope's ring.

Instead, Hadrian—Stephen—caught her by the elbows, raised her, and kissed her gently on the forehead. "There now," he said to Lucilla, standing beside him. "That's a lot better than having my ring kissed and," he continued with a quick wink at Lucilla, "it's a lot more fun."

He took Regeane by the shoulders and held her back to have a good look at her. "Lucilla tells me you were able to get Antonius away from Basil into some safe hiding place."

"Yes," she answered in an uncertain voice, thinking furiously all the while, *How much has Lucilla told him? Is he going to demand an explanation?*

But he didn't. Instead, Hadrian began to examine Regeane herself, looking her up and down and meanwhile nodding his head in approval. Then he patted Regeane's cheek and said to Lucilla, "You've done wonders with her, my dear."

Lucilla gave a self-deprecating little shrug and smiled. "She was born beautiful. A few nice clothes, a new hairdo. She has a natural grace that's all her own and shows itself even in strange surroundings. I wonder if the Frankish king knows he has such a prize among his royal ladies? If he did, he might see fit to bestow her higher than—"

"No, no," Hadrian said. "This marriage is very important. Come into my library and I'll explain further."

The library was separated from the garden by a simple curtained colonnade. The walls were lined with bound books and had niches for scrolls.

Regeane's gasp of delight stopped both Hadrian and Lucilla in their tracks.

"She liked my library, also," Lucilla said.

"The special one?" Hadrian asked.

Lucilla nodded. "My heavens, she didn't even look at our little fountain that way."

"No?" Hadrian said with a lift of his eyebrows. Then he echoed Augusta. "You showed her our fountain? Hardly a sight for a maiden."

"A maiden, soon to become a married woman. She needs to know what she's facing," Lucilla said waspishly.

"Lucilla," Regeane said soberly, "I don't think love's joy or love's delight has a lot to do with what I'm facing."

"You can never tell," Lucilla began.

"No, you can't," Hadrian broke in on her, "but on balance, I think the girl is right in learning to prefer the more sedate independent pleasures of intellectual inquiry. They often serve to comfort a troubled spirit when events in the world go awry. So, you like to read?" he asked Regeane.

"Yes," she answered. "Sometimes when I was younger," Regeane gave Lucilla a quick, warning glance. "I was . . . alone for long periods of time. My stepfather had a large library— over sixty books. They were, as you have said, a great comfort to me in my . . . loneliness."

Hadrian gestured expansively toward the shelves lining the walls. "Books are meant to be read, and mine, alas, often simply sit and gather dust since affairs of state leave me little time for them. So if there are any here of particular interest to you I would be glad . . ."

"Have you a life of Alexander?" Regeane asked. "I've often read of the doings of the noblest among the Greeks. I'd like to know more about him."

"I have three good lives of Alexander," Hadrian said. "I'll send you one. Your stepfather had sixty books. That's quite a fine library for a layman. What happened to them?"

Regeane lowered her eyes. "Gundabald sold them along with the rest," she said.

"Gundabald again . . ." the pope mused and scratched his chin. "But no matter, sit down. We have not much time. Soon I must join my guests."

Lucilla and Hadrian sat down side by side on a cushioned bench and Regeane took the high-backed chair opposite them.

"Regeane," Hadrian said, "Regeane, you notice I call you friend and I treat you as one of my intimates. Do you know why?"

Regeane shook her head.

"Because," he continued, "Lucilla calls you friend. And she dignifies very few people with that name, reserving it only for those who have done her a great service, or she feels are absolutely loyal. Do you understand?"

Regeane nodded.

The couple's hands clasped and their fingers intertwined. They looked into each other's eyes and smiled. Then Hadrian turned his attention back to Regeane.

"Since Lucilla calls you friend, I'm going to trust you, too. But what I say must never leave this room. Do you understand?"

"Yes," Regeane said.

"Very well, then, I must tell you. In the spring, Charles, king of the Franks, will cross the Alps and make war on the Lombards in my behalf. That's why your marriage is so important, Regeane. Maeniel's principality straddles his line of march. It must be secured by his submission to Charles before his spring campaign."

Lucilla leaped to her feet and strode quickly toward the colonnade that separated the room from the garden. She stared up at the stars.

"We've done it," she said quietly, almost to herself. Then she repeated more loudly, "We've done it," and stood, fists clenched over her head and shouted, "We've done it!"

"Yes," Hadrian said simply. "We have."

Regeane felt the blood drain out of her face, leaving it numb.

She seemed to hear an audible click as the jaws of the trap snapped shut. "There is no help for it then," she muttered between clenched teeth. "I must marry him."

"Yes." Lucilla gave Regeane a look of fierce delight. "But how long such a marriage will last once Charles is master of Lombardy is a matter of some conjecture."

Lucilla walked back toward Hadrian. She radiated power and had the step of a queen. "We've done it," she said, "and a peasant girl from the Abruzzi holds the fate of nations in her hand. I can't believe it. But why is my Antonius the price?"

Hadrian took her hand again, pulled her down on the seat beside him, and kissed her on the lips.

"Why is it so important that the Frankish king win?" Regeane asked.

"In a word," Hadrian answered, "peace."

"Peace?"

"Look around you, girl. Have you no eyes? Over half this city, once the most populous in the world, lies in ruins. Every day the poor troop to the churches and almshouses of this city, hands outstretched, begging for bread.

"Our fountains that once ran with the clear, pure water of mountain streams are green and stagnant, filled only by the rain. The aqueducts that once fed them are abandoned or lie in the hands of our enemies. Barbarian kings fight over the papal tiara like dogs over a bone. Each hopes to place his own candidate on the throne of the first apostle and use the church as a tool to further his own ambitions."

"I still can't see how Charles is superior to Desiderius or the Duke of Spoleto or any of these other kings," Regeane said.

"Regeane, do you presume to question?" Lucilla said in rebuke.

"No. No. No." Hadrian said, rapid as finger snaps. "I'm glad she's not a rattle-brained little ninny. In fact, her inquiry puts me in mind of you at her age and it's the same sort of point you would have raised."

Lucilla smiled. "Yes, I suppose that's true. I questioned you often at first."

Hadrian smiled back at her. He rested one hand on her hair, drew her face close, and kissed her on the forehead. "No, her question is a very good one." He settled his arm over Lucilla's shoulders and turned back to Regeane.

"Charles is like the rest—a very ambitious man and he, too, has definite ideas about the role of the church as a cornerstone of state policy. But," Hadrian raised his finger, "he has already guaranteed my independence as ruler of the Duchy of Rome and has promised to return those lands stolen by Desiderius and the other Lombard kings. And," he added triumphantly, "he is very far away. In short, Rome cannot be ruled from Franca, nor can Franca be ruled from Rome."

"I see," Regeane said slowly. Hadrian was playing off one distant state against another, closer one. "A very dangerous game you are engaged in," she said. "And when the Lombard king learns of your agreement with the Franks—and he will, it cannot be kept secret forever—he'll be wild. He'll use every means he can think of to destroy you."

Lucilla laughed. "Oh, you child. He already has."

"Yes," Hadrian said. "Why do you think he kidnapped Antonius and threatened to crucify him?"

Regeane shook her head. "I don't have any idea."

Hadrian leaned forward toward her. "He wanted to force me, at the price of Antonius' life, to anoint the sons of Carloman made into kings by my hand, those two little boys, his dead brother's sons, would be rival claimants for the throne Charles sits on. They'd be a focus for every kind of rebellion and dissatisfaction. Every troublemaker and malcontent would try to attach himself to their cause.

"Charles is young, and though he looks to become a great king, many still doubt him. Yet others will try to test him. Some out of greed or a lust for power. In short, my intervention, if it be bought or coerced by Desiderius, could make Charles' throne a very shaky seat.

"Archimedes is supposed to have said, 'If I had a lever, I could move the world.' Well, those two little boys are the lever I have used to bring Charles across the Alps to aid me in my battle with the Lombards. To yield to Desiderius' demands that I anoint them would destroy all my carefully laid plans and probably—I must mention this in passing—cost me my life as well."

Lucilla drew away from Hadrian and rested her back against the cushions at the arm of the bench. "Now do you see why Antonius must die?"

"Is that why you brought me here," Regeane shot back at her, "to be a party to murder?" From the corner of her eye, Regeane saw the glow of distant lightning. It was too far away for thunder, but a gust of wind set the curtains that divided the library from the garden to flapping and rattling.

"Hush, girl," Hadrian replied sternly. "There's no question of your killing Antonius or anyone else." Then he reached toward Lucilla and placed his hand on her face. "No, my dear. I won't give the order and neither will you."

"But you must," Lucilla cried desperately, hysterically, "You must. My God, yesterday . . ." She seized him by the shoulders and shook him. "Yesterday the mob gathered around my litter and threw stones at me, called me the pope's whore and accused you of being tainted by the devil's curse, the vile disease. Hadrian, don't you think I love Antonius?"

He embraced her and she rocked back, pushing him away with her hands as though she would deny comfort to herself. "There was a time when he was my life. I lived only for him. But I won't, I can't let you be pulled down, broken by the corpse of a man rotten already before he lies in his winding sheet."

Regeane shivered, dulled both by the cold blast of air driven before the storm and by her memory of the ghosts waiting in their temple high above the sea.

"No," Hadrian said implacably. "No, I won't give the order and neither will you. Not only because I love you both, but because I know myself and I know what I can live with. No. I called him brother for far too long. Besides, even his death might not save me. There already is talk of a synod of bishops being convened—no doubt inspired by my good friends Desiderius and Basil the Lombard—to try me and determine my fitness for the office of supreme pontiff. If I should be judged tainted by Antonius' disease, well then . . ."

He drew Lucilla toward him and she rested her head on his shoulder like a tired child. Tears streamed down her cheeks.

"And so," she asked, "after we've come so far, will we fail in the end?"

"Perhaps," Hadrian answered, his lips in her hair. "Perhaps, but we'll fail as we began, honorably, honestly, because I can't believe however . . . irregular . . . our love has been or seemed in the eyes of the world, it has never been less than honest and honorable."

Lucilla drew away from him slightly and smiled up at him through her tears. "Yes, that's true, isn't it? We've both tried to do our best for this beleaguered, war-weary city and its people, haven't we?"

Hadrian nodded. "Yes, my friend. We have, and that's why I won't yield to your demands or Desiderius'. You spoke a while ago of having the destiny of men and nations in your hands."

"And do I find in Antonius' fate only a rebuke to my pride?" she asked.

"No," Hadrian answered, "but of its price, the price of responsibility. If worse comes to worst, I'll abdicate. And rather than allow harm to come to you or Antonius, I would abdicate. After all, others can pursue my policies as well as—or better than—I can. It doesn't do for a man in my position to start believing he's indispensable."

He chuckled. "After all, countless men have occupied the see of Peter and doubtless many more will sit where I'm sitting and try to convince themselves they, and they alone, are God's anointed singulars and cannot be replaced. But I'm not so naive, Lucilla. I understand perfectly that I am but one link in a human chain stretching back through the ages and forward into generations yet unborn. I will not save myself at the price of infamy."

"Infamy, no," Regeane said, "but . . ."

Both Hadrian and Lucilla started, and Regeane realized that they'd almost forgotten she was there.

"I believe," she continued slowly, "that I can help Antonius, perhaps even save him. Only don't . . ." She stuttered the words a little and realized now that she was bargaining for her future. She was terribly afraid. She gathered herself together and pressed on. "Don't ask me too many questions about how . . ."

Hadrian smiled and Regeane saw, even in the half-darkened room, the same glint of authority in his eyes she'd seen when they first met.

"Don't ask too many questions, eh?"

"Please don't," she quavered.

Hadrian grinned. "Never fear," he said. "As I told you, over the years I've learned those who Lucilla calls friend are discreet and reliable. I've also learned not to question them too closely about their activities."

Regeane breathed a deep sigh of relief. "Thank you."

"A polite girl," Hadrian said ironically.

"An unusual girl," Lucilla said. "A very unusual girl."

Hadrian turned toward Lucilla and raised one eyebrow.

"I beg you, my love. Listen carefully to what she has to say," Lucilla said.

Regeane took a deep breath. "I will want something for myself."

"What?" Hadrian asked.

"I want you," Regeane said, "to draw up the marriage contract, not my uncle, Gundabald; and I want the contract to contain a provision allowing me my own domicile, my own servants and men-at-arms."

The pope's eyes narrowed as he studied Regeane. "You really are afraid of this man, aren't you? So afraid you want to live apart from him."

"Yes," Regeane answered simply. "I do."

Hadrian's brows drew together into a deep frown as he looked from Lucilla to Regeane and back again. "There is no help for Antonius."

Lucilla didn't answer. She stood up. She was as beautifully dressed as the rest of the pope's guests in a long chemise of green silk, embroidered with white roses that brought out her splendid strawberry blond coloring and fair complexion. She drifted away from Hadrian toward a doorway in the far corner of the room. "I've been crying," she said. "I'll need to repair my face. I need a mirror."

"You are as lovely as always," Hadrian said with sweet gallantry, "but if you don't believe my assurances, there's a mirror on the table by the door." Then he turned and stared at Regeane. "I can see," he said, "that neither of you intends to tell me anything more about your plans."

Regeane's fists were tightly clenched in her lap. The knuckles were white. She didn't answer.

"No," Lucilla said, standing over the table. It was cluttered with books, loose parchments, wax tablets, pens, ink, and other miscellaneous administrative paraphernalia. "A mirror here?"

"A great deal of chancery work goes on in this room," Hadrian said. "All sort of things end up here."

"But a mirror," Lucilla commented, beginning to sort through the objects on the table.

Outside, Regeane saw the lightning cut a bright jagged path across the sky. She heard in the distance a faint rumble of thunder.

Another breath, not strong enough to be called a breeze, wafted from the distant rainstorm and freshened the stuffiness of the room. Regeane was conscious of the wolf's silent, sullen rebellion.

What had she to do with politics, or feasts, or costly raiment?

Outside, the rain would be sweeping across the Campagna. The wolf wanted to run with the rain, watch the storm fires sweep across the heavens, and thrill to the thunder rolling through the clouds. Be a part of the storm's majesty as it moved across the winter countryside.

But the woman shouldered her aside and realized Hadrian hadn't given her an answer. "The marriage contract," she repeated.

"Yes," he said shrewdly, "the marriage contract. Tell me, how much of this man's wealth do you plan to take as part of the bargain? A third? A fourth? As much as he will yield for the privilege of being married to a woman of the royal house?"

Hadrian's eyes fixed on Regeane, cold and compelling in the candlelight.

Regeane was surprised at the ferocity in her voice as she answered. "His wealth? I hadn't given his *money*—" She spat the word contemptuously. "—one single thought until you brought it up. I only want to assure my own safety. I'm *afraid*."

The word seemed to carry the whole fright of her terror from the black depths of her own soul out into the open. "I'm afraid," she cried. "Can't you see how frightened I am?"

Hadrian drew back. "Yes, I can see. Your fear is immense. I

don't quite comprehend the reason for it, but yes, I can see that it is."

"Perhaps," Lucilla said, "that's because you've never been a woman."

"Yes," Hadrian answered, "and perhaps it's because you and this girl with the pretty, innocent face are up to some tricks so nefarious you don't dare acquaint me with the details."

Lucilla had found the mirror and was walking back toward Hadrian with the silver circlet held down against her gown.

"I seem to remember you taking the matter of Paul Afartha on yourself," Hadrian snapped back at her, "signing his death warrant."

"I signed nothing," Lucilla said. "I only let the Archbishop of Ravenna know that you wouldn't be prostrate with grief if Paul died suddenly. And he did—die suddenly," she said with cold satisfaction in her voice.

"So suddenly," Hadrian said, "that he had no time for contrition."

Lucilla seemed stunned into fury by his words. "In the name of God, Hadrian. How much time did Paul give Sergus for contrition? He was blinded, beaten, half strangled, and thrust into his tomb while he was still struggling, to die of suffocation in agony and despair. I'd like to remind you, Sergus was your friend and mine."

All at once Hadrian looked old and tired. "Very well," he said quietly. "The bargain is made. The terms of the marriage contract will be as you wish."

Regeane took a deep breath and let out a long, fluttering sigh.

Lucilla looked into the mirror in her hand. Her shriek echoed through the room. A second later the silver clattered and rang on the stone floor as Lucilla flung it away from her as though it were a living serpent.

The mirror skittered across the marble and came to rest at Regeane's feet. She leaned forward in the chair and looked down into the silver reflecting surface.

The face she saw was not her own. Regeane started back, jerking her eyes away. Lightning flashed, this time close enough to illuminate the room brightly for a second. The curtains belled out in the wind.

"Adraste's mirror!" Lucilla screamed. "Adraste's mirror here!" Her face was the color of ash, blue around the mouth and eyes. Regeane knew she had also felt the presence pass.

"Nonsense," Hadrian snapped impatiently. "Calm yourself, Lucilla. How could Adraste's mirror be here?"

Lucilla stood still, one hand pressed against her breast for a moment, then regained her composure with an obvious effort of will. In the distance, Regeane heard the music begin.

In the garden, big, fat drops of rain began to splat against the flagstones and splash in the fishpond.

Hadrian rose from the bench. "We must go now," he said. "My guests will be gathering in the triclinium, waiting for me to greet them."

Regeane picked up the mirror at her feet. She felt the same as she had at Cumae. The same dazed sense of unreality she had felt when the ghostly procession passed her by. She knew the mirror was there for her, sent to her somehow, but why she couldn't begin to guess. Still she took it, and dropped it between the silk lining and the heavy brocade outer dress.

Hadrian paused next to Lucilla and gave her a quick kiss, saying sadly, "Tonight after the feast, we can be alone."

Their faces, the way they looked at each other, reminded Regeane very much of an old, married couple who had seen many changes in fortune, many struggles, but who still clung together, and bound by ties shaped over a lifetime, and by love, by laughter, and by tears until they had now reached a kind of peaceful understanding that no worldly crisis could breach.

"My love," Lucilla said and touched his face. Then Hadrian was gone and they were alone.

"Come," Lucilla said. "Hadrian's right. We must hurry." She lifted a lamp from the table and began to guide Regeane through the shadowy maze of rooms back to the triclinium where the feast was being held.

They had reached a long, covered colonnaded porch when Lucilla stopped, shielding the lamp flame with her hand to wait for the wind to die down. It drove the rain across the porch in wavering curtains and water streamed in silver sheets from the overhang.

Regeane and Lucilla stood as the wind twisted and turned the bushes and trees in the garden and the rain fell in torrents.

"I don't know what you're planning," Lucilla said softly, "but I advise you to keep Antonius hidden." She seized Regeane's arm and Regeane felt her nails bite into the flesh. "And if you think to terrorize me with your other shape, think again. I'm not afraid of wolves. I saw them often when I tended my father's flocks in the mountains. They are cowardly beasts that can be driven off by stones and curses."

Regeane twisted her arm out of Lucilla's grip with one, quick movement, saying, "I cannot be driven off by stones and curses."

Outside the wind died. The rain poured straight down, a dense, roaring flood. The storm was at its height. A haze of moisture drifted through the portico, settling on Regeane's hair and face.

Lucilla stepped forward. "Come away. You'll ruin your dress."

Regeane stayed where she was, feeling the wolf rise strong and uneasy inside her. "Something's wrong. There is danger. The wolf feels it. I feel it," she whispered.

"Of course there's danger. You're in danger right now from me, if only you had the wit to see it. I'm not Hadrian. Hadrian is a man. He can afford to be complacent. The mob would weep if he abdicated, but that selfsame mob would blame me, sack my villa, and drag me through the streets to face a Lombard tribunal that would be only too happy to take my life. Any and all of these things might happen if Antonius is found. My life depends on you, and I'm not even sure what you are."

"It won't comfort you to know," Regeane said, "that I'm not sure either. I've never had a chance to learn."

Regeane turned to Lucilla and Lucilla took a step backward and gave vent to a hoarse cry. "Don't . . . don't look at me," she stammered. "Your eyes reflect the lamplight like . . . an animal's."

"Like a wolf," Regeane said. She could hear the harsh sound of Lucilla's breathing. "Lucilla," she implored. "Please . . ." She extended her hand into the darkness, but Lucilla only drew a little further away from her. "Lucilla, are you losing your nerve? Tell me what's wrong? What's really wrong?"

"Regeane, why did you take Adraste's mirror? I know it's Adraste's. The pattern is original, her own. She drew it for the silversmith who made it. The same pattern was on all her personal possessions."

"Because the mirror was sent to me, meant for me," Regeane said. She moved toward Lucilla again.

"Don't come any closer. Don't come near me," Lucilla whispered. "The last time I saw that mirror was when I placed it in Adraste's coffin. Then they closed the stone lid of her sarcophagus forever over the mirror, over Adraste's lovely, evil, greedy face. I know where that mirror came from . . . because I put it in her hand."

XIV

REGEANE WALKED TO HER COUCH IN THE TRI-clinium over a carpet of flowers.

The room was as beautiful as any church Regeane had ever seen. The flower-strewn floor was patterned with green and white marble.

Couches covered with purple silk velvet were arranged around two enormous half-moon-shaped tables. The pope's couch occupied the space near the back wall in the opening between two ends of the tables. It was set high on a raised dais.

Musicians were gathered in the open area between the two semi-circular tables and the soft waterfall of notes from the harp and cythera mingled with the plaintive cry of the flutes.

On the curved walls, the larger-than-life frescoes of the twelve apostles looked down on the silks and velvets of the glittering guests.

From a tall mosaic panel in the center of the room behind the pope's couch, a stiff Byzantine Christ gazed down, his hand raised to bless the pontiff at dinner.

The apostles in the frescoes weren't stiff or formal. They strolled together in groups through the lush beauty of a Roman summer. They resembled a crowd of peasants taking their ease at siesta time beneath the trees, heavy with fruit and foliage. Looking out over meadows alight with scarlet poppies and golden wheat ripening in the fields. Mark's lion played like a kitten in the long, green grass. Matthew's eagle soared like a falcon on the hunt. Peter lounged under a tree, his keys in his belt, nets folded beside him.

"Antonius!" Regeane said sadly.

"Yes," Lucilla answered. "At first I thought he was mad hanging around those silly painters' workshops, grinding colors, messing with plaster and stucco when Hadrian could have sponsored him. Assured him of a brilliant career in the church. But then when I saw what he produced . . . Alas, we poor Romans, floundering in a sea of barbarism, can still comfort ourselves with beauty. As though it were important," she added bitterly.

Regeane, still gazing at the magnificent painting, said, "It is."

"Yes," Lucilla said thoughtfully. "Yes, you're right. Perhaps these things are our immortality. Perhaps it is for them that we will be remembered when all else is dust."

Elfgifa was standing beside Regeane's couch. Augusta's friends were making a big fuss over her. Indeed, dressed in adult clothing, her hair braided with pearls as Regeane's, she looked a perfect little doll.

A big woman, dressed in the sober garb of a nun, pushed her way through the crowd around them and introduced herself. "I am the Abbess Emilia, and that, unless I miss my guess," she pointed to the child, "is Elfgifa."

The ladies around the child parted to let Abbess Emilia through. Emilia confronted Elfgifa with hands on her hips, an expression of disapproval on her face.

"Aunt Emilia," Elfgifa said.

"Don't 'Aunt Emilia' me, you naughty child. Your father has been frantic with worry about you."

Elfgifa's lower lip began to slide out and Regeane knew this was a danger sign.

"It wasn't my fault I was captured by pirates."

"Yes, it was," Emilia boomed. "You know very well you were told not to run away and play with the fishermen's sons. Our coast isn't safe," she explained to the rest. "The Northmen prowl everywhere, looking for loot, trying to take our people as slaves and sell them to the Greeks. Your father was afraid you were lost forever. In fact," Emilia shook her finger in Elfgifa's face, "you've grown up so much that even if I had found you, I don't know if I'd have recognized you."

Elfgifa appealed to Regeane. "Why do they always say you've grown? What do they expect at my age, for me to get smaller? You've grown, too," she said to Emilia. "This way." The little girl spread her arms in a measuring gesture. "Stout."

A wave of soft titters swept the group of women around Emilia.

"Outrageous!" Lucilla said. "Young lady, not another word. Greet your aunt properly with a kiss on the cheek. I believe we had a discussion on the way here about the differences between private and public behavior."

"I remember," Elfgifa said, looking chastened and guilty.

Emilia folded her arms and stared down at the child. "It's Elfgifa, all right." She grinned and pinched her cheek and said to the child, "Fat is the word you want."

Elfgifa looked annoyed. "My father says 'fat' isn't nice," she insisted. "Stout."

Emilia gave a whoop of laughter. "My brother's daughter in everything. He's always twitting me about my girth. Happens whenever I see him, though that hasn't been for a few years now. God bless him. I tell him I'm not one to confuse piety with misery. My ladies in the convent spend their time in works of holy charity. We care for orphans, visit the sick, and feed and shelter those pilgrims that come to our door. Believe you me, a girl who's spent her night in sleepless vigil beside the bed of a dying man, or a long day supervising the education of a bunch of active youngsters doesn't need to come to the table and find a bowl of thin gruel and a few slices of black bread. We laborers in Christ's vineyards need to keep up our strength."

"I'm sure you do," Augusta murmured. "Now, as for the child . . ."

Elfgifa spun around and looked at Regeane accusingly. "You're going to send me away, aren't you?" Then she ran toward Regeane and threw herself into her arms.

Regeane clasped her and lifted her up, setting her on her hip. Elfgifa wrapped her arms around Regeane's neck and rested her cheek against hers.

For a moment Regeane was simply overwhelmed with love. She trembled with its intensity. "Don't you want to go home? Your Aunt Emilia will take good care of you until your father can come get you. She's a kind woman, isn't she?"

"Yes," Elfgifa said, "but she makes me study my letters. And she lectures me all the time about right and wrong. If I sneak off to play, she acts like I committed a sin, and she thinks I should work in the kitchen and scrub the pots. She won't let me climb trees and I have to stay inside when it rains. She nags, 'Stand up straight or you'll get a hump in your back.' 'Don't get your dress dirty.' My father says if you wear clothes they're *supposed* to get dirty and—"

Lucilla clapped her hands, bringing Elfgifa's tirade to an end. "Headstrong should have been your name, not Elfgifa. Regeane loves you. Try not to give her any more pain than you have to. Besides, a little work and discipline will do you good. Quickly enough you'll be returned to your father and allowed to run wild as usual."

"Oh, heavens," Emilia said, throwing up her arms. "It's true. He treats the child more like one of those wayward men of his. He treats her as though her thoughts and opinions mattered."

"That's because they do," Lucilla snapped. "She is the daughter of a thane, is she not? At the very least she'll become the mistress of a large household."

Emilia looked flustered for a moment, then gave Lucilla a quick smile. "I've never heard it put quite that way, but yes, I suppose you're right."

Lucilla spoke then to Elfgifa. "Regeane is sending you with Emilia because it's . . . at present, a lot safer. She loves you and wants what's best for you."

The child threw her head back and her deep, blue eyes looked sadly at Regeane.

Regeane's free hand stroked the soft curls at the back of Elfgifa's neck. "I want you to be happy and to preserve you from harm, little one," Regeane said in a very low voice to her, "and you wouldn't be either happy or safe with me. I want to see you with people who love you and can care for you properly." She shook her head. "Circumstances . . ." Words failed her for a moment and her eyes filled with tears. "Circumstances being what they are, I can't."

Elfgifa stared at Regeane solemnly for a moment, then tightened her arms around Regeane's neck. Her soft kiss was a whisper of love and trust against Regeane's cheek. "I'll be good," she promised, "and I'll try to do what Aunt Emilia tells me."

"Mother," Augusta said. "The pope is going to his couch. The feast is beginning. We must recline."

Regeane set Elfgifa down and found herself enveloped in Emilia's quick, unexpected embrace. "Thank you for your sweet compassion. You'll never know how happy it's made us to get the child back. My brother adores her. You have our eternal gratitude." Then she hurried away to join the other nuns seated across the room.

Lucilla nodded to Regeane as though she were a mere acquaintance and she, too, walked away toward her seat near the foot of the table.

Regeane stood for a moment, watching her, holding Elfgifa by the hand, Augusta beside her. "How strange," she murmured. "She must be one of the most powerful personages in Rome and yet propriety consigns her—"

"Be quiet," Augusta interrupted harshly as she looked quickly around. "Someone might hear you. My mother is continually a disgrace and an embarrassment to me," she added with an air of martyrdom. "She has sufficient fortune to live modestly—as a proper Roman matron should—and devote herself to the church, to relief of the poor. But instead she consorts openly with the lowest element in the city. She dabbles in politics and other matters unbecoming to a woman of rank. And above all, she continues to see a man whose company she should properly avoid as occasion of sin."

Regeane bit back the retort already forming in her mind. Elfgifa broke in on her angry thoughts to ask, "Are we going to eat lying down again?"

"Yes," Regeane said sternly. "It's the custom here and, as guests, we must do honor to our hosts."

"I didn't object," Elfgifa replied in an injured tone. "I was only asking."

THE MUSIC WAS SOOTHING AND BEAUTIFUL. THE conversation among the guests civilized and subdued, the food and many wines a complex tapestry of color and flavor, an embarrassment of riches.

Regeane was bewildered, but delighted by the first courses of the banquet. She and Elfgifa feasted on thrushes and bobolinks braised in a white wine sauce, their flesh permeated by the sweet taste of the figs used to fatten them.

Augusta gave them both a look of disapproval and contented herself with a salad of endive, watercress dressed with oil, a little honey, and some wine, saying, "At my age I have to watch my weight. The two of you should be more careful," she warned darkly. "The eating habits you form now will follow you all your life."

Elfgifa dutifully tried some of the salad and made a wry face at the bitter taste of the greens.

They were seated near the pope's couch and Regeane saw him smile at Elfgifa's reaction to the greens. Then he sent over a dish from his own table.

"For the child," the smiling servant said as he presented it to Elfgifa.

Augusta stiffened into complete disgust when she saw the contents of the dish—pears cooked in cinnamon honey and wine in a light sauce thickened only with a few egg yolks.

Elfgifa ignored Augusta's admonition that she would ruin her appetite for dinner and gorged herself saying, "I don't care. I like what's here now."

Servants then cleared away the heavy, scrolled silver dishes and the guests washed and dried their fingers. The serving man poured rosewater over their hands.

Elfgifa got rosewater up her nose because she tried simultaneously to sniff the scented water and wash her hands at the same time. She began sneezing violently.

Rigid with fury, Augusta lay propped on her right elbow, pretending Elfgifa didn't exist, while Regeane, scarlet with embarrassment, tried to repair the damage and stop the sneezes by bathing Elfgifa's face with a napkin steeped in the offending rosewater.

"Oh, good heavens," Regeane whispered, completely exasperated. "Can't you stay out of mischief for even one second?"

Elfgifa's little face scrunched itself up and she looked like she might begin to cry. Regeane was immediately consciencestricken.

"I'm sorry," Elfgifa said. "I didn't mean it. Only the water smelled good and I wanted—"

"Hush," Regeane said, taking the little girl's face between her hands and kissing her on the forehead. "There's a good girl. Now, don't cry."

Elfgifa refused to be comforted and hung her head. "Is that why you want to be rid of me? Because I'm not a good girl? I must be bad, because everyone's always telling me things to do and not to do and—oooh! Look how pretty!" she said, her grief forgotten like a passing shadow.

One of the serving men was offering the guests cups. They were glass, each in the shape of a different flower.

"Can I have any kind I want?" Elfgifa asked as the servant paused before them holding the tray laden with the glass confections. Elfgifa bounced up and down with delight. "I like the sunflower. No, the harebell. No, I don't know. The lily is so pretty."

"Don't kick so," Augusta said in a dreadful voice. "Make up your mind and don't break it."

Elfgifa subsided immediately and her two large, blue eyes instantly became pools of tears.

"Don't be cruel, Augusta," Regeane snapped. "She's only a child."

"So I've noticed," Augusta hissed. "A nasty, sloppy, hateful little . . ."

Elfgifa looked stricken and pressed close to Regeane's side.

Regeane could feel her own passionate anger drain the blood from her face and she draped her arm over Elfgifa's shoulders. "Yes," she said softly. "You can have any one you like."

"I think I like the blue harebell best," a subdued Elfgifa whispered to Regeane as she looked up fearfully at Augusta.

Regeane glanced at the servant. The handsome, young man was staring at Augusta with dislike.

"Very well," Regeane said. "I'll take the lily and," she added maliciously, "since you like it, Augusta will have the sunflower."

Regeane's lily was of rare, clear crystal, the petals each tipped in white, while Elfgifa's harebell was a pale blue streaked with darker sapphire markings, each placed to suggest the delicate coloration of the spring flowers.

The beverage served in the cups was a dessert wine. Regeane chose a sweet raisin, Elfgifa one scented with roses, and Augusta, predictably, took the beverage redolent of violets.

A young girl strolled into the opening between the tables and took her place near the musicians.

Conversation among the guests stilled as they waited expectantly for her to begin singing.

"Doesn't look like much, does she?" Augusta said.

Indeed, to Regeane's eye the simply dressed girl was plain, almost ugly. She was dark-haired, her high-cheekboned face was distinguished only by a hooked nose, but when she began to sing, Regeane forgot the tall, thin body and the almost ugly face. The girl's voice was a golden thread of liquid beauty winding among the strings. The flute accompanied her with a sad, lilting melody.

She sang a simple lyric about a poet who begs the gods to spare his mistress' life. The girl's voice and the poet's lyric phrases painted a heartrending portrait of a helpless, lovely young girl stricken by a dangerous and frightening disease and her lover's terror and grief.

Regeane found her eyes filling with tears, but Augusta affected not to be moved at all by the music. When the song ended and the girl bowed and slipped away, she sniffed and said, "Dulcina, another one of Mother's charity cases. She found her swamping out taverns. The child was a slave and her master didn't feed her very well. She sang for the few coppers the patrons threw at her feet and so was able to earn a little extra food. Now, thanks to Mother's patronage, she's the most popular entertainer in Rome. But, dear me, Propertius and here of all places."

"Propertius?" Regeane asked.

"The poet who wrote the poem Dulcina set to music. So passionate the verses about his Cynthia, how deplorable. Many churchmen disapprove of them. But that's my mother, ever the sentimentalist. Despite all her cynical talk, she believes in love."

Regeane remembered Hadrian and Lucilla together, their oneness even in sorrow for Antonius and in the face of failure and perhaps, defeat. "Possibly that's because she has known love," Regeane said.

"Ha," Augusta said. "Nonsense. That odious, but I must admit, profitable connection should have been broken off years ago. It's nothing but a source of trouble for both of them now. She is not so much loving but, as I said, sentimental. I've noticed she never lets sentiment stand in the way of destroying her enemies."

Regeane didn't answer, but privately agreed that, much as she hated to admit it, Augusta had a point. She had sensed a certain ruthlessness in Lucilla and she considered dispassionately if she failed to either find a cure for Antonius or keep him hidden, Lucilla probably would see to it she paid the price.

Elfgifa was growing restive. "I like the pretty music," she said. "And the cup is nice, but are we going to get any more to eat?"

Augusta's lips thinned to a cruel line as she glared down at Elfgifa. "I would think after making a pig of yourself with those pears, you would—"

"A pig!" Elfgifa cried, and for a second, Regeane saw the wild barbarian chieftain who was her father etched plainly on her features. Her mouth was hard. The small, blue eyes had a steely glint in them.

Regeane rolled over, pinning Elfgifa to the couch with the weight of her body. "Stop it," she hissed into the struggling little girl's ear. "Stop it now. Don't you dare throw a tantrum here."

Elfgifa stiffened and complied. "She called me a pig . . ."

"I don't care what she called you," Regeane said in a hoarse, furious whisper, "and she did not call you a pig. She meant you ate a lot of the pears, and so you did."

"Shocking," Augusta said. "The way you and my hare-brained mother spoil that child. What she needs . . ."

Regeane looked up and realized Hadrian was watching them with a sly grin on his face. It seemed he found the entertainment emanating from their couch to be equal or superior to that of the musicians. She felt her face burn.

"For heavens sake, stop squabbling, both of you," Regeane begged. "The pope is looking at us. You're making a spectacle of yourselves."

Directing a look of freezing contempt at both Regeane and Elfgifa, Augusta said, "I *never* make a spectacle of myself."

"All right," Elfgifa said with ill grace and throwing an equally unpleasant look at Augusta, "I'll put up with her for your sake."

"Thank you," Regeane said sarcastically and noticed with much more sincere thanksgiving that the servants were entering carrying the main course on platters.

When the soberly garbed young servant made the rounds of the tables picking up the delicate flower cups, he paused at the table and spoke softly to Regeane. "Since the young lady," he indicated Elfgifa with a nod, "likes the cup she chose so much, His Holiness begs her to accept it as a gift."

Elfgifa threw a smug, triumphant glance at Augusta and clutched the cup to her bosom.

Augusta looked daggers at Elfgifa.

Regeane, very tired of both of them, concentrated grimly on selecting supper from among the many offerings. She settled on a loin of young, wild boar smothered in a delicious, plum sauce, and a dish of peppered sea urchins.

Augusta contented herself with a baked trout in a sauce of honey and almonds.

Elfgifa shared Regeane's wild boar, but turned her nose up at the fish and sea urchins.

At the first taste of the wild boar, Regeane's eyes closed with delight and she managed temporarily to forget Elfgifa and Augusta. She lost herself in the joy of eating a really perfect dish and she gave a regretful sigh when she and Elfgifa polished it off.

Augusta's prediction proved false. The pears affected Elfgifa's appetite very little, if at all, and Regeane turned her attention to the sea urchins.

The spicy little morsels provided the perfect finish to an experience Regeane considered both more subtle and spectacular than merely dining and she was searching her mind for words to describe her own inner satisfaction to herself when Augusta's words broke in on her thoughts.

"A young, unmarried woman shouldn't be seen eating such a dish in public, my dear," Augusta said patronizingly. "Sea urchins are said to be even more aphrodisiac than oysters."

"What's a frodisiac?" Elfgifa asked.

The muscles in Regeane's temples twitched as the wolf tried to lay her ears back and didn't succeed. "Never mind," she said impatiently and began reaching for the dish of colbainan olives when she saw Gundabald.

The room blurred away as the shock of terror ran through her body.

He was seated at the very end of the table opposite her, Hugo beside him. Preoccupied by both the food and the antics of Augusta and Elfgifa, she hadn't seen him before.

He caught her eye and raised his cup to her, a self-satisfied smirk on his face.

Regeane's fingers pushed at the velvet of the couch as she tried to rise. And if she had been strong enough, the mindless terror she felt at the sight of him and the realization of the cruel significance of his satisfied smile might have propelled her to her feet and sent her into precipitous flight.

But she found she couldn't do anything at all. The room was spinning. Nausea twisted her belly muscles. She felt the sweat of pure terror break out all over her skin.

The wolf tried to come to her aid, but was trapped in her twisting body by the light. The torches blazing against the walls. The candles burning in the ceiling fixture above. The sconces on the pillars of the colonnade separating the dining room from the dark garden. So many candles, the columns suddenly seemed to be draped in fire.

Sounds were overpoweringly loud, the babble of voices, the threads of music twining among them.

Regeane realized the wolf was in her eyes and ears and the brilliantly lit dining room was a place of terror to the wolf. The lights blinded her. The packed mass of people and the stench of sweet, over-spiced food and perfume going sour on hot, moist flesh. The sound of voices roaring like a mountain torrent in her ears.

Regeane let her head fall to the cushions under her face. Augusta's voice thundered like storm surf in her ears.

She clucked at Regeane with mock sympathy. "Poor dear, have you had too much wine?"

Too much wine? Regeane knew she hadn't had too much wine, only a few sips of the beverages served with the meal, and the amount of raisin wine in the flower cups hadn't been enough to make her drunk. Not unless there was something else in it.

Darkness flooded her brain, blurring away the edges of reality. Bile choked her while inwardly she fought the frightened wolf with all her strength. Fought her for control over her body.

Voices were all around her and she realized through the waterfall of sound far away she could hear Gundabald and Hugo, hear them speaking, pick out their words among all the rest around her. And the wolf listened, listened with the intentness of a creature who can hear the rustle of a moth's wing, or a mouse moving in the grass, or the footfall of a stalking cat.

"She's looking peaked already," Gundabald was saying.

"Our patroness has served us well. We can take her in the confusion . . ."

Then she lost them as the wolf's power faded. The whole room seemed to be moving, and the lights were a blur of brightness, but the nausea quieted for a moment.

Regeane gathered herself against the drowsiness stealing over her, allowing her time to think.

Lying beside her, Elfgifa stared up at her in bewilderment.

On Augusta's face, Regeane saw a look of smug self-satisfaction.

Regeane bent and whispered in Elfgifa's ear. "Get to the pope. Tell him to muster his guard. We're about to be attacked."

Elfgifa stared up at Regeane for a second in consternation, then acted. She slid backward off the couch.

Augusta gave an exclamation of dismay and snatched at her, but the little girl was off the couch and then under the table before she could catch her.

Elfgifa surfaced three couches down, crawled under the table, and began to walk toward the musicians grouped in front of the pope's dais.

Regeane saw Augusta's eyes dart this way and that as she sought some way to stop her. Regeane would have laughed if she hadn't been in mortal fear. It was beneath Augusta's dignity to duck under the table and chase her.

Instead, she snatched up the child's treasured harebell cup and held it out over the hard, marble floor. She caught Elfgifa's eye.

The battle of wills that ensued was brief, but poignant.

Regeane saw the expressions chase themselves across Elfgifa's face: dismay, followed by fear for her treasure, then grief, and, at last, rage. The little body stiffened and again Regeane saw in Elfgifa's features the Saxon lord who was her father.

Her eyes flashed blue fire and she turned, ignoring both Augusta and the cup, and continued her march straight toward the papal couch.

Regeane heard the cup shatter on the floor just as Elfgifa reached the couch. The child flinched, but gave no other sign of distress.

One of the men seated near Hadrian made as if to stop

Elfgifa, but Hadrian welcomed her and eased her up beside him. A second later she was whispering in his ear.

Regeane saw Hadrian turn quickly to a hard-faced layman resting near him. The man rose and hurried away.

The buzz of conversation among the guests dropped for a second, then resumed more loudly as a thrill of anxiety flowed through the throng. Had the child brought him some sort of message?

Regeane tried to rise again.

"Don't you dare," Augusta said, pushing her back down. "It's improper to rise at a feast before the host does."

But the pope was already on his feet, addressing his guests. "My friends . . ." he said.

Regeane twisted, trying to escape Augusta's grasp. The room reeled.

Hooves thundered on the cobbled street outside the square in front of the Lateran.

Regeane heard someone scream in utter terror. "The Lombards! The Lombards!"

The room erupted around her as the guests fled, knocking over couches, tables, even the tall candelabra in wild flight.

Regeane was jerked from the couch, one arm twisted behind her back in Hugo's grip as the big room emptied around them. The screaming guests almost trampling each other in their haste to flee.

Gundabald's bearded, pock-marked face loomed before her, only inches from her own. He patted her cheek gently. "I have a cage for a wolf," he said quietly, "a cage and an iron collar. This time you won't escape."

Then he slapped her a backhand slash across the face that snapped her head back. A flash of pain knifed through her skull. She was deaf and blind for a moment. Then a choking wave of blood filled her mouth and throat.

Behind her she heard Hugo's terrified whine, "Hurry, Father, hurry, before she changes."

"She can't change," Gundabald replied with an evil chuckle. "There's too much light."

Regeane felt the cold touch of iron fetters at her throat. Mad with fear, she twisted in Hugo's grip, ducking her head to escape the collar and chain, and saw Gundabald's hand draw back to hit her again.

Behind her, Hugo's grip loosened on her arm and she heard him say, "I'm on fire." He sounded as though he didn't believe it.

"I'm on fire," he repeated, sounding astonished.

"I'm on fire!" he screeched and, letting go of Regeane's arm, he fled in the direction of the fountains outside.

In Regeane's brain, the wolf seemed to go mad. She lunged at Gundabald, her nails clawing at his eyes.

He leaped back and slashed at her with the chain in his hand, lost his footing, and fell heavily to the marble floor.

Regeane turned. A dark hallway leading to the interior of the villa beckoned. Nearby, Elfgifa was dancing up and down, shouting delightedly, "I set him on fire. I threw the lamp oil all over him."

Regeane snatched the child's arm and burst into a staggering run. It seemed an eternity before she gained the darkness. She was going down and wondered what drug Augusta had put into the raisin wine.

She shoved Elfgifa hard in back and shouted, "Run for your life! Hugo will kill you." She was rewarded by the sound of feet scurrying ahead into the distance and Emilia's welcoming cry.

Then abruptly she turned a corner and the corridor was pitch black. The woman's eyes could no longer see anything.

The wolf seized her, throwing her to the floor. The change was a savage convulsion. Not the lovely, ethereal moon darkness that floated over her like a veil, but a terrible silver wave that broke over her, sending her into a black undertow of madness.

Her body writhed and the breath was squeezed out of her lungs in whimpers and moans. The drug burned out of her body in a flash of brilliance.

The wolf's paws scrabbled amidst the silk and brocade of her gown as she burst free to stand triumphant. She had only seconds to get her bearings when Gundabald thrust a torch into her eyes.

The fire blinded her for a moment, but she could smell him—

the scent of food and stale perfume. And, under them, the sour stench of a body she had been familiar with for so long.

She met him with a roar of such primal fury that it seemed to shake the very walls around them. For a second, Regeane wanted—with an absolute purity of purpose unknown to humankind—to feel her teeth meet in the soft flesh of his throat.

Gundabald drew back. His face had blanched even in the torchlight. He fled the way he came, to the safety of the triclinium.

XVI

THE WOLF RAN TOWARD THE LATERAN BASILICA. It smelled cleaner than the palace. The raw fury and pain in her heart swept the woman aside as though she'd never been. She fled trying to find the clean, green hills beyond the city.

In a few moments, she was trotting among the tall columns supporting the church roof. They seemed a forest of marble to the wolf's eye.

The giant church edifice was drenched in the scents of candle wax and incense mixed with the cool, musky damp of a building hidden from sunlight for a long time. As much a place of innocence as the forest glades that haunted the woman's dreams. And then abruptly the torchlight from beyond the portals of the cathedral flashed in her eyes.

Rage still burned hot in the wolf's heart. She ran toward the torches seeking she knew not what—an enemy to fight, freedom to be won?

She skidded to a stop in the shadow beside Hadrian where he stood facing the Lombards. He made his stand alone. The woman, a remote figure in the wolf's mind now, hadn't warned him in time.

The square was filled with mounted Lombard troops, all armed to the teeth.

Hadrian had his arms raised to command silence. "Why do you come here?" he shouted. "Why do you dare to threaten the vicar of Christ himself?"

The troops seemed to pull back, huddled together, abashed by the pope's words.

But Basil rode to the forefront. "Your day is done," he shouted back at Hadrian. "We have taken the fortress of Nepi, Palestrea, and Piastem, and now Rome is our prize. Yield to me before we put you to the sword."

From the shadows, the wolf could see Hadrian's profile above her. He was a head of Caesar on a silver coin, unyielding, jaw tight, mouth firm below the sharp-bladed nose, his eyes were like stone reflecting the torchlight. Churchman and warrior both. Threaten him with the sword or not, the wolf knew he would never yield.

The wolf heard a smash, the sound of rending timber and stone. Shouts came from the deep, shadowed darkness surrounding the square. Lights sprang to life in every window and balcony. A mob, culled from every quarter of the city, gathered. The Romans were preparing to protect the pope.

The mounted men behind Basil cast uncertain glances at them, but Basil rode toward the slender, white-garbed figure.

The wolf lunged forward in front of Hadrian. In the torchlight she appeared almost a creature without substance, a silver shape composed of moonlight and black shadow. But her head was lowered and her ivory fangs gleamed golden in the flaring lights.

The wolf heard a whisper travel through the mob. "Lupa, the wolf of Rome, herself."

For a moment the crowd and the soldiers were absolutely silent. The horses stirred and the soft click of their hooves on the cobbles was the only sound.

The wrong sound, the wolf thought. *There should have been a drumming.*

It was so when she had hunted them before. Ah, the plains had been a sea and the long, wind-tossed grasses sang with the music of freedom in a boundless land where soft, white clouds hung in masses casting long, cool shadows on the green eternity as they passed. The horses had run in herds so vast as they thundered over grassy expanse that they rivaled the very clouds above. Brown and roan, black and red, their coats shimmered in the sun, prey, and yet companions in freedom. The hunter and the hunted tethered to each other by an unquestioned necessity, challenging each other forever in their need, and the freedom of their hearts.

The stallion Basil rode reared and screamed a challenge. The wolf knew he'd fought her kind before. He was blind with rage and the desire to destroy her. The wolf leaped forward like an arrow leaving the bow. The stallion's hooves came down, striking at her skull. But the woman was gone. The wolf was present and she understood with a savage intensity what she had to do.

At the last second before the first slashing hoof struck her skull, she dodged and lunged for the stallion's hamstrings. The stallion lashed out with his heels.

One hoof caught the wolf on the shoulder. She was kicked into the air, flying for a second, then falling, rolling over and over the cobbles.

The risk was a nasty one, really dangerous. Left to herself, the wolf would have run. She staggered, in terrible pain from the kick in the ribs. A few felt as if they might be broken. The woman was in command again. If she could enrage or terrorize the horse, he might throw Basil on the ground. The man would be at the mercy of her fangs. She wanted to kill him. She could still feel the bite of the iron collar around her neck. With cold, conscious ferocity, she charged the stallion.

The horse reared, and with a whistling shriek, met her halfway. She leaped up, going for the soft, sensitive nose.

The stallion, enraged, with incredible swiftness in an animal so big, slashed at her with his fore hooves, ready to follow up his advantage and trample the wolf into bloody scraps of fur and bone. But the man on his back hampered his efforts.

The stallion bucked, throwing Basil to the ground. He landed at the base of the steps to the Lateran basilica with a crash of armor and a howl of fury. The stallion charged the wolf, striking sparks from the stones as he galloped toward her.

The wolf barely had time to get her feet under her before the stallion was upon her. The hooves slammed down on the cobbles like a rain of bludgeons aimed at her face, turning her back away from the pope and Basil.

Damn him, the woman thought, *I want that human bastard who is even now trying to shake off the stunning effects of the fall.*

Basil was screaming at the top of his lungs, "Kill the unnatural bitch . . . kill it . . . kill it!"

But the Lombards were having problems of their own. Fear spread among horses the way lightning flashes across the sky; their mounts were a milling, rearing, dancing mass.

The stallion was a maddened juggernaut. No one and nothing wanted to be in his path. The wolf was. Woman and wolf melted into one. Locked in the logic and commitment of battle. Now, there was no more running away. It was kill or be killed.

The wolf lunged at the horse's hocks again and again, trying to hamstring him. Round and round they went, a wild melee of horse and wolf, spinning toward the empty center of the square as Basil's men and the mob both drew back before the furious animals.

Dimly, the wolf was aware the mob around the square was chanting, "Lupa! Lupa!", cheering her, egging her on.

But the horse was too fast, too powerful.

Every time she lunged toward him she met flying hooves, flailing heels, and bared teeth, and she had to leap back to avoid death beneath them.

The wolf knew sooner or later one of them would make a mistake.

The stallion's foot slipped on the wet stones. He didn't lose his footing, but he staggered.

In a flash, the wolf was back on her haunches. A second later she was in the air. She landed on the stallion's neck. Teeth met with a crunching snap in the spine where it is thinnest, just below the head.

The horse reared and plunged, flinging the wolf back, then down toward the stones.

The torchlight whirled before her eyes. The wolf spun as she was flung wildly from side to side. The world vanished. Fear vanished. Nothing was left but her grip at the back of the horse's neck. A wolf's jaws can break a man's thighbone, the longest, strongest bone in the body. She closed them. The spine snapped under her fangs. The stallion's death scream was a horror.

The wolf was flung free and again she slammed down gasping, aware her mouth was filled with a wave of blood, this time not her own.

But wolflike she'd landed, rolling, realizing even as she got her footing that Basil's men were bunched at the end of the square beyond the dead horse, still trying to control their frightened mounts.

The wolf didn't hesitate. Lowering her head, her muzzle dripping blood, her pelt glowing golden in the torchlight, she went for Basil's cavalry like a streak of flame. Whatever discipline had held them down before, snapped.

Madness flowed through the horses like the ripples spreading from the center when a stone is cast into a pond. In seconds, they were all over the square, bucking, plunging, rearing, screaming in a frenzy of mindless, animal fear.

At the same moment, more torchlight flared at one of the entrances to the square. Dimly the wolf knew the papal guard was arriving and, because of her, they had come in time.

They smashed into Basil's demoralized cavalry the way a battering ram strikes a crumbling gate and the mob followed them.

All around the wolf the square exploded into violence. She found herself twisting and turning and dodging a barrage of flying hooves as pain-drenched horror and exultation warred between beast and human in her heart.

She fled into the welcoming darkness of the Lateran church. She didn't afterward remember how the wolf found her dress in the dark corridor. She only knew that after a short time, her paws scrabbled on silk and the scented cloth that had been in contact with the woman's skin.

The wolf fought her, wanting, desiring the night, dreaming of running free. A sweet hunger pervaded her mind. An image of endless grasslands, drenched and freshened by rain, beckoned her. They flowed away like a vast sea as she ran under a bowl of starry heavens untainted by human light. The wolf dreamed, but the woman knew. This time, the woman won.

With the wolf's heart-hunger echoing in her veins, Regeane

found herself kneeling on the rags of her dress. Feeling hideously naked and vulnerable, she scrambled into the obligatory three layers of clothing worn by a respectable Roman woman.

She was overwhelmed by pain. Her face and mouth were covered with blood. Shivering in the darkness, she wondered how much was splattered on her dress. It seemed as though blood drowned the world. The taste was hot and sweet in her mouth. Enough of the wolf was left in her to relish the taste and revel in the sense of power the killing brought, but the woman felt defiled.

She had killed. She had taken life. The horse's blood stank and steamed on her face and hands.

Dimly, even through the heavy stone walls, she could hear the sounds in the square as the people and the pope's men drove out the Lombards.

She stumbled to her feet, reeling, and leaned against the wall. She struggled through the empty silent corridors until she found a courtyard where a fountain danced and played.

She washed out her mouth and scrubbed her face and arms. She could see by the faint starlight that water poured from a Gorgon's head into a scallop-shell basin. Spray from the fountain watered a patch of sweet fennel and she fell to her knees, her cheek against the cool, marble basin, feeling the feathery touch of fernlike leaves against her face. The gentle licorice scent of the herbs drove the anguish and confusion from her mind and set her quivering nerves to rest.

The wolf rose in her mind gently, quietly this time, not trying to change or control her, but simply present, reveling in the peace of the dark garden. Away from the battles and perplexities of humankind. The wolf's nose told her there were other herbs here, their perfumes drifting in the moist, dark air. The thick sweetness of mint and the sharp scent of thyme at her feet.

The woman wanted to question her dark companion, but the wolf didn't reply to questions. She simply was and, as always, brought all her being to bear on the moment's problems. She sensed the woman's suffering and wished to bring her to peace.

Here, together at last in this little splinter of wilderness, caught amidst the vast matrix of human works, unthreatened and alone, they became one.

To the wolf there was no right or wrong, good or evil. There was only the pattern and she was part of the pattern. To judge as the woman did was as foreign to her nature as were hope and despair.

To the wolf, the world was a tapestry of things given—sunrises scarlet, then gold; sunsets arrayed in purple shadow and bloody light; plains awash in tall grasses and mountains drifting against blue skies; and gray storms that rose, coalescing seemingly out of nothing in the upper air, then roaming at random, drenching the earth with rain. Spending their fury in wild bursts of lightning.

Life was part of the pattern and death, too, as were blood and pain. She herself had struggled uncountable times, sodden with suffering, down the long, dark path into starless night. But this, too, was part of the pattern, part of the seamless tapestry of light and darkness whose only assurance was in its own endless, ever-changing repetition, always different, yet the same forever.

The pattern was beauty, somehow always in everlasting harmony with itself. Beauty was! Ugliness, sadness, despair were human judgments imposed by lesser, frightened minds on the whole shining spectrum of reality whose boundaries the wolf couldn't even dimly comprehend.

She knew only that it was, and she was part of the pattern and content with being itself and engulfed by endless and everlasting love for her reality and her world.

The wolf's mindset faded slowly as she slipped into silence, leaving the woman's mind fully awake, still questioning, but at peace.

She rested quietly on her heels beside the basin, listening to the musical sound of falling water, drinking in the sweet air cleansed by the storm a few hours before.

I am human, Regeane thought stubbornly, *and more than the wolf is. Or am I less?* She couldn't answer her own question, and didn't care to try.

The wolf's ears, ever alert, told her someone was coming. The woman's mind knew the step.

Lucilla.

XVII

LUCILLA RAISED THE TORCH, ILLUMINATING RE-
geane kneeling by the fountain. "My, but you're hard on
clothes," she said, giving a disapproving look to Regeane's gown.

Regeane got to her feet and looked down at the dirty, blood-
spattered brocade. Her long hair hung around her face. "I'm
sorry. Next time I'll wear something dark. It won't show the
stains as much."

"Whose blood is that?" Lucilla asked. "Yours or the horse's?"

"Mostly mine," Regeane answered. "Gundabald slapped
me. My mouth and nose bled. He means to chain me up and
lock me away forever."

"He won't succeed," Lucilla said. "It's much too late for that
now. He just doesn't realize it. As soon as you broke free, you'd
kill him."

"Yes," Regeane said bitterly. "I would."

"Don't sound so downcast," Lucilla said. "Why shouldn't
you?"

In the torchlight Lucilla's face was hard. Deep lines of strain
were etched around her mouth.

"I didn't want to kill the horse," Regeane said. "I've never
killed so much as a chicken before tonight."

"Then it's time you learned," Lucilla said harshly. "Sometimes it's necessary. Here." She thrust a comb and the pearl
snood into Regeane's hand. "Fix your hair. I must have something presentable to bring before the pope. Besides, you killed
an animal, not a man."

"We are all animals," Regeane said. "No more, no less." She
pulled the tangles out of her hair and coiled it in the snood.

"Perhaps," Lucilla said. "I can't say. I believe men die harder, kick longer at the end of the noose that wrings their life away. Be the noose in the hands of man or time, it closes just the same. We all come to it in the end. At least the horse died quickly and without pain. I'll wager if you're caught, you won't be offered as quick and clean a death as the horse had."

Regeane flinched at Lucilla's words.

"Stop it!" Lucilla snapped. She took a few, deep tearing breaths and Regeane realized Lucilla was shouting at her because she was having difficulty controlling herself. Regeane's fear was contagious. "Be still," Lucilla continued. "The whole city is aflame by now. The riots are spreading everywhere. I have to find somewhere to put you. My house isn't safe anymore."

"I don't understand," Regeane said. "What happened? Didn't the pope's militia drive off Basil and his men?"

Lucilla laughed softly. Terrible laughter, laughter that took the place of tears and screams. She raised the torch, reached out, and caught Regeane's chin between her fingers. The fingers and thumb squeezed Regeane's cheeks. "You don't understand, do you?"

Regeane tried to shake her head, but found she couldn't. Lucilla's grip on her face was too tight. "No," she whispered through lips made numb by fear.

"Very well," Lucilla said. She paused and Regeane felt the tremor flow through her fingers and her body as her control over terror was tightened by an iron will. "We are riding a tidal wave and no one can tell if it will bring us safe to shore or drown us. Time out of mind, this city has ruled itself. And its citizens remember they have toppled popes and dethroned emperors. Even Desiderius and Basil fear them.

"Tonight they helped the pope's forces drive off Basil," she continued, "but tomorrow if Hadrian can be discredited, they may throw open the gates and welcome Basil and the Lombard king as their saviors. If . . . if, as I said, Hadrian can be discredited. In the meantime, they, the people, rule here. Tonight, at this very moment, I have no doubt they are plundering Basil's villa and putting such of his servants that haven't been able to flee to the sword.

"Tomorrow they may plunder mine, or even the Lateran itself, if Hadrian can be proved to be tainted with Antonius' disease. To do this, all they need do is produce Antonius in his present state, alive or dead! You . . ." She shook Regeane's face lightly for emphasis. "You will see this doesn't happen, or I promise I will include you in my fall."

Regeane pulled back, and Lucilla's hand fell from her face. "You needn't threaten me, Lucilla," Regeane said. "I have as little choice as you have. Only the pope's promise protects me. Win or lose, succeed or fail, we're in this together.

"But," Regeane continued, "I can't help anyone if Gundabald gets me. He said he had a cage for a wolf. And you know he has. If he can win Hadrian over, I won't be able to help anyone ever again.

"Don't you see?" she said desperately. "He'll torture me until I no longer have the strength to withstand him. Until my heart, my spirit, my will is broken. Forever. I'll end up like my mother, doing anything, everything he tells me to do."

"Gundabald!" Lucilla spat out choice words in gutter Latin. "How did he get here tonight?"

"Augusta," Regeane said. "Didn't you know Augusta betrayed me?"

Lucilla's teeth clenched. "Bitch, whore," she whispered. "Daughter or no, I'll have the heart out of her body for this. How dare she interfere with my plans . . ."

Lucilla paused. Her face paled and the skin seemed to tighten over her bones as though she were struck by some terrible realization. "Christ," she whispered, "even now Gundabald's probably pleading his case before the pope. We must get you away from here. Hide you. God in heaven above knows what he'll tell Hadrian, and after what happened in the square tonight, Hadrian will listen."

At the same moment the terrifying realization struck, the wolf heard footfalls.

"Hurry," Regeane whispered. "Someone is coming."

Lucilla raised the torch. Her eyes searched around the little courtyard feverishly. Regeane realized she was trapped. There was only one entrance.

A moment later Regeane and Lucilla were surrounded by torch-bearing soldiers. A tall man wearing ornate armor bowed to Lucilla, saying "I see you found her, my lady. His Holiness wished that you return to the triclinium at once. Her uncle is there and some," he paused, then continued, "some . . . very . . . serious charges have been made."

Regeane hadn't realized the wolf was still present until she noticed the torches seemed unnaturally bright. The creature endured suffering for only a few heartbeats, then slipped away into the depths of Regeane's being in dreary resignation and defeat. Leaving the woman alone, an icy knot of anxiety in her belly as she prepared to confront the worst.

The wolf might dream but the woman had to live if the wolf was to fight back. All Regeane felt was an icy determination to survive no matter what she had to do.

She looked down at her ravaged finery in fear. Fear for the impression it would make. She would need every possible advantage if she were to persuade Hadrian not to yield her back to Gundabald.

"I'm afraid I'm in no condition to be presented to His Holiness," she said softly. "May I . . ."

She saw the soldier's mouth tighten—saw the refusal ready in his face, and so she modified her request. "May I borrow someone's mantle so that I may cover myself decently?"

One of the soldiers handed her a dark mantle of heavy woolen stuff.

Regeane threw it over her shoulders and wrapped it around her body, concealing as much of her clothes as possible. Then, she accompanied the men into the villa. Lucilla followed.

The big room was darker than it had been earlier. Many of the lamps had burned out and the candles guttered in their sockets. Overturned tables and couches lay where they had fallen amidst splatters of spilled food and puddles of wine. Shattered crockery and a scattering of fallen silver vessels littered the floor.

The walls and corners of the room were in shadow. The few remaining lamps and candles illumined the pope and the red-garbed cardinal priests of the city where they stood gathered beneath the stiff, glittering mosaic of the Byzantine Christ. They waited in the center of the room below and in front of the pope's couch.

The chaos within the once-graceful room seemed to Regeane to mirror the disorder in the square outside. She could hear clearly the shouts and screams of the rioting mob as they exulted in their victory and plundered the dead Lombards.

Then across the room she met the pope's eyes. The chill of terror in Regeane's belly seemed to radiate upward to her heart, turning her whole body cold.

The dark eyes probed her face relentlessly as though trying to reach into her soul and pull out the secrets hidden there.

He knows, she thought. *Perhaps he doesn't want to know or really believe what he knows, but he knows.*

Regeane lifted her chin and met the pope's stare unflinchingly. *I'm innocent,* she thought. *Innocent and guilty. I didn't will the wolf into existence, but she is there and I must defend her. Her and myself. We are one and whatever I am, I had no choice. I will not turn away from her or you or Antonius.* She tried to will the thought into her gaze, into Hadrian's mind. *Please protect me, protect me from this man who wants to destroy me.*

Hadrian's eyes dropped first and he turned to Gundabald.

Regeane felt something brush the edges of the mantle at her arm and she realized Lucilla stood beside her. "He's dangerous," she said in fearful realization.

"Yes, my dear," Lucilla said. "Dangerous as only a man of principle can be. Dangerous to himself."

Regeane glanced around and realized most of the guests at the feast were still present, though they were dressed as she was, their battered finery covered by dark mantles. They gathered like black-winged moths around the little light left and the comforting presence of the pope.

"Your niece, I believe, my lord," Hadrian said to Gundabald.

Regeane could feel her heart hammering in her breast.

"My dear niece," he said, starting toward her with his hands outstretched.

Regeane felt an instant's confusion; then she realized the game he was playing and decided she must play it, too.

His hands clasped hers and she met his eyes. Eyes malicious, not even raging, but cold and dark as the entrance to a tomb. She felt fingers slowly closing ever more tightly as if he wanted to crush the fine bones in her hands. She curled her fingers over and her nails, longer and sharper than most women's, sank into the soft flesh of his palms.

Nothing in his face or eyes changed, but the crushing grip on her hands slackened and he bared his big, blunt, yellow teeth in what he obviously hoped was a fond smile.

Regeane showed her teeth to him, too. "Alas, my kinsman," she said, "I fear we were separated in the confusion."

"Never fear, sweet niece," he replied heartily, "we're here to take you home."

Regeane pulled her hands free of Gundabald's, brushed past him, and fell to her knees before Hadrian. "Your Holiness, please!" she whimpered. "Hear my plea!"

Hadrian looked down at her, his eyes narrowed, the dark brows drawn down toward the nose, the eyes questioned her. "Certainly," he said, seeming slightly bewildered.

"Oh, please, I know my kinsmen wish nothing but my best interest, but please—oh, please—I am afraid. No, 'fear' is too weak a word." She extended her arms toward the pope, palms up in beautiful supplication. "I am quite distracted with terror at the riots and confusion in this unhappy city. Is there no convent, no establishment of holy virgins dedicated to Christ's love where I may find shelter until this dreadful confusion and madness is ended? I have the deepest trust and affection in my kinsmen, yet they are but two men."

Regeane wrung her hands and, to her surprise, found real tears running down her cheeks. "What if some evil chance," she gasped, "some terrible moment should come when they are powerless to protect me? Brave as they are, two men alone might be easily overwhelmed and I would fall victim to a dreadful fate, with the added burden of being guilty of their deaths in my heart. Oh, please," she said, clasping her hands, "find me some quiet refuge among the blessed ladies, a safe harbor where I may rest until these troubled hours are over."

"Your Holiness," Gundabald exclaimed in a shocked voice, "I believed the matter of my niece's residence to be settled."

Hadrian continued staring down at Regeane, his eyes opaque. "Did you?" he asked. "I didn't. All I promised was that I'd hear your petition. And I did. I didn't promise anything."

"But," Gundabald sputtered, "it's as I told you. She's . . . The girl is wild and her mother was a baneful influence . . ." Gundabald seemed to flounder.

Regeane jumped to her feet forgetting to look pathetic. The thought of Gundabald maligning her mother to Hadrian was too much for her. "How dare you!" she hissed in furious incredulity. "You despised my mother. You abused—"

A voice broke in on her. "Why, of all the brazen effrontery."

Regeane recognized Augusta's voice. She was standing next to Hadrian with Lucilla beside her.

"How dare she present herself as a frightened innocent," Augusta snapped stridently. "She wasn't afraid. She was . . . uh." Augusta's eyes goggled, her mouth opened and closed like a gasping fish. Regeane realized Lucilla's elbow had caught her hard in the breadbasket.

Abbess Emilia appeared out of the shadows near the triclinium porch, holding Elfgifa's wrist in a firm grip with the little girl trailing behind her.

She reminded Regeane of a war galley under full sail towing a tiny fishing boat.

"Your Holiness, if I may be so bold? I have every reason to believe the young lady's fears may be . . ." She stopped in front of the pope and gave Gundabald and Hugo a hard glance before continuing. ". . . well-founded."

Regeane remembered that Elfgifa also had a glib tongue and apparently she had used it to talk to Emilia.

Emilia continued rather breathlessly. "Now, if the young lady really desires the shelter of the convent, she would be welcome among—"

A roar of fury interrupted Emilia's words. Hugo had seen Elfgifa and finally realized who she was. He started toward her, his eyes bulging with fury.

Elfgifa dodged behind Emilia. Hugo reached out to grab her. Emilia clouted him soundly on the ear. Emilia was stout, muscular, and her aim was unerring.

Hugo sat down hard on the floor, his eyes glazed over.

Gundabald strode toward Regeane. His face was flushed with rage and, as always, he exuded the same aura of raw violence that had always terrified her.

Regeane wanted to cringe away, to run, but she didn't. She realized she had to defy him now or perish. "Stop," she said quietly. Her whole body was quivering. She could feel the need to change gathering around her like the shimmer of moonlight in a darkened glade.

Their eyes locked. His face was inches from her own. His outstretched hand almost touching her hair. She realized in spite of the gallery of interested spectators and the pope, they might have been alone so long as they spoke quietly.

So Regeane's voice was a soft, throaty whisper. "Put one hand on me and you die. I know they'll kill me, but it might be worth it to see you writhing on the floor, your life blood spurting out of your torn throat. Put one hand, one finger on me and you will. I swear it."

Hatred and malice hovered palpable as a mist between them.

Gundabald bared his teeth and Regeane realized he was a hair away from blind, murderous rage. "You little bitch," he whispered. "I'm going to kill you."

Yes, Regeane thought. *He won't now, but as soon as he can, he will.*

The sharp sound from behind her struck the wolf's ears almost as loud as a crack of thunder. She spun around toward the pope and realized he'd only clapped his hands together hard.

"You will stop this unseemly bickering at once. I rule here and until I'm dead or deposed, I'll make the decisions. Now, what in the name of God ails you?" he asked, pointing to Hugo.

Hugo, still sitting on the floor, was blinking as he returned to full consciousness. He pointed a shaking finger at Elfgifa. "She . . . she . . ."

Gundabald clouted him on the other ear, saying, "Shut up, you moron."

"It appears he has some grievance against the child," Emilia said. "If he has, I'd like to hear it." She folded her arms and glared down at him.

Hugo got to his feet and, casting a dazed, fearful glance at Emilia and Gundabald, he began backing away muttering, "Nothing . . . nothing."

"He doesn't have a large vocabulary, does he?" Lucilla commented. Hadrian gave Lucilla a glance that could have ignited a bonfire.

Both women backed away, covering their faces with the mantles.

"Augusta," he said, "Both the young lady's reputation and safety are at stake here. If you have anything cogent to say in the matter, then speak up. And by cogent, I don't mean malicious tale-bearing and spiteful innuendo. I mean any fact of which you are aware that has any bearing on the matter."

Augusta shook her head slowly.

"Very well," Hadrian said. He turned again to Gundabald. "We are both concerned with the young lady's safety and virtue amidst the tumults and temptations of the world, and I believe a convent would serve both our purposes equally well. Abbess Emilia, have you a penitential cell?"

Emilia looked nonplussed. "I don't know . . . I . . . We seldom have call for such a thing."

For a moment it looked to the terrified Regeane as though the abbess was going to object to having her convent turned into a prison, but finally she said, "Yes. I do believe we have a few doors with bolts on the outside, rather than on the inside. If this is really the sort of accommodation you wish for the young lady?"

"I do," Hadrian said. "She is not to go out. She is not to receive visitors." He glanced at Lucilla. "Any visitors. She is to be kept under lock and key until the marriage contract is signed and she is handed over to her bridegroom."

XVIII

THE BOLT WAS A BIT RUSTY, AND IT GAVE A LOUD, metallic screech when Emilia shot the bar into the socket.

It was, Regeane thought, *an only-too-familiar sound.* She stood and listened to Emilia's retreating footsteps and the silence descending.

They had been returned to the convent under heavy guard. The pope's militia rode three deep around the mule litter carrying Regeane, the Abbess Emilia, and Elfgifa.

The whole of Rome seemed to have taken to the streets. A good-humored crowd for the most part, dancing, drinking, and wenching. All the taverns and many brothels were doing a brisk business.

They were ablaze with lights and the frolicking mobs spilled out into the streets at their doors. They cheered the soldiers of the papal militia and parted willingly to let them pass. People on balconies threw flowers, and women blew kisses and sometimes shouted raucous promises of more intimate entertainment if they would care to dismount and tarry for a while.

But Regeane was not fooled for a moment. Twice they found themselves riding through the smoke of burning villas. The screams coming from the flaming houses behind the high walls turned Regeane ice-cold with fear. And she wished herself rid of the wolf. The creature with whom she shared her body could hear only too well.

In the more populous parts of the city, the litter jolted past the gutted ruins of taverns and wineshops that hadn't opened their doors quickly enough to the roistering throng.

Many private houses and insula were tightly shuttered and dark. The people inside hid, fearing to show a light, cowering behind their barred doors, wondering who the mob might see fit to turn on next.

Abbess Emilia leaned back, her arms protectively embracing Elfgifa, her eyes closed, her lips moving in silent prayer.

Regeane, on the other hand, peered out through a slit in the curtains, terrified yet fascinated and appalled by the spectacle, at the same time powerless to shut out the sensations of pity and fear that surged through her. Feeling all the while the wolf's silent wonder at this incomprehensible human madness.

When they reached the gates of the Saxon quarter, Emilia opened her eyes, signed herself with the cross, and whispered, "Thank God." The streets were silent here, guarded by relatives belonging to the households of the Saxon nobles residing near the Vatican.

"These Latins haven't a scrap of common sense among the lot of them. In my humble opinion, just to show the Lombards they're not afraid of them, they're going to pillage their own city and burn it to the ground before their enemies can get around to it," Emilia said.

The litter came to a stop before the convent gates. Regeane jumped down and Emilia handed Elfgifa to her and followed.

"God in heaven above," she said, puffing a bit as she hauled Regeane and Elfgifa along. "This wretched city is mostly in ruins already. I see no earthly reason to wreck the rest of it. And His Holiness, God preserve him, is no better than the rest. Half his people out destroying the place, the other half, God help them . . ." She let go of Elfgifa's hand to make the sign of the cross again. "Hiding under their beds.

"That worthless cousin of yours, a debauchee without even the saving grace of courage. And that uncle of yours, Gundabald . . ." She crossed herself again. "One only has to look into his eyes to know he would have sold Christ more quickly than Judas and congratulated himself for profiting by the transaction. He could tutor Lucifer himself in evil. And . . . and." She plunked Regeane and Elfgifa down at the table and presented them with bread, cheese, and wine.

"And," she continued rattling on, "His Holiness can't think of anything better to do than imprison you. A virtuous girl if I ever saw one. Just like a man: one helpless innocent in all this confusion and conflagration and he must lock her up at once."

Regeane said, "I . . ."

But Emilia rolled on inexorably. "Be of good cheer, girl. There are worse things than marriage. Do you know I was once a married woman myself?"

Regeane managed an "Oh?"

"Oh, yes," Emilia said. "My dear, I sat weeping the whole week before I was to be wed. I nearly went into hysterics when I saw him. He was fat, bald, old, and covered with warts like a toad. His disposition was no better than his looks. He was as annoying as a grease spot and as smelly as an untended chamber pot."

Regeane said, "Ah . . ."

"Oh, no, my dear," Emilia said cheerfully. "You see it all turned out for the best. One week after we were married, during the wedding festivities, he consumed the best part of an ox, two and a half barrels of my father's excellent ale, fell down in a fit and choked to death on his own vomit, leaving me a wealthy and independent widow. I would wish you similar good fortune.

"Men," Abbess Emilia sniffed. "I can't think why God created them," she sighed. "I suppose for the same reason he created rats, mosquitos, and fleas. Another cross for women to bear so that their salvation may be all the sweeter. I know they're good for some things, though put to it, I can't imagine what. I think we could do with a great deal less of them. They say that in heaven there will be no marriage or giving in marriage and I suppose that means we may all go our own way in peace. And I for one look forward to that pleasant state with blissful anticipation.

"Now, don't worry, my dear. No matter what His Holiness says, you're welcome here among us and I'll do my best to make you comfortable."

And Regeane thought, standing in the narrow room within the limitations of the pope's orders, Emilia had done so.

The bed was a cot, but a comfortable one. Fitted out with a feather tick, linen sheets, blankets, and even a goose-down comforter in case it grew cold. A brazier stood in the corner and in it Regeane saw a fat heap of red coals. They warmed the room against the growing chill outside. At her elbow was a table with a bookstand, a book, and, beside it, a tall candle that cast a fitful light in the tiny room.

Weariness lay over her shoulders like a yoke, bowing her down. As she began to pull off her ruined dress, her fingers brushed something hard in the lining and she remembered Adraste's mirror. She withdrew it carefully from its place in the silken lining. She didn't want to look into the polished silver face again. Not here. Not alone by candlelight.

The silver was icy to the touch. It seemed as though her fingers had no power to warm it.

She studied the flower pattern on the back for a second. Red valerian. The flower of Rome. It grew wild everywhere, shooting up pink rockets of flowers among the ruins, even rooting itself in small pockets of soil in the brickwork of inhabited buildings, blowing and bowing from walls and eaves high in the air.

The flowers on the mirror were inlaid with coral. The exquisite workmanship perfectly simulating a starburst of bloom.

A pretty trinket, Regeane thought, *an expensive bauble that once must have graced the dressing table of a lady of fashion.* Her fingers stroked the back of the mirror.

Who was she, Adraste, and why did she send me her mirror? Regeane wondered in the silent room.

All at once she felt the touch of a presence that gathered like the shadows cast by the ·flickering candle. A presence that seemed held in abeyance only by her will.

She set the mirror on the table beside the candle and the presence dissipated, seeming to fade like a shadow when a cloud crosses the sun.

The room had one narrow window near the foot of the bed. Simply a long slit, not big enough to admit a human body. It looked out over a garden and the roofs of the Saxon quarter below. Beyond she could see the Tiber and the city perched on the rolling hills.

The wolf's ears could hear the faraway sound of tumult, of

violence. Fires burned against the night sky. The people of the ancient town killed with the same abandon that they devoted to laughter and song.

Two quarreling kings, Desiderius and Charles, and each one wanted this city; each wanted to dictate papal policy.

Urbi et Orbi, the city and the world, Regeane thought. *I am Peter and upon this rock . . . I will build my church and the gates of hell will not prevail against it.*

The pope, the papacy—things not of this world, but in it. And what was she herself, but a thing not completely of the world.

The wind blew hard, bringing an icy chill into the room. It carried the smell of smoke from the city. The waft of burning stung her eyes, then passed as the air cleansed itself. From beyond the city, carried on the wings of distant winds, the wolf smelled snow and the tang of frost. Air from distant mountains, where millions of stars glowed like crystal light, filled the room. She saw high peaks, floating pure and unapproachable as a divine dream. High granite precipices mantled in sparkling glaciers and sweeps of pure untrodden snow. The changing, moving sun sometimes cast back rainbows into the dazzled eyes of travelers. At other times, the peaks boiled with storm clouds or draped themselves in the morning mist. Veiling themselves like eastern queens until the air cleared, the fog burned away by pure light.

Valleys whose springtimes were like bowls of flowers set in the snow, slowly turning to green in the long, summer silences then brown with thick, rich hay in autumn when the eternal winter of the heights reached down and reclaimed them.

A wave of almost unbearable longing rose in the wolf's heart, bringing a hard, painful lump to Regeane's throat and tears to her eyes. A feeling that she could forever abandon the world of men and run out across the Campagna.

It was growing colder there, now that the wind was blowing. In those coldest hours before dawn, the ground mist would settle on the grass and the long blades would be covered by a soft frosting of crystals. They would crackle beneath her paws as she passed. She could find a place to lie up and sleep. A place to den where a soft woman's body would remain warm while the long, daylight hours passed. When night came again, she could run on and on until she lost herself in the green solitude of those deep valleys and the vast silence of the peaks beyond.

Regeane opened her eyes and the dream faded.

Bolts and bars. Narrow rooms like this one were her life, not the freedom of mountains and forests. Conventions that tied her hand and foot and dictated what a woman must do and be. Crystal streams, and storms that set the night sky aflame. It might be that all the world had for her was an iron collar and a chain. That might be the best the world had to offer her. Someday she might stand at the stake and pray for dry wood, a soft breeze, and a hot fire.

She felt so tired, she staggered toward the bed. Oh, sleep. Blessed, blessed sleep. Her clothes dropped to the floor and she crept between the clean, soft linen sheets in a sweet relief. In spite of the brazier, the air in the room grew colder and colder. Regeane pulled the covers up to her chin. Her head touched the pillows. Sleep washed over her. The wolf dreamed of mountains. She hunted in dark woods among stands of fir, laden with snow, below ice-coated pines whose long needles glittered like frost daggers . . . under a drowsy moon.

SAD, SO SAD. THE NAKED PAIN IN THE WORDLESS voice was so terrible it jolted Regeane out of sleep. She woke thinking Elfgifa. She knew Elfgifa had been bedded down in the dormitory room with the orphans in the nuns' care. Had she perhaps been awakened by some nightmare and was she even now crying for the comfort of Regeane's arms?

Regeane turned on the cot and stared into the darkness open-eyed. The room was illuminated now only by starlight glowing through the window slit. The candle had burned down. The flame extinguished in a cascade of hard wax.

But the wolf knew the hour as she knew the hours of the passing day by the changing slant of the moving sun and the night by scent and sound, the position of the wheeling stars. She matched them against the template engraved since before the beginning of time on her mind and heart. It was close to dawn, that darkest hour when even the four winds seem to feel the weight of night and a breathless hush precedes the coming of dawn. The room was freezing and Regeane could see the cloud of mist created by her breath on the air.

She listened and found that even the wolf's ears heard nothing. *Only a dream,* she thought. *I had a nightmare of my own.*

In the profound darkness and silence something sighed. *No,* Regeane thought, remembering the face in the mirror. *No.* But she knew however much she wanted to deny it, the dead called to her from beyond the world.

Another sigh—this one louder followed by low laughter, brittle and cruel that seemed to mock her fear. And shadows began to gather themselves and grow darker near the table and the mirror.

It's coming, she thought in terror, *coming to visit me.* Suddenly, the air around her grew colder. The shadows were an ugly phosphorescent mist. Mist the color of a corpse candle.

She gasped, choked, and tried not to breathe as an almost intolerable stench of decay pervaded the room. Regeane threw the covers aside and leaped to her feet.

The cold was more than cold, a freezing shock wave that seemed to chill her to the bone and then she remembered she couldn't run. She was locked in with the thing. She retreated toward the door. The awful stench nearly gagging her. She would scream, she decided. Hammer on the wooden panels. Surely someone would come.

At the thought, another sort of terror overcame her. What would the good ladies think of her? But the thing was taking shape now and what she could see a ghastly blasphemy of the human form.

Regeane shoved her shoulders and back against the door. She found she was afraid to turn her back on it, afraid she would throw herself against the bolts and bars in vain and in a few seconds she would feel a hand on her shoulder. She would turn, she knew—she would turn and look into the face of God alone knew what horror.

No, it was better to confront it, no matter what grisly shape it might assume.

The thing was almost solid. She heard it move. It squelched and plopped as it took a step. It seemed wet, coated with rivulets of decay, like a piece of rotten meat. All at once she realized the step it took was away from her. It was backing away, fleeing.

The sudden breath of perfume was almost as dizzying as the stench had been. A scent, sharp, yet sweet and fresh like crushed wild mint, subtly mixed with something even sweeter. The heady fragrance of an orchard blooming in the sunlight or a meadow at springtime when in the cool morning the grass is wet with dew.

The very air around Regeane had changed and it seemed as laden with promise as when God first touched the rich, fertile earth with His hand and called forth life.

She was suddenly aware that she could see the room clearly. Light was streaming in under the door and around the frame.

Someone, Regeane thought incoherently, *someone in the hall with a torch or lantern.* But that couldn't be. No torch or lantern she'd ever seen shed such a fierce white light. A light so bright she could see the whole room in the glow of the few rays stealing in around and under the heavy door.

The ugly thing was only a shadow now. It gave another cry laden with loneliness and loss as it faded and fled away into nothingness.

The room grew cold and dark around Regeane again. But she realized the cold was only that of a winter morning and the dark only the empty night.

Regeane stumbled toward the bed, shivering, her teeth chattering, and dove under the covers. The other world was reaching out for her now. She was sure she couldn't sleep and not sure if she would ever sleep again. But when she next opened her eyes, the sun was sending a shaft of transparent yellow light through the window slit. And the room was full of the low cooing of doves welcoming the morning.

XIX

EMILIA SENT UP BREAD, CHEESE, RATHER WELL-watered wine, and wild strawberry and fig preserves. The bread was fresh baked, the preserves so honey-sweet Regeane ate every bit and scraped the dish. Folded on the table Regeane found a soft linen shift and a robe of fine, brown woolen.

Washing water arrived in a ewer carried by a nun wearing the same soft shade of brown robe as that on the table.

She was a woman of severe mien with an eye that glittered like an eagle's. Despite a webwork of wrinkles, her face held the same threatening bird of prey profile that dominated the monuments of the past scattered through the city.

She fixed Regeane's silk shift and satiny pepulous with a stern, disapproving eye. "I am Barbara," she told Regeane, "and despite the name, I am Roman born and bred. I am the cook and you are assigned to the kitchen. Wash and dress. I'm already behind in my work. I will expect you there promptly. Please hurry." She stalked out.

Regeane hurried. She was given an apron by Sister Barbara and set to placing a joint of meat over a fire pit just outside the door.

Most of Regeane's life had been spent locked up or on her mother's endless pilgrimages. Her meals had been taken in wayside taverns and religious hostels. She knew very little about cooking.

The meat began to char. At the first hint of a stink, Barbara arrived like a thunderbolt. She directed a look at Regeane that nearly struck her dead on the spot and then she moved the spit up six notches higher on the rack.

"Don't you know anything?" she asked witheringly.

Regeane protested with the utmost meekness. "But so high up, it won't cook?"

"You mean it won't burn," Barbara snapped. "Meat needs must cook slowly. The hot smoke seals the outside. The inside bastes itself in its own juices. And don't question me further. I am," she said grandly, "the greatest cook in Rome. Perhaps the best in the entire world.

"I myself have studied the Frankish culinary arts. The few rude, but delicious innovations of the Saxons and the masterful tradition of our own Roman Apicitis. I need herbs. Now! I will want sage, basil, thyme, and rosemary to stuff the pork roast for supper. You will fetch me a sufficiency at once!"

Barbara clapped her hands. "Hurry. There is not a moment to be lost. This is the best time of day to pick them, after the dew has dried and before they lose their savor to the sun."

Regeane had no idea what a sufficiency was. She managed to get a basil plant and a sage plant up by the roots and she was seriously threatening a rosemary bush when Barbara arrived at her elbow like a striking hawk.

This time, the resulting blast of fury backed Regeane up several paces, clutching the unfortunate plants in her hand. But her feelings must have shown on her face because Sister Barbara broke off in midsentence and peered at her with interest.

"What?" she said. "No tears? Usually I have them in tears by now or red-faced with anger. Not looking at me with mild irritation and even," she peered at Regeane's face, "perhaps contempt. I can see you have some spirit."

Regeane was angry. She could feel the flush of it burning in her cheeks, but then she consulted the wolf and found the creature amused. The images that arose in her dark companion's mind were those of a mother bird cleverly feigning a broken wing to draw a predator away from her nest or a toad squirting and creating a stink, puffing himself up, warts sticking out all over his body, trying to convince the owner of a pair of jaws with long teeth that he was both ferocious and inedible. In a word, a bluff.

"I can see," Barbara said, "that you are an utter neophyte and must be instructed."

In a few moments she had the herb plants back in the ground, soil tamped down around their roots.

"Do you think they'll grow again?" Regeane asked anxiously.

"Bah . . . who knows?" Barbara said with a flip of her hand. "I think so. They are not very far from their wild relatives that flourish in the open places on the Campagna or on hillsides overlooking the sea. If they don't, I have many more."

She did have many more, all growing in brick-sided, raised beds between neatly swept flagstone walks.

Each type of culinary wonder was confined in its own special cubicle. The plants seemed to stand at attention in the morning sun and Regeane could see from the occasional bald patch of soil between them that no weed dared raise its head in this well-ordered place.

Barbara shot a glance at the meat roasting slowly over the fire near the kitchen door, then she led Regeane to a rude seat under an arbor near a wall where they could both sit and enjoy the beauty and delicate fragrances of the morning garden.

"Behold," Barbara said, gesturing at the kitchen and the garden behind it. "Behold my kingdom. I am mistress here and absolute monarch of all I survey. And if you allow yourself to be instructed by me, you, too, will lord it over your own kingdom one day even if it is only a walled garden."

Two trees guarded the small arbor, bending over the iron trellis. Regeane reached out a tentative hand toward one of the leaves.

"Go on, child," Barbara said. "Pluck one and savor its fragrance."

Regeane did. "Bay," she said. It reminded the wolf of the night she seemed inexorably driven toward the ghostly temple, high above the sea.

"Yes," Barbara said, drawing Regeane out of memory. "The bush that provides us with crowns for our conquerors and savory pot roasts."

Regeane laughed. "And which one do you prefer?"

"Why, the pot roasts of course, but not for the reason you think. Not because I'm a cook."

"Why then?" she asked.

"Because conquerors come and go, but the pot roast endures forever."

"Surely not," Regeane said. "It's eaten at the next meal."

"Quite the contrary. Great Caesar himself delighted in the flavor of meat cooked with mushrooms and wine, and a thousand years from now men and women will make pilgrimages to a place where they can eat a meal prepared in the same way.

"No, my dear, it is the conqueror who is ephemeral and the pot roast which is eternal. That is why Christ in his wisdom made His greatest sacrament a simple meal. Because the need is not simply for nourishing, but good food binds all mankind into one. Together they sit down three times a day to share the riches of the earth and the fruits of their toil with one another.

"The pope may eat his from a silver dish with cardinals at his side, and the laborer sits on a stone with a piece of bread and a single jug of coarse wine in the company of a few friends, but they both give thanks to God for the same thing. And who knows?" Her eyes twinkled. "The laborer may enjoy his bread and wine more than the pope his ample repast. 'Tis said appetite is the best sauce. In any case, Emilia has chosen me to be your instructor in this greatest and most ancient of all arts."

Regeane stared at a patch of dill pensively. The umbeliforous heads were almost ripe and ready to drop their hard, brown seeds. "I'm not sure how long I'll have to learn what you can teach me. I'm to be married soon."

"Yes," Barbara said, "so I hear, to some wealthy mountain lord. No doubt a drunken ruffian who goes to bed every night in his boots."

Regeane first sighed deeply, but found herself smiling and then laughing outright. "Not you, too?"

"So Emilia told you her story, did she?" Barbara said.

"Yes, the last night when we returned from the Lateran."

"I hope you got the short version," Barbara mused. "Sometimes she embellishes it describing how he first turned pale, then gray, followed by blue, then . . ." Barbara threw up her hands. "Black!" she exclaimed. "How he clutched at his throat." She clutched at her throat dramatically. "How he arched his back." She arched her back.

"Oh, stop!" Regeane cried. She was holding her sides and

tears were running down her cheeks. "Stop. It's not funny. The poor man died!"

"Very so, he did," Barbara said, easing her body back on her seat. "God rest his soul. Though if even half the things Emilia says about him are true, I doubt if he did. Find rest, that is."

She patted Regeane lightly on the knee. "Never mind, my dear. What else can you expect when you come among a group of women who have retired from the world. We . . . most of us have our reasons. Besides, don't you think it's as well to be prepared for the worst? In this world our hopes for the best are so often disappointed." She smiled kindly at Regeane.

But Regeane looked sadly past her at a sundial standing amidst a patch of calendula in the center of the garden. Each flower was a small sunburst, a frolicking ground for bees as they went their ever busy way among the newly opened blossoms and the sundial cast its long morning shadow on its stone mounting.

Hope for the best, Regeane wondered. *What is the best she could hope for? Someone so brutal and dangerous that she could meet him in the darkness with a clear conscience? If her conscience could ever be clean after such a sin.*

But Barbara took her hand. "Oh, come now, don't let my idle speculation cast a shadow for such a bright morning as this. Besides, if he is as I have said, no doubt you can disarm him with your beauty and grace. And as for cooking, I should say if he is wealthy, what you'll need to do is learn to manage the cook. I can teach you how to do that in a word."

"In a word?" Regeane asked.

"Yes," Barbara said, "and the word is flattery. Taste the man's food and if he seems at least halfway competent to you, lay it on with a trowel. For if cooking is the greatest and most ancient of all arts, it is also the most unappreciated and praise is rarer than gold and more precious than rubies to even its most humble practitioners.

"Only flatter him and he will draw on all his skills to please you and your husband. As to that other thing of which men are so fond, pay close attention to Lucilla and faithfully follow her precepts and I'm sure you'll be rewarded with deep devotion. After all, a lout like him must be delighted to be offered a woman of the royal house. And if he wants to keep a whole skin, he'll cherish you. You might point out gently to him—oh, so very gently—that if he doesn't, the Frankish king might take it as a personal insult. I'm sure he wouldn't want that." Barbara smiled a perfectly sweet, ingenuous smile.

Regeane turned and stared apprehensively at Sister Barbara for a second. "Lucilla?" she asked. "How do you know about Lucilla?"

"By now, my dear, everyone knows about Lucilla. Have no fear. Lucilla's not a connection that will damage your reputation. Lucilla has many friendships among the women of this city. Among the powerful as well as the humble and weak. She is greatly esteemed, sometimes I think in places where even she doesn't realize it."

"The pope has forbidden her to visit me," Regeane said.

"So I heard," Barbara said, producing shears from her pocket. "How Emilia does talk." She put the shears in Regeane's hand. "Now, go fetch me those herbs I asked for and take your time. Meet my friends, the beautiful, harmless things growing here. Because by learning them and their proper uses one can turn even simple peasant fare into a delight that would charm princes and kings. And don't be afraid to cut anything, for nothing noxious or evil grows in my garden."

Regeane took the shears and wandered out. Barbara's herbs and flowers enchanted Regeane and the wolf, also. The shadow on the sundial was much shorter when she returned to the kitchen and found Barbara up to her elbows in bread dough.

Regeane set the herbs on a chopping block and turned her attention to a task about which she felt full confidence— scrubbing pots and pans.

The kitchen was airy and pleasant. She tackled the pots with a will as Barbara finished forming the bread into loaves and began chopping herbs with a two-handed curved knife while she began Regeane's initiation into the culinary arts.

"Basil," she said, lifting a sprig to her nose. "The regular kind and also cinnamon and clove. I hope you noticed the difference."

"I did," Regeane answered. "I'm sorry if I got too much. I hope they won't go to waste."

"Not at all," Barbara said, laying some aside. "The cinnamon and clove will do nicely to spice the baked apples I plan for lunch. Here," she said, stripping the leaves from another stem. "Clary sage, an interesting choice, my dear. Long-stemmed thyme. Ah, you know something at least: a bit of rue, the merest tinge of bitterness, corrects the sweetness of a wine sauce. Rosemary, ever indispensable to the cook, and I will add a touch of garlic and the bread crumbs and we have our stuffing. This evening you may taste and see if any of your choices went awry."

Regeane was immediately alarmed. "You're going to trust in my choices?"

"Not entirely," Barbara said wielding the knife with what Regeane recognized as a highly skilled rocking motion. "But as I told you, cooking is an art and even a beginner must be allowed some experimentation if he or she is ever to reach full potential. And when you are finished with the pots, my dear, you may give the floor a good scrubbing," Barbara said grandly.

"Thank you," Regeane murmured quietly.

Regeane scrubbed while Barbara held forth on the flesh of every member of the animal kingdom of which Regeane had ever heard and several the more conservative Franks didn't think of as food, i.e., snails and songbirds, and when she was finished with these, she moved on to descriptions of less animate life, beginning with fruits and nuts and working down at last to the lowly cabbage. Wherein she paused, not for breath, but to inform Regeane it was time to rake out the bread oven.

"I set the fire myself," she said, "when I came down at dawn and it will be burned to cinders by now, and the stones will be hot and ready to puff the dough to golden fullness." She handed Regeane a bucket and a long-handled rake. "Now, be careful. The door is hot and the stones, too. Don't get too close. I'll open the door for you."

Barbara was holding the oven door open and Regeane was raking like mad, trying to get the still live coals into the bucket before the stone oven cooled when Emilia entered the kitchen.

"Barbara, just what in the world do you think you're doing?"

"We're working," Barbara snapped. "What does it look like we're doing? You told me to teach her to cook."

"Teach her to cook, yes," Emilia cried in horror. "Not turn

her into a scullion. She is a royal lady. I meant for you to let her gather a few herbs, perhaps peel a turnip or two."

Barbara slammed the oven door. Regeane was only just able to jerk the rake clear in time to prevent its being broken in half.

"What!" Barbara shouted. "You object to my teaching her that cooking is work?" She drew herself up proudly. "I . . . I, the daughter of one of the first families in Rome. I don't scruple to get my hands dirty in the service of our community. Why should she?"

Emilia threw up her hands. "Barbara, people talk . . ."

"How well I know," Barbara said grimly.

"No matter. No matter at all," Emilia said. "I'm aware I'm not blameless, but what if her royal kin should get wind of her cleaning out ovens? And what else have you had her doing this morning?"

"She gathered a few herbs."

Emilia nodded approvingly.

"Cleaned the pots and scrubbed the floor."

"Scrubbed the floor!" Emilia moaned. First, she clutched at her chest, then pressed the back of her hand to her brow. Then she snatched Regeane by the arm and towed her out of the kitchen, barely allowing her time to drop the bucket and rake.

They were off down the hall, Emilia pulling Regeane behind her, muttering to herself. "What will His Holiness think?"

"I don't—" Regeane began, but Emilia cut her off.

"What will the king think?"

"Please—" Regeane said.

"What," Emilia almost shouted, "will Lucilla think?"

They turned at the end of the short corridor to the kitchen and started up the stair.

Regeane snatched at the newel post, locked her elbow firmly around it, and brought them both to a halt.

"Eh, what?" Emilia said.

"Please, Emilia," Regeane implored. "Please let me wash my hands and face."

"Hands and face?" Emilia asked as if she'd temporarily forgotten the meaning of the two words. "Oh, yes. Definitely the hands and face. Definitely."

"Thank you," Regeane said, "and I wouldn't worry too much about my royal kin. I don't know any of them."

"But don't you see?" Emilia answered in some distress. "Whether you know them or not is unimportant. They are bound to know you, and that's what matters. Come, we'll see how Sister Angelica likes you. She teaches a more ladylike skill—embroidery."

"Oh, dear," Regeane said.

SISTER ANGELICA DIDN'T LIKE REGEANE AT ALL. She made that plain from the outset. Obviously used to training the younger and more nimble-fingered daughters of the poor, she found an older noblewoman a definite embarrassment.

She gave Regeane a glance lightly glazed over with ice and lost no time in assessing her needlework skills. Those were, as far as Angelica was concerned, nil—confined to weaving, mending, and patching. In other words, the activities required of a girl of shabby, genteel birth who wanted to keep her back decently covered. The skills with gold and silver thread required by fancywork had always been beyond Regeane's means.

So she was set to doing a simple cross-stitch in one end of a plain linen altar cloth.

Regeane was submissive, but perfectly disgusted. She much preferred scrubbing the kitchen floor in Barbara's company. She, at least, treated Regeane as a willing pupil and, in some ways, an equal, whereas Sister Angelica tried, with some success, to pretend she didn't exist at all.

So Regeane sat quietly at the table with the rest, her head bowed quietly over the cross-stitch, and endured. She soon discovered there was much to endure.

Sister Angelica announced to her, as if making an important discovery, that idle hands and idle minds were the devil's workshop, and no talking among her pupils was allowed. Instead of chatting among themselves, they listened to readings intended for their edification and entertainment. Today, she told Regeane, it consisted of an account of the persecutions of Diocletian.

At first, Regeane only half listened. But then the very ordinariness of the people she was hearing about drew her. They were not in the least like the magnificent and often tragic characters she found in the histories she sometimes read. But rather the humble, who are never of much note in the great march of human affairs.

They were servants, slaves, artisans, small shopkeepers, and the occasional poor priest or prelate—shadowy figures moving quietly among their flocks preaching courage by their example.

And their only sin was that they had the misfortune to cross an imperium so bloated with conceit that it could find no more fitting object to worship than itself, a self personified by the goddess, Roma.

Not to worship at this shrine of naked power was, to the imperial government, a dreadful crime deserving the cruelest punishments. Their deaths were horrible and depicted in meticulous detail.

As the stories continued on and on, Regeane found her imagination begin to clothe the actors with life.

When men were spoken of, Regeane saw Hadrian, a man willing to sacrifice himself rather than commit what he considered an evil act or Antonius who, even lost in the darkness of his crippling disease, had found the courage to be kind to her when they first met.

When women walked into the gruesome spotlight of torture and death she saw Lucilla, proud and ruthless, but also kind and courageous. Or her mother, bringing her crushed heart to a God she believed she'd failed and whose love she felt she didn't deserve.

The children, though, were the worst because they brought Elfgifa to mind. The child's Saxon pride and her impudent innocence.

The story of one mother, who fought with her child and taking the little hand in hers forced the lifesaving sacrifice, tore at her heart. Surely she herself would burn incense to a thousand gods rather than see Elfgifa perish.

Adherence to principle was well and good and Regeane could understand it. But a mother's love, so deeply rooted in the fabric of life, was a force that could transcend even the power of law and the state and made nothing of principle.

As Regeane's needle flew back and forth through the cloth,

she began to feel at first depressed, and then weighed down by the inevitability of the stories. She had not known there were so many imaginative and cruel ways to deprive human beings of life. The stubborn resistance of the Christians must sometimes have brought out the worst in their executioners.

Regeane began to feel that if she had to listen to another account of branding, flogging, roasting alive, or flaying, she would leap to her feet, throw the altar cloth at Sister Angelica, and storm out of the room when a solution to her problem presented itself.

During a cheerful description of molten lead being poured into someone's open wounds, a shaken Regeane missed the cloth and slashed her palm with the needle.

The cut wasn't deep, but it hurt and bled copiously. Regeane dropped the needle and cloth into her lap and clutched at her wrist. The blood ran between her fingers and dripped on the linen in her lap.

Sister Angelica had hysterics. She had them with great determination and skill.

Abbess Emilia arrived. She clucked, tished, and tut-tutted, applied cold compresses and aromatics . . . not to the still bleeding Regeane, but to Sister Angelica.

A few minutes later, Regeane found herself back in the kitchen with Sister Barbara. She washed the cut on Regeane's hand with wine.

"Nothing," she said. "A mere trifle. It will heal in a few days. Tell me, my dear, what did it? Patient Grizelda, the sufferings of the holy church under the Emperor Nero, or the persecution of Diocletian?"

"Diocletian," Regeane said.

"Ah, well," Barbara answered, "you were spared the worst."

"I can't imagine anything worse," Regeane said.

"I can," Barbara said. "Patient Grizelda. I find the worthy woman's sufferings both boring and infuriating. Sister Cecelia, a rather learned woman you have yet to meet, tells me the tale was written as a moral lesson to young girls that they might learn to respect and obey their husbands. But I firmly believe Angelica has it read as an inducement to virtue and new vocations.

"Given weekly doses of patient Grizelda, even the less impressionable of her pupils emerge, if not confirmed man-haters, at least cherishing a firmly rooted distrust and fear of the whole sex. This she feels makes it easier for them to forgo the more transient delights of the world and," she added piously, "fix their eyes on the eternal lover." Barbara promptly belied the piety of this statement by laughing uproariously.

"It isn't funny." Still caught up in the story, tears started in Regeane's eyes. "It was terrible and all the poor people wanted to do was live in peace and practice their religion . . . and I don't see how you can laugh."

Barbara's face sobered and she reached out one hard, calloused hand and touched Regeane's cheek. "Oh, my dear, how young you are. Sometimes I forget my years and the distance that separates me from children like you.

"I laugh, my dear, because time has given me a besetting sin called perspective. The dead are dead, and nothing we can do will help them. Besides, one hopes they will have forgotten the griefs of the dust in eternal bliss. And because I know many of God's people saved their lives, and no doubt their families also, by committing apostasy, which makes me feel better. It shouldn't, but it does."

Barbara patted Regeane's cheek gently and gave her a smile so infectious that Regeane found herself smiling back in unabashed delight.

"There now," Barbara said, "that's better." Then she stepped back and daubed at Regeane's cut with the wine-soaked cloth. "See," she said. "It's stopped bleeding."

Regeane shook her head. "I can't understand how she can listen to all those horrors day after day, and get so upset about a little blood."

"Tell me," Barbara asked, "did you bleed on the piece you were embroidering?"

"Yes," Regeane answered.

"Then that's what she was upset about. Better you had cut your throat and bled on the floor rather than spoil any of her handiwork. Besides, they are not horrors to her."

"No?" Regeane asked. "How could they not be?"

"They are only words to her, my dear. You see, she has no

imagination and you do. Now, come help me set the table for the afternoon meal."

Barbara led Regeane to the refectory. It was a long, low-ceilinged room beamed in oak. The room had no windows, but looked out past a porch supported by wooden uprights on a small garden filled with late-blooming roses. The bushes were arranged in a circle around a waterfall fountain whose flow trickled down from a pipe over mossy stones.

Regeane immediately walked to the porch and gazed longingly out at the sunlit garden. "Oh, how beautiful they are," she said. "I didn't know so many of them bloomed this late in the season."

"Yes," Barbara said. "That is why they are called the 'roses of the double spring.' This was Abbess Hildegarde's favorite garden. When she came here to found her convent she brought some exquisite white-flowered ones with her from the chill mist of her northern land. Everyone said they would die in our warm southern clime, but they didn't. They thrived and even made love to our own native varieties and now we have several the like of which have not been seen before. People come from all over Rome to cut canes and start them in their own gardens."

"Made love?" Regeane asked.

"It's as good a word as any," Barbara said. "Though flowers do it in all innocence with the help of bees. But come, let's get the table set. It's almost time to ring the dinner bell."

The refectory had one long, plain wooden table with benches stretching its length on either side. A big sideboard stood against the wall of the room opposite the garden. It held plates, cups, spoons, and serving dishes.

The table was very simple—long boards set in a row but polished to a high gloss.

Regeane jumped back when she saw a lectern on one end. "Oh, no," she said.

"Never fear," Barbara laughed. "Abbess Emilia chooses the readings at meals and she doesn't like to hear anything that disturbs her digestion. She likes a bit of Boethius or some psalms, the more cheerful ones. And occasionally, a story about the Eastern fathers, happy ascetics living in the desert, fed by manna from heaven. Now set fourteen places. Give everyone a plate, a bowl, a spoon, a cup, and a napkin."

When Regeane was finished, Barbara surveyed her work and pronounced herself satisfied. They both brought in the food.

Barbara rang the bell and the nuns hurried to their meal. To Regeane's great relief, there was no reading at all.

By the time Regeane was finished eating, she was convinced Barbara's claim to being the best cook in the world was true.

The first course was a thick lentil soup spiced with herbs and chopped ham. The second, roast meat in a sauce made with the drippings carefully combined with chestnuts, mushrooms, and wine. The dessert was honey-glazed apples, lightly seasoned with the cinnamon and clove basil, topped with rich cream.

Regeane ate until she could eat no more. Then she rose and helped Barbara clear the table.

The nuns drifted out of the room slowly to their afternoon siestas, leaving Emilia, Barbara, and Regeane alone.

"Well, how was it?" Barbara asked Emilia impatiently.

"Incomparable as always, Barbara," Emilia said. She spoke as one paying the usual tribute to superb fare, but Regeane noticed she looked worried and preoccupied.

"What's wrong?" Barbara snapped.

"Nothing," Emilia said hurriedly. "I was only wondering what to do with the girl."

"That's easy. Send her up to Cecelia. She can spend a quiet afternoon with her."

"I don't know," Emilia said hesitantly. "Cecelia's such a butterfly. Her accounts never balance, her letters go out only after I've prodded and urged for months on end and . . ."

"And," Barbara said, "all her students love her."

"Yes," Emilia said, "because she stuffs their heads with dreams."

"I see nothing wrong with a few dreams, Emilia," Barbara said glancing at Regeane, "especially at her age. Better dreams than nightmares."

"Oh, very well. I suppose it's the best place for her right now. Explain to her about Sister Cecelia and send her upstairs to the scriptorium. When you're finished, come back. I have something important to discuss with you."

"Very well," Barbara said. "Regeane, come to the kitchen. I'll prepare a tray for Cecelia."

Regeane followed Barbara and waited while Barbara began slicing the roast.

"Now," Barbara said as she arranged the slices on a silver platter, "you will notice when you enter that Cecelia wears a heavy veil over the lower part of her face."

Regeane was spooning cream over the baked apples. "Why?" she asked.

"Because," Barbara said, "she has no nose."

CARRYING THE TRAY, REGEANE ENTERED THE scriptorium with some trepidation. As Barbara had said, a heavily-veiled woman sat near a book stand in the corner. "Ah, my dear Regeane," the veiled woman greeted her. "Barbara told me she would find some way to send you to see me before the day was over. Set the tray on the table and please sit down. I hope Barbara sent up enough for two. As you see, I have a guest."

Regeane frowned for a moment, puzzled, then recognized Dulcina, the singer she had heard at the pope's banquet last night.

"If I know Barbara," Dulcina said, smiling, "she sent up enough for three." She rose, took the tray from Regeane's hands, and set it on the table. Then she embraced Regeane.

Confused for a moment, Regeane stiffened and almost drew back, but deep within her the wolf gave a soft, inaudible cry and she relaxed in Dulcina's loving embrace.

The wolf fully awakened and her memories filled Regeane's

mind. Memories of singers long ago. Singers so gentle, so much a part of the living world that their voices had the power to call even the savage wolf packs of the mountains from their dens down into cool, green, high meadows, dotted with copses of silver birch and red-berried rowan, where she, like the rest of the wolves, lay at the singers' feet. The fiercest among them at peace with God and man, enraptured with the glory of the song.

"Daughter of Orpheus," Regeane greeted her almost adoringly.

Cecelia applauded, clapping her hands softly. "Excellent," she said. "Were we all not Christians today, Orpheus would indeed be your patron, Dulcina."

Regeane studied Dulcina's face. She remembered Augusta's cruel story of how her life began—a waif singing in taverns for a few coppers to buy extra food. The sadness of such a beginning still lingered. Dulcina was thin-faced with high cheekbones, startling emerald-green eyes, and dark, fine, mouse-colored hair. She managed somehow to look even more aristocratic than Augusta. But a shadow of sorrow hovered in the brilliant, jewel-like eyes and in the soft curve of her lips. She seemed confused and even a little embarrassed to be so praised.

"But we are all Christians now and a daughter of Orpheus is an outcast among the godly," she said.

"What foolishness," Cecelia said with a merry laugh, the laugh of a happy child.

As Regeane drew closer to her, she realized Cecelia's eyes, the only part visible above the heavy veil, were a child's eyes. Soft blue, clear, wide, and innocent, they confronted the world with the same open enjoyment as Elfgifa's. It was as though she were always ready to be amused and delighted by any new experience that came her way.

As Regeane took Cecelia's hand, she was close enough to see, in the shadowy planes of her cheeks and outline of her lips, the vibrant glow of what once must have been great beauty.

Cecelia took Regeane's hand in both of hers and patted it. "My dear, I quite agree with Lucilla. You are everything she says and more: intelligent, sensitive, and beautiful. Come, sit down and join us. Dulcina has a message for you from Lucilla."

"Yes," Dulcina said, taking her seat at the table. "She asked me to tell you that her house is safe again, guarded by a company of Frankish mercenaries. And you may shelter there whenever you wish."

"Thank you," Regeane said.

"A clever woman, Lucilla, though devious at times," Cecelia said. "But given her rather equivocal social position in Rome, I suppose it's necessary."

Devious, yes, Regeane thought, meeting Dulcina's sad, but somehow wise eyes. *Lucilla had managed to obey the letter of Hadrian's orders while disobeying them completely.*

She had contrived to send a message to Regeane without visiting her or even dispatching a messenger. Regeane exchanged glances of perfect understanding with both women. Cecelia, in spite of her almost childlike innocence, understood this as well as Regeane and Dulcina. Mirth flashed in Cecelia's eyes and the breath of her soft chuckle disturbed the heavy linen veil over her lips.

"Lovely Dulcina, I hope you won't be in a hurry to leave now that your real business with me is concluded. Autumn or no, the streets of Rome are crowded and dusty and a long, stuffy ride in a curtained litter would be tedious and fatiguing."

Dulcina's fair-skinned cheeks flushed slightly and she lowered her eyes. "I would do anything Lucilla asked me to," she said. "Noble lady, if I seemed to use you, I can only say I'm sorry."

"I did wonder what was going on," Cecelia said, "when the foremost songstress of Rome presented herself at my door, bearing a cherished and long-coveted gift. As soon as you asked to see Regeane, I understood. And don't dare apologize for your unswerving loyalty to your distinguished patroness. Would that we all had such faithful hearts. I have no qualms about being used in such a noble enterprise as keeping Hadrian in the papal chair."

Regeane gave a start of surprise. "How did you know . . ." she began.

Cecelia waved a hand at her, motioning her to be silent. "For years," she said, "everyone has known Lucilla served Hadrian's interests in every possible way. Her intrigues as much as anything were responsible for his election as pope. Please convey my greetings to her and request that she visit me at her convenience, for I have observed her career from afar for many years and often longed to meet her."

Dulcina's reply was equally formal. "She, too, I believe, has longed to meet you, but I think she feared the humiliation of being turned away. Many have. You are more accessible to the poor than to your old friends. Indigent young girls find a home in your literature and music classes, while the first families are turned away from your door."

Cecelia sighed. "Yes. I suppose I have been guilty of excluding a few of my former acquaintances. But I fear many of those who called were only seeking a moment's titillation, an opportunity to gossip about my . . ." She sighed. "My great misfortune. I can hear them now. 'Oh, my dear,' " she mimicked, " 'How is she bearing up? Is it true she is as ugly now as she once was beautiful? Pray, tell me, did you get a glimpse of her face? Or does she remain always veiled as they say? And banishes all mirrors from her chambers?' What they offered was not true friendship, but only a kind of morbid curiosity. Being the object of such attention is at best unpleasant, at worst infuriating."

Dulcina smiled ruefully. "My lady," she said, "I believe you may have outlived that morbid curiosity, as you call it. During the time you were in society in Rome you were known as the arbiter of beauty and good taste. Now your approval is sought by every aspiring poet and artist, often in vain."

"Truly," Cecelia said, seeming to preen herself behind her veil. "Ah, but then it is 'the unattainable' all poets and artists seek." She sighed. "I suppose my goodwill has simply become another unattainable thing."

"I don't know," Dulcina said. "All I know is that you are both sought after and feared. A kind word from your lips opens many doors. A harsh judgment closes them for you are famed far and wide as the most formidably learned woman in Rome. 'Too prolonged,' you say of one poet, and he, in fear of you, shortens his verses. 'Bombastic' you say of another and he tempers his hexameters with lyrics. Praise or blame from you is valued indeed. That's why I both hoped and feared I wouldn't be sent away after I brought my message to Regeane because whatever you think of my little songs, the ultimate obliquity would be to be dismissed by you without a word. No matter whether your judgment be for good or ill, I cannot bear to think I inspire indifference."

Cecelia began to applaud again. "Wonderful. Never have I been approached with such grace and charm. Of course, I'm as vain as the next woman. More so, I should think. Flattery will get you anywhere with me. But come, my dear," she said, placing a hand on Regeane's arm. "In this conversation between Hera and Athena, we are forgetting Aphrodite."

Regeane colored to the roots of her hair. "Oh, my goodness. Aphrodite, surely not."

"Who would you be then?" Cecelia asked. "Dulcina's words crown me as Hera, the all-powerful goddess. She herself must surely be Athena, wisdom enthroned. So, for the purposes of this little symposium, who are you?"

"Diana," Regeane said. "The virgin goddess, lover of wild things, the forest dweller, patroness and protector of maidens, the lady of moonlight."

"Diana, the huntress?" Cecelia questioned. "What would the virgin goddess know of love?"

"She would be," Regeane said, "an acute and objective observer."

Cecelia began to laugh. "I daresay she would be."

Regeane took her seat on a long book chest beneath a window that looked down on the rose garden. Wooden louvered blinds covered the window. The dusty rays of the afternoon sun shone through the partially open slats, creating a pattern of gold on the floor.

Dulcina stepped into this tracery of light and shadow holding a lyre in her hand.

"Do you know Propertius, my dear?" Cecelia asked.

"The name, no more," Regeane answered. "Augusta, that's Lucilla's daughter, spoke of him."

"I know who Augusta is," Cecelia said. "I also know she would rather not claim that redoubtable woman as a parent."

"Yes," Regeane said. "She's ashamed of her. In any case, when Dulcina sang at the pope's banquet, Augusta mentioned Propertius as the author of her song."

"I have written a musical setting for many of his works," Dulcina said. "I would like to present them to you now." So saying, she struck the lyre and began to sing.

Gradually, almost imperceptibly, Regeane found herself transported back in time. To a world where Rome was the glittering queen of cities and to be a prosperous citizen of this ruling city was the very pinnacle of good fortune.

Dulcina sang of a young poet newly come from the provinces, and told in his own words how he met his fate in the eyes and face of the loveliest of women, his Cynthia. The tormented power of his passion spilled from the verses Dulcina sang and vibrated in the dusty air of the room.

The music of his poetry was alive, as vivid, as real to Regeane as the day when the poet penned them. Regeane was as seduced and enraptured by this world as the poet was.

A world where conquerors reveled uncaring amidst the spoils of whole continents. A world where men and women drank the fairest vintages and reclined on silken couches amidst the splendor of colored marble, gazed at paintings by the finest artists, and ate delicacies spiced with flavors of lands so far away they were only legends.

A world where married women like Cynthia draped themselves in coan silk and the softest linen. Aglitter with jewels, they ignored their complacent husbands and dispensed their favors when and where they willed.

A world where lamps burned all night and a lover and his mistress could drink together till dawn and then couple in savage passion on the very couches of the banquet hall.

Regeane listened as the poet moved from infatuation to adoration, his delight in his goddess-like mistress seeming to lift him as far above mere mortals as the immortal gods, finding both ecstasy and peace in her arms . . . until the darkness crept in.

Love, Regeane thought, seems to demand eternity and desire possession of its object. The poet realized he had neither one.

Was Cynthia really a loose woman or only too frail a vessel for the poet's immortal fire, she wondered. Slowly, over the time of their affair, the poems change. They become even more brilliant. The verse sings more beautifully as the poet descends into savage jealousy and morbid self-loathing as his obsession with the woman begins to destroy him. In the end, his hatred for Cynthia seemed as great as his love had been. He dreamed of her death and, perhaps, desired it.

Did she die or not? Regeane wondered. Or did the poet only want her to be dead to him? No matter, because the poet found there is no freedom from love, even in death.

Cynthia's shade comes to trouble his sleep. Even as her voice calls from the world beyond death, it is drenched with passion and desire. She promises a restless eternity. The serpents that guard the tomb will weave among our mortal relics. Thy bones will twine with mine. Threat or promise? Who could tell? Perhaps neither, but only a statement that love once given is stronger than death and she would remain his real and only love all the days of his life and beyond.

But Propertius' songs end on a strangely high note. The last poem, mock-heroic in tone, tells how a very much alive and angry Cynthia drove the whores from his bed, the pimps from the triclinium. She purified the house and opened her arms to him. And the poet leaves us with a picture of himself and his mistress lying together in contented bliss. The first man to tell us that love is better than power or conquest sleeps at last, forever, in his Cynthia's arms.

Regeane came down to earth with a bump. She sighed and stretched.

"A little unwatered wine, my dear," Cecelia said. "Some for all of us."

Regeane poured three cups. Cecelia wouldn't and didn't remove her veil to drink. The thing was long and loose. She lifted it out.

"Well?" Dulcina asked, putting the lyre back in its case.

"You need no praise from me," Cecelia said. "Certainly you know how good you are, but you'll get it nonetheless. I will recommend you to the first houses in Rome. And I'll never speak to anyone again who denies you admittance. But come, we're neglecting Barbara's largess."

They gathered around the table. The food was still edible, warm and as delicious as it had been earlier.

Regeane found herself embarrassed to be eating another

lunch so soon. The wolf wasn't embarrassed, however. Regeane got a sneer from her alter ego. And both she and Dulcina fell to with a will.

"It seems," Regeane said, lifting a particularly generous portion of roast dripping with gravy toward her mouth, "love gives one a tremendous appetite."

"I wouldn't know," Dulcina said. "I've never been in love."

"Ah," Cecelia said as she managed the complicated process of spooning baked apple under her veil without getting a drop on herself or the cloth. "But you do have a lover."

"Albinus?" Dulcina said. "My lady, the man is rising seventy. He doesn't even bother to hide his bald spot and never worries about his paunch. If I went into transports of ecstasy about him, the shock might kill him. I'm an artist. I may sing of love and while I'm singing I may believe in it, but I don't plan my life around it. I'm far too practical."

"And you, Regeane?" she asked.

"I'm to be married to a man who commands a pass in the Alps," she said.

"Oh, you poor dear," Cecelia said. "Some ferocious barbarian, no doubt. Yet many of these northern lords are tall, handsome men, fond and respectful of their womenfolk. And," she said as if trying to soften, "it may be you will come to love him."

"I hope not," Regeane said. The words popped out of her mouth before she thought. "I don't plan to love him. I plan to survive him."

"How very wise, my dear," Cecelia said.

Dulcina nodded her agreement. "Look at Propertius' love, a theme for poets, a sickness of the soul, a curse."

"But my dear," Cecelia said, "don't we women live for love and build our lives around it?"

"A king and a warrior are going to make a pact over my body," Regeane said. "I see nothing there around which to build a life."

"I see that you're a sensible woman, as I am," said Dulcina. "Lucilla found Albinus for me. He's a very pleasant sort, she told me. 'Of course you'll stand somewhere in his esteem between his water organ and the antique cythera he bought last year in Greece. So don't let his attentions go to your head. But he's generous and if you're prudent and thrifty, I'm sure you'll do quite nicely.' She was right. He is, and I have. Besides she didn't tell me how kind and considerate he was and, believe me, a little kindness and consideration go far with someone who's as well acquainted with neglect and abuse as I am."

"In your unhappy childhood, no doubt," Cecelia said.

"Unhappy isn't the word, my lady," Dulcina said. "All the words I can think of are too impolite to use in your presence. I can remember the day Lucilla came into my life as though it was yesterday."

Regeane was shocked to realized there were tears in Dulcina's eyes.

"She offered me a silver coin to sing for her. I remember I snatched the thing at once and held it tightly clenched in my fist behind my back. For I was afraid if my voice displeased her, she'd take it back, and a little money meant I could lie down in the kennel I slept in, for a few nights running, with a full belly. And you can't imagine how important that was to me at the time.

"I sang the prettiest song I knew for her. A vile, filthy ditty the muleteers who drank in the tavern taught me. They delighted in teaching me all the dirtiest songs they could dredge up. Such foul language falling from a child's innocent lips was always funny to them.

"But Lucilla didn't laugh or blush. When I was finished she put another silver coin in my hand and paid a visit to my master. Then she led me away to paradise. Or at least what was paradise to me. Clean bed linen, good abundant food, and a life lived among people who didn't turn the back of their hand to me for pleasure, as the tavernkeeper did."

"And to think you might be a child belonging to one of the first families of Rome," Cecelia said.

"What?" Regeane asked. "How is that possible?"

"Don't you know, my dear?" Cecelia asked.

"No," Dulcina said. "Her people are barbarians. No doubt they have such tricks among them, but they aren't so widespread or so generally approved of.

"Many families, Regeane," Dulcina explained, "don't bother to raise all the children they have."

"The rich are worse about it than the poor," Cecelia said. "They often don't want to divide an inheritance or pay out a dowry. So the child is abandoned in some public place. They are frequently taken by slave dealers who raise them for future sale."

"Better to strangle them at birth," Dulcina said, "than let them live to endure such suffering as I did. Believe me, life is at best a dubious gift under such circumstances."

"But," Cecelia said, "suppose you had been born beautiful?"

"All the worse for me," Dulcina said. "Then the brothel keeper wouldn't have sold me to the tavern where I learned to sing and came to the attention of Lucilla. As it was, I didn't completely escape the attentions of his . . . customers and it was years before I could endure the touch of a man without cold chills going through me."

"How strange," Regeane said. "Yet you live with Albinus, an old man."

"I never feel afraid of Albinus, and I'm safe, Regeane. So he can never really hurt or disappoint me. You see, I can't love him."

"So you're free to like him," Cecelia said.

"Exactly." Dulcina looked down into her wine cup. "Much more of this and I'll have to be poured into my litter and make the journey home unconscious."

Cecelia pushed the tray toward her. "Eat a little more, my dear. What about you, Regeane? What does the virgin goddess think of love?"

Regeane lifted the wine cup quickly to hide her face because she remembered she had surrendered her first kiss to a nameless shepherd on the Campagna. She had felt only pity for him at the time, yet she vividly recalled the silken brush of those soft lips on her own. Afterward, she had dreamed of caresses far more intimate than that one. Delivered to other places in far more pleasing ways.

She thought of the long nights she had spent alone. In the slow drift between sleep and waking she had journeyed with the wolf across a world of beauty, enchantment, and freedom.

She had run with others across Arctic wastes, through mountain valleys, played in the shallows of rivers by moonlight and . . . they . . . she remembered dimly . . . had always been beside her. Brothers, sisters, and friends. But had the fierce silver beauty lovers? The wolf didn't know and couldn't, or wasn't ready to remember. Had the warm, quivering, eager emptiness of the female desire felt the hot, pulsing power of the male?

And then the awareness surged over her consciousness like the rush of an oncoming tide. Of course the wolf did, and one day the wolf would, but not just yet. No, not quite yet, but soon—very, very soon—she would want . . . what?

Regeane jumped to her feet, turned, and walked quickly to the louvered window. Oh, God, here was a complication, an event she hadn't counted on at all.

She pushed aside the slats and stared down into the garden. The thick heady scent of roses enveloped her.

The wolf reared up in the darkness of her being and examined the world through her eyes. The beast who won the wolf would have to do more than bare his fangs at his rivals. He would have to best all of them at single combat because she wouldn't yield herself for less. The woman could be taken, moved like a pawn on the chessboard of men's power games, but the wolf was free. A lean silver mass of fury who would yield herself only to the best, the strongest, the fiercest of her suitors.

Cecelia's voice broke in on her thoughts. "Excuse me, my dear. Have I been indiscreet? Asked a question I shouldn't have? Perhaps you have a lover?"

Regeane shook her head, her fist clenched at the bodice of her dress. "No," she said. "It would be very dangerous for me to have a lover. My prospective husband might not be jealous of me, but he will certainly be jealous of his honor. No, I was merely thinking. I often dream of love, but when I wake, I find my pillow wet with tears. For if a lover would be a danger to me, it would be even more dangerous for me to learn to love my husband. The length of my marriage depends on the success of my illustrious kinsman, Charlemagne. Should he fail, I'm sure my husband would look around for another match. Divorce is common among the Franks and so is . . . something even cheaper than divorce . . . murder."

Dulcina began to laugh. "Good heavens," she said, "you're even more of a realist than I am."

"Yet your pillow is wet with tears," Cecelia said.

Regeane turned from the window and faced Cecelia. She was sitting at the head of the table and the slanted rays of the westing sun shone on her face and body, covering her with bars of golden light and black shadow.

One struck the veil rendering it for a moment transparent to Regeane's eyes. Under it Regeane could see clearly the soft outlines of a face so beautiful it took her breath away. A sweet, sensual mouth, cheekbones planing down into hollows that made the faces of other women seem broad and squat. Above them, the wide-set, flower-blue eyes. And below, the stark, black triangular hollow where the nose had been.

Regeane tried not to allow her face to show anything as she averted her eyes. She wasn't horrified, but grief-stricken at the destruction of so much beauty. "I wonder what the ancients would have thought of our little symposium?" she said.

"If you mean Plato," Dulcina said. She made a sound of disgust. "Pah! I can imagine that pack of male fools sitting around a table discussing the existence of love, a complete abstraction to them. As though love in the abstract ever existed. Love is always particular, never general."

"Besides," Regeane commented, "I think the philosopher once said women never discuss the nature of love, only lovers."

"Indeed," Cecelia said. "Perhaps Dulcina is right. The philosophers haven't the remotest understanding of love."

"Of course they haven't," Dulcina said. "Any woman who's ever borne a child, nourished it at her breast, cleaned it, protected it through all the years knows more of love than the most intelligent of those fools. But why are we going on about love? Look at your precious Propertius. He was killed by it, or so they say. I'm disgusted by it." She pointed to Regeane. "She's afraid of it, and your life was destroyed by it."

Cecelia flinched and Dulcina clapped her hand over her mouth. "Oh, God," she said, "I'm sorry. I've had too much wine. It must be loosening my tongue."

"Not at all," Cecelia said. "Don't apologize, my dear. I always encourage my pupils to speak freely to me. I like to know what they really think when they read Livy or Cicero. I like to hear about their lives, their hopes, their dreams, their aspirations. They often come and bring their troubles to my ears. Sometimes they ask my advice about their own lives. Nothing they say ever leaves this room. I, in turn, often confide in them. I have told them more than once my story. If it hasn't come to your ears, then they must have been more discreet than I supposed.

"You must understand my family is an ancient one. I even number a few Caesars in my line. It is said we are the purest blood in Rome. We trace our ancestry back to the imperium. But we are poor now, our great estates in Gaul and Britannia long gone, our Latin lands confiscated by the Lombards. All that remains of our once-vast wealth is a villa on the Via Latia and a few vineyards and castalia near Nepi.

"However, given our distinguished position in society, we were not surprised when one of the wealthiest men in Rome asked for my hand in marriage. He was a good thirty-years older than I, but I knew my duty. He offered to restore the family fortunes."

"Yes," Dulcina said, "distinguished ancestors won't repair the leaks in the roof, replace threadbare clothing, or put bread on the table."

"Only too true," Cecelia said. "I was married in my great-grandmother's wedding dress, the only truly magnificent garment our family still possessed, a gown of old-fashioned silk and gold thread embroidered with citrines and seed pearls. The only reason it hadn't been sold was because citrines and seed pearls simply don't fetch enough. Semiprecious stones, you know.

"After the wedding I had no scarcity of magnificent garments or beautiful jewels. Indeed, I was surprised at my husband's generosity toward me, for he was notoriously tight-fisted with everyone else.

"Until one day he presented me with a large black pearl. That night at a dinner party, I failed to wear it. And when the tables were taken down and the guests were gone, I felt the weight of his hand. Then I understood. I wasn't a wife to him or even a human being, but another of his possessions like his huge villa, his horses, or his dogs. I was there to crown his success. To provide the proper setting for his magnificence.

"When I picked myself up off the floor, I told him that I was sorry I hadn't fulfilled my part of the bargain. I told him my omission of the pearl from my finery had been quite inadvertent. It simply didn't go with the dress I planned to wear. He hit me again and said, 'Wear a different dress.' At that moment I understood my worth to him.

"Very well, I told him. I will make you the envy of Rome. Your house will be a showplace, floored with the finest marble. The wall paintings and furniture will evoke gasps of admiration. I will never fail to set myself as a showpiece for your wealth. My attire will always be impeccable. My behavior toward your sometimes dubious business associates will be anything you direct, from the cold to the cordial. But never, never touch me again . . . in any way . . . either in love or in hate, or I will leave on that very day, and no matter what you say or do, I'll never return.

"Suffice it to say, I kept my part of the bargain even as he kept his, though I can't think being deprived of my company was burdensome to him. I was a grown woman, a drawback where he was concerned. I noticed on those rare occasions when he chose to amuse himself he almost always picked something quite a bit younger than I, either boy or girl."

Regeane saw that Dulcina froze for a second, her face stiff with revulsion; then she hugged her slender body tightly and her teeth embedded themselves in her lower lip.

"As for myself," Cecelia continued, "my life became one long loneliness. I hid my misery behind a mask of wit and excruciatingly well-bred politeness. But most of the time, I felt as alone as that unchaste vestal must have, when the earth was sealed over her head and she was condemned to expire in her solitary living tomb. At least, until Rufus appeared at our table.

"He was not especially handsome, but he was strong, wellbuilt, with an infectious grin. He was full of fun, always good humored, and ready with a jest at all times. Whenever I looked into his green eyes, I forgot my sorrows and my loneliness. From the moment we met, he paid close attention to me. At first, it was all very innocent. Small gifts, flowers, a book of poetry, short visits when my husband happened to be away attending to business. We were, you understand, closely chaperoned by my many servants.

"I wasn't about to compromise myself for a barbarian. That's what Rufus was—a Lombard lord—however wealthy or powerful he might be.

"But, as time passed, the visits became longer and longer. We spent whole afternoons together, lost in the fascination of each other's company. You see, Rufus was not like my husband—interested only in increasing his wealth. The whole world was his province. I could be myself with him. He found amusement in the trivialities of running a large household. I often had my hands full with mine. We gossiped for hours about the tangled politics of this great city and the all-too-human personalities behind the politics.

"He had many correspondents in distant lands and never arrived without some new and engrossing tale of the doings of kings in Gaul or Britannia and the intrigues of their barbarian courts, of men made and unmade, and battles won and lost. For you must understand, my dears, when I spoke of these things to my husband, I met with either mockery or anger. But Rufus was never angry with me. And he never mocked me, even sometimes when I think I might have deserved it.

"His gifts, too, became more elaborate and expensive. Priceless, really. Yards of fancy lace made in Byzantium, normally unobtainable in Rome; a packet of some precious fragrant spice from the Far East never found on the spice seller's table in the market here; a psalter illuminated with exquisite knot work made by those Celtic monks who sequester themselves in beehive cells by the stormy northern seas. He brought the world to my door. My shriveled, frightened soul began to open as a flower does to the morning. In short, I began to love him.

"Finally, in desperation, I asked my husband if he was completely indifferent to the connection between Rufus and myself. He answered me in a word: 'Completely.'

"A week later, Rufus invited both of us to visit his villa in the country. The day after we arrived, we all rode out to hunt. My horse pulled up lame. Rufus remained behind with me."

Cecelia paused, turned, and looked at a bouquet of roses in a glass vase at her elbow.

Her attention drawn to them for the first time, Regeane realized they must come from somewhere else than the garden below the window. The roses blooming in the convent garden were mostly single and either pink or white. These were double and so red they seemed almost black in the shadowed room. They showed their true colors only when medallions of broken sunlight found their way between the heavy shutters and brushed the soft petals. In its rays they smoldered like the scarlet coals of a dying fire, glowing as though illuminated from within.

Cecelia reached over and caressed a velvet-soft petal with her fingers. "I have often thought if one could impart the doings of humankind to a rose, the only thing it would understand would be the sweet, drawn-out lovemaking of a drowsy afternoon. The long grass is a bed draped in emerald velvet for lovers. Bees dance drunkenly through a peach orchard. The only clock is the sun moving silently across the sky . . . as it slips toward the cool, blue shadows of a summer twilight.

"When my husband returned from the hunt, I was an adulteress. Rufus and I were lovers. My husband continued to pursue wealth relentlessly. Rufus and I pursued each other. We were lovers by day, by night, under the moon and the stars, at dawn we found each other and at dusk. Whenever we could escape and spend a moment alone, we delighted in the mingling of our bodies and minds. For we were fast friends as well as lovers. The sight of his face and the touch of his hand were enough to fill me with an almost unimaginable joy.

"The years slipped away, one by one, very quickly it seemed then. Until one day I returned home one rainy afternoon and found a man waiting at my door. A supplicant. He begged me to receive him and listen to his plea. I listened at first willingly, and then only because he drew a knife from his sleeve and threatened to cut out his own heart in my presence if I didn't hear him out. So, to my despair and my everlasting sorrow, I did.

"I can't reproduce his speech here. It was rambling, incoherent at times, but the gist of what he told me was this. Many wealthy families draw their income from lands they lease from the church in the countryside around Rome. They pay their dues in kind to the church. The diocese of Rome uses the produce to feed pilgrims and the poor. If the Lombards raid across the border during the harvest, they could not pay in kind, and so must borrow to pay in cash. Should more raids occur, then the landowners go bankrupt and lose everything.

"Now, my husband was a great moneylender. Many important families were in debt to him. My lover was a Lombard count. Need I say more?"

"Your husband was using your lover to systematically ruin his creditors one by one," Dulcina said.

"Just so," Cecelia answered, "and I had been bought and sold like the lowest whore in Christendom and my happiness founded on a quagmire of misery and deceit.

"I can't remember much of what happened in the few hours after this revelation, but the servants ended by hiding all the knives and sharp objects from me. When I tried to hang myself from the ceiling beams in my bedroom, they cut the rope and pulled me down. When I was calm enough to think, I knew what I had to do.

"I summoned all of my husband's creditors I could find to the house and emptied the contents of his strongboxes into their hands. We had wonderful things at our villa. I had the discrimination and good taste to pick the very best. My husband had the money to assure acquisition of anything I desired. I piled everything in the atrium. Tapestries, rare and precious glass, antique statuary, illuminated manuscripts, sumptuous clothing, in short the lot and let them take their pick. When my husband returned home, well . . . there really is no more to be said."

The sun was low now. Long rays were pouring through the louvered windows. The furniture in the room cast heavy shadows, thick and dark amidst the flares of orange brightness.

Regeane stared aghast at Cecelia, a grim suspicion forming in her mind. "You did it to yourself," she accused and she saw the beautiful lips move in a smile under the veil.

Cecelia didn't deny the accusation. "Why yes," she said. "You are quite perceptive, my dear. Very few guess. May I ask how you knew?"

"Your husband wouldn't have done it. Rufus really loved you. He'd have killed Maximus. He was too cold, too crafty to have mutilated you."

"Yes," Cecelia answered, "he was. All I had done had barely injured him. Most of his wealth was invested in his many enterprises in his broad lands, the produce of his vineyards and orchards.

"No, he laughed at me and said, 'What! Tantrums! And from you of all people. Don't be a fool. In the morning, you'll return to him.' But I didn't. I couldn't and I never will. You see, to do so would have made me their accomplice and that I couldn't face."

"So you had your revenge," Dulcina said. "Who can say you were wrong?"

"Strange you should say that," Cecelia said. "Abbess Hildegard used much the same words when I came here seeking shelter from a world that had in one awful day become so unkind. She said, 'You will have a long time to meditate on your revenge.' And I have."

"What happened to your husband?" Regeane asked.

"Rufus saw to that. My husband's estates were as combustible as his creditors. He died a beggar. He was found one morning beside the steps of the Lateran palace where the poor draw their ration of bread and meat for the day. He was dressed in rags, the rain falling into his open eyes."

"And Rufus?" Regeane asked.

Cecelia turned to the roses at her elbow. "How strange," she said. "The moment they go into bloom all over Rome in the spring, they come and keep on coming until the cold autumn wind finally sends their ragged brown petals fluttering to earth. Almost every day, bunches and bunches of them come to the convent door. At first, letters came with them. Of course, I always burned them unopened."

"Of course?" Regeane exclaimed, tears pouring down her cheeks.

"Of course," Cecelia repeated firmly, "but the letters stopped some years ago. Now there are only the roses. And I remember, as he remembers, I'm sure, that for six beautiful years I was the happiest woman on earth."

"I hope to God," Regeane whispered, her hands covering her eyes, "that I never love or hate anything as much as that."

"You will, and I have," Dulcina said thickly, raising the wine cup to her lips. "Only I haven't Cecelia's courage or perhaps I'm simply not sure my destructiveness would hurt the whoremaster who raised me to sell myself in the streets, or the tavern keeper who starved me. My best and only revenge is success."

"And mine," Regeane sighed, "a victory over death."

Cecelia turned to the roses on the table again. "Without love," she said, "we are as the painted images on the glass windows of a church are without the sun, only shadows. Love illumines our lives. When its rays cease to shine into our days, we are nothing.

"Come . . . do we despise the rose because its beauty is fleeting? Some do, and seek comfort in glass or marble. But true love is close to the divine and, like all of God's creations, its beauty unfolds from within. Glass shatters, marble is eaten away by the tides of time. But the rose has unfurled its banner every spring to the sun and will do so for God knows how many uncounted ages more.

"Dulcina, you have your Lucilla and your song. Regeane has something which she will not name and I . . . I have my roses."

She tapped one gently with her finger. The scarlet petals fell, drifting down to lie like a pool of blood on the table beside her hand.

XXI

THE DINNER BELL WAS RINGING AS REGEANE SAW
Dulcina to the door.

Dulcina embraced her once again, then drew back, but kept
her hands on Regeane's shoulders. Her thin face was somber,
her lips set in a hard line. "Take care of yourself," she said. "No,
don't worry. Lucilla didn't tell me anything about you. God
knows, she's close-mouthed about any secrets she has. She has
to be. She probably knows enough to ruin half of Rome. But
there was much in her manner when she asked me to deliver her
message. Don't fear to take shelter with her if you must."

"Thank you," Regeane said.

"No thanks required. An afternoon with Cecelia is more precious than rubies. My fortune is made. No society dinner will be
complete without me. My fees will double within a month."
She caught Regeane in a hard, almost crushing embrace, then
hurried on her way.

Regeane joined Barbara to help set the table.

"How did you like Cecelia?" Barbara asked slyly.

"Oh, God!" Regeane said, almost dropping a serving platter.

"Don't waste your sympathy on her, or my dishes," Barbara
snapped. "In her way I think she's perfectly happy. She brought
about her wretched husband's death, and as for poor Rufus, he,
I might add, is one of the few human beings I have met capable
of life-long devotion. And she has successfully tormented him
for over ten years. Those damned roses don't arrive alone, you
know. Every year he asks, and every year we return the same
answer. Tell me, did she give you her famous speech about
love?"

274

"Er, yes," Regeane answered slowly.

"Humpf," Barbara said. "If that's love, I'd rather be an alley cat."

Regeane had to duck into the corridor near the kitchen since tears of laughter were streaming down her cheeks. "Oh, Barbara, stop," she pleaded, stifling her mirth with the apron.

"Not at all," Barbara said. "Just what you need after Cecelia, a dose of sturdy common sense."

The nuns had begun to file in and sit down. Regeane went to the kitchen and returned with a platter of bread. To her immediate dismay, she realized she hadn't put enough place settings on the table because as the nuns seated themselves, an old woman limped into the room. She was bent with age, her body supported by a heavy, black thorn staff. She was dressed as the others in the same brown woolen cloth. She walked in the direction of the seat beneath the lectern across from Emilia.

As she passed Regeane, she turned. Regeane saw her face was as wrinkled and lined as a withered leaf, but the smile she gave Regeane was both benign and loving. It was so beautiful it lit up her worn features the way the fire in an alabaster lamp sifts through the translucent stone.

"Oh, dear," Regeane said. She set the platter on the table and hurried to the sideboard for another set of eating utensils as the old nun seated herself at the table.

Regeane scurried back to set the plate and cup before her and because she was certain the old woman couldn't be very strong, she poured some wine into the cup and set the jug of water close by her hand.

The old nun acknowledged her courtesy with another beautiful smile and blessed her gently, tracing a cross in the air.

Regeane curtsied politely as one does to a no-doubt-distinguished elder. She was sure the old woman must be someone important to deserve such a high seat at the table.

It wasn't until she stood upright that she realized complete silence had fallen and that Emilia stared at her in something like horror.

"What's wrong?" Regeane asked.

Emilia didn't answer. Instead she jumped to her feet so quickly the bench crashed to the floor behind her and the other nuns on that side of the table who also rose rapidly only saved themselves from falling by clutching at each other's gowns. In a moment, every one of the nuns was across the room, their eyes wide with terror and fixed on Regeane's face.

Regeane looked for the old nun, but there was nothing there, only the plate with the spoon neatly set in the center and a half cup of wine.

"No!" Regeane cried. "No!" She'd backed away from the table, her fists tightly clenched in her apron. "Sometimes I do see them," she babbled, "but I almost always know. She wasn't like the rest—so calm, so polite."

"Who do you see, Regeane?"

The question came from the kitchen door where Barbara stood, a platter of pork roast in her hands.

"The dead," Regeane answered wildly.

Barbara nodded. "What did this one look like?"

"She was old, dressed as the others here are. She limped and leaned heavily on a black thorn stick."

"Abbess Hildegard," Emilia gasped. Her eyes closed and she made the sign of the cross.

"Yes," Barbara said. "That black thorn stick was seldom very far from her hand for the last ten years of her life. She never had a day's sickness, but old bones creak and crack. Ah, well, it's nice to know she still thinks of us and visits us from time to time. A bit unnerving, of course, but nice. Now, let's sit down and have our supper."

"Good heavens, Barbara," Sister Angelica shouted. "How can you be so calm about it? Surely Hildegard didn't visit us for nothing."

It was apparent to Regeane that Sister Angelica was working up to a terrific bout of hysterics. She toppled over like a falling tree. Two of the younger nuns tried to catch her while a third fanned her vigorously.

"And what are we to do about this girl?" Angelica screeched, pointing at Regeane. "She can't embroider and she sets places for the dead!"

"She can hardly be blamed for being polite," Barbara said with a certain grim relish. "She didn't know Hildegard was dead."

"I wish you would stop using that word," Emilia wailed.

"What word?" Barbara asked innocently as she entered the room carrying the roast. When she came close to Regeane, the girl shrank back. "Don't worry," Barbara said. "I'm very much alive."

"No!" Regeane said, gagging and turning her head away. "It's the roast. Can't you smell it?" She retched and clutched at her throat. "The thing reeks. The stench is overwhelming."

Barbara stood for a moment looking nonplussed, then whispered a soft curse under her breath, one at least as bad as anything Regeane had ever heard from Lucilla. "I thought the butcher sold it too cheap."

She placed it on the table and began to slice it carefully, cutting through the thick crust the open-fire cooking had left on the meat. Deep narrow slits had been cut into the roast and some sort of green leaf had been thrust into the openings.

Barbara removed one with the point of the knife and teased it open. The thing was dark and limp from the heat of the cooking fire, but still recognizable.

"What is it?" Emilia asked, stretching out one hand toward the leaf.

Barbara slapped the back of her hand with the flat part of the knife. "Don't touch it. People have died of handling the plant and if Basil is behind this, he can afford the best, or should I say, the most deadly quality of goods. If we had eaten this nice pork roast, it could quite conceivably have killed us all."

Emilia stepped back, making the sign of the cross again. "So Hildegard did have a reason for appearing. What is that leaf?"

"Monkshood," Barbara said.

Wolfsbane, Regeane thought, and for the first time in her life, she wanted to faint. She found it an unpleasant sensation. First there was nausea, followed by dizziness, and then everything started to go black.

The wolf, as usual, saved her. Wolves don't faint. She was energized, wanting to take the corridor to the kitchen on all fours, jump the garden wall, and go find Basil. The wolf's thoughts were very direct and involved tearing flesh, spurting blood, and snapping bone. The fact that the room was lighted and public got her under control very quickly.

"I was the target," she said.

Barbara looked over at her from the other side of the table. "Maybe you flatter yourself, Regeane."

"No. Barbara, I have to get out of here."

Barbara shook her head slightly as if to say, not here, not now.

A loud shriek from the other side of the room interrupted them. "Poisoned!"

"Oh, no," Emilia sighed.

"Ah, dear Sister Angelica," Barbara said.

Sister Angelica was having hysterics in earnest.

Barbara rapped the staring Regeane across the knuckles lightly with the knife. "Pay close attention, my dear. Every woman needs to learn the right moves. This is what you want to do anytime you wish to make an already bad situation worse or, better yet, reduce it to complete chaos and drive all the males in the immediate vicinity to drink."

Sister Angelica shrieked again. "Poisoned!"

The only sound louder than her voice was the clangor of the bell at the gate.

Angelica was on her knees, arms extended toward heaven. Emilia supported her, trying to keep her from falling further.

Barbara spoke to the young nun who was still futilely fanning the air where Sister Angelica's face had been. "Stop creating a draft, Cornelia, and answer the bell."

A few seconds later Cornelia ushered in two soldiers attired in the purple and gold arms of the papal guard and two small boys, one blond, the other dark.

The blond one launched himself at Regeane like a projectile.

The child was in her arms before she realized it was Elfgifa. Regeane goggled at her stupidly for a second, then asked, "What happened to your hair?"

"Postumous' mother cut it off," Elfgifa explained. "She said I was safer as a boy. That was after the riot started in the street and they sliced the man in half and he bled everywhere and the Lombards came looking for us."

"Stop," Regeane said. "What were you doing in Postumous' street in the first place? I thought you were supposed to be here studying your letters with the other children and . . ."

"She's been missing since this morning," Barbara said.

"And you didn't tell me?" Regeane asked furiously.

Barbara shrugged. "What could you have done about it besides worry yourself sick? We had the pope's soldiers out looking for her."

"And," Elfgifa said, nodding, "they didn't find us until a few minutes ago when we started across the bridge and I told them who I was." She hugged Regeane tightly and spoke in her ear. "I only sneaked out to see Postumous because he's my friend and my father says friendship is sacred, but that's not what I want to tell you. Please listen. It's important. I know it is."

Angelica screeched again, interrupting her.

"Why is she hollering?" Elfgifa asked.

Regeane put Elfgifa down, snatched her hand, and led her down the short corridor and into the kitchen. Barbara followed, carrying the roast and setting it down on the table.

"Now, what's so important?" Regeane asked.

"You know the place where we ran when the soldier was chasing us, the place where we met Antonius? Lucilla told me not to talk about it. It's secret, but it can't be a secret from you."

"It isn't," Regeane answered. "What about it?"

"I told Postumous about it," Elfgifa said breathlessly, "and he wanted to see it. So we went around to the drain where we climbed through it the first time, but something was wrong. The place had blood all over and there were bodies in the courtyard. Then the soldiers saw us. We ran. When we got to Postumous' house the soldiers tried to take us, but they were Lombards and the people in the street wouldn't let them. That's when the fight started and the man got sliced in half and Postumous' mother cut my hair." Elfgifa ran out of breath and stopped talking.

Regeane stood up. The kitchen was dark. Regeane looked out the window.

The last rays of the sun were outlining a band of cloud near the horizon with fire. The new moon was an alabaster crescent in an indigo sky spiked with stars. Night was upon her.

What could the Lombards possibly want with the poor people Hadrian had protected along with Antonius, she wondered. Then she remembered with horror that a synod of churchmen was to convene soon here in the city to examine

Hadrian's fitness to be pope. Testimony from them about Antonius might damn him.

"Barbara," Regeane whispered, "I have to go."

Barbara rose from the stove with the lamp in her hand. The light was dim and illuminated only their three faces. From the other room, Regeane could still hear the loud sounds of Angelica's wailing.

"I can't let you do that, dear," Barbara said.

"You can't stop me," Regeane answered. "No one can."

A bucket of water stood near the kitchen fire. Regeane snatched it up and hurled the contents into the flames. A noxious mixture of smoke, steam, and ash boiled out of the fire. The stinking cloud filled the room.

The wolf took Regeane. She went flying into the change so quickly she had no time to flee. She heard Barbara gasp and begin coughing. Elfgifa shouted in glee.

Regeane flew out of the kitchen door at a dead run. Taking tremendous bounds, she was across the garden in seconds. She cleared the wall in one gigantic leap. She found herself on the riverbank looking across the Tiber at Rome.

XXII

THE WOLF STOOD FROZEN IN THE DARKNESS, sniffing the wind for a moment. The rank scents of the city and the river disgusted her. She remembered Lucilla's words and realized the mob must reign there now. Even from across the water she could see the glow of a few fires against the sky and hear the sounds of fighting.

The green open spaces of the Campagna and the mountains beyond it tugged at her soul. A breeze blew from the water and an even more ghastly smell drifted to her nose. Her animal eyes picked out the shapes of bloated corpses stranded on mud flats near the shore.

Grim as it was, she knew her duty. Even the wolf bowed to a law so ancient the wolf could not remember its inception—we do not abandon our own. Antonius' and Lucilla's struggles were part of her life now. She had so chosen, both as wolf and woman, and must keep faith. She trotted out past the reeking corpses and plunged into the water.

During her swim the current carried her toward the crowded heart of the city near the Corso. She emerged from the water and shook herself dry amidst the rabbit warren of twisting streets near the Tiber. It was an area so subject to floods that only the poorest of the poor lived there.

The narrow cobbled streets were wet and slimy with urine. Household refuse and rotting garbage clogged the gutters. The smells from the tumbledown human dwellings scalded her senses.

The fighting must have been fierce, since she passed a corpse here and there. One, lying in an alley, had an intact lower body, but the face and head were pounded to a bloody pulp. Another dangled by its feet from a balcony, head down, except it didn't have a head and its entrails bulged out of the split-open belly, gleaming wet and slick in the faint moonlight.

The silver wolf trotted on, thankful that these dangerous streets were almost deserted. Ahead she saw the lighted windows of a wineshop near the Corso.

She melted into the shadows at once as she tried to edge quietly past the door . . . Until she saw him.

At first, she took him for a large dog, perhaps a mastiff. Her hackles rose as she prepared herself to fight, but then she realized she was looking at one of her own kind.

She'd been fooled at first by his color. He was brown, but shading to red. The slenderness of his muzzle, the mask of darker fur at the face, and the slanted eyes all proclaimed wolf to her. He was not interested in her. As far as she could tell, he hadn't seen her at all.

He sat to one side of the wineshop door. His ears stood erect, eyes eager and expectant. His mouth was open, its red tongue curled in a big doglike grin.

Two drunken men emerged from the wineshop and helped each other down the street. The wolf ignored them.

The next two who came through the door were a young girl with a painted face wearing a tattered silk gown leading a much older soldier—a prostitute and her customer.

The soldier staggered and leaned heavily on the girl's arm.

The wolf ducked down with an expression of unabashed delight and came up with his head under her skirt.

The silver wolf saw surprise, then consternation chase themselves across the girl's face as the cold nose and the wet tongue reached their goal. She shrieked and jumped away. While making her escape, she let go of the soldier. He fell heavily to the cobbles.

The girl kicked hard at the wolf. He fled into the darkness of an alleyway next to the wineshop.

Then she turned back to assist her prostrate customer. She bent over, trying to pull him to his feet. A mistake, the silver wolf realized as she soon saw the other wolf's head appear from around the side of the building.

In that position, she was obviously irresistible. In a second his head was under her skirt again. She gave vent to a scream of outrage and fury as she fell forward over the soldier and they both rocked together on the cobbles.

The soldier lurched to his knees and drew his sword. He swung hard, a mighty and terrible blow had it landed. It didn't. The edge of the sword struck sparks from the stony street. The wolf was behind him in a flash. Sharp teeth nipped him hard on the backside.

A threatening snarl set every muscle in Regeane's body quivering for a second until she realized it wasn't directed at her, but at the red wolf. The soldier gave a soft screech, dropped the sword, and clutched at his backside. The red wolf scurried away from the pair, moving back into the alleyway where he sat down, tried to look innocent, and scratched his ear with his hind leg.

Two other wolves appeared beside him. One was gray, and

only a shadow in the gloom, and the other so black it seemed at first only a pair of eyes suddenly catching the light.

The gray snarled at the red wolf again. This time there was less menace and more reproof in the sound.

The soldier and the girl got to their feet. They both looked around wildly for a few seconds, then bolted into the door of a lodging house next to the wineshop.

The three wolves slipped silently into the light streaming from the tavern door. Then, they all froze as they caught sight of her.

The red wolf grinned, his tongue lolling as it had when he was waiting for his victims. He started toward the silver wolf. She brought him up short with a snarl so vicious she surprised even herself. She was going to take that red wolf apart if he came near her.

His mouth snapped shut, and he gave a soft whine that might have represented an apology and stepped back toward the other two.

The gray wolf glided fully into the light from the door. He was to Regeane's eyes the most beautiful creature she had ever seen. In the absence of mirrors in a wolf's life or standards for comparison to herself, Regeane had forgotten how magnificent wolves were, and even she herself was.

He was the deep matte-silver-gray of a shadow on snow. His belly and the backs of his legs were as pure a white as a high-piled drift near a glacier. His shoulders and chest were massive and deep. Below them the slender, delicate legs seemed to tread the earth with a touch as light as a dancer's. The head and soft upright ears were framed by a ruff as thick as the powerful musculature below. The darker markings on his face set off a pair of eyes so beautifully expressive they might have been those of a lover gazing on his beloved.

The silver wolf felt a tremor run through muscles that had unconsciously stiffened for combat. She relaxed her threatening posture and raised her head.

Were they her kind? she wondered. *Surely they must be. These weren't the diminutive, skulking wolves found on the Campagna, but Arctic giants, mountain predators.*

The big gray seemed to carry a whiff of the high fastness with him. A memory of meadows awash with flowers, of slopes dotted with the graceful whorled shapes of snow-mantled spruce and fur. Of cold so deep it cleared the air of all other scents and drenched every breath with pure lightness.

On his hind legs, he would top most men by a foot or more. And he'd be a formidable opponent for even a thing so large as a bear.

Yet, the silver wolf knew she need not fear him. The knowledge ran deeper than the wolf's thought or even her savage memory. Instead, she felt an incredible femaleness for the first time as a wolf. A sheness not in the sense of feeling smaller or weaker, but a sleek awareness of her own wild beauty. Though there was no question of a contest between them, she was more than a match for him in speed and her jaws were just as powerful as his. The silver wolf met him as an equal. She encountering a he, each knowing in their coupling they could ignite a brief, exquisite fire in each other's flesh.

The silver wolf felt a quick stab of heat in her loins. A tightening that sent a shiver of delight over her skin. Every hair on her body stood erect for a second.

The gray made a soft sound in his throat. It was not a growl, but something akin to the purr of a great cat. The ruff at his neck flared out almost like the folds of a fur cape, as if to say "Look upon me. Am I not everything you could desire?"

The silver wolf was stunned. She was too young to reciprocate this first mating gesture, but was secretly delighted. The woman was horrified. The images flooding the wolf's mind were so deliciously sensual . . . The antics of a long tongue in certain places, the fangs in that magnificent muzzle could probably groom the fur in a number of excruciatingly sensitive spots with sweet tenderness, and how comfortable to spend an icy night cuddled in the curve of a big, warm, strong body. The woman wanted to be disgusted with herself, wanted to be angry—and was afraid. If only there hadn't been that almost anguished delight mingled with the fear in her heart.

Suddenly there was a flash of bright light and a loud babble of voices sounded in her ears as the tavern door swung open. Another of its customers tumbled into the street.

The silver wolf was in motion almost before she thought, and she found herself dodging into the inky cover of another dark street, her mind a turmoil of warring emotions.

THE THREE WHO HAD BEEN WOLVES DONNED their clothing amidst the charred and blackened timbers of a burned-out house.

"I don't see what's so awful about having a little fun," the one who had been the red wolf said. "What's the good of being shape strong if you can't enjoy yourself?"

"Wash your face," the woman who had been the black wolf said. "You stink of those women."

"Oooh, I love the musk," the red wolf moaned delightedly.

"And men talk about bitches," the black wolf said.

The man who had been the big gray belted on his sword. "Wasn't she beautiful?" he asked.

"Magnificent," the red wolf agreed.

"Obviously a lady," the black said.

"She didn't like me," the red wolf said.

"That proves my point," the black said. "One more step and she'd have torn you limb from limb."

"She's certainly one of us," the gray said in a dreamy tone, "though she doesn't know how to communicate yet. She didn't understand."

"Oh, yes she did," the black wolf said. "That one little gesture when she seemed to turn her whole body to silver flame says more than whole volumes to an experienced eye."

"I must have her," the gray said, looking up through the tracery of broken timbers at the pale wash of moonlight.

"So ardent," the black wolf said. "I can't believe it. I've never seen you this way before."

"My blood runs hot by night," the gray said. "All I remember by night is that I am a leader. The semblance of humanity in me is just that—only a semblance, and I lust after enemies to overawe, to tame and then rule; for a mate before whom I can flaunt my strength and power, one who will match the heat of my passion with her own."

"Then you likely picked the wrong one," the black said. "She probably thinks of herself as a human woman at most times. And human women are more abject slaves than our cousins the dogs." She spat into the thick jumble of wood ashes at her feet. "I'll wager she's married to some lout who beats her by day and rapes her every night."

"I hope not," the gray said ominously, "for his sake. Otherwise he'll make the near acquaintance of my teeth. Mayhap that is all I can do for her. But if her man is a brute, I shall certainly rid her of him, that I promise. I don't find these Romans all too difficult to kill."

The woman who had been the black wolf chuckled nastily.

"I take it you're not hungry then," the red said.

"We dined tonight," she said, "on an unwary footpad who was foolish enough to try to slip a dagger between his ribs." She gestured toward the gray. "The fool was tender. A bit fatty for my taste, but tender."

"Hmmm," the red said hopefully, "do you think we could find another? I'm starving."

"Let's go try," the gray said. "I hope we see that silver beauty again. Maybe we can follow her home and, if her husband is minded after the fashion of most humankind, I'll crack his bones and lap the marrow."

THE SILVER WOLF CROSSED THE CORSO AND paused to sniff the wind lightly. The mixture of odors blunted her nose, confusing the wolf, and frightening the woman. At least a dozen fires were burning in the city. Beyond the overpowering smell of wood smoke hung a miasma of death and decay. She realized the city belonged neither to the pope nor to the Lombards, but only to itself.

A tide of Caesars, barbarian conquerors, and kings had passed through it and over it, but in the end its real rulers had always been its turbulent and stubborn people. They held it now. The tide Lucilla had spoken of was at the flood. The magnates who controlled the lands that fed the city and its angry, independent people would decide the issue between the Lombards and the pope.

She thought of the others she'd seen. *Were they really like her?* For a moment a dream she'd believed dead had possessed her, the dream of love. *Who had the gray been? What kind of man was he by day? Churchman, warrior, thief, or madman?*

The silver wolf wanted to go back and find his spoor. To follow him. Find him and begin the long frolic that would end in . . . what? Did her kind, partaking as they did of the nature of both beast and human, make love as men or wolves? Or was their coupling some secret beauty denied to both beast and man? Something unique only to themselves?

She suspected it was. The wolf's free heart cried out for the gray, urged her to find out who and what he was. Images flowed freely through her brain. They could carry their dance of love across a world that was a garden to them. They could consummate their desires high on a mountain peak where no man's foot had ever trod. There, the snow packs so deep and the crust freezes so hard their wide paws can fleet across it the way a flung stone skips over water. Comfortable where the windchill alone would kill a man in minutes, they could find a trysting place for a pair of lupine lovers. Did the deep woods beckon, they might easily penetrate places pathless to humankind. Hidden among trees so tall, with trunks so thick they would laugh at the bite of an ax. They could explore the endless possibilities of desire in moonlit glades and worship the mistress of the night together.

Oh, God, the dream was real. A gnawing hunger in the wolf's heart, a pain in her throat.

The woman cringed in terror. Whoever he was by day, how could he have the power to protect her from the wrath of both king and pope? In the instant their eyes met, he had wanted her as much as she wanted him. She was caught in a trap and she could not pull him down to perish with her.

No, she would grit her teeth and embrace a man. And try to forget the mysteries of moonlight.

The stench of a slaughterhouse jerked the wolf away from her thoughts.

She eased along the Corso, moving stealthily from shadow to shadow. When she smelled it, she realized the horrible odor was coming from the insula where Antonius had lived with the rest of the maimed outcasts of the city. Two Lombard soldiers guarded the door. They had set torches in brackets above their heads and the street was brightly lighted around them.

The fierce brilliance burned the wolf's eyes. She faded back into the shadows, remembering that there was a back way into the insula down the sewer pipe.

She wasted a few minutes wandering among the alleys around the insula until she found the pipe.

The wolf hesitated, whining and snarling softly at the woman's will that drove her so inexorably. Finally she plunged into the narrow opening.

They were lying in the courtyard helter-skelter. Blood and even more noxious substances congealing around them. Even in the faint light, the wolf's superior vision could recognize a few of them.

The one with stumps for legs had been beheaded. Before they beheaded him, he'd been castrated. The larger pool of blood was between his legs. *Why had they done it?* She couldn't imagine. Maybe only for fun.

The girl with the hole in her cheek had died under torture. She dangled from a balcony, head hunched between her disjointed arms. She'd been strapadoed, then flogged. What remained of both her ragged gown and her flesh hung in strips from her body. She no longer moved, but blood still dripped from her flayed carcass, drop by drop on the stones below.

The hunchbacked idiot boy had been eviscerated and left to die. The wolf could see and smell the foul trail he left on the stones as he dragged himself round and round in agony as suffering and blood loss took their toll.

A few soldiers wearing the livery of the papal guard lay among the dead. They, at least, had been able to die fighting. Hadrian had made an effort to defend the place.

The woman melted perfectly into the wolf and they became one. Death on four legs slinking toward the entrance to the church. In the distance ahead of her through the darkness she heard someone scream. It was a horrible outcry, more animal than human, one of agonizing pain. It ended in retching sobs.

The wolf went forward like a silent silver thunderbolt through the church and came to a halt at the entrance to what had been Hadrian's quarters.

It took a second for her eyes to fully absorb the scene.

The once-beautiful room was almost bare, having been stripped of everything that could possibly be of any value except the table. Tied to it was the young shepherd boy in whose care she had left Antonius.

They had roped him to the table faceup, leaving only one arm free. A black-bearded soldier held the arm by the wrist. Two of the fingers were mangled and bloody. The man was reaching out with an iron pincers toward a third.

"Please," the boy pleaded, his eyes rolling in agony. "Please, gentle sirs. I know nothing."

The wolf recognized the black-bearded soldier. He was one of Basil's men—the one who'd pursued her into the alleyway. She had escaped him through the drain. Elfgifa had been right. The child had wanted to cut his throat. Hadrian should have done it.

A man standing next to him said nervously, "Sirus, perhaps we should have left a few more of them alive."

"Alive to do what?" the black-bearded one snarled. "Even had they been willing to speak against their master, their protector, do you think the men in the synod would listen to the drivelings of such as these? I thought for a while the girl knew something, but she died too quickly." He smiled at the young man tied to the table. "I plan to go more slowly with this one.

"Now," he said, tapping at some silver chains dangling from his belt. It was Lucilla's necklace. "Tell me how a creature like you came by such rich jewels as this."

The wolf could see the animal terror in the boy's eyes as he raised his head. He didn't answer, only stared at the pincers in the black-bearded soldier's other hand in horrified fascination.

"Very well," he said. "I'll break a few more fingers. Then maybe you'll become more talkative. Hold the lamp higher," the one called Sirus said as he forced the boy's arm down over the edge of the table and reached with his pincers for the fingers.

The boy's eyes screwed themselves tightly shut. His body bucked against the ropes that tied him to the table.

The wolf felt every muscle tighten in her body. It seemed to her she was moving very slowly. She took out the throat of the one holding the lamp first.

He stumbled away from the table, gurgling. The only sound he could make. He gave a very surprised look at the blood spurting everywhere as he died.

The bronze lamp hit the floor with a clatter. The oil splashed and eerie blue flames spouted from the mouth and began to play over the metal. The light in the room turned to purplish twilight.

A second later, Sirus went over backward, both hamstrings severed by the wolf's teeth. His neck fell like ripe fruit into her waiting jaws. She snapped his spine low down so that he didn't die immediately.

The wolf thought of the girl. She even remembered her name—Crysta—while she closed her jaws on his throat, suffocating him slowly.

It seemed to the boy still tied to the table that the choking and gasping sounds went on a long time. Finally, they stopped and all he could hear was the drumming of heels on the floor. Then that ceased, too, and there was only silence.

A few strokes of a knife freed him. He rolled from the table and fell to his knees, clutching the wrist of his maimed hand, holding it high before his face, his eyes averted from Regeane's naked body. She had removed Lucilla's necklace from Sirus' belt and wore it around her neck.

The fallen lamp had relighted itself and the flames spouted high. Shadows danced frenetically on the wall.

"I told them nothing, my lady," the boy whispered, peering at her through his fingers.

To him, Regeane seemed truly a goddess. Her long silver-tipped hair hung like a garment over her body, covering her nakedness, the curve of her breasts and stomach made a pattern of light and shadow in the flames flowing upward from the lamp. Her eyes compelled him. Glowing in her shadowed face, they seemed to see into the innermost depths of his soul.

"I told them nothing, my lady," he sobbed out again. "I cannot say it was out of loyalty to you or the poor leper, Antonius, but because I knew they'd kill me as soon as I talked. Kill me the way they killed the others. They didn't," he gasped, the tears flowing down his cheeks. "They didn't have to be so cruel."

No, they didn't, Regeane thought as her woman's mind tried to cope with the simple amazement of the wolf. *Why all this madness?*

"How did you come here?" she asked.

"The leper Antonius sent me," he answered. "Told me to warn the priest. To tell him where he was hidden."

Of course, Regeane realized. *Antonius would have wanted Hadrian to know about his hiding place.*

"But when I got here," the boy continued, "there was no priest. Only the soldiers, and then the Lombards came . . ." The boy giggled hysterically. His nose ran and he mopped at it with the back of his good hand. He was still holding the injured one like a claw before his face, looking at Regeane between the fingers.

"The only reason I escaped so easily is that they were occupied with the girl—the girl they whipped to death."

"Where is Antonius?" Regeane asked.

"At Cumae. There are many caves in the rock. No one goes there at night. It's said to be haunted."

"It is," Regeane answered. "Here." She took the necklace from her neck and threw it over the boy's head. "You've earned your pay and double. Now, can you find the villa of one Lucilla?"

"The pope's . . ." His voice trailed off. He was unwilling to use the word in front of one who might be their protectress, too.

"Yes. She will help you."

"I don't fear for my safety once I'm away from here," the boy said. "These Romans have no love for the Lombards."

"Were the two outside part of this also?" Regeane asked.

The boy nodded. "They came in force, killed the pope's guards, and then left these four to question the prisoners. They helped flog the girl to death. They took turns."

"Blow out the lamp," Regeane said. "Unbar the door and call them inside."

The boy looked up at her fearfully. "They're armed."

"These two were armed. It didn't matter."

The boy lifted the lamp in one trembling hand. Just before he blew out the last flame he looked up. The woman was gone and the wolf looked back at him, teeth gleaming in the half-open jaws, eyes glowing with a red light in the flare of the one tiny flame.

XXIII

THE TOPS OF THE ORCHARD TREES WERE GRAY IN the moonlight when Regeane leaped the wall into Lucilla's villa.

She was thinking that killing wasn't difficult if you knew what to do and took your victims by surprise. Dogs and real wolves gave warning of their intentions before they struck. She needn't and hadn't.

She moved soundlessly through the dark garden. She remembered Lucilla's message that the villa was guarded by a company of Frankish mercenaries. She didn't want anyone to see her and raise an alarm.

She peered into the atrium and saw Lucilla alone, pacing up and down beside the pool.

The atrium was dark, the only light the sickle of the new moon, shining both in the water and the sky.

The change was easy to call now. A second later, Regeane rose to her feet a woman, and walked toward Lucilla.

She blinked and stared at the pale figure confronting her. "Regeane? Or are you only some ghost?"

"I came," Regeane said. "You knew I'd get here somehow, didn't you?"

"Yes." The word was a sigh. Lucilla reached out to touch Regeane as if to reassure herself that she was real. She drew back her hand as if she'd been burnt. Staring at her fingers covered by blood, she exclaimed, "Christ!"

"It isn't mine," Regeane said indifferently.

"Whose is it?"

"I don't know their names. They were Basil's men. Basil sent soldiers to the insula where Antonius lived. They killed every-

one there. Mutilated some of them before they killed them."
Freed of the wolf's indifference to violence, she felt suddenly
sick with horror. "I found them torturing someone—a boy . . .
The shepherd I paid to hide Antonius. I . . . the wolf . . . No, I
and the wolf killed them. I sent the shepherd boy safely into the
night. He may make his way here. You'll know him by his
broken fingers. Please receive him kindly and don't try to extort
information from him. After I reach Antonius, not even the
shepherd boy will know where he is anymore."

Then Regeane cleaned herself by turning wolf and jumping
into the pool.

Lucilla made a half-stifled sound under her breath and
averted her face, covering it with her mantle.

The wolf shook herself dry like a dog and Regeane reappeared in front of Lucilla a second later.

"God!" Lucilla whispered. She was gasping, one hand pressed
to her breast. Her face looked pale in the faint moonlight.

"I'm sorry," Regeane said. "Did I startle you?"

"Startle me? Oh, my, yes," Lucilla said waspishly. "Startle is
a bit too weak a word for what I just felt."

"What do you see?" Regeane asked. "I can't see the change.
I'm inside it."

"Nothing," Lucilla answered. "But then one doesn't see a
hummingbird's wings when it's in flight. Only a shimmer, a diffuse sparkle like the reflection of moonlight on moving water."

"I'm cold," Regeane said. "Double cold when the wolf is not
with me, because I have killed and I never wanted to."

"There's another mantle on the bench and some wine." Lucilla pointed to the one nearest the door of the triclinium.

Regeane wrapped herself up and poured a cup of wine. The
ewer was the same one she'd seen on her first night with Lucilla. The vessel had a snarling wolf's head spout.

"You saw the pitcher, didn't you?" Lucilla asked. "It frightened you when you first came here."

"Yes. For a little while I'd managed to deceive myself about
my true nature, but the sight of the pitcher brought it all back."

"And you're still trying to deceive yourself, aren't you?"
Lucilla said. "I can see the tears running down your cheeks.
Why all this grief? Is it the men you killed?"

Regeane found herself shivering. She cradled the wine cup in both hands and drank deeply. "I don't know."

"Think about it," Lucilla said bleakly. "What other choice did you have?"

Regeane shook her head. "None. I couldn't let them torture the truth out of the boy. In fact, I couldn't bear to watch them torture him at all . . . and some of the other things they'd done there . . . were unspeakable. They must have killed some of those poor wretches slowly, simply for the sake of watching them suffer. Basil's men deserved to die. The wolf knew it. I knew it. But the wolf doesn't remember their eyes as the light goes out of them the way I do. She doesn't care. To her everything is simple. You do what you must. She protects me while I'm with her."

Regeane's face twisted with pain. "But I'm not wholly her. I'm myself, also, and so I suffer."

"I can't help you," Lucilla said. "If you do such things, you have to find some way to live with them. I know I have."

"Do you?"

Lucilla laughed. "Do you remember what Hadrian said about Paul Afartha? That I murdered him?"

"You didn't deny it."

"What would be the good? Half of Rome knows I did, and he was not the first. Paul belonged to the Lombard king and for a time he controlled the chair of Peter, as much as if he sat in it himself. When the Roman nobles banded together, defied him, and elected Hadrian, Paul promised he'd tie a halter around Hadrian's neck and drag him captive before Desiderius. But by then I'd charmed the Franks into an alliance with the Holy See. Antonius was my ambassador to the Frankish king.

"It's one of the reasons Hadrian loves him. Faced with a possible war with the Franks, Desiderius didn't send troops to help Paul and he had to flee. Fool that he was, he went to Ravenna where, if possible, the archbishop loved him even less than I did. He took Paul captive.

"Hadrian favored a public trial and exile. I journeyed to Ravenna in secret and told Archbishop Comus that I would be less than prostrate with grief if Paul met with some mischance. That fool was as chicken-livered as Hadrian. Men! With all their talk of law and due process!" Lucilla spat. "What nonsense. As though such as Paul Afartha ever worried about law. As though he would worry about law if our Frankish alliance should fail and I or Hadrian ever fell into his hands."

Regeane was warmer now, the wine flowing hot in her veins, emboldening her. She took another sip. "And?"

Lucilla chuckled as if amused at her own cleverness. "I rented a large house and gave a feast for the archbishop and Paul and his men. I hired nearly every whore in Ravenna to entertain them. Certainly they expected no less of me. I am, after all, the very dissolute Lucilla.

"When they were all far gone in drink and the ecstasies of carnal pleasure—there was not one, but three beautiful girls to every man there—my men and I took Paul down to the cellars of the bishop's palace and garrotted him."

Lucilla looked down at her hands. "I turned the stick that snapped his neck. He didn't make it easy for me." Her voice shook. "He pleaded, he begged, he made promises that weren't worth the breath it took to make them. He died, all in all, a most unmanly death. Archbishop Comus got the credit for Paul's untimely demise and he took it rather than admit he'd been hoodwinked by a woman."

"Killing sickens you even as it sickens me," Regeane said.

"Yes," Lucilla said, looking at her helplessly. "It does. I don't think I'd be going to confession to you if it didn't."

"I can't offer you absolution."

"Nor I you."

Regeane drank again. "How will I kill my husband? That's what Gundabald wanted, you know."

"Do it in such a way that you won't be caught, and," Lucilla cautioned, "only if it's absolutely necessary. That's the best and only advice I can give you. And never learn to glory in death as some men do. Women have the power of life and death. We, after all, give birth and the fate of humanity is in our hands. That's why men try so hard to rule us, my dear.

"They know if we once looked well on what they have made of the human existence, we might close our legs and within our barren wombs bring the comedy to an end."

"Would you really, Lucilla? Could you?"

Lucilla threw her head back and an expression of almost unbearable pain crossed her face. "No. I can remember when Antonius first kicked in my womb. I believed then that anything was possible. Ah, God above, he was my life. My life was in him. I continue to hope though all hope is lost. We women are accursed with life. It binds us fast and we continue to believe with every child we bear that the world will be better than it has been in the past, that it will receive them with love."

"Not always," Regeane said.

"Never," Lucilla said. "A child, my dear, is often only another mouth to feed. Perhaps we're lucky when some man finds a kind of honor in the fact that his little squirt of spunk made our belly swell. And he sees fit to protect it."

The wind picked up. High clouds flew past the moon.

"The north wind is blowing," Lucilla said. "Tomorrow there will be frost on the grass and even the flowers in my garden will feel the chill."

"Who is Adraste and why did I get her mirror?" Regeane asked.

"Adraste is a dead woman, a dead whore. What does she matter to you?"

"I don't know," Regeane said, "but somehow I think the dead are as important in this as the living. Tell me, Lucilla, who was she?"

Lucilla shrugged. "Since you ask, I'll do better than tell you about her. I'll show her to you."

There was a lamp on the bench beside the wine pitcher. Lucilla lit it by striking a flint on a steel ring she wore.

"I have another dining room." She shielded the flame from the wind. "One I don't use anymore," she said laughing. There was a cruel edge to her laughter.

She led Regeane around the atrium pool to a dark, curtained doorway on the other side, and stepped inside the room. When the curtains fell, the room was almost pitch black. The tiny flame created only a small circle of light around the two women. Lucilla walked toward one of the walls, lifted the lamp, and said, "Behold Adraste." Lucilla turned her head away and covered her face with her mantle.

Adraste sat painted as Venus at her toilet in a cushioned chair, naked, with her maids clustered around her. One stood behind her, coiling her long, blond hair. Another graceful beauty proffered jewels for her inspection. Yet another, head bowed almost in adoration, laced sandals onto her small white feet while their mistress gazed at the handiwork of the hairdresser in a silver mirror.

So fine was the detail of the painting that Regeane could recognize the mirror with its spray of pink blossoms. Her eyes shifted to Adraste's face and she knew she looked not on some idealized vision of the artist, but on the face of a living woman. The large green eyes had a sparkle of mischief in them and there was a sprinkling of tiny freckles across the beautifully shaped nose. The slightly too full lips smiled invitingly. The naked breasts were lush and jutted slightly, turned upward at the pink blond nipples. The waist was slender and the belly a sweetly curved platform of desire where nested a sex covered with curly reddish-blond hair.

"How Antonius must have loved her," Regeane said.

"Yes," Lucilla answered. "I can't bear to look at the paintings in this room and I can't bear to destroy them either. They were some of the last he did before he contracted the disease that was his ruin.

"She came from the east, fleeing, as she said, from a cruel and dangerous lover highly placed in the government. I should have known better than to take her in. Should have known that nothing good ever comes to us from Constantinople. All those accursed Greeks ever do is make trouble. Better she had ensnared any man in Rome—yes, even my Hadrian—than to have taken my son. You see, she knew. Even when she first lay with my son, the bitch knew she had the disease that would end both her beauty and her life.

"When my son fell ill I began to inquire as to the cause of his disease. I sent word to a correspondent at the emperor's court in Constantinople. I asked him about Adraste. It seems her last lover was not only not a high official, but he already walked the roads robed in black with a clapper in his hand.

"I had her dragged out of her house, the fine house my money bought for her. For you see I indulged Antonius in everything. I had her brought here. My maids washed the paint from her face and body. The lesions, those pale numb marks that slowly destroy the leper's flesh, were everywhere."

Lucilla stopped speaking. Her rage left her gasping for breath. In the lamplight her face was set like a stone. Her eyes glittered like dagger points.

"I'll say this for her. She carried herself at the end better than that puking Paul Afartha. She had the grace to be contrite. She didn't plead for her life. The only excuse she offered was that Antonius was her last hope, the last flare of a dying lamp before the oil is exhausted and the night closes in. I cannot say I was moved. I wanted to watch her die screaming. But I didn't want Antonius to hate me, either. So I offered her the same choice the Caesars offered their enemies—the dagger or the public executioner. As it happens, she chose white arsenic. I gave her a magnificent funeral. It was what Antonius wished."

"Does he know?" Regeane asked.

"I can't say," Lucilla answered. "We've never spoken of her fate."

Lucilla walked away from the shadows into the center of the room and hurled the lamp to the floor. It shattered and the flames flashed through oil like a bonfire, roaring up almost to the ceiling.

The two women looked at each other. The one in the painting frozen in time, caught in those last moments before beauty is extinguished by disease and death. Lucilla, the living woman, standing on the other side of the flames, her face a naked mask of pain.

"My son, my son," she cried. "The bitch took my son. Is it my sins, Regeane? Is Antonius paying for what I've done? Is he?"

Regeane backed toward the curtains that covered the entrance to the triclinium and she pushed them aside. The wind tugged at her mantle. She could feel the change coming toward her the way a cloud shadow moves over the plain.

"I don't know about sin, Lucilla. I've never understood it. It's a thing of the church. Am I to believe in a church that will brand me a witch and burn me? I can't. All the years on my knees and all the penances my mother offered couldn't make me, and they can't now. All I hope is that somehow I can give you back your son."

Lucilla saw something like summer lightning glow around Regeane and the wolf ran like a silver shimmer, elusive as the high thin clouds above that, one by one, danced with the moon.

XXIV

"WHAT IS IT, SILVER ONE?" THE WOMAN ASKED OF the wolf. As one, they flew across the Campagna. "Will you now try to do the impossible?"

The wolf couldn't answer in words, but the woman understood her joyous reply. "Why not? I am an impossible thing."

The lights of Rome behind her, the wolf paused at the top of a high hill to survey her kingdom. The cloud-haunted moon cast a bright light to the wolf's eyes. Below her stretched a sea of grass broken only by lines of small bushes and low trees. These marked gullies and watercourses where the wolf could, if she so desired, find refreshment and prey. Deep in her savage heart the wolf remembered and exulted.

The memories that flooded the woman's brain were almost unbearable in their poignancy. The wolf not only remembered joy, but pain also and pain's sometimes inexorable ending, death. Often swift death under the sharp, crushing hooves of the beloved prey. Death equally quick as she faced the weapons of her own kind, the long, white fangs, and bone-crushing jaws. Death, most feared, inflicted by the lingering slow torture of disease.

She also remembered life, not as humans sometimes lived it—an experience of constant anxiety and fear of tomorrow's misfortunes, dreading displeasure of the great and powerful among their own species—but life fully realized and lived to the fullest amid the love of others of her kind, the exultant triumph and sometimes bitter disappointments of the hunt.

A life sharpened by the pangs of hunger. Alternating with utter satiation. Of desire, potent and passionate, reaching its fulfillment in love untouched by guilt or regret. A life shaped by the freedom the woman longed for, a sense of power over herself and her own world, a savage strength that could never be betrayed or enslaved into the stupid, mindless barbarity of human servitude.

The woman or the wolf could be killed. She might die tonight as one or the other. But she wouldn't go stumbling down the road to death hating life or the world around her. She would not be a driven slave, born to drag her burden from birth to death. She would go free, free as the wolf was free, incapable of being subjected by terror or cruelty. Embracing existence, even its pain, to the very last extremity. Herself at one with the wind-tossed grass, the high arch of the dark heavens, urged on by the keening cry of the wind that seemed to speed her on her way.

For one last moment wolf and woman looked up at the moon and then almost with a soundless sigh, Regeane yielded to the wolf's joyous freedom from fear and she lunged forward toward Cumae.

THE CLOUDS WERE THICKENING AND AN ICY MIST was creeping over the Campagna when the wolf reached the foot of the rock. The temple lifted its empty shell against the sky, clouds its only companions.

The wolf took the holy path to the top. Just before she reached the summit she saw two figures, hooded in black, waiting. Neither held a torch or lantern. Moonbeams found their way between the fissures in the thick overcast, and they seemed blackened shadows in its lambent light.

One of them saw her and spoke. "He said a wolf would come, brother."

"Yes," the other answered. "A wolf bigger and more powerful than those of the Campagna. A wolf that didn't act like a wolf."

"We greet you, Lupa," one of the figures said, lifting its hand.

The silver wolf raised her head and stared proudly at them.

"Not everyone has forgotten that God once spoke here," one of them explained. "A few still remember. Come, he waits beside the hearth."

Antonius was sitting beside the tall cone of the sacred fire. He raised his hand in greeting to Regeane.

"Lupa," he said. "What do you want with me? What can you want with me?"

Regeane stood before him, a woman. The wind chilled her to the bone and sent her hair blowing like a dark veil around her body. The two hooded hierophants hid their faces in their mantles and bowed down beside him.

"I come," she said, "to bring you healing, if I can."

"The only cure for me is death," Antonius answered, rising to his feet and facing her. He pulled the mantle around his features. "Even so," he said. "Do I hide my ugliness from a creature of such beauty as you are, Regeane?"

Regeane looked down from the rock. The fog below was a thickening pall in the ever-changing moon glow. It was covering the landscape with its moist caress, blanketing the outlines of the coast, blurring away the vast plain of the Campagna. The clouds above roofed the high rock, and the silver moonlight came and went as they thickened, then thinned in their racing passage across the sky.

Like the rock and the temple, Regeane seemed suspended between heaven and earth. Not wholly either one, but something different and, perhaps, more powerful.

"Ugliness and beauty don't exist for the wolf, Antonius," she said. "At least not in the way you see them with your artist's eye."

A gust of wind whipped her hair, lashing it around her face like flame. Dust from the cone of dead ash coated Antonius' robe, and he ducked his head to escape its fury.

"You were," Regeane continued, "my first friend. The first to help me. Neither the woman nor the wolf can forget that. Yield yourself to me. I will try to make you whole."

"How?" he asked.

"By going where the dead go."

She turned away from him toward the entrance to the temple.

The two black-robed hierophants took up their positions on either side of the temple portal, a door that opened now into darkness.

"Mine." Regeane recalled her own words to Cecelia. "A victory over death." She forgot Antonius for a second and quailed back. But the woman no longer fought the wolf. They were one.

There was a light inside the temple. Its brilliance showed the temple for what it was. The big gaps in the cella walls, the broken stonework under foot, the cracked pedestal. An emptiness now, where the statue of the god once stood. The glow emanated from a bent figure that leaned on a heavy staff. And as the figure drew closer, Regeane recognized Abbess Hildegard.

Regeane lifted her arm and raised her hand in salute to her, remembering and recognizing the light that had succored her in the night when evil seemed to outweigh everything, when the creatures of darkness had reached out toward her.

The bent old woman paused at the temple door before Regeane and spoke. "I would not have you face the forces of night without a word. Do not think we of the worlds beyond death are all alike. Because you loved my sisters while you were among them, take with you my blessing and the blessing of God." She lifted her hand.

Regeane went to her knees on the temple steps. She felt the bite of chilled marble on her flesh. The wind was blowing harder. The fog seemed to be rising more quickly. Long scarves of vapor trailed between the tall, white columns.

"May God protect you on your journey," Hildegard said as her fingers traced a cross of light in the air.

Then she was gone.

Regeane faced the woman out of time. Age and youth flickered across her face like the change of seasons across the mind of God.

"Are you a creature of time?" Regeane asked, rising to her feet.

"I am," the woman said, "how time looks to eternity. Each thing contains the seeds of its destruction. Its failure is ever compensated by the moment of rebirth."

"I can't understand you," Regeane said.

"No," the answer came. "And, as you are mortal, you never will. Are you ready for your journey?"

Regeane stretched out her arms to the being almost in desperation. "I am. Can you tell me, will I ever return?"

There was a titter of laughter from the shadows gathering behind Regeane, from the ragged ghosts. It sounded like the squeaking of bats. But the face of the thing before Regeane did not change except to age and then grow young again.

"Some do," it said. "Some don't. And some don't care. Such is their sorrow. Journey with us or not; we are indifferent."

Regeane felt a moment of hesitation. Even the wolf was afraid as Regeane sought the protection of her lupine shape. For a moment she was lost in the wolf's memories. She saw destruction as a lightning-kindled wildfire poured across a plain, killing everything not swift enough to flee, an avalanche moving like a cloud down a mountain to carry the corpses of men and beasts embedded in its violence, depositing them, kindred in death, in a valley below. The earth shook. Chasms opened at her feet and fire erupted from the top of a mountain. Scalding, killing ash rained around her.

So many were the ways to die. The universe was death, and death ruled it. All life took a thousand roads to destruction. Yet life lived on, sparkling, illuminating, burning like a candle in a tomb. A star flaring on the horizon's edge at dusk, returning ever resurgent, like Cecelia's roses, forever.

Regeane had never felt more woman or more wolf.

The wolf trotted up the steps to the endless tittering of the ghosts and passed through the door.

When Regeane was a child, years before, she reached her womanhood and met the wolf within her. She'd lived on her stepfather's estate in Austrasia. Even then she'd been a lonely child. Her mother, still beautiful, always hung on the arm of her stepfather, Firminius. The socially ambitious, corpulent thug had worn her fragile mother like an adornment.

Regeane had often been alone. In the evening, before one of her mother's maids put her to bed, she would peer out of the narrow window of her chamber at the sunset. The last flare of the daystar glowed a golden mist down the road to their villa. She would dream of following that road into the haze of gilded splendor. For she understood as a woman that a child looks into the realm of absolute possibility not with fear, or desire, not with love or loathing, but simply with clear-eyed acceptance.

The child waits for time to fling it forth into that strange realm that it cannot yet fully comprehend. And this was how Regeane began her savage journey, speeding like an arrow into a blaze of golden light.

Now she stood, woman, birth, naked, in a temple of darkness. The pillars of the hall reared up to reach the sky. From the top of each was a throat belching forth roars of flame and black smoke. The smoke was an inky cloak that blotted out the stars. The floor was polished black glass and reflected the bloody glow of the fires roaring from the pillars above.

"Welcome," a voice said, "to the ruined land."

Regeane knew she stood in the midst of a court. A ruler's entourage, and this ruler's subjects were horrors. They were clearly visible in the light from the dreadful fires burning above lining the long aisle between the flaming pillars of the hall. The aisle led to a throne and on it was seated the skull-faced woman who had greeted her when she first entered the temple. Only this time the vision was worse. Then, Herophile had been wrapped in a mantle that covered all but the ivory face. This time she was draped in gossamer that covered a lush woman's body. The soft breasts had dark nipples straining at the thin fabric. At her neck the flesh stopped and teetering on the column of bones was a naked blackened skull. Wrapped around her body, the tail at the neck, the coils embracing the breast and waist, was a serpent. Its head deeply thrust into her loins.

The voice echoed in Regeane's mind again. *I, the Queen of the Dead, welcome you. For know you, Woman Wolf, the road to paradise is through the gates of hell.*

The crew surrounding her was no less terrible than their queen. Some of them seemed to be dead, for surely no living thing could look so. Eyeless horrors blackened by fires. Rags of flesh dripping from shiny red bone. They looked like carcasses being cleaned by vultures.

Others glowed with the evil blue light of putrescence. They were puffed out with rot, running with the juices of decay. Yet they all moved with a horrible life. Laughing, howling, weeping, they surrounded the throne of the queen. Outside the temple of the dead queen, Regeane could see between the columns surrounding her, a pitted, pockmarked waste. In the distance ground fires flared in the inky gloom.

Regeane realized she could recognize some of them. Those who had lived in the insula with Antonius. Drusis, legless and blind, the entrails spilling from his split belly. Sirus, one of his murderers, the one she'd killed slowly, his face black, eyes bulging. Hideously, he groped his way toward her, arms outstretched. The girl, Crysta, whipped to death, crawled in her direction, she also leaving a trail of bloody slime.

Nightmare. This must be a nightmare. Regeane's mind gibbered and shrieked.

"There is nothing," the voice continued, thundering at her from the black stone throne, "nothing between you and what you fear."

In a few moments, the throng of horrors would be upon her. Their vile, rotting hands, clutching at her naked flesh. Regeane gasped and tried to twist herself into the change, but this time the wolf failed her. She wouldn't come to Regeane's aid. She was alone.

Regeane could feel her body collapsing slowly as she fell to her knees. In dreams, one doesn't fall. But here her senses were awake. Her hands seemed to move like tentacles through thick liquid as they groped toward her own eyes, not to cover them, but to punch them out of their sockets. Her knees contacted the stone floor and the icy cold rock sent a shock of pain through her naked flesh.

Eternity. Regeane's mind stumbled and groped for the concept. She seemed to see an endless loop, herself standing there locked in insane terror. While the dead struggled to reach her, a madness that would begin ever again in endless repetition. A nightmare from which one could never escape, never break free. She would stand there, lost in everlasting anguish as the dead groped toward her forever in vain.

Then Regeane felt the wolf and realized she was not gone. The she-beast remained with her always, and as she looked out at the demonic throng through her eyes, the woman's heart almost burst—not with horror—but with compassion.

She was more than wolf and woman, she was wolf-woman.

Neither one nor the other, but a being embodying both creatures at once, immeasurably more powerful than either, immeasurably stronger.

The wolf, as she had said to Antonius, saw neither ugliness nor beauty as the woman saw them. She saw only humanity caught in the shackles of time.

Time causes the dead to fall to dust, time maims. Time kills. Time corrupts. Here at the gateway to eternity the dead still bear the scars of their journey not only through time, but the wounds we humans, in our vainglory, inflict on one another.

Then the vision of cruelty faded, and the crowd around her grew taller and taller. She saw they were becoming transparent. As they did so, they seemed more sad and more harmless. Then they vanished like a gust of smoke captured by the wind. They left only the roar and stench of the fires burning atop the high pillars and the endless keening of the blast that blew like the breath of some dreadful curse over the wasteland. All were gone except for the eyeless ghost of the girl who had been whipped to death at the insula. The girl who had once cursed Regeane for being young and beautiful. The girl Regeane had avenged. Crysta.

She was no longer a horror now. Regeane saw her as she had been when she was young; at the moment of her first youth when her life began. She was gowned in white, a garland of flowers in her hair. She carried a sword in her hand.

One other remained. Herophile still sat in her chair. She also had undergone a change. She was no longer the obscenity of lust and death that met Regeane's eyes a few moments ago, but the white-robed, laurel-crowned priestess who stood at the gateway to the underworld. She lifted one hand and beckoned to Regeane.

"Approach my throne, girl," she said. "For you have seen truly. You have looked on the dead, not with the eye of fear, but of truth, and so escaped the first danger of your present state."

Regeane walked down the long aisle between the black columns toward her throne. The stone was icy under her feet and the wind-borne grit from the desert beyond the temple stung her naked flesh painfully. The wraith of Crysta, sword in hand, trailed behind her.

The wind howled more loudly and dust devils whirled at the edges of the temple and whipped across the floor. Regeane's eyes teared and she raised her hand to clear them.

"Weep not," Crysta whispered, "for the pains of wretched human flesh. For you have trespassed where no living flesh was meant to go."

Regeane paused before the throne and looked up. She could see the woman's face. Not old, yet not young; she was ageless.

"What do you wish?" she asked.

"I ask to heal Antonius," Regeane said.

"Then," Herophile answered, "you must search out someone who can heal him."

She stared down the aisle of the temple past the tall pylons that seemed like deadly trees spouting leaves of flames, on into the distant waste. The hot dry wind gusted again, and Regeane heard the whimpering cry, the same cry that had awakened her by night in the convent. A cry of sorrow so profound, so bitter, that it seemed beyond hope or even love. A desolate lonely sound, the weeping of one condemned to wander forever without either consolation or rest.

"The one who will guide you there—to him—in whom you hope, cries out for you."

Regeane looked around. Only a desolate expanse of broken rock and sand lit by the temple fires met her eyes.

"I see no one," she said.

"She is there," Crysta said, "waiting. You gave her the mirror and hope." She extended the sword toward Regeane.

Regeane turned and looked her in the eyes. Before she had seen only a shadowy wraith, though a beautiful one. Now, she seemed a real woman, auburn haired with hazel eyes and a pale, milky complexion. She smiled at Regeane, almost impishly for a second, then her face sobered and hardened.

"What I must do is not easy for me," Crysta said. "For I must take your blood that the spirit may drink and become one of us and then so that you will bleed and know the path to return. You will travel as wolf to the garden and each time your forepaw touches the ground, the blood will be an offering. It marks your road back. But before I do, I would have peace between us. When we first met, I hated you. Your beauty reminded me of all

I was and all I never could be again. Will you forgive me my spite? When I died, my troubled spirit hovered near, thinking all the world was cruelty and pain and as life had been, so also must be eternity. But you came."

"I avenged you," Regeane said.

"No," Crysta said. "You brought me justice."

Justice? Regeane wondered as she extended her hand toward Crysta's sword, remembering the bloody melee in which she'd killed the guards at the insula. She wondered if even the dead were at times deluded. Had that been justice? Perhaps it had. Surely she had shown no mercy.

Herophile answered her thought. She leaned forward and rested her chin on her fist. "We, too, have our debates and our divisions, even here. The poor soul that cries out to you asks salvation, sees you as her savior. For our sins do not always find us out, Regeane. Sometimes we become the sin we commit and that is its own punishment. Her will cannot forget the pattern of an earthly human life. You are, as I have said, her salvation. Say you will give it to her."

"I will," Regeane said and extended her hand.

The sword bit deep, cutting a slice across the palm of her hand. Blood began to drip from her fingers. A shadow flitted into the red light surrounding the three women and began to sip greedily at the blood. Then a second later, cold bony hands clutched at her wrist.

Regeane refused to flinch and held her hand still as the thing formed into flesh before her eyes. First it became a skeleton; then flesh slowly clothed the bone—the pale, tallowy flesh of a corpse, the face, a sunken horror, withered lips drawn back, eyes lidless holes. But as it drank, sucked, and drank, the thing took on the lineaments of life. The pale flesh ripened, took on the flush of a living thing. The lips returned, the eyes glowed in the black hollows and then were covered by soft blue-veined lids, until a woman knelt there, whole and lovely as she had been in life. She released Regeane's hand.

She was bejeweled, painted, and gowned in silk. As beautiful as she must have been when Lucilla dressed her for her journey into the tomb.

She stood and spun in joy, looking into her mirror. "I am myself again."

Herophile, sitting on her throne, sighed deeply. "Come, Adraste," she said. "It is as you have long desired?"

"Yes," Adraste whispered, but she couldn't seem to tear her eyes from the mirror in her hands. "All my beauty is returned to me. I have it now for eternity."

Regeane curled her injured hand and clutched it close to her breast. Waves of pain ran up her arm, jolting her right to the edge of consciousness.

"Tell me, Adraste," she whispered, through dry lips. "How may I save Antonius?"

"Find Daedalus' garden," she said, almost absently. Her gaze riveted on the mirror. "Cross the waste until you reach a river of fire. Many ghosts flit along its banks, unable to cross. Some of the ghosts will not see you. Many will not care even if they do. But you must search there until you find one willing to carry you across. But take care when you do. If you exchange one word with that vagrant throng, or answer when they speak or if they answer you, then you are doomed to wander among them forever. Beyond the river is Daedalus' garden."

"Antonius saw you as you were, didn't he?" Regeane asked. "I mean when he painted you with the glass in your hand. He was just another mirror to you."

For the first time Adraste tore her gaze from the mirror and directed a malevolent glare at Regeane.

"That's all love means to you, isn't it?" Regeane asked. "To see your loveliness mirrored in the pleasure of another's face and eyes. Because of that, you took him for your lover and your victim."

"Unnatural thing," Adraste shrilled. "Not beast and yet not human, who are you to condemn me? You who are destined never to know love unless it leads to death."

Then she turned back to the mirror in her hand and smiled, crooning softly to herself in a comforting way. "I have my beauty. It's all I ask, and if I doubt, I can always look into my mirror and see it there."

Slowly she began to drift away; but even as she did, Regeane saw her body was begining to fall into the ruin of the grave again. Yet the reflection in the mirror remained unchanged—a face young and beautiful forever.

Then, from the timeless current of air that blew across the waste, a zephyr took her and she drifted like a fallen leaf taken by the wind into the immense reaches of eternity.

"She is in hell and doesn't know it," Regeane said to Herophile and Crysta.

"I cannot say," Herophile answered. "In time she might come to know herself better."

"But there is no time here," Regeane answered.

"True," Herophile answered. "No time, but many mysteries. So there is hope that one day she may forswear self-love for compassion and regret. But to do so would bring pain, so she would rather stay as she is. Know well, Regeane, that the price of paradise is pain. Now if *you* have the will, go seek it and heal Antonius."

When she ceased speaking, she also seemed to cease to be. Wherever Herophile went she took Crysta with her, and Regeane found herself alone. She heard only the endless moan of the wind and the roar of the fires at the top of the pylons.

Whatever compulsion had kept Regeane woman was lifted also, and she found herself wolf again. She started out across what Herophile had called the ruined land. Every time her forepaw touched the ground, the pain was like a red hot iron slicing into the sensitive pad of her foot, but the wolf, controlled by the woman's will, held to her task and drove on.

The ruined land was rock and sand, the sky a dark starless pall, and Regeane found her way by the light of burning cities. As she drew close to each one, she found they were inhabited, filled with the senseless cruelty and blind tragedy that has afflicted man since time began.

In the streets, illuminated by flames pouring over burning rooftops, leaping from the windows and doors of dying dwellings, wives wept over their fallen husbands, men cried out against heaven as they stared down at ravished and murdered mothers and daughters.

In places the gutters ran red with the blood of the slain and the victors rioted drunkenly amidst the slaughter even as they, too, were felled by disease and ran themselves on each other's

swords to escape the pain of water running from their bowels
and lumpish swelling of armpit and groin that drove them wild
with misery. Others were beset by torture, flaying, branding,
blinding, burning and they writhed in agony even as they turned
on their torturers and sent them by the same road.

All these visions tormented the wolf as she dragged herself
onward. Her suffering consisted in wondering if she saw actual
spirits locked in an endless repetition of cruelty, pain, and despair. What little comfort she felt lay in believing they were
only shadows of what had been, and somewhere the souls of
those enduring so much agony, suffering were free.

The last city was only rubble filled with bloated corpses eaten
by dogs and flies. Ahead of her she saw a forest and through the
forest ran a river of fire.

The wolf stumbled into a painful lope, her heart hungry for
the trees, for the coolness under the heavy boughs. The ash was
a torture almost as intense as her wounded paw. Perhaps in the
forest she could find clean water to drink and she would smell
something besides smoke dust and burning flesh.

But when she drew closer to the forest she saw it was a ruin
also. Charred dead trees lifted a tracery of leafless branches
against the sullen sky. A sky reflecting the bloody light of burning cities. In a few moments she was among the skeletal undergrowth at its edge. She felt the dead branches snap against her
body as she passed. They were brittle and rotten.

Down the slope she struggled, toward the river of fire. Many
trees were fallen, shattered into tangles of sinister branches and
thorny growth, the deadfalls traps for her tired feet.

The only water she found there stank of mold and was heavy
with the tannins released by rotting wood. Bark hung in strips
from the trunks of trees still standing like flesh falling from
the bones of a corpse. The forest was no sanctuary. Still she
struggled on down and down toward the river. Its fires glimmered through the trees.

At the rocky bank, Regeane found the ghosts of which
Adraste had spoken. Some of them she could see, but even the
wolf turned her eyes from them. Some walked unseeing, lips
moving in silent communion with themselves. Others wept or
raged, teeth clenched, spitting out the bile and fury of a lifetime

at the empty dark. Others were only sad, lonely voices drifting on the wind. Their words were a torment to her ears and seemed to demand she speak if only to offer them what little comfort she could.

They cried out of the heart-wrenching tragedy of being human. And Regeane, soul locked in the wolf's body, wept silently that her wolf shape could not weep with them.

"I died in childbed . . ." one moaned. "Oh, the pain—the pain."

"I was captured and taken as a slave," a man's voice cried in anguish. "My life was impossible without freedom. I died under torture after the third time I ran away."

A child's voice wailed, "I died of hunger. My mother starved me after my father left her."

No, the wolf thought. *No.* And despite the wound in her paw, she began to run along the rocky river bank away from this cauldron of human pain. The fires blazed from the water, scorching her side.

The voices followed like a swarm of furies dinning their misery into her ears.

"I adored my sons . . ." one voice whimpered, "but they poisoned me for my gold."

"I was strangled," another screeched. "My husband accused me of adultery. I was guiltless, but he had me strangled anyway because he wanted another richer than I."

No, the wolf thought, trying to return to the poor shelter of the dead trees. A heavy thicket of thorn bushes drove her back.

Then abruptly she was a woman again. The hot rocks near the river seared her feet. There was blessed, blessed silence.

The figure of a man stood before her. He was only a shadow backlit by the flames. Strangely, he alone, of all the shapes that wandered by, seemed to see her.

"I am Wolfstan, the wolf stone," he said.

Father, Regeane wanted to say, but didn't. She didn't dare let the words pass her lips.

"Hush," he said. "Be silent as Adraste warned you. Only one of us can be heard here."

He turned slightly. The fire illuminated him, and Regeane

saw the broad wound made by the crossbow bolt that let out the life from his chest.

"How many sunsets and sunrises has it been, Regeane, since you leapt in your mother's womb? I have followed you from the time you first opened your eyes on the day. I remembered and loved you, and I have waited here."

Regeane was woman now and she could weep. She walked toward him, the tears streaming down her cheeks.

"Cup your hands," he said, "that I may drink and feel my mortality again."

Regeane cupped her fingers. His lips touched her bloody palms. He solidified before her into a man.

The first thing he did was undo his mantle and wrap it around her body to cover her nakedness. Adraste's warning was forgotten. Many words choked Regeane's throat. Her loneliness was a bitter ache that held her to silence.

"Hush and be still." He pressed a finger to Regeane's lips. "Do not speak.

"I have followed you all the days of your life. Not just through sunrise and sunset, but through the hours of the night when the stars turn in silence about the world. Through the days when the sun burned hot on your back, and the fields baked a golden shimmer in its glory.

"I heard your voice on the summer wind, and through the lonely nights of winter when great trees crack with cold and snow blankets the earth in silence.

"I knew your dreams and fears. I peered with you and puzzled over the words in books. And I, too, struggled with you in your loneliness and pain. My daughter, my beloved daughter, you have never been alone.

"I looked through your eyes in the springtime when new growth was a green mist on the trees and meadows, and in the autumn when the bright leaves were a gay chorus of color against the brown land.

"All the days of your life have I followed and loved you. And I have waited, walking here, denying my own peace that you might know how much."

Regeane felt his arms lift her. He carried her into the flames, roaring up from the burning river. She could feel the heat rise around her, stifling, furious, malevolent, almost a living thing reaching out tentacles of fire to pluck her from her father's arms. Then they were across and walking through a meadow aglow with the new light of a rising sun.

Wolfstan set her down on the grass and took her face between his palms, and she looked up at him. He was a big man with a thick thatch of sandy hair. She wondered that his face was so ordinary. He had a kind, strong man's face with a heavy nose broken more than once in combats, scarred by the battles he had fought.

"Your mother," he said, "never understood my double nature. She hated and feared it. God forgive her! For your mother, the Almighty always wore Gundabald's face.

"But here on the riverbank, this chasm between self-delusion and eternity, one must leave not only the griefs of the dust but its injustices before one can seek the light eternal.

"So here I leave my love betrayed, my loss, and my bitter sorrow."

Regeane tried to speak and felt again his finger on her lips.

"Hush, for I have seen your tears and they are stars that will light my way on all my journeys . . . forever."

Then he was gone and a giant gray wolf stood where he had been. The wolf turned and ran to the edge of the meadow where the greenwood began. He turned once and stared back at Regeane and then was gone. His abiding, eternal love washed over her in a wave.

Regeane stood quietly by the edge of a forest of living green, scented by the clean pure air of morning.

She trembled with both grief and joy for a long time. Wolfstan's mantle was made of coarse, heavy woolen stuff, edged with a narrow band of gold embroidery. It might have been part of a king's hunting dress. She wrapped it around herself and started forward without looking back.

The grass was soft and cool under her feet and slightly damp with the morning dew. At the top of the hill, the sunrise glowed in a scattering of mackerel clouds. Her hand bled. Her blood sparkled and glowed in ruby droplets on the green grass.

Following the path the wolf took, she reached the forest. The light there was gray. The soft moss on the barks of the trees glowed deep emerald. In the morning stillness, no bird sang.

The forest floor was carpeted with fern. The crisp, dark fronds bent under her gentle footfalls, then sprang back again, leaving no trace of her passage. The forest belt was narrow, and Regeane left the trees atop a high hill and looked down into a garden. It was cradled between the rolling forested hills like a child on the breast of its mother. She understood she had, at last, reached her goal.

She paused for a moment and stared out into the distance. The sun was over the horizon's rim and something even brighter shone in its first rays. Was it a fair white city that gathered all light into itself? She didn't know and couldn't be sure because the sunrise was too bright for her eyes.

She started down into the garden. She almost cried out with pain when she reached the edge. It was fenced by a hedge of brambles—the soft four-petaled white flowers scattered over hard, black, thorny stems.

Regeane paused for a second. She was so tired. Her hand ached with a cold, dull pain. She didn't know if she had the strength to bear any more suffering, but she stretched out her torn hand toward the rigid, dark-green stems and they parted easily at her touch.

She found herself on a flagged path walking toward a distant fountain. The path was bounded by flowers. They bloomed everywhere, riotously, indifferent to the season. Some of them Regeane knew and could call by name. Rank on rank of velvety purple lavender, thick clary sage, clover white, yellow, and purplish red, hugged the path as a border.

Behind the lower plants stood tall foxglove and abundant lilies. Ah, and such lilies as she had never seen. White with stripes of lavender, heads drooping, heavy with the dew. Other, taller ones behind them lifted crisp petals twisted back, orange and scarlet as though they waited breathlessly for the sun.

Behind them twining among the tall cypresses were the roses. Single, double, red, pink, and white, and on their petals scattered as stars are across the night sky, lenses of dew catching the light of the rising sun and turning it into a thousand tiny rainbows.

I have been here before, Regeane thought. *Walked here in those dreams I have in deepest sleep. Those dreams I only dimly remember. I have walked here and my troubled heart has longed for this place. For its cool healing and peace. I will find him near the fountain.*

And so she did.

His hair was white and his short beard gray, but his face had the same ageless beauty Herophile's had. She must have made some sound as she came into his presence, or perhaps, he caught her thought because he lifted his eyes from the book he was reading and studied her face.

"You are Daedalus?" Regeane asked.

"Yes, I am, and what does a creature of such beauty as you want with me?"

"I seek," she said, "healing for a man. Is this within your power?"

"Though I am one of the lesser creatures here, yes it is."

Regeane wondered if he were one of the lesser ones here, who the greater might be, but she didn't ask. She was content to sit down on one of the stone benches and stare at the play of water in the new sunlight. She was very thirsty, as she had been when she sought the river.

"May I drink?" she asked.

"Yes," Daedalus said. "But," he cautioned, "do not bathe your wounded hand in that water, for it is the water of life and the wound is the only thing that ties you to the earth. Heal it, and you may not return."

"I'm not sure," Regeane said, "that I want to return."

Daedalus smiled. "I perceive you are a very young creature and your life has been harsh, but fear not, things may soon grow better. But if you remain here, nothing will ever change for you. For better or worse. I was old when I came here, a dried-out husk of a man. I had reason to believe I had experienced all that life had to offer.

"My sight was blurred and my ears could barely hear the sound of a thunderclap. My spirit was as dry and withered as the rest. I was no use to the world any longer and the world was no use to me. I had long forgotten my youth and its struggles. Accidea had taken hold of my spirit. I had drained life's cup to the lees. I wanted only to rest here in the sun."

Regeane knelt by the fountain and began to drink. As she did, she began to feel the fatigue and the weariness leave her. She felt a sense of quiet victory enter her heart as she realized she'd won. Antonius would be as he had been and the poetry of his fingers, the magic his nimble brushes could trace on a wall, would be renewed to the greater beauty of the world. She had not spent her blood, her pain, for nothing.

"Where is he?" Daedalus asked, putting his book aside. "This one you want me to heal?"

"At Cumae," Regeane said.

"Ah, Cumae," Daedalus said. "I dwelt there long and loved the priestess. I remember the Acropolis, the sanctuary high on its rock beside Homer's wine-dark sea."

Still on her knees at the fountain, Regeane looked up at him, sadness in her eyes. "It is a ruin," she said.

Daedalus frowned. "So Icarus informs me."

"Icarus?" Regeane questioned.

"My son. Tell me, what do men say of him?"

"That—" Regeane's tongue stumbled as it was borne upon her that it was very strange to talk to a legend about a legend, but she continued. "That he flew too high and the sun melted the wax on his wings and he fell into the sea."

Daedalus laughed. "What folly. There were wings, but there was no wax. No, Icarus was one to test the limits of everything. I tacked upon the air as ships skim the broad bosom of the sea with a sail. Icarus tested the limits of my craft and came to grief on the rocks below. But that was only in one of his lives. He has had many since."

"While you remained here?"

"Yes," Daedalus answered. "You see, my dear, for some men one lifetime is enough, but for others, a thousand would not suffice. Icarus is one of these. So he comes and brings me news of the world I left behind so long ago. A world, I might add, that astounds me.

"Though it doesn't tempt me to leave my garden very often, but seldom do I meet such a creature as you are, and never before has one penetrated my sanctuary."

Regeane asked hesitantly, "You see me as I am?"

"Yes, I do. I see the graceful woman, all delicacy and intellect, also your fleet companion of the night. She who glories in the freedom of moonlight.

"While I lived, I saw your kind as the stuff of dreams and illusion. But when I came here, I met a few wanderers in the forest, children of life's most intimate beauty, and I understood. Men see the world past the blinders of reason. No ruler, tyrant ever existed worse than reason. For those blinded by it cannot search out what lurks at the corners of their eyes, half unseen."

"Reasonable men," Regeane said, "would rope me to a post and burn me."

"Indeed. How could they ever endure such power in a woman? It smacks of the witch."

"Is it so terrible, then, to be a witch?" Regeane asked.

"No." Daedalus smiled. "For the earth is a beautiful soft woman, and the witch is her voice."

Daedalus stared out into the distance with eyes that didn't see Regeane any longer.

"I remember many years ago, in my youth, I was born on Crete, that fair island set in a lapis sea. Ah, it was the earth's morning then, and we were the first to taste her bountiful fruits. We tamed the wild grapes grown on the mountainsides. Soft tiny, purple globes, fair and round as a woman's lips. Our fields were golden with wheat, bowing before the sea's breeze. Long dead as I am, I can still taste the soft, white loaf that wheat made. Still scent the bouquet of the wine we drank with it. The olive, gray queen mother of trees, lent us fragrant oil to tease our palates when we feasted on plump partridges, doves, or partook of prawns and fishes, the ever-present bounty of the sea.

"The days ran into one another, woven together like the threads of a tapestry, or like the notes of a wonderful melody. One of those played by a shepherd as he dozes among his sheep on a summer afternoon. A threnody that cannot be written down. I cannot separate those days from one another because they were all delight.

"I built Ariadne's dancing floor that we might give thanks to the earth, ancient and benevolent mother of man, for all her gifts. For then, Regeane, we did not think of rape or conquest.

We knew how to woo the earth and went to her gently as a lover goes to a virgin. We had of her infinite pleasure and fulfillment. And the witch was a priestess who treaded the measure of life abundant and joyous on her dancing floor."

Regeane rested her head against the porphyry basin of the fountain and her eyes closed. "What happened?" she asked.

Daedalus laughed harshly. "A dream of power, girl. The Egyptians came to our island. They coveted our wine and oil. Before they came, Minos was only a man who was sometimes possessed by a god. They taught him to believe he was a god, in fact, and so could take what he wanted.

"The precious oil and wine went into the storage jars in his palace. The plump partridges and doves to his table, and only the splendor of his house from afar was left to fill the hearts and bellies of his people. His hands reached out, grasping for more and more—and I, who had once but wonderful things for him, could not do enough.

"When I spoke out against him—he imprisoned me in a villa atop a high cliff. I escaped by sailing away on the wind. I did not live to see Minos' end, but my son tells me it came in a cloud of fire."

"And the witch?" Regeane asked.

"Why, men hate and curse her," Daedalus said, "because she is the incarnation of their shame. She reminds them of their beautiful mistress, the earth. They have forgotten how to love her. Now they fear her her tempests and her torrents. Her winter cruelty, her summer heat and dust. Her passionate hours, when her crest shakes and fire boils from mountain tops.

"They say that this is her face, pretending not to know that it is only one of her faces, forgetting the hours when she smiles on them and stretches out her arms in love. They forget that when they see her darkness and cruelty, it is only their own they see mirrored in her eyes. Having condemned her, they feel free to despoil and pillage her. Even as they despoil and pillage the witch."

Regeane rose to her feet, her father's mantle was still wrapped around her. She threw back her head and took a deep breath of the morning air. "I understand why I find you in the garden."

Daedalus shook his head. "I didn't make the garden. It was a gift given to me by love."

Regeane looked down at her hand. It was still bleeding. The red droplets staining the flags at her feet.

"We must leave," she said. "I believe I have not much time. I'm still bleeding."

Daedalus stretched one of his hands toward her torn one. She jerked her own hand back for a second and looked out over the garden, wanting to see it again in the morning light and drink in its beauty: at the flowers, their blossoms splashes of color against the green gold grass; turf, sparkling so brightly in the sunlight that she couldn't tell where the green stopped and the gold began; at the roses whose scent was beginning to fill the air; and the tall cypresses shadowing the orange ball of light on the horizon.

"I want to remember it," she said. "Remember it all."

"So that someday you can find it again?" Daedalus asked.

"Yes," Regeane answered. "So that someday I can find it again."

Then he took her hand.

Regeane felt a tremendous pull, a pain. She knew nothing of giving birth, but it was similar to what she imagined that must be like. A second later, they stood together on the rock at Cumae before the sacred fire. The fog was gone, the stars were a cascade of light above her, and the wind tore at her father's mantle. The garden was only a memory.

Antonius lay at their feet, his naked body stretched over the cold fire. He seemed dead. His eyes were closed and his skin was blue with cold. The results of his disease were plain, fingers and toes destroyed, white and crumbling nose, mouth fallen away. Yet over him still hung the shadow of ancient beauty.

The moon was down and the land lay in darkness beneath the rock. The ghosts were no longer in evidence. The temple, with its empty cella, loomed behind Regeane.

The two black-robed heierophants waited on the temple steps beside the cella, looking like statues poised at the door to a tomb.

Then the wind dropped and the night was still. Regeane seemed to hear the silence.

Daedalus lowered his arms and while Regeane watched, he

slowly raised them. As he did, fire flared in the stone circle of the ancient sacred hearth. The flames looked real, and Regeane started with surprise and alarm.

But then she realized the flames shed no heat. Antonius seemed to take no hurt from them, rather he seemed to float among them like the salamander that lives among the flames. But as Daedalus' arms continued to rise, the fire turned white and flared into a star of coruscating brilliance that blinded Regeane for a moment and then was gone.

She looked again. Antonius lay before her in the fullness of his youth and strength. His flesh glowed against the gray ash with the flush of life. As she watched, he shivered in the chill night air, turned on his side, and drew his knees against his chest as he felt the cold.

Regeane took the mantle from her shoulders and dropped it over him. Daedalus walked around the fire and took her still-bleeding hand.

"My garden?" he asked. "Will you come back with me?"

Regeane stood before him, conscious now she stood clothed only in shadow and her own moon-tipped hair.

"No," she answered. "I will try the world and see what it holds for me before I sleep."

"Ah." Daedalus stepped back. "So then it is farewell, lovely lady of moonlight. Looking upon you, I can well see why immortal gods could find surcease from desire in the arms of mortal woman. And what my foolish son so thirsts for that he drinks again and again at the fountain of life."

Then he was gone, leaving Regeane standing alone with the bitter winter night and the stars. She turned toward the two hierophants waiting at the temple steps. She pointed at Antonius.

"When he wakes," she said, "return him to his mother."

A second later, she was wolf. Favoring her still bleeding paw, she limped down the processional way toward Rome.

XXV

WHEN REGEANE CROSSED THE STREAM, HER PAWS
shattered a coating of ice at its edges. The night was bitterly
cold. She was aware that her energies were seriously depleted.
She didn't know if she could reach Rome and the safety of Lucilla's villa tonight.

She paused and looked out over the desolate Campagna. The
fog that earlier had boiled over the sweeping grasslands had
settled on the ground and then frozen into hoarfrost on the
tangled grass blades. They cracked under her limping feet. The
moon was down and the stars in their myriads blazed a cold
light above her.

The woman's mind was almost as weary as the beast's.
Sooner or later, she thought, *death will be upon me. Why not
here? Why not now? And then . . . what? Daedalus' garden?
Who knows?,* she thought, looking up at the icy splendor above
her. There had been as much ugliness as beauty in the world
beyond the temple doorway, but how much of either beauty or
ugliness was real? How much illusion? The woman's mind, imprisoned in the wolf's narrow skull, faltered before the problem. But no matter.

A jolt of pain traveled up her wounded paw when it struck the
ground. *That is real enough,* she thought. Fatigue dragged at
every screaming muscle in her body, tempting her to lie down
in the frost-covered grass and sleep. The wolf's memories were
like music, a continuous flow of images that threatened to over-
whelm the woman's mind and will.

The woman was too confused and disheartened to beat them
back. She was near the end of her strength. The cold that had

never bothered her before, now bit through the heavy guard hairs on her coat, chilling her to the bone.

Rome, she thought, and tried to force herself onward. But the woman knew Rome was very far away. The images shadowing her consciousness told her death was very near. Certain, if she were caught out in the open day, naked and alone. She had spent too much of her strength, her life blood, to save Antonius. Now perhaps, she was doomed.

To the woman's dismay, the ever-confident wolf accepted this. If it was so, then why struggle to the last? Simply lie down beside the stream. There would be a little pain and then darkness would come. A darkness not much different than sleep, and then might she not be allowed to run forever by her father's side, across the vast reaches of eternity?

She lowered her muzzle to the stream at her feet. Drink now, and then curl up and rest. Let her blood ooze away slowly into the frozen grass. Numbed, she lapped at the frigid water.

The shock of cold snapped her back to full alertness. To drink too much of the icy water in the condition she was in was hideously dangerous. Her head came up and she staggered back from the water, snarling, ears tight against her skull. No, that water would be a virtual death sentence to her already chilled body.

Fury overwhelmed her. She raised her head and for the first time in her life, she lifted her voice against a monstrously unjust world, a cruel universe, and the distant, indifferent stars.

The sound from her throat began in a roar of rage and ended in a wail of agony. It echoed across the empty night like the clarion call of a trumpet. Then she dropped her head and staggered, realizing to the fullest, both woman and wolf, what her own weary body was telling her. She could go no further.

A second later she was galvanized by terror. She was being answered! The calls were very far away, just the faintest of cries, but clear on the still night air.

Her whole body shook. Her first impulse was to run, but the moment her injured paw struck the ground, the pain paralyzed her. She no longer had the strength to run.

Brief, ironic laughter flickered in the woman's consciousness. She had cried out against death and succeeded only in calling it to her. Then red rage flooded the wolf's thoughts, sweeping aside the woman and her civilization. The wolf snarled with contempt at the mewing creature who turned her eyes away from blood and trembled before death.

She was very conscious of her power, one wounded paw didn't strip it all away from her. She was one hundred and ten pounds of hard muscle and flexible sinew, with fangs that could tear out the throat of a bull and jaws so strong they could snap a man's thighbone like a twig. More than a match for any natural wolf ever born.

The howls came again, this time closer, and she was briefly shaken as she seemed to discern a plea in the cries. As though they were asking her to reply and tell them where she was.

So be it, she thought. *It could go one way or the other.* If there were too many of them, she might lose. Well, better a fight than the slow death by night and the cold. The images in the wolf's brain were of warm blood and hot red meat steaming in the freezing air. If she won, she would feed and regain her strength.

She lifted her head and cried out again, an unearthly yell that was both challenge and invitation. A few moments later she could hear them coming. A soft crackling sounded as they fleeted over grass stems made brittle by ice.

The wolf limped quickly back toward the stream. The water wasn't much, but it might protect her if they tried to encircle her. A second after she took up her position, they topped the hill in front of her, black yellow-eyed shapes in the gloom. They slowed as they came down the slope toward her and came to a stop at its foot.

They were the same three she'd met in the city. The red, the gray, and the black. Her first reaction was a profound shudder of relief, but her second was bewilderment and fear. They hadn't been unfriendly before, indeed, the giant gray had been amorous, but what would they do now when they saw she was a cripple? Yet she confronted them proudly, head lifted, ears erect, her wounded paw curled under her breast.

For a long moment, they simply stood looking at each other. Then the big gray turned toward the black, as if making a request. He touched noses with her. Her tail waved once as if in acquiescence. The red wolf, probably remembering Regeane's hostility, hung back. He sat back on his haunches with a big doglike smile and began to scratch vigorously with his hind paw at his ear.

Fleas, the wolf wondered in revulsion. *How could one of her noble kind sink so low as to allow himself to get fleas!*

The black wolf approached her slowly, unthreateningly, muzzle extended. The intent was unmistakable. *Do you wish to be friends?*

The wolf did. She didn't know if they could help her; she didn't know if anyone could. But their companionship was infinitely better than being alone with her suffering. So she extended her muzzle toward the other, gently.

Their noses touched. The wolf didn't know what she expected to smell, but what she did surprised her. There was a hint of red meat, the scent of the cold night air caught in the pelt of the other, and rather sweet breath, a warm bread smell.

The black made a gentle sound in her throat, like a soft whine. It was as though she said "welcome." Then, oh so gently, her head slid along the silver wolf's jaw until her muzzle rested on her back at the shoulder.

For a moment, the silver wolf was at a loss how to reply and then she understood. In this position, the other's throat was bared to her teeth as was her own. It simply said, I trust you.

The silver wolf placed her head on the other's shoulders. Their bodies were close together, breast to breast, and the warmth of the black wolf's body was like a conflagration to the silver wolf's chilled one. She trembled with the cold, with excitement, with fear. She could scent the black wolf's warm, clean fur, and the gentle tang of the femaleness that hung about her like some exotic perfume.

The other broke the contact first by stepping back. Her tongue washed the silver wolf's face so quickly she didn't have time to object to what was, to Regeane, an indignity. Then the black's muzzle dropped to her injured paw.

The silver wolf's hackles rose, and she snarled softly, more in fear than in anger. Fear of the pain. The big, black wolf's eyes looked up into hers. The silver wolf read compassion and some amusement as her long red tongue flicked over the inside of the pad. The touch of the wolf's tongue eased the spasms of pain that had been a background to the wolf's thoughts since Cumae.

She uncurled her paw and extended it toward the black wolf to let the gentle caress do its healing work.

Meanwhile, her attention shifted to the big gray. He had been watching closely while she and the black became acquainted. He broke off his scrutiny and was tiptoeing carefully through the long grass and low scrub surrounding the stream bank. His neck was arched, muzzle lowered, ears pricked as he studied the ground below him carefully.

Abruptly, he leaped into the air and came down, forepaws together, pinning something to the earth. The big jaws snapped with an audible click. A second later in a motion so quick even the silver wolf's eyes could barely follow it, he tossed something small at her. It landed with a soft thump at her feet.

The silver wolf looked down and saw a mouse, its small body, neck broken, still quivering in its death throes. The silver wolf backed up quickly, one hind foot went into the icy stream behind her. She jumped to land with a shrill whine.

The black wolf made a grunting sound and turned her face away. The red wolf didn't bother to hide his merriment. He bounded into the air and came down hindquarters elevated, forepaws and muzzle against the earth and then rolled over on his back, waving all four paws in the air, managing to give the general impression of a human paralyzed with mirth.

In rapid succession, a second mouse landed next to the first, and then a third. The black wolf stared at the silver wolf patiently, then reached down and pushed one of the mice toward the silver wolf with her nose. Her intent was unmistakable.

The gray looked at the still laughing red wolf and snarled. He turned his eyes to the silver wolf and stared at her imperiously.

Strangely, the woman made the decision, not the wolf. The wolf in her own way was a traditionalist, but the woman knew she was, at least in part, dying of hunger. So if mice it was, then mice it would have to be. Besides they were no stranger than other things she had eaten as a woman.

She gulped the first, barely letting it touch her tongue. The taste wasn't bad—nutty, crunchy, a bit more mushroom than mammal. She took the second more slowly. The third she savored. *Not bad*, she thought. *A new delicacy. Not bad at all.* She wondered what Barbara, the cook at the convent, would think.

Five mice later she was feeling almost like her old self again. When she touched her paw to the ground, she began to wonder what magic the black wolf's tongue had worked. The pad was still sore, but she could walk—and without being too uncomfortable. She no longer limped.

The big gray gave her a look of approval and began to lead the pack slowly along the stream bank, looking for more mice. He ate the next himself and gave the silver wolf a long, meaningful look.

She was filled with a wild excitement. He wanted to teach her how to hunt. His next stalk was a slow, measured demonstration of how it was done.

One walks slowly, quietly, through the grass, eyes and ears alert for the slightest sound, the quick scurrying, the soft rustling sounds the rodents make while foraging among the grass stems. Then the high leap and the lightning pounce.

The silver wolf began to imitate his movements. Head bent, her eyes and ears probing the thickened brush and dried winterkilled weeds. She froze inadvertently when she saw her first one, a fat brown fellow feeding on the remains of a dried sunflower. She leaped. Her paws came down on nothing.

The mouse darted away, right into the waiting jaws of the red wolf. He crunched happily, then gave her a big, canine grin.

She had no better success with her next. He darted toward the black wolf who made a meal of him.

The silver wolf gritted her teeth and continued grimly to imitate the big gray. The next time she saw movement, she leaped at once and pounced on a hare. He slipped through her front paws and pushed off on her face, then bounded away, leaving her blinking and shaking her head in the aftermath of a hard slap across the muzzle.

The red wolf evidently thought this was hilarious. He leaped into the air and came down rolling. The gray made an eel-like turn and nipped the red wolf sharply on the rump. This time the red wolf's jump wasn't one of mirth. He yipped and sat down, licking his backside furiously between glares at the big gray.

The gray turned back to the silver wolf and looked at her as if to say "Shall we continue?" The silver wolf's next effort met with better success. Something soft and furry wriggled under her paws. Her jaws snapped. Mouse and delicious.

After that, hunting seemed to come easily to her. She had the inborn predator's skill of absolute concentration. All she needed to do was rely upon her senses. She found, much to the red wolf's chagrin and the big gray's approval, that she was one of the best at the game.

When they had all taken their fill of mice, the gray wolf led them out onto the plain. They began to run. Now that she was well fed and rested, the silver wolf could run with them.

The whole world seemed to sleep around the four wolves and they flowed like shadows over the frozen hills. *This is,* the silver wolf thought, *the night of my nights.* This must have been what it was like before man with his cities, his cruelty, and his wars . . . A primal innocence. Only the stars were their companions.

Once they started a sleeping deer from a copse of trees near an abandoned farm house. The wolves gave chase, more in fun than out of any idea of bringing her down. The silver wolf stretched herself, running flat out, and was amazed by her own speed as she paced the terrified creature.

Then she looked up and saw the brown head, the wide staring dark eye, the throat that throbbed with blood and life. She smelled the thick acrid musk of terror, and realized what was fun to her was agony to this creature. She saw the deer was a pregnant doe.

And the woman reined the wolf in sternly.

She broke off the chase and dropped back to join the rest.

At that moment, she smelled the city. *Rome,* she thought, *and Lucilla's villa.* In her heart, she felt a pang of sorrow as the woman's mind understood the night had come to an end.

The wolves dropped from a run to a lope. They turned toward an abandoned village hidden in the fold of one of the hills very near the city. The silver wolf followed. Her nose picked up the tang of wood smoke coming from one of the dark tumble-down houses. She assumed this must be one of their dens. That was what she would have done, had she the power. Found a base where clothes and a fire were waiting for her before she returned to the city. A safe way station between the world of men and that of wolves.

The silver wolf paused just before they reached the village. The rest stopped, too. They turned and looked at her. And the silver wolf understood she was being invited to join them. The big gray took a step toward her.

Desire raged through the woman's mind like a fire through dry twigs. The wolf wasn't ready for her initiation into the arts of desire, but the woman was. More than ready.

If she was moonlight, he was starlight. The gray coat spangled like the fiery arch of the heavens above her. She saw the breadth of his shoulders and felt the overpowering presence of his maleness and, at the same time, the vast mystery of the night.

Once inside the hut, the big gray would be a man and she a woman. The other two could dress quickly and go. They would be alone. He would not need to speak to her. She would not speak to him.

They could, as they did now, look at each other's eyes, tell one another every secret of their private universes without words. He would be strong, very big and strong. She could, in her imagination, feel his caresses.

And she knew that once he held her in his arms, she would refuse him nothing. She would, instead, yield up her innermost being to him, eagerly and without shame.

If only she could blot out the knowledge, the foresight that made her human. These three were safe, careless and carefree in their double state. All the things she could never be. What would happen to their lives if they were suddenly hunted by a king, a pope?

The black wolf glided toward her. She joined in again: the touch on her nose, the head on her shoulder. The sense of love and trust. A blessing. A farewell.

Then the silver wolf turned and without looking back, ran. As she crossed the first hill and looked down on the city, she saw a strip of light on the eastern horizon; the stars were dying in its glow.

LUCILLA MET THE WOLF AS SHE LEAPED THE WALL into the villa. She was standing near one of the peach trees with a lamp in her hand. She extinguished the flame when she saw the wolf gliding toward her.

"Thank God," Lucilla breathed.

Regeane stood before her as a woman.

Lucilla wrapped her mantle around Regeane's shoulders.

Regeane clutched at it tightly as Lucilla helped her back to the villa.

"Antonius?" Lucilla snapped.

"He's well," Regeane replied. "You'll see when he returns. I'm exhausted." As she said the words, she realized how great that exhaustion was. The fury that had saved her from death at the stream and then the exhilaration that carried her across the Campagna with the other wolves had completely drained away.

"It's been a day and a half since I last slept," she told Lucilla as she guided Regeane across the villa porch toward one of the cubicula.

Regeane sat down on the edge of the bed. Lucilla handed her a cup of wine.

"You say he's well?" Lucilla asked, furiously. "How can that be?"

"Lucilla, please," she pleaded. "I haven't the strength. All I can tell you is I've accomplished this night all you could ask and more. Now, in the name of God, let me rest."

"Yes, yes. To be sure," Lucilla said.

As Regeane gulped the wine, Lucilla asked, "Food? Do you need food?"

Regeane shook her head and smiled. "I've eaten," she said.

Lucilla shuddered. "I guess I'd better not ask where or how."

Regeane chuckled as she slipped between the covers and sheets on the bed, then yawned.

"Only mice," she said.

"Mice!" Lucilla exclaimed, repelled.

"Mice," she whispered, intrigued.

"Mice." Then puzzled, she asked, "Do wolves eat mice?"

"Sometimes," Regeane answered and was an instant later asleep.

XXVI

THE THREE WOLVES DRESSED IN THE SHELTER OF the peasant hut near a small fire.

"My God. By all the gods, did you see her run?" the big gray whispered. "What a huntress she'll be. She had that deer if she wanted her."

"Beautiful," the red agreed, "but haughty. She's attracted. I could tell. Why wouldn't she join you in a little, shall we say, adventure? A bit of a tumble could only bring pleasure to you both."

"I want more than pleasure with that one," the gray said. "Though, by God, she'll be that, too."

"I think, perhaps," the black said as she pulled on her dress, "the silver one doesn't understand how truly free she is. She's timid. I could sense that, and she's ignorant of her own powers. A simple mouse hunt was a revelation to her."

"The wound," the gray said, "disturbs me. Very few things injure us in a way that survives the change."

"It was not a normal wound," the black said. "I knew that when my tongue touched it. Only heaven knows what torments she went through before we were able to rescue her. I could tell when we found her she expected not her own kind, but our wild cousins. You suggested a run on the Campagna tonight," she said to the gray.

"I had ulterior motives," the gray answered. "I hoped we might meet. The Campagna is where I would go if I lived in this stinking city."

"Oh, I don't know that the city's so bad," the red said. "I'm kind of learning to like it."

"Indeed," the black said dryly. "I know what you like. Is that how you picked up the fleas?"

"I don't have fleas," the red said, belying his words by scratching his ribs vigorously as he slipped into his shirt.

"Whatever you say," the black answered maliciously. "But stay away from me until you bathe and fumigate yourself."

"Even as a shape changer," the gray said, "Gavin, you're a true lowlife."

"Catch as catch can, Maeniel," Gavin said, "and between one thing and another, I catch a lot."

"Fleas, among other things," Matrona said.

"There's more than one bitch in the forest," Gavin said. "I met the cutest little thing living down by the Forum our first night in."

"Dog or woman?" Maeniel asked.

"As it transpired, both," Gavin said. "We did it one way, then the other, then both. She was quite impressed the way I dealt with my rivals. She was none too tidy about her person, but what are a few fleas between lovers?"

"Pervert," Matrona said.

REGEANE WOKE SEVERAL TIMES FROM HER LONG sleep. Once she saw Antonius looking down at her, Lucilla beside him. She saw no trace of his former disease on his body.

He kissed her once, very chastely, on the forehead and then she returned to sleep.

She was awakened again by a hug from Elfgifa. Lucilla's voice scolded in the background. Again she drifted away into slumber.

She woke finally, spontaneously, to find herself fully aware. Through a narrow window flowed a shaft of morning light. She sat up and saw Lucilla had set out clothing for her. A white shift and gown were draped over a chair near the bed.

She yawned and rose to her feet, and was in the process of dressing when Lucilla came into the room.

"At last," she exclaimed. "Come out when you have finished. I was about to have my morning meal. Come join me. We have much to discuss."

Regeane followed Lucilla to a small garden set away from the main atrium. It was private and quiet. Sweet woodruff bloomed in flower beds around a fishpond and against the blank whitewashed walls of the storerooms surrounding them.

"I'm a bitch in the morning," Lucilla said, "and the servants seldom bother me here."

There was a marble table to the right of the pond. Two comfortably cushioned chairs were drawn up to the table. Regeane seated herself in one of them. Lucilla sat in the other.

"I think," Lucilla said, "that you'll find this a bit more substantial than the usual Roman breakfast. I don't follow the custom of beginning the day with a dry, crisp bread, sour wine, and perhaps if you're in the mood for luxury, a few figs. One never knows what difficulties the day will bring, and I prefer to be well fortified."

Regeane, looking at the table, decided Lucilla's idea of fortification was more than adequate. The table held sliced cold breast of capon with a raisin wine sauce, warm fresh-baked bread, honey, butter, and white cheese. All served with a mild white wine blessed with slight basil fragrance.

"How long did I sleep?" Regeane asked between mouthfuls.

"All of yesterday," Lucilla answered, "and through the night."

Regeane sighed. "I was tired."

Nothing else was said until they'd both worked their way through the food and were relaxing quietly, over their wine.

Lucilla frowned. "I have some bad news for you. I saved it until you finished breakfast. I didn't want to spoil your appetite. But you should know, Regeane, your prospective husband is here in Rome."

A wave of silent shock went through Regeane. She looked down at the wine cup in her hand, a beautiful thing made of opalescent glass resembling mother-of-pearl. She set it carefully on the marble table. Her hands shook.

"And?" she asked.

"My, but you're calm," Lucilla said.

"Remember," Regeane said, "I've been expecting him for some time. What should I do? Screech? Weep? Run up and down, scratching my face, tearing my hair in handfuls? No,

Lucilla, whatever I am, I'm not made that way. So have you met him? Tell me, what's he like?"

"From your point of view, the news is the very worst imaginable. I haven't seen him, but I dispatched Augusta to greet him at Ostia."

"Augusta?" Regeane asked.

"Yes," Lucilla said. "She whined and made pathetic noises, but she owes me something for assisting that despicable uncle of yours. In any case, she reported back to me that he's not old. I'd hoped he might be. Men in their dotage sleep soundly at night and think a lot about their stomachs and their bowels.

"It's quite easy for an attractive young woman to lead them around by the nose. Worse luck, he's not effeminate either. That class of men is often easily dealt with. One simply ignores their little peccadillos and offers them the honest friendship one gives to a sympathetic woman friend.

"But no such luck. He's a well-formed man in the prime of life. Augusta found him intelligent, mannerly, and well spoken. She thinks you are a very lucky woman. She said his understanding was quite impressive for a barbarian."

Regeane threw her head back for a second and looked up into the bright blue autumn sun. Then her eyes closed. She pressed two fingers to her lids. A voice in her mind spoke clearly. *You will have to kill him.*

"No," she whispered. "No. I don't want to."

Then she lowered her head and opened her eyes. It seemed as if a long time had passed. She found herself looking into Lucilla's face.

Lucilla's gaze was flat and opaque. She was smiling, a harsh quirk of her lips.

"Yes," Lucilla said, answering Regeane's thoughts. "I know you don't, but the less said the better. Even the walls have ears."

"Did he raise any objection to the marriage contract?" Regeane asked.

"No," Lucilla answered. "Hadrian had it drawn up by the chancery at the Lateran. Maeniel saw it."

"He is able to read?" Regeane asked.

"It would seem so," Lucilla responded, "because Hadrian

said he asked a few questions about the provisions in the contract, but raised no serious objections."

Regeane nodded. "Thank heaven for that."

"Your thanks are premature, my dear," Lucilla said. "Once you're out of Rome, that contract is just a piece of paper. There'll be no way for pope or king to enforce it in the mountains."

"I don't know," Regeane said, biting her lip. "He'll want preferment. The king will be very jealous of his honor. Abusing me might bring royal anger on his head."

"Yes," Lucilla said. "And you must present yourself as the road to royal favor. And toward that end, I have a plan. Which brings me to the betrothal feast. It will be tonight at one of Augusta's villas."

Lucilla produced a wax tablet from the skirts of her gown and set it on the table.

"You will wear white. Silk, lightly embroidered with golden daisies. There is a Frankish count in Rome now. Incidentally, he supplied the Frankish mercenaries who are guarding my villa now. His name is Otho. He's fat and has eyes like something you find hopping through a flower bed on a wet day, but bat your eyelashes at him and do your best to charm this toad. I won't say the Frankish king trusts him, but he uses him often. I'm certain he'll carry word back to Charles about what a prize he's bestowed on this Maeniel. With a bit of luck you'll be summoned to court and this unfortunate marriage may not last very long.

"I don't know, Lucilla," Regeane said. "Suppose, just suppose, I can reach an accommodation with this Maeniel, what then?"

"There's no help for it," Lucilla said. "Otho has to be invited to your wedding feast in any case. And impressing him will certainly help your cause with your husband. But that's not the important part of my plan, it's just an outside possibility.

"Think, child," she said, reaching forward and tapping Regeane on the forehead. "No matter what happens, you're going to be alone with this man for several years."

Regeane nodded again.

"What I plan to do," Lucilla continued, "is to send the same troop of mercenaries guarding this villa into the mountains with you. I don't think I'll have the slightest difficulty persuading Otho that it would be a good idea. Added assurance of this Maeniel's continued loyalty, shall we say."

"I see," Regeane said. "They would enforce the marriage contract."

"Just so," Lucilla answered. "Which brings us to another difficulty."

"Gundabald," Regeane said unhappily.

Lucilla's plucked brows lifted, and she smiled at Regeane with satisfaction. "Clever girl," she said. "How did you know?"

"Because," Regeane said, "I know Gundabald. He'd have nominal command of the mercenaries. He'd set about corrupting them at once. By the time he was finished, they'd be loyal to no one, and nothing, but him."

Lucilla laughed shortly, then leaned back in her chair and stared into the distance, a faint smile on her lips.

Regeane felt cold dread creeping over her. "What do you plan to do about Gundabald?"

Lucilla leaned forward over the table, poured herself another cup of the fragrant wine. Her face was very close to Regeane's. "I intend," she said, very softly, "to have him strangled."

Regeane jumped to her feet. "No," she shouted.

"That's it," Lucilla hissed in a soft, sibilant whisper. "Tell the world."

Regeane sat down again, very quickly. "No," she repeated more quietly.

"What?" Lucilla snapped in an undertone. "Do you love him so much?"

Regeane's fists clenched. She looked down at the marble top. "It's murder. Murder."

Then Lucilla said, "Have you another solution?"

Regeane didn't answer. She was remembering the ghost of the fiery river, the wound in his chest. "Wolfstan forgave him," she said.

"He what?" Lucilla asked.

"My father, I met him in the world beyond death. He forgave Gundabald."

Lucilla made a wavering gesture with her hand as though to

banish Regeane from her sight. She cupped her chin in her fist and leaned toward Regeane. "Now let me get this straight. You met your father in the world beyond death. When? How?"

"The night I saved Antonius," Regeane said. "I journeyed into the other world. I met my father there. He still bore the wound Gundabald had given him."

"You can speak with the dead?" Lucilla asked, breathlessly.

"Yes. I saw the Abbess Hildegard at the convent. She was dead. It frightened the nuns."

Lucilla threw back her head and howled.

Regeane started up, appalled and afraid Lucilla was having some kind of fit and then realized Lucilla was laughing.

"It frightened the nuns. Oh, my God," she chuckled. "Oh, Mother of God. Oh, Son of God. I imagine it did. No wonder Emilia was so hot to get rid of you." Lucilla was holding her sides. "The night you ran away, I sent word to them that you were here. They went to Hadrian the next day. They gave him every reason possible why he should leave you in my care. The attempted poisoning, Sister Angelica's hysterics, every excuse but the right one.

"Oh, oh, oh." Every "oh" was a hiccup of laughter. "Girl, you are most uncomfortable company."

Then Lucilla's mirth subsided. She stopped laughing and began to wipe her eyes. All at once another thought seemed to strike her. Her eyes darted quickly around the small garden.

"You don't see any here, do you?" she asked.

"No."

"Thank heavens for small mercies," Lucilla said, shaking her head.

"Though," Regeane said hesitantly, "I don't know when I do see them. Sometimes they seem so mortal."

This set Lucilla off again, and it was a while before she got herself under control. When she did, a hard, rather cold expression crept into her eyes.

"Did you see Adraste?" she asked.

"Yes," Regeane said. She looked away from Lucilla at a patch of sweet woodruff. The new sun gilded its white flowers. "She is in hell."

"And may she rot there," Lucilla shot back. She reached out and seized Regeane by the wrist. "Look at me, girl."

Lucilla's face was set and remorseless. "Your father may or may not have forgiven Gundabald. I'll assume what you say is true and you did meet him in some world we common mortals have no access to. But you haven't the luxury of your father's generosity. You can't afford it. He's dead and nothing can harm him. It's well and good to forgive past injuries, but you must consider the future harm Gundabald could do to you."

It grew warmer in the small patio, and bees visited the flowers at the border of the pool. Regeane closed her eyes and inhaled deeply. Sweet fragrances surrounded her. The delicate scent of the flowers, the heavier smell of Lucilla's clean body lent a warm human flavor in the clean air. But above all, the air itself that seemed a fresh white wine. That made every breath a draught of pleasure.

How strange it was to sit surrounded by beauty and plot a man's death.

"What's wrong?" Lucilla asked.

"The wolf," Regeane said. "Sometimes she comes and just wants to revel in the world around her."

"You're dodging the issue," Lucilla said. "And tell the wolf to go away. No mere animal could possibly understand dissimulation, or at least not the sort we're planning."

The wolf wandered back into her daytime darkness. And Regeane's mind snapped back to the present.

"What kind of dissimulation are we planning?" she asked with an interrogative lift of her brows.

"Your uncle is a frequenter of low companions, is he not? Brothels, taverns, wine bars, and the like."

"Yes."

"Good," Lucilla said. "Murder is always best and most easily accomplished when it seems to grow out of the manner of a man's life. Now, no doubt, your uncle sees you so successful at finding other friends. Friends, I might add, in a position to be of more help to you than he has been.

"I think that your charming uncle will see he has been wrong in the methods he chose in dealing with you. He will believe you're more clever and more powerful than he realized. He will arrive at my villa anxious to—shall we say—mend fences." Lucilla paused and smiled maliciously.

"You really think so?" Regeane asked. "Last time I saw him, he threatened to kill me."

"And he still intends to," Lucilla said, "but first, he will have to win you over. Because otherwise, how can he achieve his objective of lining his pockets with this Maeniel's gold?"

"I want nothing to do with him. His very nearness makes my flesh crawl," Regeane said with a shudder.

"Naturally," Lucilla said. "But when he comes, as I have said, you must seem won over by his sweet words. Mind you, don't allow yourself to be persuaded too quickly or he might become suspicious.

"Be very reluctant at first. These things require very deft, delicate handling. In fact, my dear, you may even show some measure of mistrust at the conclusion of your conversation. But above all, you must make him believe that you can, eventually, be persuaded to fall under his sway—in short, to become his accomplice, willing or unwilling. Send him away confident and you will have won the engagement. Then, of course, I'll hire my man and he'll begin his stalk.

"When Gundabald is found floating facedown in the Tiber, you will follow him to his grave, discreetly veiled in black, in tears. Now, what about Hugo? Should I include him in my instructions also?"

Regeane, marveling at her own calm, reached out and poured herself another cup of wine. "I don't think so," she said, judiciously. "With Gundabald dead, Hugo will do whatever I say. He's afraid of me."

"Excellent," Lucilla said. "It's always best in these affairs to keep things as simple as possible. Economy is always preferable to blood-lust and slaughter."

"Hugo will know," Regeane said, looking up at the cloudless sky and taking another sip of wine.

"Yes, my dear," Lucilla said. "But then, he won't talk, will he?"

"No," Regeane said. "He has no money and he'd be dependent on me for his keep and his pleasures. He'd be too afraid he wouldn't be believed and then I'd cut him off."

"Just so," Lucilla said. "And he wouldn't be frightened of you any longer. He'd be absolutely terrified. And sometimes, with some men, terror is a better guarantee of loyalty than love."

XXVII

THE SKY WAS THE SAME CLEAN, CLOUDLESS BLUE over the Forum, the wind sharp and chill. Maeniel paused in the shelter of an enormous stone block. Beside it, a flight of marble stairs led upward to nowhere. While it was warm enough in the sunlight, the dry air was cool in the shadows.

Gavin shivered. "Let's ride on," he said. "These ruins depress me and besides, you never know who might be lurking about, waiting to—"

"Be quiet, Gavin," Maeniel said.

"Be quiet, Gavin. Shut up, Gavin. Don't take on so, Gavin. I know what I'm doing, Gavin. That's all I ever get from you in this mood," Gavin complained. "I might point out that we're carrying enough gold to buy half of what's left of this wretched city and you want to play around in lonely spots where—"

"Gavin," Maeniel said as he dismounted and began to climb the marble steps. "Have you ever seen anyone who could take anything from me against my will, ever, anywhere, anytime?"

"No, but . . ."

"No ifs, buts, or maybes," Maeniel said. "No one ever has. Besides, we're alone. If we were not, I would see something, smell something, or hear something, and I don't."

Maeniel stopped to peer down at the marble steps. They were cracked and broken, stained by centuries' growth of lichens and moss. Weeds, bearing some golden composite flower, poked up from the interstices between the treads, blooms glowing against the shadowy stone.

One side of the stair was clear, the other disappeared into a velvet mantle of greenery where vines and even small trees struggled to get a foothold.

"Was it here?" Maeniel mused softly. "It's all changed so much. Augustus is supposed to have said 'I found a city of wood and left one of marble.' In fact, I think he found something alive and left only a cenotaph."

"Maeniel, what in the hell are you talking about?" Gavin asked.

"Caesar," Maeniel answered.

"Which one?" Gavin asked, sourly.

Maeniel reached the top of the steps and gazed out over the ruins of the Forum. Seen from this slight elevation, the place had a parklike aspect. Though a night of frost had dulled some of its lush vegetation and even stripped a few trees bare, the verdigious color of the hardy ones still prevailed. Here and there a patch of autumn goldenrod among crumbled blocks still flaunted its saffron banners. At his feet in a mossy dell formed by two broken columns, small blue flowers were a cerulean carpet welcoming the sun.

"The first one, Gavin," Maeniel said.

"The first one," Gavin smirked. "Who cares about the first one? I doubt if there's enough left of his dust to raise a sneeze." Then he suited the action to the words and did sneeze. "Maeniel, I'm going to catch my death—"

"I doubt it," Maeniel said coldly as he closed his eyes and tried to remember. The sun was hot on his neck. It had been equally hot on that day almost . . . what . . . eight hundred years ago. And it hadn't been winter as it was now, but spring . . . the ides of March.

The cobbles under his feet had been slick and wet after a night's rain. The sights, sounds, and smells had almost overwhelmed his wolf senses. For they had been extended against his will, driven by a deep visceral knowledge that this day might be his last on earth.

Street hawkers advertised their wares, sausages, wine, cheese, in voices that were a violent assault on his tender ears. He was surrounded by toga-clad bodies that jostled his, each with its own particular miasma of perfume and perspiration. Above all the smells of stale food, sour wine, hung the smell of burning bone from the morning sacrifices in the temples that surrounded the Senate.

Maeniel had pulled away from the crowd that filled the ancient marketplace and stood by the plinth that supported the statue of some Arabic goddess with a thousand breasts. He had brought his wolf senses sternly under control and waited for Julius Caesar to reach the long flight of stairs leading to the Senate. Their eyes met for a second and Maeniel, young creature that he was, was stunned by the terrible look in them. He saw before him a greedy, needy face. The face and eyes of someone who had wanted, desired with a poignancy beyond mortal flesh, something for so long that he has forgotten what it is. A face alive only to the pointless, futile energies driving it from within.

Even now after the passage of so many years, the sheer futility in that face drained Maeniel's arms of strength, his soul of will. His hand had been on the hilt of his sword. In that moment, it slipped and fell away.

Gavin broke in on his thoughts of the distant past. "Maeniel, are you just going to leave all that gold on the horse?" He pointed to a leather saddle bag on Maeniel's big roan.

"Gavin," Maeniel said, quietly. "Don't trouble me about a few trinkets."

"I like what you call a few trinkets," Gavin said, outraged. "The best of all the wealth we've ever won. I can't remember how many years of hard fighting—"

"A few trinkets," Maeniel said firmly. "What we've won over the many years of fighting is our valley, our mountains, and above all, our freedom. Compared to those, I consider a little gold a trifling matter."

"We're riding to meet your prospective bride, Maeniel," Gavin said. "I'd like to get on with it. I want to find out what's wrong with her before we go much farther. Did you see that marriage contract? She demanded everything, her own court practically. Maeniel, that woman can ruin you. She'll have her own soldiers. What will we do if she decides to . . ."

"To what?" Maeniel met Gavin's gaze.

"Well, I don't know." Gavin threw up his hands. "But I'm sure if this marriage lasts, she'll think up some form of treachery to practice.

"In God's name, at times you worry about everything. The damn hay, the damn harvest, the damn firewood, even all the way down to the mold on the damn cheeses. But here when all we've won is in mortal peril, you're standing in a patch of weeds, muttering to yourself about Julius Caesar. I ask you, what the hell has Julius Caesar to do with anything? Besides, you couldn't have known much about him, you're not that old. You can't be that old. No one is that old."

"That's it," Maeniel said. "Try to convince yourself. But I'll tell you the truth, Gavin, I was a boy your age when I came here at the behest of my master to kill Julius Caesar."

"No," Gavin exclaimed, turning his back. "I won't listen to this. It's impossible."

Maeniel laughed harshly.

Gavin spun around again and faced him. "I've never known you to have a master. Who was he and how did he persuade you to . . ."

"He didn't have to persuade me," Maeniel said. "I was willing, even eager. Caesar destroyed my people."

The breeze blew hard, whipping around the two men, the noise deafening them. Gavin felt the back of his neck prickle.

"What was he like, this Caesar? He's nothing to me . . . only a name in a history book the priests made me read a long time ago."

"I'm not sure I know," Maeniel said. "After all, I'm only a wolf who is a man. Sometimes I'm not sure I understand any man, not fully."

Gavin ducked his head and looked away from his chief toward the crumbling ruins of the Colosseum on the horizon. "But," Maeniel continued, "he destroyed a whole people and their way of life to pay his debts. In the process, he ruined countless human lives. Killed hundreds of thousands and led as many away into slavery. I know," Maeniel said, "I saw them here. So many with wounded eyes, enduring the Romans' alien ways, learning, painfully, to speak in another tongue. A few of them recognized me for what I was when I traveled here. Sometimes they spoke to me, not asking for succor or even comfort, but I think simply to hear, for one last time, the music of a world they had been commanded to forget. But I wasn't of their world, even as I am not fully of yours. So there was little I could do. The only reason I stopped here today was that I seemed to recognize and remember this place. But everything is changed now."

"How about that?" Gavin said, pointing to the Colosseum.

"It wasn't even built then," Maeniel said.

A sense of age washed over Gavin as he realized that Maeniel had been here before a thing now falling apart had been constructed.

"How long have you been alive, then?" Gavin asked.

"I don't know," Maeniel said. "It is for such as Caesar to count the sands of time. I am wolf and never felt the need."

"Then," Gavin said, "how did you get to the city, get close enough to kill him?"

"My master, Blaze . . ." Maeniel said.

"Blaze taught Merlin," Gavin said. "And Merlin is only an old story."

"Perhaps . . . or perhaps not," Maeniel said, strolling a little farther away from him. "I forget. You don't know how strange it is to be old, to know that events that once seemed of catastrophic importance in my own life are only the dry bones of history to you."

"All right," Gavin said. "I'll bite."

"I hope not," Maeniel said with a grin.

"What I meant," he said with exasperated patience, "is you're telling this story, so tell it your way."

"Very well," Maeniel answered. "My master, Blaze, spent a year preparing me to be a Roman. After all, he said, Caesar's friend Dacidicus managed it. So should I. I learned all I could of their dress, their language, their manners and customs. By the end of the year, I could pass among the Romans as one of them. I learned quickly enough when I came here that I needn't have bothered. The city then as now was an aging whore always ready to sell herself for the right price.

"Posing as a wealthy landowner from Crisalpine Gaul, I

quickly found out all I needed to know to accomplish my objective. The location of Caesar's residence in the city, the hours when he went to visit the Senate, who his friends and habitual companions were.

"But I had not seen the man himself until I shouldered my way through the Forum to the very steps of the Senate and waited with my hand on my sword."

"How did you plan to escape after you killed him?"

"I didn't." He turned and faced Gavin with a half smile on his lips.

Gavin was struck by his eyes. They were a peculiar color, a deep steel blue in some lights, dark as a troubled sea in others, and now, sunstruck, they were the hazy color of a storm wrack when the day fades into purple dusk.

"Strange," Gavin said sarcastically, "I always thought you were intelligent."

"I was young then," Maeniel said, "and headlong courage was what was expected of a warrior."

"If you ask me," Gavin began.

"Nobody did," Maeniel answered.

But Gavin finished anyway. "Those Gauls had too much headlong courage and not enough common sense. That's why Caesar found them such easy prey."

"Perhaps," Maeniel said. He was looking away again over the quiet ruins basking in the clear autumn light. "At any rate, I waited for him there. And I met his eyes. He was a lean man, hollow cheeked, and in their deep sockets the eyes burned with the unquenchable hunger."

"I suppose," Gavin said, "it's my function to ask for what?" He tried to sound bored.

Maeniel turned toward him, again with a slight smile on his lips. Then his eyes followed a ring dove as it flew overhead, its wing feathers a sunlit fan against the sky.

"I don't know," Maeniel said.

"Maeniel,'" Gavin said, in a warning tone. "I don't like you when you get enigmatic."

"Men," Maeniel said, "weaken things by naming them sometimes. Thank all the gods that they have not found a name for this. But I know what it is. I have it, you have it, even the bird has it. How else would they trust their wings to the invisible air? How else would the pinions of a hawk ride the heat rising from a sunlit mountainside? A wolf has it when he curls in his den after a hunt, not caring for tomorrow, knowing he must hunt again but sure of his strong legs and sharp fangs. I had it, too, even in Blaze's house, cut off as he wanted me from the world of beasts. I knew the transcendent confidence when I crossed the meadow, breasting the ground mist, to bathe in the river at dawn. An infant knows it when he seeks a mother's breast with his lips and finds his pleasure and ease. I had it even in my own magnificent stupidity and showed it by not caring what happened to me, if I could but sink my blade into his body.

"But I could read the truth in his restless, hungry gaze. All his power had brought him no ease, no hope, no joy. So I watched him, sickened, pass toward the top of the steps. Then I smelled it. A reek that drowned out the myriad other smells that hung like a foul miasma surrounding me. The powerful odor of human rage, human fear, and desperation. And I realized it came from the men around him. The smell of a pack closing in.

"Damn it, Gavin, did he know those he thought of as his brothers were going to kill him? Was that the reason for that heart-hungry gaze? I think now perhaps he did not care. He was tired of life. Perhaps he would have preferred me to finish him. A clean kill by an avowed enemy. I don't know. I only know they paused at the top of the stair. As if to urge a petition on him. A moment later their steel was in him. Even the blade of one who they say was his son.

"Men make such a fuss over a kill," Maeniel mused. "A wolf would simply have left him for the carrion birds.

"I left quickly, a riot was beginning. I brought the news to his wife, Calpurnia. A great, stately lady very much like the Romans of old. Strange, women preserve the virtues of a people longer than men do."

"That's because they're forced to," Gavin said. "Give them any choice at all . . . well, I ask you, look at Matrona."

"That's your problem, isn't it?" Maeniel asked slyly. "She won't let you look at her often enough."

"Maeniel," Gavin wailed. "I have. I go in search of a little adventure and she cuts me off for months."

"In any case," Maeniel continued, "I told Calpurnia and ordered the servants to keep a watch over her. I was afraid she might take some Roman way out. Then I hurried away from Rome, not just Rome, but from man. Night found me fleeing toward the mountains. A wolf."

Maeniel turned and walked back toward the horses.

"He was a great man," Gavin said.

Maeniel paused and looked out again over the sweep of ruins and the wide empty sky. "No, he wasn't. Great men always leave the world a better place than they found it. He didn't. He destroyed a state that could have stood as a buffer between his people and those beyond the Rhine who have washed over them since, like a tide. And he wrecked his own government."

"It may be," Gavin said, "that those Romans saw his seizure of power as a choice between disorder and despotism."

Maeniel gazed into Gavin's eyes again. "That's no choice at all, and you know it, growing up as you have among people who make their own laws and obey them. No, Roman government was contentious, disorderly, and all too often corrupt. But it had room for growth and change. And above all, when one attended deliberations, it was possible to hear more than one voice.

"After he passed by, it was never anything more than the projected will of one man. That's why I said Augustus found something living and left a cenotaph. Just as Caesar in Gaul found something living, a people who might have become mighty and magnificent and stood as a bulwark against the savagery beyond the Rhine.

"No, he was not a great man, only a talented, small one driven by greed and a lust for power beyond the common run. Be glad we have no Caesars and no faceless legions to be his instruments." He turned away abruptly toward his horse.

As Gavin hurried after Maeniel, he only half believed what his war chief was telling him. Still, the quiet that surrounded the big man frightened him. He was in the saddle and the two of them were setting off for Lucilla's house when he asked, "Why are you telling me all this?"

Maeniel reined in his horse abruptly. "Because," he said. "I want no Caesar to come to my valley in the mountains, be his name Charles or any other, and destroy my friends.

"I am explaining to you why the stakes are too high in this marriage for me to behave otherwise than as a father to my people. I will marry the girl, whatever she is. And she will be honored in my house by the rest of you. And we will keep our secrets as well.

"So, I hope you enjoyed the freedom of the Campagna last night, because that freedom is about to come to an end. Understand, Gavin, an end. For the time she is with us, we will be men, not wolves. And you will behave yourself at the villa of Lucilla. All of you."

Gavin showed an uncharacteristic meekness when they reached Lucilla's house. Maeniel lifted the heavy saddle bag from the horse as Gavin announced his identity to the gatekeeper. The gatekeeper was a pretty young girl and Gavin didn't even roll his eyes at her.

He followed Maeniel at a respectful distance when they entered the atrium garden. The girl paused, looked at them once, giggled, and disappeared into the house.

Gavin sat down on a marble bench beside the pool. "I suppose we are to make ourselves at home," he said.

"Not too much at home," Maeniel warned.

"Oh, no," Gavin said, trying to sound reassuring.

Maeniel placed the saddlebag on the bench beside Gavin and stood, waiting expectantly. A few minutes later a very dressed up Elfgifa stepped out of the door of the triclinium. She wore the silk shift and the stiff gold and white brocade overgown she'd worn to the pope's banquet. A string of pearls was wound into her short golden hair.

She looked up at Maeniel, expectantly, and said, "Aren't you going to give me a kiss?"

Both Gavin and Maeniel stared at her in complete bewilderment for a second. Then Gavin dissolved into roars of laughter.

Maeniel glared at him.

"Did the letter . . ." Gavin said, choking with laughter, "did the letter they sent you say anything about your future wife's age?"

Maeniel turned and kicked him hard in the ankle.

Elfgifa's lower lip shot out.

"I knew something was wrong," Gavin said. "I knew something had to be wrong," he moaned. "Now I know what it is."

Elfgifa's lip protruded even further. "There's nothing wrong with me," she said, stamping one little foot. "Everybody said I was very pretty. What's the matter with him?"

"Gavin," Maeniel said between his teeth. "Shut up. Yes," he said with forced cheerfulness to Elfgifa. "You are very pretty." Bending over, he dropped a soft, very gentle kiss on the child's forehead.

"Poor Maeniel," Gavin said, wiping his eyes. "You're going to go without for a very long time."

"Without what?" Elfgifa asked innocently.

This set Gavin off again. Faint sounds of incipient hysterics emanated from behind the curtains that shielded the triclinium. Maeniel knew every servant in the villa must be there listening.

"My lady," Maeniel said to Elfgifa. "If you don't mind, would you bring me a cup of wine and when I'm finished strangling my friend, here," he directed a quelling look at Gavin, "I'll join you and we'll talk over the future."

Elfgifa studied Maeniel darkly for a moment. "If he's your friend, why would you want to strangle him?"

Gavin was nigh paralyzed but he managed to jump off the bench and sidle well away from Maeniel.

"I always thought," Elfgifa went on, "that you strangled people you didn't like."

Gavin staggered against one of the columns supporting the porch roof. "It's going to be wonderful," he said, "waiting for this consummation."

"What's a consummation?" Elfgifa asked. "And why is he acting that way? Is it because you're going to strangle him? And if you are, can I watch?"

"Yes," Maeniel said between his teeth. "Only I may not strangle him, I may just drown him, slowly."

Suddenly Gavin stopped laughing and stared at the two women walking along the porch from the garden.

"Look," Elfgifa said to Regeane, clutching Maeniel's brown mantle. "This is the man who's come to marry you."

Regeane stopped dead in her tracks. The blood left her face

in a rush, leaving her almost as pale and waxen as the lilies blooming beside the pool.

"Oh, good heavens," Lucilla whispered.

A volley of half-stifled giggles erupted from behind the curtains to the triclinium.

"What's going on here!" Lucilla demanded.

"This is the Lord Maeniel," Elfgifa said, excitedly. She still had hold of Maeniel's mantle. "You know, the mountain lord who's going to marry Regeane. The servants said to greet him properly and be nice to him. And since I'm going to be one of Regeane's ladies, I came out to talk and that red-haired man there," she gestured at Gavin, "started laughing. I don't know why. I don't think I'm funny." She pointed at Maeniel. "He said he was going to strangle him and promised I could watch."

"He won't," Lucilla said, "and if he did, you couldn't, and thank you for bringing me up to date, you terrible, terrible child."

Elfgifa's face clouded over, the lower lip protruded. "I'm not terrible. I'm very nice. Regeane says so. I told you where she went when she ran away. I set Hugo on fire and made him let her go—"

"Enough," Lucilla roared. "Besides, as a lady's maid—"

"I'm not going to be a lady's maid," Elfgifa piped up. "I'm going to be an attendant. Postumous says as the daughter of a thane I am too highborn to be a lady's maid. I'm—"

"I said, enough," Lucilla commanded in a voice like a boulder dropping to earth. The murderous look she directed at the closed curtains of the triclinium promised dire consequences for the authors of this particular mischief.

"Having a little fun with the bridegroom, are we?" she asked in artificially dulcet tones.

Sounds of feet moving away quickly followed her words. Elfgifa stood her ground. She tugged twice at Maeniel's mantle and whispered. "Bend down." She looked anxiously at Gavin.

Maeniel obediently bent down. Elfgifa placed her lips near his ear. "Do you know what my father says about red-haired men?"

"No," Maeniel whispered back.

"He says Judas had red hair," Elfgifa whispered breathlessly.

Maeniel's face convulsed with mirth.

Gavin, who had been standing openmouthed a second before, drew himself up in fury. "Now wait just a goddamn minute . . ."

Maeniel straightened up, his hand on Elfgifa's golden curls. "Gavin may have red hair," he said, "but I don't think he and the apostle are related."

"I certainly hope not," Elfgifa said, casting a second suspicious look at Gavin. "My father says . . ."

"That is quite enough," Lucilla said. "That father of yours has filled your head with every manner of nonsense. You will go inside and trouble us no more. At once." She clapped her hands.

The young girl who had answered the door reappeared, looking suitably abashed. She took Elfgifa by the hand as if to lead her away, but Maeniel sank to one knee beside Elfgifa and looked up at Regeane. To his relief, her waxen pallor had faded and color flooded her cheeks.

"You will be a good lord to Regeane, won't you?" Elfgifa asked. "My father told me that if a man is the head of the house, the woman is its heart. And a man without a heart is no more than a corpse." Elfgifa spoke quickly but clearly, as if to make sure Maeniel understood.

"Yes," he promised. "I will. I could never forsake my heart, little one. So go with an easy mind. I will welcome you to my home as one of my lady's attendants."

The girl sped Elfgifa away. And Regeane stood face to face with Maeniel. She saw a tall man. He was a little over six feet, thick bodied. His bare arms rippled with muscle, massive and powerful, that clothed his frame.

He wore trousers with cross-gartered leggings and over that a heavy white linen shirt, long enough to be a tunic. Over that a cuirass of chain mail. His brown mantle was secured to his shoulder with a golden brooch, a lion's head with large ruby eyes.

His face was the most striking of all, powerful, with a strong nose and cleft chin, and an air of seeming sternness. But the deep laugh lines around the mouth and crow's feet at the corners of his eyes indicated that this man smiled often and loved laughter. Overall, a kind face, sure and strong.

His hair was thick, dark, and coarse. It curled freely at his neck and forehead. It was roughly cropped, short. Long hair was a hindrance to a warrior and wouldn't fit properly under a helmet. It was clear he was a fighting man. He wore a long sword, very plain, utilitarian, suspended from a heavy ox-hide belt and baldric.

Fascinated, Maeniel stepped toward Regeane as if they were alone. She'd been in the kitchen garden with Lucilla, and was wearing a tabard of brown wool over her simple white gown. She was holding up the skirts of the tabard. In it were pouched a few late peaches from Lucilla's trees.

Her hair was drawn back in a loose fall from the top of her head, streaming down her back, the silver ends shining in the sun. The wolf in Maeniel rose and smelled the perfume of the peaches, sun-warmed flesh, the clean wind.

Thus, Maeniel thought. *Thus I was captured long ago. I was a wolf, but Blaze made me into a man and a warrior. So I was captured then and, in the same way, now by a fair woman.*

Maeniel took another step closer. Regeane's hands were locked in the tabard, and she thought absurdly as Maeniel's arm went around her wrist, *I can't let go or the peaches will fall.*

His kiss was a chaste one, closed soft lips on her own, but there was such an immense naturalness in the strength of the arms around her and her presence in their embrace, that Regeane quivered all over. Afterward, she was never sure whether she trembled in fear or desire. She relaxed against a body so strong it seemed made of sun-warmed stone.

Her lips parted slightly and her mouth opened. But Maeniel didn't press his advantage. The kiss eased and he took a step back, releasing her both from his arms and his spell.

"Happy," he said, "are the words of the poet. 'She is,' " he quoted, " " 'a fair gem from the realm of sun and wind, a cup of honey. A man might drown himself in such sweetness.' May I have a peach?"

"A what?" Regeane asked, bemused. She came back to herself with a shake. She stretched the tabard out toward Maeniel. "They are touched by frost," she said.

"Like your hair, exquisite one," he answered as he selected one of the velvet-covered fruits. He ate it in a few bites, holding Regeane's eyes with his own. He tossed the pit into a flower bed.

"Rich, ripe, and rare," he said. "Like she who gave it to me." The juices gleamed on his lips.

Regeane permitted herself a little shake as she tried to regain her wits. Somewhere she knew the wolf was lying on her back in a bed of flowers, all four paws in the air, wiggling with delight. Regeane shot a thought at her dark companion, *You're thoroughly disgusting.* The wolf really didn't care.

Lucilla stared at them both in something like horror. Gavin stared too, his mouth open.

"Shut your mouth, Gavin, before your brains fall out," Maeniel said. "And fetch the presents we brought the lady."

Lucilla quickly removed the peaches from Regeane's tabard and brushed soft wisps of curling hair from around her face. "We didn't anticipate seeing you so soon," she said.

"Yes," Regeane said. "I expected to meet you at the feast tonight." She looked down at the brown tabard and the white dress. "I'm afraid I'm not properly attired. I'm sorry . . ."

"Don't apologize, please," Maeniel said. "It is I who should be contrite, coming unannounced."

"Ahem," Gavin said. He emptied the saddle bags on the marble table top.

Even Lucilla, who was used to wealth, gasped to see so much gold of every kind spill out of it. There were necklaces, rings, coins, pendants, torcs of twisted gold and silver, brooches of every kind. Gems, precious and semiprecious, glowed among the gold. Rubies, deep red, sapphires blue as the sky at twilight, the clear water of aquamarines, and sun-colored topaz all lent fire to the mass of riches.

"A wedding gift for my future wife," Maeniel said.

Lucilla gave him a quick narrow look. "You're a generous man to make your wife independently wealthy before your wedding day."

"She is," Maeniel said, "a lady most royal and must properly support her state."

Regeane stood, simply gazing at the wealth spread out in front of her. She bit her lip, uncertain what to do. She looked up at Maeniel. When she was in his arms, she had felt as if she had

known him for a thousand years, but now he seemed a stranger.
A pleasant stranger, to be sure, yet still a stranger. And then it
was borne upon her that this was a man she might one day have
to kill.

He would, she knew, dress the woman in gold. And the
woman would find all desire quenched by ecstasy in his arms.
But what had he for the hunter, the silver hunter of midnight?
No, he could never know the wolf.

She looked at the pile of wealth on the table and the wolf
thought of the shimmer of sunlight on a mountain lake at dawn,
or a waterfall wreathed in rainbows, seen through the cool
green gloom of a summer forest. And the jewels seemed like the
cheap trinkets offered to serving girls in the thieves' market.
No, the wolf was not so easily bought or sold.

Maeniel looked at her with a fixed, speculative expression.
He stirred the deep heap of gold with his hand, carelessly.
"Please," he said, "select something to wear tonight. As a com-
pliment to me."

"Of course," Regeane said mechanically.

He lifted a beautiful pure gold necklace from the pile. It
was clear to both Regeane and Lucilla that the thing was very
old and of such fine workmanship that it must be precious
even above the intrinsic value of the shining metal it contained. A confection of tiny pitchers interspersed with flowers
of amethyst suspended from a thick flat golden chain.

Regeane touched the necklace, her hand closed around it,
and the day vanished as it had when she touched the brocade
dress, the day she met Lucilla. She was in a long hall, brightly lit
by torches. Feasting and revelry surrounded her. The guests occupied couches stretching the length of the room. In the center
acrobats capered and leaped. A boy played a double flute. Its
music sent a thrill of abandoned desire along her veins. She sat
near her love.

He occupied the high-ended curved couch opposite hers.
How strange is the heart, the girl who was Regeane and was not
Regeane, thought. He was hardly an impressive man. He had a
short, curly, dark beard and equally dark, tightly curled hair. His
skin had the weatherbeaten look of a sailor. The gold and
amethyst necklace was his gift. She fingered it gently as she

looked deep into his eyes. There was a proud, knowing look in them as he gazed on her and she was serenely aware he would share that knowledge with her as they lay together on his couch before dawn.

He lifted a cup, a thing of beauty, black-on-red ware, its bottom, half obscured by the wine, was a picture of Venus lying with Mars, trapped by Vulcan's net. Their bodies were locked in a frenzy of desire indifferent to the meshes containing them.

He crooked his arm and raised the cup to her lips. She lifted her cup and offered it to him. Arms entwined, they drank together. The scene vanished. Regeane almost screamed as raw-edged pain crashed through her mind and body like a storm surf.

Regeane was somewhere else. Now, she lay on a bier. She was decked for a burial. She was not yet dead. She was wearing her finest white gown, embroidered with rosettes of gold, the necklace, and a diadem. She couldn't see the diadem, but she was sure she would know its shape. A crown of finely wrought golden willow. She didn't move because she knew instinctively that even the slightest movement would bring her intolerable pain. She must have broken nearly every bone in her body when she fell.

Through the window, she could hear the thunder and crash of the sea against a rocky shore. But here in this dim chamber only darkness surrounded her. Someone spoke in the darkness. The utterances were thick with tears.

"She has awakened. I had hoped she wouldn't."

The girl who was Regeane and not Regeane recognized her mother's voice.

The woman stepped out of the gloom. She was veiled in black, her face pale against the darkness. Beside her stood a priestess, who also wore black and carried a staff. The priestess wore a gorgon mask with mouth twisted in fury, snakes dripping from her hair. The staff she carried was surmounted by the poppy goddess. She wore the crosshatched pods as a crown and her eyes were closed.

"The flower of sleep," Regeane whispered.

"You shouldn't have walked so near the rocks," her mother sobbed. "Not in your condition. You fell."

"I didn't fall," Regeane heard the girl say, weakly.

"No," the priestess said, her voice muffled by the mask. "I thought not. Well," she continued, "it is now as you wished. The man you loved is no more, the child you carried is no more, and soon you will be no more." She extended a cup toward Regeane, the same black-on-red ware. The picture on the side of the calyx was of the genus of sleep, a beautiful youth. His eyes were closed and he had wings on his shoulders.

"Drink now," the priestess said, "the water of Lethe and find rest."

The girl closed her eyes and tightened her lips. "Carry me to the hearth," she said. "I would not die here with the sea sounding in my ears. The sea took him from me. Her waves beat him down, the water strangled him, leaving only a rag of flesh tumbled by the surf. I would not hear her rage in triumph as I sink into night."

They carried her on her bier to the center of the red-pillared hall. The hearth was high and round, plastered and painted around its border. The fire flared and leaped toward an opening in the ceiling. The flames painted the faces of men and women as they gathered round. Some wept, some glared in stony-eyed disapproval, but each raised a hand, one by one, in farewell.

Then the calyx touched at her lips. Smoke from the hearth fire filled her nostrils and its light blinded her eyes.

Regeane watched from afar as the funeral cortege wound in and out along the roads, through the patchwork of ripening grain fields. The heads tossed yellow-gilt, rustling like whispers of grief under a mild blue sky.

Darkness . . . a long darkness.

The tomb robbers' torch broke through the roof. Where once there had been beauty, there was now only bone blackened by an age under the earth. The teeth were still white, though, and the thief knew as he reached for the glimmer of purple and gold at her throat that she must have been young.

He jerked at the necklace and the dark skull went flying, shattering, leaving a scattering of teeth on the floor. Then the necklace was his, but one hand had been placed on her breast as he leaned over to grab it, braced one palm on the stone couch. The bone hand fell, the long nails caught his arm, and it gashed to the bone. His scream rang in Regeane's ears as she tore her hand from the necklace and backed away, gasping, trying not to show either Maeniel or Lucilla the shock and horror in her face.

"I . . . I . . . think not."

"No," Maeniel said. He was still holding the necklace. He dropped it with a clatter among the rest of the gold.

Regeane stood, shivering with the terror of her vision. She got another look at Maeniel's face. She was being tested, probed.

Maeniel reached down and lifted a torc, simple but made of heavy gold with inlaid knobs at its ends. "What do you think of this, then?" he asked.

Regeane braced herself, stretched out her hand, her fingers closed around it.

Again there was darkness and the sound of the sea. A pyre flared on a headland. All around Regeane were the sounds of anguished grief. The wind blew the flames aside for a second and Regeane saw the dark figure within. And she knew, with the perishing of this woman, all her world perished also. In the night vigil of her mourners she understood darkness was the elegy, the violent sea a dirge not for one woman, but for a whole people.

Regeane drew her hand away very quickly. "No," she whispered, stone-faced. *What is he doing to me?* she thought.

"Perhaps you're right," he said as he laid the torc down gently. "It is said to have belonged to a mighty queen never defeated in battle."

"It would not be suitable for me," Regeane said.

Maeniel reached down and lifted a mass of golden chain by one crooked finger. It emerged as another necklace made of fine golden chains in red, yellow, and white gold secured by fruiting grape vine with each grape picked out in pearls.

Tentatively, Regeane took hold of it, wondering what sort of trick he might be playing now. This time the vision she saw was of morning. Maeniel himself lay on a stone in the center of a circle of menhirs. He was naked. His youthful flesh was beautiful in the gentle light. His face was that of a much younger man, the long muscular limbs stretched out in voluptuous relaxation were those of a stripling youth.

Again, as with the shepherd on the Campagna, Regeane felt

an awareness of utter vulnerability in his innocent sleep. A woman sat beside him. She wore the necklace Regeane held and nothing else. Silver comb in hand, she was dressing her long dark hair. There was an unmistakable air of complacency and power in her gaze as she stared down on the sleeping Maeniel.

Regeane drew her hand away from the necklace. "This one, I think," she said.

Maeniel placed it gently around her neck. Then he took Regeane's hand and kissed it. "I will take my leave of you ladies and say good-bye. Until tonight then," he said to Regeane and strode from the garden followed by Gavin, leaving Regeane and Lucilla standing beside the golden baubles on the table.

XXVIII

WHEN SHE WAS SURE HE WAS GONE AND SHE heard the entrance doors closing, Regeane ripped off the jewels and flung them onto the table with the rest. "He is more than he seems," she gasped and staggered toward a bench. She sat down heavily.

"What was wrong with those things?" Lucilla asked. "What did he do? Did you see visions?"

"Enough," Regeane said, "to make him as no ordinary man. But I cannot think what he is. A magus . . . I don't know."

"Girl," Lucilla said, sweeping the gold into a pile and beginning to replace it in the saddle bags. "Speak to me coherently. Tell me what's wrong. I saw your face when you touched that first necklace. You looked as if you'd seen a dozen ghosts."

"I did, in a way," Regeane said. "Some objects, Lucilla, carry the memory of events, evil and good, they've been associated with. They are, in a sense, alive. Remember the dress on the cart when we first met? The one I described as vile?"

"Yes," Lucilla said.

"Well, all of those pieces of jewelry were alive in that way. I'm certain he selected them deliberately."

"If he did, you gave yourself away completely. Deception is not an art native to your character."

"No, it isn't, is it?" Regeane admitted as she sat on the bench, twisting her hands despairingly. She could feel the tears trickling down her cheeks.

"Stop that," Lucilla commanded. "This is not the time for tears but for clear thinking and planning. We must both decide what to do about this man. Now, while he's here in Rome. I have the ear of Count Otho. If I can convince him this Maeniel might betray the Franks . . ."

Something warm and soft fell gently into Regeane's lap and she felt a comforting hand squeeze her shoulder. She blinked away her tears, looked down, and saw her father's mantle. She clutched it to her breast and gently dried her tears on the soft woolen cloth. Love, and then a sense of almost unbearable loss, flooded through her, blinding her to the world around her. They had failed each other, her wayward parents, and in a sense had failed her, she thought, remembering her mother's wounded love. But however twisted by religious teachings and the world's malice, her mother had loved her. And her father's arms had been her strength in the very canyons of hell.

She had seen him enter the forest. Did Gisela await him there, assured of his forgiveness and God's? Was death only a sleep from which we awaken into a garden of light? Regeane looked up and saw Antonius standing by her side, smiling.

He was handsome again. A few faint, pale scars marred the fine-boned aristocratic face, but otherwise, he looked for all the world like a healthy man in the prime of his life. He was slender, clad in the long, embroidered tunic and the ornate toga of a Roman aristocrat. The fingers on her shoulder were intact and powerful. His grip was firm and strong. She had won. And the sense of victory over death drove out the demons of doubt, uncertainty, and despair, the way the sun scatters mist.

"Let her cry if she wants, Mother," he said, gently. "There is a time for tears and, believe me, I know they can heal the heart."

"Be quiet, Antonius," Lucilla said. "I'm on the track of an idea. If we can convince this Count Otho that—"

"Ever the intriguer, aren't you, Mother?" Antonius said.

"Yes," Lucilla answered. "You know my mind. The best of all my children and you are the cleverest. I own it. Now tell me how you would set about convincing Otho this Maeniel is dangerous."

"I wouldn't bother," Antonius replied. "At least not now. Since this morning I visited Otho."

"Yes," Lucilla said. "Of course, he must have urgent political reasons for being here."

Antonius nodded.

"He wants to see if there is any truth to the story that the Lombards are spreading about Hadrian's family being tainted by leprosy," Regeane said.

"She's not slow, is she, Mother?" Antonius commented. "In any case I called on him this morning and denied all the rumors. I even stripped naked in his presence."

"Did he try to seduce you?" Lucilla asked.

Antonius shook his head in negation. "I don't believe that's one of his weaknesses."

"What a pity," Lucilla said. "That's always a good point of leverage with these barbarians. They affect to despise effeminacy."

"Yes," Antonius said. "It was something of a test. However, when I was sure he was convinced these disease allegations were only a Lombard trick, I then persuaded him that it might be a good idea if I were appointed a captain of Regeane's guard."

Regeane gave a soft sigh of relief.

Lucilla clapped her hands together and rolled her eyes heavenward. "A masterstroke," she shouted as she embraced Antonius. "Oh, my son, my most beautiful, perfect son." Tears were streaming down her cheeks. "How can I ever thank you, Regeane?"

Antonius pried himself from Lucilla's embrace ever so gently and kissed her hand.

"I'm sure you will think of something, Mother," he said with almost tender irony.

"You darling boy," Lucilla said.

But Regeane saw a twinkle of equally subtle malice creeping into her eyes.

"Your father would be proud of you," Lucilla continued.

"Which one is that?" Antonius asked with an air of innocence. "The black-bearded Thracian pirate with the muscles and scars? I believe I recall he sailed to his death in a violent storm. Or was it the Sicilian poet who won your heart with song? He, I understand, was a bit too fond of wine. Didn't you say he was murdered in a tavern brawl?"

Lucilla looked at him sourly for a moment. "I was trying to get you to study your letters at the time. You have no idea how difficult it is to get an adolescent with a roving eye to apply himself. Or at least you won't until you have children of your own."

Antonius winked at Regeane. "This ghostly procession of fathers has goaded me on all my life," he sighed. "I believe the best one was the Umbrian muleteer who stank of garlic and onions. You invented him when I was about to take up with Adraste."

"I didn't approve of Adraste, but I notice it didn't deter you," Lucilla said.

"No," Antonius said, settling himself on the bench beside Regeane. "Thank you for not saying 'I told you so'. Tell me, would my father really be proud of me?"

Something changed in Lucilla's face. Her eyes took on a haunted look. For a second, she seemed to shrink into herself and looked almost old, but her recovery was immediate. She drew herself up, eyes flashing. "Dear boy," she said. "I'm sure he would. But I have an even more important question to ask you. Are you in love with Regeane?"

"Lucilla," Regeane cried, outraged.

But Antonius threw back his head and laughed. "You mean, Mother, am I going to use my subtle skills as a courtier, my polished personal charm, my aristocratic air, to ruin both her and myself?"

"In a word, yes," Lucilla snapped.

"No," Antonius answered. He ticked off the reasons on his

fingers. "First, I owe her too much ever to place her in the kind of danger that would be occasioned by an affair of the heart. Second, she's not my type. You know the kind I like, raunchy, a little stupid, shameless, and just a tad bit cruel."

"You forgot to mention greedy," Lucilla said.

"Yes," Antonius answered. "There's that, too. Believe me, Mother, my behavior will be above reproach."

"See that it is," Lucilla said. "Make absolutely sure that no possible suspicion can be raised against you. And remember, appearances can deceive, also. Even innocent actions can be misinterpreted and guilt may be implied where none exists."

"Mother," Antonius said. "You have a tendency to preach."

Lucilla swept the rest of the gold into the bag. "The sermon is over," she said. "I hope you both took it to heart."

Then she left, carrying the gold.

Regeane continued to sit where she was. Antonius was silent.

A brocaded butterfly paused in its search for nectar among the flowers and perched on her knee, folding its wings neatly into a sail. Regeane's and the wolf's eyes traced the hardened veins that held the dusty wings into their shape. Then the butterfly's wings opened into a tapestry of yellow and black, and it fluttered away.

"What did you think of Maeniel?" Antonius asked.

"I like him," Regeane said. "When he embraced me, I wanted to be his wife."

"Is that possible?" Antonius asked.

"I'm not sure," Regeane answered.

"Yes, I know," Antonius said. "When I was reassuring my mother about our future relationship, there was another reason in the deepest part of my heart why I could never look on you as a lover—you're not human."

"No," Regeane agreed, quietly.

A dragonfly flashed past Regeane's face. One hand flicked out. She caught the dragonfly by the thorax. She held it, wiggling and buzzing loudly and indignantly, for a moment before she released it and let it go on its way in peace.

"How many humans do you know who could do what I just did so easily?" she asked.

"Very few, perhaps none," Antonius answered. "Cage the wolf, Regeane."

"No," she answered. "The night Basil kidnapped you, he came here to kill me. On that night the wolf found her freedom. I will be free or I will be dead. It's as simple as that. I can't disavow her. We are one."

"Then you will always be in danger," Antonius said.

"I know," Regeane answered. "And this Maeniel is a formidable opponent."

Antonius nodded. "I'd already assessed him. Why do you think I got myself appointed captain of your guard? I did it to protect you and to forestall any lethal little plans my mother might be hatching."

"Someone," Regeane said, "should tell your mother that murder is frowned on in some circles."

"Not in the circles you and I are going to travel in, Regeane. In those circles, it's an instrument of policy. Do you understand?"

"Yes," she said. "Or at least, I'm beginning to. The blood of a king runs in my veins as well as the blood of a wolf. And I can never escape the dangers wrought by both. I must learn to defend myself."

"As for my mother," Antonius said. "I won't make either excuses or apologies for her. She doesn't need them. You don't know what it was like here in Rome when the Lombards controlled the papacy."

He bowed his head. "Every day another murder, usually the killing of one of Mother's friends or Hadrian's. Hadrian was too popular with both the people and the nobles to attack openly, but there were many clandestine attempts on his life. I remember very well the night he was poisoned—at a dinner in the villa of a man he believed to be his best friend.

"My mother fed him emetics while I held the basin. He vomited a very good dinner that would have killed him if it had remained in his stomach. For many years, my mother rarely dared go out openly by day and never by night. You see, she'd been set upon by a party of Lombard soldiers. I think the only reason she survived was that she put almost superhuman heart into her men by snatching up a sword and fighting alongside them. I, myself, crossed the Alps to the Frankish court to lay my mother's wager. She left it to me."

"Wager?" Regeane asked.

"Yes, wager on which Frankish king would prevail. Charles or Carloman."

"I assume you made the right choice," Regeane said.

"Charles," Antonius nodded. "I got letters from him supporting Hadrian's candidacy for the papal chair. As soon as the Lombard pope's health began to fail . . ."

"I hope your mother didn't have anything to do with that," Regeane exclaimed.

Antonius paused, a speculative expression on his face. He brought one finger slowly to his lips. "Mother," he whispered, half to himself, "is a thoroughly unprincipled virago, but I don't think . . ." Then he began to sigh, flashing a set of strong white teeth. "Well," he said, "I'll never ask. In any case, those letters circulated among priests and patricians here in Rome charged with electing the pope, virtually guaranteeing Hadrian's victory. But it was a very near thing, Regeane. Twice Mother's friends, her girls, uncovered plots against Hadrian's life. And once, he was forced to flee the city and hide on the estate of a friend."

Regeane shuddered even though the air was warm. The wolf looked wonderingly through her eyes at the sunlit garden. Regeane felt the beast's helplessness in the face of intrigue, treachery, and deceit. Her own heart longed for savage simplicities. One hungered, one hunted. Angered, one fought. Love was a shadow play by moonlight, governed by chance and choice. Never by force and politics. A final yielding of all of oneself to pleasure and desire. The female is respected. She gives life, she is life. Her body is a temple. The beast doesn't use force. The strong-sinewed, powerful killer. The lord of the hours between midnight and dawn worships at the temple of love.

"Yes," Antonius said. "There is a certain temptation to reject the world."

Regeane gave a little start. "How did you know?"

"I think," Antonius said, "that if I could do what you can do, I would be tempted, too."

"You seem to enjoy the game for its own sake," Regeane answered.

"Yes," Antonius answered. "And if you are wise, you will learn to enjoy it also. Because I'm very much afraid, Lupa, that you will play it all your life."

"How so?"

"This King Charles," Antonius said. "Men are already beginning to call him Charles the Great, Charlemagne. I was with him the night he wrote the letters that secured Hadrian's election as pope.

"Those letters were written in secret, Regeane. His brother, Carloman, was still alive. Charlemagne was married to a Lombard princess and his mother leaned heavily toward an alliance with the Lombards. But Charlemagne was already laying the groundwork for what is now Frankish policy."

Antonius lifted one hand and his words brought the scene to life for Regeane.

"We were alone in his chambers except for the scribe. Charles, you see, cannot really write, though he can read three or four languages well. We had only a few rushlights and the scribe toiled in their glow. Charles strode up and down, hands clasped behind his back. He must have carried not only the import of those letters in his mind for a long time, but each and every word he wished to use. For the scribe didn't have to blot or correct a single line on the parchment. And he spoke not merely with the confidence of a king, but his mien was that of an emperor.

"When he was finished dictating and the scribe was sealing the letters I was to convey to Rome, I asked him how he could be so sure that he would ever be able to carry out his plans. He put it to me very simply. 'Carloman, my brother king,' he said, 'is sickly. As you have no doubt observed.' I had. 'It will be a miracle if he survives another winter. The Frankish lords will not support his wife, a foreign woman, or her children, not against me, they won't. And as for my mother's leanings toward the Lombards, well,' he said with a faint smile, 'that's a family matter and I'll deal with it when the time comes.' And he has, Regeane. This Charles—Charlemagne—is going to become a very strong king. Your connection with his family will become even more valuable and possibly more hazardous for you. It is given to you to learn the path of worldly power, or you will die."

Regeane could feel her heart hammering.

"Regeane, if you will not cage the wolf, at least learn to be discreet." Antonius leaned forward and brought his fist down on his knee. "Too many people in Rome already know."

Regeane leaped to her feet and stared down at Antonius, fists clenched. "The shepherd boy," she gasped. "You didn't . . ."

Antonius raised one hand as if to quiet her. "No, Regeane, but I was only just able to talk Mother out of eliminating him."

Regeane turned away, shaking. "What am I that I spread death wherever I go?"

Antonius gave a snort of laughter. "Contain yourself, girl. Death is a part of this game. Death for the great as well as the simple. You will see failure, defeat, and yes, death, around you as long as you live. The boy hazarded his life not only for you and me, but for pearls and silver. Enough to buy a farm. He will have his life and his fine farm, I've seen to that. So save your tears and self-reproach for the better cause."

Regeane walked toward one of the columns supporting the porch roof and set her back against it. "How like your mother you are."

Antonius laughed. "Yes," he said. "I'm not only like my mother, you'll find in time, I'm even worse. But dry your tears because this is your afternoon to be charming."

Regeane closed her eyes for a second. Her mind drifted. She remembered Maeniel's hands on her body. That wasn't love, but it was something. Would the rest be as good? The wolf gave a soft grunt of pure enjoyment. Her desires right now were clear to Regeane. The sun was warm on the woman's face and its brightness shone through her eyelids. The air was cool, but the stones in the wilderness beyond the city would hold the sun's heat. The wolf wanted to stretch out on one of those stones and drowse through the long afternoon. She would dream of springtime, of mountain torrents that are frozen all winter and swell to a flood in the snowmelt, of meadows where the delicate scent of new grass and spring flowers madden the senses into ecstasy. Of sun-dappled valleys where birdsong is the only sound and even that turns to silence when the long blue shadows of twilight become a star-filled night.

She opened her eyes and Antonius smiled up at her.

The wolf reached out past the woman. She felt his cold, but sad intellect. This man knew what the world was, but did not glory in his knowledge. Yet beyond the intellect burned the flame of an abiding, gentle love. The wolf gave him her trust.

"Who am I to charm?" Regeane asked.

"First, you will greet the men who are to be your household guard. I entreat you, reach down into that bag of gold Maeniel gave you and give each of them a fine present. They must know who pays them. Also, a hint of 'I'm so pleased that you strong, handsome, stalwart men are going to stand between my flower-like beauty and danger,' wouldn't hurt either."

Regeane smiled.

"Oh, my yes," Antonius said, admiring the smile. "Bestow those beauties freely, also, and they will buy you more than gold."

Regeane nodded.

"After meeting them, you will see Rufus."

"Rufus?" Regeane repeated, her brow furrowing. "Who is . . . ?" then she remembered. "Cecelia's Rufus?" she exclaimed.

"Yes," Antonius answered. "You recall Cecelia."

"Yes," Regeane whispered. "How could I forget her? But how did you know about Cecelia? I met her at the convent. They say she never leaves."

"You are a child, Regeane." Antonius shook his head. "True, she never leaves the convent, but she has an almost constant stream of visitors. Often very aristocratic visitors, I might add. Both you and Dulcina have received her approval and her accolades. She says she found you sweet, compassionate, passionate, ingenuous, and charming. Not to mention attractive."

"Only attractive?" Regeane said. She was a little disappointed.

Antonius lifted one hand in a graceful gesture and mimicked Cecelia. "A beauty, my dear, which does not stun, but compels. One that will not fade with time, but increase into a magnificent presence."

Regeane dimpled and curtseyed.

"Be that as it may," Antonius continued. "Her accolade came to the ears of Rufus. He begs that you intercede with her for him."

Regeane looked away from Antonius at a moss-grown statue of the girl pouring water into the pond. A light breeze ruffled the surface, breaking the sun's reflection into splinters of light. A carp came to the surface and took an insect skating among the golden reflections, and then vanished with a snap of its muscular body into the depths.

"It won't help," Regeane said.

"I know, Regeane, but you need not promise Cecelia will listen, only that you will go."

"Very well," she answered dully. "I will go."

"Good," Antonius said. "Rufus' lands are very close to Rome. So far he's persevered in his loyalty to the Lombard duke. But if Mother and I can persuade him to throw in with us, Basil will find himself unable to besiege Rome any longer. In fact, he'll be cut off and operating in hostile territory. Rufus has his own men and they are experienced fighters and deeply loyal to him. Don't forget, Regeane, this beautiful garden may be peaceful, but outside, the city is in chaos. Only Basil's fear of attacking the Franks openly protects us right now. So do your best to please Rufus and win him over."

Regeane nodded sadly.

"Last of all, of course, is Gundabald."

Regeane's lips tightened into a thin line. "Your mother made it plain what I was to say to him."

"Well . . ." Antonius looked down at his knees with a wry smile on his face. He refused to meet the burning gaze Regeane fixed on him. "Well then," he repeated. "I believe the less said the better."

"THERE IS NOTHING WRONG WITH HER," GAVIN said as they rode off down the street away from Lucilla's house. He sounded chastened.

"There is plenty wrong with her," Maeniel answered. "But I'm not sure what."

"Maeniel," Gavin began in a warning tone. "You're getting on my nerves again."

"Didn't you watch her when she touched the jewels?"

Gavin gave himself a little shake, then remembered he wasn't furred at present. The gesture was one of puzzlement among wolves.

"I'll put it another way," Maeniel said. "By all accounts, she's poor, that girl. Did she act like a normal woman receiving a magnificent present?"

"No-o-o-o-o, she certainly didn't," Gavin said. "She seemed suspicious and a bit reserved."

"She had her reasons," Maeniel said. "The first necklace I handed her was badly haunted. I've never been able to bear the touch of the thing for more than a few moments. She must have seen, as I did, the evil fate of the woman who first wore it. The second belonged to Guinevere."

"What?" Gavin shouted.

"Guinevere," Maeniel repeated.

"*The* Guinevere?" Gavin said.

"None other," Maeniel answered.

"She was a great whore," Gavin said.

He hit the ground a second after with a crash. It took him about one dazed minute to realize Maeniel had knocked him off his horse. By this time he was on his feet, reaching for his sword hilt.

Maeniel pulled his horse to a stop in front of him, sidewise, blocking his way. Maeniel laughed. "Want to try your teeth on me, cublet?"

Gavin shook his head as if trying to clear it. "I've never seen you like this before," he said, bewildered. "What has this city done to you? We were happy in our mountains. What did I say? And don't tell me you're going to start yammering about how you knew Guinevere."

"I did," Maeniel said.

Gavin marched toward his loose horse with an air of injured dignity. "No," he shouted. "I won't fight you, you're much too good. I'm not suicidal. Besides," he said, stopping and staring up at Maeniel. "It would hurt me almost as much as if I won as it would if I lost. I've followed you faithfully since we met in that Irish wood."

Now Maeniel noted there were tears in Gavin's eyes. He sighed deeply. Gavin was chasing the horse around in a circle, trying to mount him. The beast rolled his eyes and kept stepping out of the way, just as Gavin reached for him.

"Stand still, goddamnit," Gavin yelled.

A small crowd had gathered and some of them were laughing at Gavin's efforts to catch the horse. Maeniel took pity on him and caught the brute's bridle and held him still. Gavin pulled himself into the saddle.

"Very well," he said stiffly, once he was seated and again in charge of the horse. "I take it you believe I insulted the lady."

"Yes," Maeniel answered. "I do. She was, as I said, a mighty queen never defeated in battle. But how can I explain to you a world that has long gone? A world that was only a dim memory in your grandsire's grandsire's time? I'm sorry, Gavin, sometimes I hate being human. This is one of them. But I shouldn't take it out on you."

They were riding away from the populated streets and entering the empty ruins. The sky was a clear bright winter blue and the wind played softly across the green and brown wasteland.

"I never thought," Maeniel said, "to be so haunted by memory. You're right, Gavin. The mountains are clean. There, we wander at will and can give free rein to our natures. Here amidst this ancient corruption, I find the face of mankind too appallingly real."

"I was," Gavin said, "a man first, but you, the way you tell it, if you're telling the truth . . . You were a wolf first." He seemed shocked, no, worse than shocked, almost shattered by the realization. "I didn't know *that* ever happened."

"It did in my case," Maeniel answered. "I've never asked any of the others. Have you?"

"No," Gavin answered, his voice was shaking. "I'm not sure I want to know."

"Nor I," Maeniel said. "And I'm not entirely certain I should have told you. Except that you're the first friend I've made in several hundred years. And I have been . . . lonely."

Gavin was silent for a long moment. "All wolf and no man," Gavin said. "Wolf by chance and man by choice."

"No, no," Maeniel answered. "Not by choice. Blaze chose for me. God, sometimes I despise you, Gavin."

"Maeniel," Gavin said.

"No, not you personally." Maeniel made a sweeping gesture with his hand. "All your kind. You speak of the wolf as a ravening killer and yet what wolf could ever equal you in cruelty and debauchery? As cowards you are without rival, as killers without peer. Even you run on four legs to find a multitude of loves. Places to lodge your prick and whimper with ecstasy. The shape change to you is the road to abandonment."

Gavin jumped off his horse and sliced a piece of broken marble at Maeniel. "Down now," he shouted, "and have at it."

Maeniel pulled his horse easily out of range of Gavin's missiles. Gavin gave up, panting, staring at a laughing Maeniel.

"You believe that, you poor damned innocent. Don't you?" Gavin said. "Now I understand so many things about you. Things I saw before, but couldn't work into a shape I could understand.

"God, I remember the way you treated Riculf. Christ, he was sent by that Frankish king Martel to hold the pass. He didn't understand what he was ruling." Gavin's voice rose to a shout, "But you and the others treated him like a god. Now I understand why. You have a . . ."

"Are you going to say something about dogs?" Maeniel interrupted, his voice heavy with menace.

"I was thinking about it," Gavin said.

"Revise the sentence," Maeniel said. "Say, 'You have the ethics of a wolf.' "

Gavin's mouth was suddenly dry. He swallowed quickly.

Maeniel threw back his head and laughed. "Animals. We animals don't need ethics. We are not corrupt. You humans do. You are."

Gavin grabbed his horse's trailing reins. "I can't see how you've lived so long," he complained as he remounted.

Maeniel dropped the horse's reins across the withers. He sat, hands flat against his thighs, staring out across the tumbled, green-mantled ruins around him. "I can't understand that very well myself," he replied. "I remember when this city was very young. Rome eternal. The center of the world, teeming with people. I hated her, but thought her invincible. Now, I find where Caesars ruled, where her patrician nobles betrayed each other and fought for power, nothing. Nothing, but wind and silence. It's a shock, that's all."

Gavin shrugged. "Wolves have no history."

"No," Maeniel said. "I think no words can compass the way we get along together and fit into the world. We worked out our arrangements between ourselves long ago. We have words, wolves do—words for love, chase, kill, fight. For snow, mountain, grass, fire, and star. Those and many others. But we have no words for sin, corruption, and evil. Those are human inventions. When I first changed, my mate said to me—frightened. I didn't change again for a long time. I didn't change until I saw some girls bathing in a stream."

Gavin whistled between his teeth. "It's as the priests say. Women are our downfall. Lust our undoing."

"Considering how much you like it," Maeniel replied dryly, "I can't think you're entirely against it. I crouched in the bushes and found myself standing up a man—in both senses."

"Let me guess," Gavin said, "they all ran away."

"All, but one," Maeniel said quietly.

"Did you turn wolf and eat her?" Gavin asked, leering.

"I wasn't hungry," Maeniel said. "And, besides," he directed a cold look at Gavin, "I was a wolf and wolves don't kill those with whom we share our bodies. She was safe. I was an animal, still. I hadn't yet learned human cruelty and perversion. I hadn't yet learned human possessiveness. Our coupling was gentle and yet, fiercely passionate. I left her safe, sleeping contentedly beside the stream bank. I even stood guard nearby in my natural state, until her people, carrying torches against the fall of night, came and found her there."

"You were seduced by human love?" Gavin asked.

"Yes," Maeniel said. "So I was drawn away from the innocence of the animal toward the profound tragedy of humanity. Because your love mirrors the paradoxes of your kind. At worst, a cruelty inflicted without a shred of decency. But, at best, something a poor beast . . . ruled by laws his ancestors agreed to before the dawn of time, at best, a passion of such sweetness as the beast can never understand. As wolf I obeyed the laws of my kind. When I transgressed them, I know not what god gave me the power to so disobey—I lost my soul.

"Over the centuries, Gavin, I have tried to escape the human in the wolf. I have even tried, once or twice, to escape the wolf among humans. I can't do either one. Now, I'm facing a choice again. And my mind harks back to the laws that rule me."

"Maeniel," Gavin said, "you think too much. What choice?"

"Never," Maeniel said, "in all the centuries I have lived, has a gift like the silver one been offered to me. The girl at the villa back there calls to my loins, but the silver one cries out in my blood. Whatever debaucheries have been inflicted on her as a woman, as a wolf, she is a virgin. I know it. Virgin and ready for the intimate fire that burns in me as man and wolf. I, alone, can be both to her."

"Christ Jesus God," Gavin said, "you must be mad. You don't even know her name. She may be a slattern, a slut. She may have a husband."

Maeniel smiled. There was nothing human in the smile, rather an enraged baring of teeth. "What care I? Do you think he will wish to face me as man or wolf?"

"No," Gavin said, staring at the savage expression on Maeniel's face. "I wouldn't. Not the way you are now. Hell, man, why not take both of them. Many a husband—many a man—has."

"That's just the trouble," Maeniel said with an ugly laugh. "I'm not a man. I can't." With that, he picked up the reins, put spurs to his horse, and rode away at a gallop.

REGEANE WENT DOCILELY FORTH TO DO AS SHE was told by Antonius and Lucilla. She greeted her men, playing the charming patroness, giving the role just the right touch of fragile innocence. She smiled beautifully and innocently at each of them, offered her hand to be kissed, and seemed to blush on cue.

She asked every man's name and surprised herself by re-membering all of them. She finalized the occasion of the first meeting by giving each of them a ring or brooch from the treasure bestowed on her by Maeniel.

When they filed out of the reception room of the villa and the last passed through the curtains that led to the street, she turned to Antonius and asked, "Well? How did I do?"

"Beautifully," Antonius replied. "Two or three of them look as though they'd been poleaxed, and the rest are thoroughly bedazzled."

Regeane looked down and smoothed the soft linen of her outer dress with her fingers. The dress was, as Lucilla had said, tastefully understated. Fine Egyptian linen lightly embroidered with silver at the neck and hem. It had long sleeves so deeply cut they almost trailed on the floor. Under it, she wore a thick silk shift with long tight sleeves, and, under that, a sleeveless linen shift. The outfit left a lot to the imagination. It was hot.

When Regeane had first seen it, she shouted, "Good heavens—the expense."

"Nonsense," Lucilla snapped. "Your men must know you are a proper wealthy maiden, and modest. Besides, this Maeniel is paying your expenses now. I don't think you quite grasp how wealthy he's made you. There was a king's ransom in that sack. Whole families in Rome live for years on what just one of those pieces is worth."

Lucilla then tried to foist off on her a heavy body chain of elaborate wrought gold, telling her such burdensome jewelry was presently all the rage in Byzantium. Regeane dug in her heels. The exchange was spirited. Elfgifa contributed her opinion. "It is very ugly."

Lucilla was infuriated. "Ugly or not, they're in fashion and I will not be criticized by the representative of a people who believe proper court attire is a shift covered by shirt, long for women, short for men, held in by a leather belt. So keep your opinions to yourself, young lady."

Antonius was helpless with laughter. When he dried his eyes, he said, "Mother, you don't care about the damned thing. You're only trying to get your own way. Forget art and leave a little to nature."

Lucilla turned her back in a huff, and Regeane departed victorious on Antonius' arm.

"I will conduct you to the meeting," he said. "I am, after all, your chamberlain."

"What's a chamberlain?" Elfgifa asked.

"I don't know," Regeane replied soberly, "but I'm sure Antonius will be a very good one."

Now that the extended interview was over, Regeane sat trembling a little, carefully smoothing the costly fabric. "Antonius," she said softly. "Do you know you were the first to tell me I was beautiful?"

"Was I?" he asked. "Well, beauty is another weapon. Learn how to use it."

Regeane sighed. "I had something else in mind."

"I know," Antonius said. "Forget it. Even a mild flirtation would be dangerous for us both. I'll go call Rufus."

"No," Regeane said, rising. "Today at least I want to be out in the open air. Take me to where he's waiting."

Antonius grinned and offered her his arm. "Come then. It's a little bit of a walk."

REGEANE WAS PERSPIRING WHEN THEY FOUND Rufus. It had been, as Antonius promised, a long walk. Down a flight of crooked marble steps, through a plowed field in the sun, and then up another stair. This one led into a grove of ancient cypresses. Their cool shade was welcome. Finally, they reached a maze of ruins bigger than the Forum.

Rufus was sitting on a bench in front of a stack of marble slabs piled on top of one another until they formed a small cliff. A faint trickle of water from the top created a tiny falls that emptied into a broken fountain at the base.

Rufus was, as his name implied, red-haired, but the fiery thatch was threaded with gray, and gray wings swept back from both sides of his ears. Regeane's first impression was one of ugliness. He had a big nose that was hooked and humped as though it had been broken several times. The white, thin scar of a sword cut marred his forehead. He had a wide, generous mouth. High cheekbones and hollow cheeks accompanied by the almost delicate pale skin that goes with such fair coloring.

All in all, she thought he did not look like the romantic lover who could have commanded Cecelia's devotion. Until he smiled. The smile had the same effect as kindling a bright lamp in a darkened room. Seeing it, Regeane thought, *Why, anyone would love him.*

He rose quickly, setting aside a paper he'd been reading, and bowed deeply over Regeane's hand. "My lady," he exclaimed, "you shouldn't have walked so far. I was perfectly prepared to come to you."

"I know," Regeane replied, "but I wanted an outing." Then she turned slowly around, gazing at the shattered piles of masonry around her. They were thickly overgrown with looping creepers, low bushes, and here and there, full-grown pines strove for a foothold, pushing their tops above dusty scrub oak. "What is this place?" she asked, awed.

"Impressive, isn't it?" Rufus grinned. "This, lovely lady, is said to be all that remains of Nero's golden house. Once the most famous and beautiful palace in the entire world. I love to come and walk here. I think on the Roman world, olden times, and our new kingdoms that replace it."

" 'So passes away the glory of the world,' " Antonius quoted. "My ancestors donned the purple and were crowned with golden laurel. They ruled the world, but we, their descendants, must humbly use—" He bowed to Rufus. "—bold, brave barbarians to be our protectors in time of trouble."

"You're being facetious," Rufus said with another one of his infectious grins. "Your personal ancestors likely knew more about homespun than the purple, were better acquainted with ox goads than golden laurels. And, as for ruling the world, they more likely spent their lives serving humbly in the legions or following a plow. The present disordered state of the world, while to be deeply deplored, offered us both our opportunities. So, let's get down to business, shall we?"

Antonius' lips twitched with amusement. "I'm glad to see you again, Rufus."

"Yes," Rufus replied, "and I, you. I don't know what happened or why it happened, my boy, but I'm very glad you're well again."

Then, the two men clasped each other's hands cordially. Rufus turned to Regeane. "Tell me, how is my dear Cecelia?"

"Oh!" The word was a gasp. Regeane didn't know what to say and tried to buy time. She pulled at the neck of the dress to let a little air at her moist skin. "Please," she said. "If I might sit down in the shade for a few moments."

"Of course, my dear," Rufus said. As he conducted her to the bench, he asked, "Will you have a cup of wine? I always take care to pack an ample lunch when I come here."

Regeane accepted the cup of wine, some bread, and an excellent, creamy white cheese. The wine was delicate. The cheese spread on the bread like soft butter. Regeane sat eating, drinking, and dreading what she would have to say to Rufus.

Until he leaned over from his seat beside her and gently lifted her chin with one finger. "Is it really so difficult, my dear?"

"Yes," Regeane mumbled shamefaced through a mouthful of bread and cheese.

Rufus' hand dropped from her chin and he sat back with his hands clasped at his knees. "Charming," he said to Antonius who was leaning quietly against the trunk of a small cypress nearby. "Is she always so forthright?"

"Usually," Antonius replied. "I haven't yet had time to instruct her in the art of seeming to promise everything without making any commitments at all."

"Well then, Regeane," Rufus continued. "At least tell me, is my darling Cecelia at least enjoying her little tantrum?"

"Tantrum?" Regeane and Antonius chorused.

"Yes, tantrum," Rufus said. "She's always been very given to them. Cecelia's high-strung."

"My God, Rufus," Antonius exclaimed. "Do you call a ten-year retreat into a convent a little snit? Besides, she cut—"

"I know what she did," Rufus interrupted, his face suddenly bleak. "I don't need to be reminded. Yet, I've always believed if that fool Maximus, her husband, had shown a little tact, a little ordinary human feeling, she'd have been back in my arms within a fortnight. But, fool that he was, he couldn't resist taunting her, enraging her. The rest was sheer folly."

Regeane shuddered as she gulped some of the wine. The perspiration was dry on her skin and, in the lengthening shadows of evening, the hollow among the ruins was cold. "If he was cruel, he paid the price," she said. "I'll never forget Cecelia's description of him dying destitute in the street, the rain falling into his open eyes."

To her surprise, Rufus howled with laughter. "Is that what she said? Oh, my. Oh, me. I hadn't heard that one before."

"Isn't it true?" Regeane asked shocked. "You don't mean to say she lied?"

"Not quite," Rufus said. "True, Maximus was never again as wealthy as he was before our little, shall we say, partnership ended, but he died at home in bed. I believe his liver got him. He turned the color of a ripe lemon shortly before he passed on, or so they say. We weren't on speaking terms by then. Yes, I do believe a bit too much overindulgence in the fruit of the vine killed him. However, whatever got him, it certainly wasn't Cecelia. But I'm not at all surprised she thinks so. She always tended to overdramatize things . . . a bit."

"What about the roses?" Regeane asked.

"The roses?" Rufus asked. "Oh, yes, the roses. Tell me, do they make her happy? Is she pleased with them?"

"Ha!" Regeane said. "I think if you stopped sending them, she might come out."

Rufus shook his head. "No, I'd never stop sending them. I couldn't. You see, my dear, I can't bear the thought of publicly humiliating her, or making her believe her lover has forgotten her and ceased suffering. Too many Roman matrons have shed tears over our unhappiness, mooned over our private misery for me to stop sending them now. How could she remain a heroine, a figure of tragedy, without them? I'll tell you a secret, Regeane. Even when I die, the roses will continue to come. I've made a provision for them in my will. Until the final breath passes her lips, the fragrance of roses will surround her . . . in my name."

Regeane set down the wine cup carefully and deliberately on the bench, got to her feet, and turned to face Rufus. "You are as bad as she is."

"Regeane!" Antonius exclaimed in reproof.

"No," Rufus said. "She's right, God help me. The girl is right. I am, lies, roses, folly, and all, but . . ." He got to his feet and faced Regeane. He looked down at her, "Regeane, I'm a happy man. As men go, I've had more than my share of the good things life has to offer. Wealth, leisure, good health, and pleasure. And I can't say Cecelia has ruined any of these things for me." He raised one finger. "But there is one thing that would make me happier still."

"Cecelia," Regeane said.

"If," Rufus said, "she would come down the path now." He turned away from Regeane and looked up the footpath as though seeing something there Regeane couldn't. "We would sit together. She would read to me from Suetonius and Tacitus. Together we would weave a magnificent fantasy about Rome in a time when the legions marched. When Nero lived here in his golden house with the beautiful, doomed Empress Poppaea at his side. We would titillate ourselves with tales of dark, ancient crimes, tortures, intrigues, and the final inexorable retribution that came to these gilded, fascinating sinners. And when our journey through time ended, we would wander away, hand in hand, to a glade I know where the moon is bright, the grass is long and soft. There were nights when I had my men spread a banquet in a meadow and warm the air with braziers so that we could lie clasped in each other's arms under an open sky. I would do so tonight for her, and for as many thereafter as she wished. And we would never know parting again."

"I hadn't thought love eternal," Regeane said. "Sometimes I hadn't thought it even possible." Her own words filled with surprise and even a little fear.

Rufus turned away from her and walked toward a stand of browning goldenrod illuminated by the afternoon sun. "Of course," he said. "You're still young. I've forgotten how young you are. Love is eternal. That is its terror and its final beauty. Love never ends. The joy may go out of it, and, in time, even the pain may end. But it lingers like a living thing and follows you every moment of your life. A day doesn't go by without my thinking 'I wish Cecelia were here to share this moment with me.' Tell me a joke, make me laugh, and I will wish I could hear her laughter. I think of her in the breathless hush of morning before the sun brushes the hilltops with golden light, and in the evening when, for a perfect moment, the sunset fills the sky with the myriad hues of purple, violet, red, and gold."

Rufus paused in the sunlight and idly broke the dusty flower heads. The dying sun burned his red hair into fire. "I walk with her in the springtime when my orchards bloom. On brief, hot summer nights, I dream of her in my arms. In the autumn, amidst the dust of the haying, she stands beside me. When my tenants carry the first sheaf to the altar, she walks crowned with wheat and autumn leaves through the shimmering, stubbled fields. She is both Demeter and Aphrodite. On cold winter nights, when the stars are brittle lights in a midnight black sky, and the wind shrieks around the eaves, I wake, reach for her, and know she is, perhaps, forever gone. Because, you see, Regeane, I know that if love is eternal, so also are folly, lies, and roses. And she may never return."

Regeane stood with her fists clenched; tears blurred her vision. Rufus walked back from the sunlight and into the shade of the cypress.

"I can't promise she will listen to me," Regeane said, "but I will go to her and I will plead your case as best I can."

Rufus grinned. He took her clenched fists in his hand and spread the fingers carefully. "Don't worry about success or failure, my dear. I'm a sensible man and I know Cecelia well. I only want you to give her an excuse."

"Of course," Antonius said. "An excuse. Something to save what's left of her face."

Rufus flinched.

"For God's sake, Antonius," Regeane pleaded.

To her surprise, Rufus regained his composure and laughed. "Antonius, how many men really fall in love with a woman's face? Was that all Adraste meant to you? A pretty face?"

"I must remember not to cross swords with you in the future," Antonius said. "You scored a hit there. A very palpable hit."

"I'm glad you felt it," Rufus said.

"I hope Cecelia takes the excuse I'm going to offer," Regeane said. "Perhaps she wants to come back, but isn't sure . . . of her welcome."

Rufus lifted one of Regeane's hands to his lips and kissed it. "Reassure her," he said.

"Come, Regeane," Antonius said. "It's late and the shadows

cast by the cypresses are very long. You will need to dress for the feast tonight."

"My men are within earshot," Rufus said. "These ruins aren't safe at night. Some of them will give you both an escort back to Lucilla's villa."

XXIX

LUCILLA WAS WAITING NEAR A GATE IN THE BACK wall of the villa when they returned. "Gundabald and Hugo are here. Where do you want them? In the reception room or the atrium garden?"

Regeane's mouth was dry, and she could feel her heart hammering. She straightened her dress and appealed to Lucilla. "How do I look?"

Lucilla fussed with her hair for a moment. "Not too bad," she said. "You're a bit flushed from your long walk, but luckily, you don't wear cosmetics and you haven't perspired too freely. Given the new clothes and jewels, I feel the effect is satisfactorily intimidating."

"Good," Regeane said.

"Now, don't be submissive," Lucilla cautioned. "That would only make them suspicious. Make it plain you intend to be mistress in your own house, but be conciliatory. Pretend that when you return to your own country, you feel you will need their help establishing yourself politically."

Regeane nodded absently.

"Do you want me to go with you?" Antonius asked.

"No," Regeane said. "He'd be surprised if I didn't come alone. He might not speak freely." With that she moved away from Lucilla and toward the curtains separating the darkened room from the atrium.

Gundabald and Hugo were cooling their heels near the villa entrance. They were seated on a stone bench. Gundabald stared gloomily out over the reflecting pool. Hugo was glancing around nervously, obviously overawed by his luxurious surroundings. He was the first to see Regeane approaching. He jumped to his feet. Gundabald rose more slowly. Both men turned to face her.

Regeane stopped, keeping about ten feet between herself and the nearest of the two men. She had expected to be frightened, instead she was surprised by her own observations.

God, they were a shabby pair. Hugo's mantle and shirt were threadbare and there were obvious sweat stains at his armpits. Gundabald's gold-embroidered mantle which had once seemed so fine to her eyes was dirty and his linen stockings were baggy at the knees. They both wore mud-stained scuffed boots that showed signs of hard usage. And, before God, they smelled foul. She had scented them often before and her wolf nose would have known them in the dark, but she realized for the first time that the rank stench she associated with them was the result of rarely washed bodies and unclean hair and beards. Gundabald stared at her with sullen eyes, red-rimmed and bloodshot with sleeplessness and drink.

For a moment, she wondered that Lucilla would bother to contemplate killing either one of them. They weren't worth the trouble. Then, Gundabald smiled. And the sight of his blunt, yellow teeth brought a shadow of the old terror returned.

"What?" he asked. "No kiss on the cheek for your uncle?"

The wolf's lip curled. Regeane could have sworn it was the wolf until she saw the spasm of rage cross Gundabald's face and the fear in Hugo's.

"You dare sneer at me, you stupid little twat?" He continued in a low voice. "I know you think you've found some strong new friends. Friends who will stand by you and so they will until you're safely married and off to your new lord's mountain fastness. But what will you do then when you're alone with him?"

"Don't try to frighten me, Gundabald," Regeane said.

He took a step toward her.

She said very softly, "Don't come near me."

Gundabald hesitated and stepped back. Hugo looked as though he wanted to flee. He made a little whimpering sound in his throat.

"Don't be a fool," Gundabald snapped at him. "It's broad daylight."

"Gundabald," Regeane said, "you aren't safe near me by day." She shook her head slowly. "Not anymore. I've changed."

Hugo went behind Gundabald.

"Yes," Gundabald said, "but then you always did that."

"Yes," she said, "but now I do it more often and a lot more easily. So, I warn you, don't depend on the sun." Deep inside Regeane, the wolf rose. Her jaws opened in a wide doglike smile, the long, red tongue curled at the powerful fangs. The look on her face was pure laughter. The laughter of the victor in a deadly contest of wills. And Regeane knew the words she'd spoken to Gundabald, only meaning to bluff him, were the simple truth.

Somewhere in the darkness of the Campagna, in the world between life and death, in the struggle to save Antonius' life, the wolf had come into her own. Regeane could call on her by day or night, and the magnificent killer beast would rise to serve her. She'd won.

"Father . . ." Hugo half sobbed.

"Shut up, you fool," Gundabald said.

"Yes," Regeane said. "Shut him up. I've no mind to listen to his whining. Dogs whine, and he is a dog. Now, what do you want? Or rather, I know what you want. Let me show it to you."

Regeane turned and swept aside the curtains to the triclinium. Some of Maeniel's treasure lay on the table, a careless scattering of gold coins, loose gems, rings, and brooches.

"Not bad," Gundabald said. "You've done well for yourself."

"This is," Regeane said, "not a tenth of what he brought. The more valuable pieces are locked away."

Gundabald went to the table and picked up a small stack of gold coins. They jingled loosely in his hand. "A tenth of what he brought?" His eyes gleamed with greed.

"Less than a tenth," Regeane said. Suddenly, she was tired. Tired and angry. She'd won. Now, all she had to do was trick this pair of fools into trusting her, and Lucilla's assassin would do the rest.

She eyed the pair of them staring transfixed at Lucilla's bait. She lifted a ring from the table, a magnificent ruby set in ridiculously complex, twisted Celtic knot work, and dropped it into Hugo's outstretched hand. "This pretty trinket will buy you a lot of women and a great deal of wine as well. Won't it, Hugo?" she asked.

Hugo backed away from her, gazing down at it, mesmerized by the gem in his hand.

"What do you want?" Gundabald asked.

Regeane met his eyes with an artificially artless glance. "What could I possibly want?"

Gundabald laughed. The laugh ended in a snort of derision. "You want something. Otherwise, your fine friends would never have allowed us past the gate. It's clear to me," he said with some chagrin, "that you're not afraid of me any longer."

Regeane's fingers played idly with the precious litter on the table. She separated a few fine Indian rubies from the rest, scraped them to the edge of the table and poured them into her hand. Then, stretched out her arm toward Gundabald. He spread his palms for her largess. They trickled through her fingers into his cupped hands. He picked out one and held it up to the light.

"This lord is plated with wealth," she said. "He must sleep and dream of gold, only to waken and find it falling into his coffers. A river of riches flows through the high mountain passes. Caravans laden with spices, silks, jewels, and gold. He is anxious for Charlemagne's favor so that he may grow even richer. I have presented myself as the road to that favor."

"And what of moonlight?" Gundabald asked.

Regeane laughed. "I'm not afraid of moonlight. You were always too shortsighted to understand. I welcomed it, embraced it, loved it. But no, Gundabald, I never, never feared it. And now, I am mistress of the night and all contained therein. For this lord of mine, I will be a tender plaything draped in silk until he reaches his home. The high fastness of which you spoke.

Fools, he is not a pigeon to be plucked, but an orchard to be cultivated, increasing its yield year by year until I have garnered all it has to give. He is a proper man, this Maeniel, and I can make him one of the greatest lords in Franca. I will be his lady, and you two my trusted companions, if you will but let me. I'll have no rivals for his favor and I will suffer none. They will meet with . . . accidents. I'll see to that. Neither of you has ever had the slightest conception of what Gisela gave birth to."

Gundabald stepped back and studied her. "Do you seriously think you can deceive him about your true nature for years?"

Regeane tried to make her face hard. "With your help, I can deceive him as long as I like."

Gundabald gave her a long, slow, brooding look. Then, he walked to the door and gazed out into the garden. "This takes a bit of getting used to," he said. "My plan, you will admit, was very simple. Take what we could get, arrange a hunting accident, and then as the grieving heiress and deeply religious widow—an appearance of piety would do you no end of good, my dear—you would spend the rest of your life under the safe supervision of your uncle and cousin."

"Yes," Regeane said, "in a narrow stone cell, chained by my neck to the wall. Was that what you had in mind?"

"Oh, no!" Hugo stammered. "We wouldn't dream . . ."

"The hell you wouldn't!" Regeane's voice cracked like a whip silencing him.

"That's better," Gundabald said. "At last, the bribes have been paid." He tossed the rubies in his hand. "The pretty words spoken. Now, we're getting down to business."

Regeane nodded. "You two gentlemen had best listen to my terms, because, Gundabald, I don't plan to spend even one day of my life under your so-called 'supervision'."

Gundabald turned in the doorway and rested his back against the wall. "What you're planning is absolute folly."

"Folly?" Regeane laughed. "You murdered my father, robbed my mother blind, and made my girlhood a hell of misery and despair. Give me one, *one* reason to trust you about anything."

Gundabald rushed toward her. "We know your secret," he roared.

He stood over the table. Regeane was behind it, only inches away. Her voice dropped into a low, hoarse whisper. "Back up, Gundabald, and get your foul breath out of my face or you will learn more of my secret than you care to. Right now!"

Gundabald obeyed. Hate glittering in his eyes, a dark evil shimmer. "I still say what you plan is folly. Sooner or later, the man will learn your secret and he will kill you."

Regeane fought for composure. "Perhaps not," she said, "or perhaps he will learn my secret and not be able to kill me. But one thing I tell you, and you had better listen well, there will be no convenient hunting accidents! This marriage is important in a way neither of you understands. Denied as you are the councils of popes and kings. Your intriguing would ruin me and I'd bring you down with me. I'd make sure of that. Be advised, Gundabald, you no longer have the power to rule me. It's the other way around. I'm giving the orders here and you'll obey my commands now or get out. One loud shout from me would bring a dozen men into this room. And I'd tell them to throw you in the gutter. Without my money, that's where you'd stay for the rest of your miserable lives. Am I making myself clear?"

With one swipe of her hand, Regeane sent some of the gold and gems tinkling to the floor. Hugo scrambled after the gold, snatching it up in handfuls and thrusting it into his purse.

Gundabald stood his ground, his chest heaving with rage. "I believe," he said quietly, "we understand each other."

"I don't know about you, Gundabald, but I understand you perfectly. The one and only throw of the dice you have is to reveal my secret to the world. And what would that get you? Tell me!"

Gundabald's eyes shifted from hers to the shadows in the half-darkened room. "Nothing," he muttered.

"Oh, you're wrong, Gundabald. It might get you worse than nothing. My new lord and husband is very pleased with his lady of the royal house. He might decide you are a madman or a liar and have you silenced himself. Or the pope who greatly supports this marriage might see you as a dangerous troublemaker. You must ask yourself, are you willing to take the chance?"

Gundabald snorted, then smiled, though rage still smoldered in his eyes. He spoke between his teeth. "My dear niece, you are a clever woman. Far cleverer than I had previously thought. I can see if I'm to benefit by our close blood tie, it will be on your terms."

Hugo rose from his knees, purse bulging. He looked from Regeane to Gundabald and back again. "Father," he said hesitantly, "I think we better do as she says."

Gundabald shot a glare at him, but the look he gave Regeane was carefully neutral. "Very well," he said quietly. "What would you have me do?"

Regeane relaxed. She was sure she had them. They waited, bought and paid for. Bullied into submission, not by her, but by their own greed. They were ready to be herded into her trap.

The wolf had a memory of this moment. A lot of memories. The memories of a huntress. Her experienced eyes scanning a herd for prey; looking for the telltale stagger where the footing wasn't difficult; heavy breathing with no expenditure of effort; the limping fawn not able to keep up with the rest; the bull or cow touched with the signs of age. She eyed Hugo and Gundabald for a second with the cold, mechanical gaze of a killer.

Hugo backed up a few paces and a muscle jerked in Gundabald's cheek.

"What do you want us to do?" Hugo asked nervously.

"Take a bath, for one thing," Regeane snapped. "All the money left on the table is yours."

Hugo forgot his fears and began snatching it up at once.

"Buy new clothes so you're in a fit state to be presented to my lord. Gundabald, you still have connections at Charlemagne's court, haven't you?"

"Yes," Gundabald said slowly.

"Very well," Regeane said. "I'll need you." She took a deep breath. "I really need you very badly. I can't turn this lord of mine into a great man all by myself. I'll have to have the help of an experienced man of affairs such as you. I've been remiss in never paying attention to politics."

Gundabald began helping himself to the gold on the table also. Nodding as though he'd come to some decision.

"I'll have Lucilla's servants show you out," Regeane said. "Come back in a few days and we can dine together quietly and talk over the future."

"To be sure," Gundabald said. "A congenial family dinner."

"Yes," Regeane said wearily. The wolf was ready to kill. There was little more to be said and she was anxious to be rid of them.

At the gate, Gundabald turned and faced her. "I'm sure," he said smoothly, "now that we've come to an estimate of your true worth, there will be no more quarrels between us."

"I'm sure," Regeane replied. "Partnership will be so much more fruitful than dissention."

WHEN THEY WERE GONE, REGEANE FOUND LU-cilla and Antonius waiting for her in the garden. She sank down on a bench beside the pool. She looked not at them, but at the dark water. "You listened?" she asked.

"Of course," Lucilla answered. "I listened closely. What do you take me for? Some silly incompetent? You're my protégé."

"Did I succeed?" Regeane asked.

"I don't know," Antonius said. "I think you might have been a little less . . . honest."

"I couldn't help myself," Regeane said. "I detest them both."

"It showed," Antonius said, turning a troubled gaze to the portico through which Gundabald and Hugo had exited.

"What they thought doesn't matter," Lucilla said. "I accomplished my objective. She was seen to receive them in a civil manner. They accepted rich presents from her. My guess is the pair of them, scoundrels that they are, will spend at least part of the money on a drunken spree in the lowest taverns and brothels in Rome. My man will take them tonight or tomorrow."

Regeane raised a stricken face to Lucilla. "You really didn't care what I said to them, did you?"

Antonius shrugged and smiled, then strolled off along the pool.

Regeane leaped up and stamped her foot as she confronted Lucilla. "You had this all planned."

"Yes," Lucilla said with infuriating smugness.

"I'm surprised you even consulted me," Regeane said bitterly.

"I very nearly didn't," Lucilla snapped back. "but you needed to know how and why these things are arranged. But, be aware of this, my dear. Once I knew your secret, I never intended to let the wretch live."

"But why?" she asked. "You hadn't even met him."

"Why would I need to meet him?" Lucilla asked. "I saw that ghastly lodging house. The stinking sty where they kept you penned up. The weals on your back. What else did I need to know? Pray, tell me."

Antonius turned and walked back toward them. "Regeane," he said, "consult the wolf. What does she think?"

Regeane turned away in confusion. "I already have," she whispered. "I know what she thinks. The wolf is . . . indifferent."

"Your better half, I think," Antonius said, "or at least your smarter half. Listen, girl, in all places among all peoples, husbands are granted by law certain authority over their wives. We . . . the three of us . . . have already taken steps to make you independent of your husband."

"Yes," Regeane said.

"Fine." Antonius spoke slowly as if speaking to a child. "Now, the other group empowered to control women are their male blood relatives. Are they not?"

Regeane nodded.

"With Hugo and Gundabald gone, how many blood relatives would you have left?"

"None, or at least none close enough to matter," she said. "I see. I would be free."

Antonius glanced at his mother. Their eyes met and an unspoken message passed between them.

"There is more, isn't there?" Regeane said.

"In a sense I suppose Gundabald is my wedding gift to you, Regeane," Lucilla said. "And possibly Hugo, too."

"I've never agreed with you about Hugo, Mother," Antonius said. "I believe Hugo is a porridge-brained, nincompoop, blabber-mouth who would spill the contents of his empty head in every tavern and whorehouse in Rome and the surrounding countryside. And sooner or later, his drunken ravings would be sure to come to the wrong ears. Take him down, too. Regeane's right. They both need a long bath. Give them one . . . in the Tiber."

"God in heaven!" Regeane exclaimed.

"Face facts, girl," Antonius said. "Neither of them can possibly do you any good, and it is in their power to do you a great deal of harm."

"Face facts? My God, Antonius!" Regeane exploded. "Do you know Gundabald once said that to me? He wanted to use me to help murder my own husband. I told Gundabald I wouldn't spend even one day under his supervision. Well, I won't accept yours either. Yours or your mother's. No," she sobbed. "No, I don't want to be involved in this heinous act. Did you see them with the gold? They can be bought off. I'm sure of it."

Antonius threw up his hands and turned away.

Lucilla sighed deeply. "A very fine-tuned moral sense you have. I'm quite sure they can be bought off . . . for a time. But what happens when you run out of gold?" she asked gently.

Regeane continued to weep quietly, tears pouring down her face. "I can't bear it," she whispered thickly. "Let them live. I hated Gundabald once, but poor Hugo. I never hated him . . ."

Lucilla embraced Regeane and rested her head on the girl's shoulder, patting her gently.

"Let them live," Regeane repeated.

Lucilla pushed Regeane away at arm's length and studied her tear-stained face. "Oh, no . . ." Lucilla said sadly.

"Let them live," Regeane insisted stubbornly.

"Mother," Antonius said, "she needs to be free. She must make the decision herself. We can't make it for her."

Lucilla looked at Antonius over Regeane's head, then gave a deep shuddering sigh. "My only son, best of sons, I believe you're probably right. Very well, Regeane, I wouldn't do this for another living soul, probably not even Antonius, but I will spare them for you, my dear daughter in love. But—" Lucilla raised one finger. "There is something more you need to know."

Regeane wiped the tears from her eyes with her fingers and looked up at Lucilla.

"Regeane," she continued, "I suppose, once in the wonderful realm the Romans created, a man or woman could carve out a niche for themselves and live an independent life. This is no longer possible. In this disorderly, broken world there exist only the rulers and the ruled. You must decide for yourself which one you would rather be."

A FEW HOURS LATER, REGEANE FOUND HERSELF alone in a mule litter riding toward her betrothal feast. She'd been the recipient of advice from both Lucilla and Antonius before departing, lots of advice.

While she was dressing there was a short, sharp conversation with Lucilla about piercing her ears.

"They don't stay pierced," Regeane said.

"What do you mean?" Lucilla asked.

"They just go away."

Lucilla sat down on a couch, looking shocked. "Are you telling me the holes just go away?"

"Yes," Regeane replied. "What's wrong?"

"I was thinking about your hymen, my dear. Things might become very uncomfortable for you if your hymen were to perpetually be, ah . . . renewed."

"I'm not worried," Regeane said. "My mother told me she didn't have a moment's discomfort. I don't think I will have, either."

Lucilla sighed. "In a way, it's a pity . . . a real pity." Then she turned and began fumbling through the contents of her dressing table.

"What's a pity?" Regeane asked. She was wiggling into a coan silk shift. The shift was embroidered with crystal and seed pearls at the neck, sleeves, and hem.

"Be careful of that. It might tear," Lucilla chided.

"What's a pity?" Regeane repeated.

"A woman able to perpetually renew her virginity would drive men wild. You would have been an immense financial success as a courtesan," Lucilla said.

Antonius was standing in the next room behind a curtain. "Mother!" he said in reproof.

"I know, I know. 'Don't give the girl ideas.' In any case, I have a little jar of ointment here. You rub it on just before the act and it decreases the discomfort. Here," she said, extending a small glass bottle to Regeane. "Take this and keep it with you."

Regeane staggered back and sat down heavily on Lucilla's bed. "Tonight?" she gasped. "Is it tonight?"

"My dear girl," Lucilla said, "you will never be more married than you are now. Yes, certainly tonight."

Regeane's head was spinning.

"Considering the way he greeted you," Lucilla said, "I think he will be eager."

Regeane remembered Maeniel, the gentle chaste kiss he'd given her as a greeting. The wolf, deep in her brain, started up from sleep and eyed her with a knowing expression. This might be fun. Regeane leaped to her feet, palms against her burning cheeks. "We've been longing to try it," she said.

"Both of you, eh?" Lucilla gave her a look of disapproval as she tapped one foot.

Behind the curtain, Antonius burst into gales of laughter.

"Hush up!" Lucilla exclaimed in the direction of Antonius. "Regeane, you must listen to me. Virgin brides aren't supposed to be eager. You must be diffident, timid, a little afraid."

From then on, the cascade of advice rained down around Regeane's ears.

"Let him take the lead," Lucilla said. "When he does it, pretend to be in pain."

"But suppose I'm not in pain," she replied.

"Pretend you are anyway," Lucilla said. "They expect it."

"Mother, stop frightening her," Antonius said. "I'm sure she'll be fine. But Regeane, don't let yourself get too frightened. No matter what happens, remember you can't be hurt permanently."

At this point, the advice degenerated into a shouting match between Lucilla and Antonius. Regeane dressed quickly and fled.

Lucilla had planned to ride in the litter with her, but Antonius put his foot down, saying, "Be quiet, Mother. She doesn't need you making her any more nervous than she is already. She needs a bit of solitude to compose herself."

So she rode alone.

The wolf scented the night breeze, and Regeane wondered if it would be permissible to push back the litter curtains. There was no one to ask, so she did.

The air was chilly. They were passing the Colosseum. It

lifted a wall of dark ruins on her right. There were few houses and shops there and the streets were nearly deserted in the gathering gloom of evening. Somewhere in the distance, a dog howled. Or had it been a dog? She, even with her superior senses, couldn't be sure.

The wolf lifted her head and sniffed the air. Power games. Antonius and Lucilla were instructing her in how to play them. The bulk of their advice had been concentrated not on what she was to expect or do, but on how to please him. Maeniel.

Regeane consulted the wolf. Her midnight sister wasn't afraid of him. She knew, in the same way she had known Lucilla was a friend, that Maeniel would never abuse or harm her. But did she want him? She thought of the gray wolf. Who was he? What was he when he walked on two legs? She had no idea. Not a young man, she surmised. His first youth was past. Certainly not old, either. He had been the undisputed ruler of the pack. She could not imagine any creature bold enough to challenge him. Yet, perhaps, he was an ordinary man, a tavern keeper, a priest, or small merchant.

She wondered what it would be like to be the wife of a commoner. Living in a small apartment above his shop, caring for a brood of children. Cooking and cleaning daily. Washing clothes in a tub in a courtyard and hanging them out on a line strung over the street.

A life of simple day-to-day routine, coping with small crises, teething children, colicky babies, getting meals ready on time, keeping business and household accounts. Yet, also, a life of laughter. Life with a man she could trust with her innermost self. A man of whom she would never be afraid.

The wolf waited in the darkness, ears up, alert. Ready to serve her. Change, slip down to the cobbles rattling under the litter's wheels. Run away. Go find him, the gray one, and yield herself to him. Together they could flee across the world. To Byzantium, to Franca where no one would ever find them.

But she was stopped, held immobile by the woman's cold knowledge that the man the gray wolf was by day might not be one the woman Regeane could ever consider loving. She could speculate. She could guess. She could hope, but she simply did not know. To chain herself to such a one without knowing would be absolute folly.

Outside the litter she heard the sudden sharp clip-clop of a horse approaching the side of the litter. A second later her eyes picked him out of the blue twilight. She realized he was the captain of the escort conducting her to Maeniel's villa.

He had a grizzled spade beard and a fall of salt and pepper hair hanging at his shoulder. "My lady," he said sharply.

And the wolf looked back at him from Regeane's eyes. *So quickly,* Regeane thought in alarm. *I never summoned her.* But then, perhaps, the wolf was angry at not being allowed her freedom. Regeane's will pushed her firmly back, out of the world.

The man on the horse appeared slightly taken back. As though warned by some instinct of another presence. "My lady," he said more quietly, "please close the curtains. With all due respect . . . if someone should see you . . . well, you would not wish us to have to shed blood to protect you. A rare prize such as yourself might tempt even the most craven thieves to recklessness."

Regeane forced herself to smile. "I'm sorry," she said. "I hadn't thought." She pushed the curtains closed and lay back against the cushions.

The litter was dark and stuffy. The perfume from her own body mixed with the dusty scent of the thick, silk cushion nauseated her slightly. That was how she knew the wolf was still with her.

She and the wolf met eye to eye in her mind. The lips drew back over the wolf's teeth. Regeane felt as though she had never before fully confronted the beast's power. She'd acted on raw instinct in killing the stallion. She'd put the wolf in motion in the insula and allowed her animal reflexes to carry her forward. But now, she and the beast were alone together. She realized the beast rebelled against the game of lies and deception she was carrying on. The wolf was making her bid and trying to drive her toward freedom.

"No," Regeane said softly. "You have your wisdom, but I, the woman, have mine. Giving you free rein might kill us both.

Have done! Trouble me not at the banquet and after on the marriage bed. Be still tonight even when the moon is high in the sky. Wait! While I do what I must to free us both."

THE BEAST CAME UNSUMMONED INTO MAENIEL'S dreams.

By day, by month, by year, he was chained by the man. But in sleep he returned and was always remembered, loved.

Maeniel the wolf lifted his head and read the wind blowing from the glacier above him. Spring was in the air. The sky was an azure crystalline pool. The mountains reared their clean, white crests against the blue.

In the pure air and clear light, the wolf tasted the greatest freedom of all—the freedom simply to be. The freedom simply to exist without thought, foresight, or memory. Those yokes that seem to burden humans' every waking moment from birth to death. In this world, the wolf simply was, and every continued moment of life was a joy.

He gulped a drink from a freshet created by the snowmelt. Shuddered at the cold and stared out at the mountain meadow before him.

Emboldened by the warm air and melting snow, the herds of mountain sheep, wild goats, and aurochs drifted up from the lowlands to reclaim their summer pasture.

The wolf leaped easily to the top of a flat rock. He lay down, head on his front paws, watching a small group of wild cattle drift past. They were a tough-looking bunch, lean, rangy, some with dun coats, others spotted and blotched red on white. They all sported horns nearly as long as his body.

These were cows, most accompanied by a half-grown calves. They eyed him nervously as they passed, but without fear. None was even slightly intimidated.

Nor did he underestimate them in the slightest. One blow of a forehoof could cave in his skull or snap his spine, leaving him to thrash himself to death in a bloody froth of snow. The gigantic horns could toss and disembowel the strongest wolf.

These were not destined to be easy prey for anything. One barren cow unencumbered with a calf, paused, pawed the ground lightly, then snorted as if in derision.

The wolf lay still, seeming to doze, but his belly muscles tightened slightly. No, he would not choose her as an opponent. The cow moved on, casually switching her tail at a few flies.

Following the cows came an old bull. He was dark-bodied with a thick mane of lighter hair on his chest and shoulders. He was still powerful, but his muzzle was gray with age. His body jerked sideways when he caught sight of the wolf resting on the rock.

The wolf laid his ears back, then they flicked upright.

The bull walked on, blowing heavily from the climb. He paused at the same freshet from which the wolf had drunk earlier and dropped his muzzle into the water and quenched his thirst. Then, he pawed at the icy stream bank and bared the winter-killed grass. He began to eat.

On the rock, the wolf felt the spring sun warm his back. Slowly, he yawned, then sat up. Behind him, he could hear small noises among the boulders. The pack had seen him move and they were coming down toward him.

The gray wolf dropped from the rock and loped toward the bull.

Their eyes met.

Come, the bull's eyes said. *Come if you want. Come if you will. We have met before. I have always prevailed. If I do, I'll trample you to bloody scraps. If I don't, so be it.*

The gray wolf glided from a lope into a run.

The aurochs threw up his head with a snort of fury and fled.

The pack exploded out of the rocks around the gray in a semicircle behind the old bull.

He was slow, but seemed to gain speed with every bound, outrunning Maeniel easily.

The chase was silent. The old bull had no breath to bellow. No herd of cows to protect. The only sound was the thud of his pounding hooves, the whisper of the wolves' pads in the snow, and the heaving breath of the hunters and the hunted. Too far away to be involved, the other herbivores in the meadow simply lifted their heads to watch the drama of pursuit.

The young females passed Maeniel easily. They were swift as racing greyhounds, and closed in on the bull's flanks, leaping and slashing with vicious efficiency. Within seconds, the pale snow was stained with scarlet blood, trailing in streams from the bull's hindquarters and flanks.

Maeniel began to drop back, then he saw the bull's strategy. He was running for a pile of rocks near the center of the meadow. They were still black with the damp snowmelt and, here and there, stained by vivid patches of white.

When the bull reached the rocks, he turned and, with incredible swiftness, swung his horns at his pursuers. The females scattered, but one young male caught the blow full on. His spine snapped; his body, a bloody rag, was flung into the snow yards away.

The other wolves drew well back, but Maeniel increased his speed, charging faster and faster.

The bull dropped his head and, for the first time, bellowed a challenge.

Maeniel's flying momentum carried him past the other cowering wolves and took him right into the bull's horns. From the corner of his eye, Maeniel saw the horn hook, the blunt tip moving like lightning to impale him. But, at the last moment, he flattened his body. He felt the horn cross his back, pushing his belly into the snow. Then, his back legs were under him and he was up, leaping with all the force of his powerful hindquarters for the bull's throat.

A last bellow deafened him to everything else . . . ending in a wheeze as his jaws crushed the bull's windpipe. He clung. Up as the old bull in his death throes reared almost like a horse. Then, down, down, smashing into the snow that rose in clouds around the thrashing bodies of the killer and his prey. The breath in his body wooshed out between his grimly locked fangs. His ears caught the sickening snap of a breaking bone. His or the bull's, he didn't know. A sense of utter rightness filled the wolf. Incomprehensible in human terms. Only as this is why we live and the way we are supposed to die. A moment's straining from the lungs against his jaws. A pulsing in the throat from arteries insulated from his fangs by ripples of muscle and tendon echoed a heartbeat that faltered, struggled, and . . . stopped.

Maeniel the wolf rose, shook himself. He accepted the homage of his pack. They mobbed him, pressing against his body, giving him wolf kisses on the face and jaws.

His body felt strange to him. And he fought against the uncanny sensation taking hold of him. He wanted to go back, to stay with his companions, feed, sleep, and then sing with the rest in the blue moonlight.

He struggled, but was drawn away more and more quickly. *This is not real,* a voice whispered in his mind. *It is only a memory.*

He woke human, his body feeling leaden on a couch in the villa he'd rented in Rome. Through the door, he could see servants lighting torches in a peristyle garden. He sat up on the side of the couch, running his fingers through his coarse, dark hair.

Matrona came into the room. She brought no lamp or candle. She could see as well as he in the dark. She turned to face him, and the opalescent glow of her eyes reflected the torchlight outside. "Time to get up," she said. "Bathe and dress for the feast."

Maeniel rose to his feet. "Matrona, who is the strongest?"

"You are," she said.

"Would any dare challenge me?"

"None," Matrona said. "Gavin is, I think, the closest, but he only comes up to your shoulder. You are the oldest, the wisest, the fiercest, the best."

"I must wed the woman," Maeniel said.

"You are the leader," Matrona said grimly. "A leader pays for his prowess by sometimes being the first to die."

"This is hardly death," Maeniel said.

"Don't be a fool, O leader," Matrona said. "The girl stinks of intrigue. Look at her friends. First, she has the backing of the pope."

"How do you know all this?" Maeniel interrupted.

Matrona chuckled. "Augusta," she said. "The scrawny wench was angry with Lucilla and wanted only a friendly ear to complain. She wouldn't dream of gossiping, but was very anxious to impart information. Almost as anxious to communicate it as I was to hear it."

Maeniel began to stroll toward the bath, shedding his clothes as he went. Matrona paid no attention. She had seen him naked often before.

"The pope wrote the marriage contract," Maeniel said, diving into the pool.

"Yes," Matrona said as he surfaced. "She snubbed her own blood relatives. A source of some shock to Augusta, but a sure sign of intelligence to me. They sound little better than what is found growing at the edges of stagnant pools."

"Scum." He scrubbed his face and body with a coarse sponge.

"Yes. And she is very close to Lucilla, the pope's mistress. And, I understand, Lucilla's very favorite son, Antonius, is to be Regeane's chamberlain. You are surrounded."

Maeniel stepped out of the pool. He began toweling himself dry. He was frowning, deep in thought. "What about this Frankish Count Otho who is to be here tonight?"

"Maybe the worst of the lot," Matrona answered. "He has a reputation of being devoted to Charlemagne's interests, but otherwise he's unprincipled and completely ruthless."

"Now why would he be so interested in my marriage?"

"This Charlemagne," Matrona suggested. "He is going to be a very strong king. He is quick about bringing his noblemen to heel."

"And I will obey," Maeniel said.

"A little too quickly, perhaps," Matrona said. "The fortress we inhabit is unique. Given a stout defense, I should say, impregnable."

Maeniel began to dress himself. White linen drawers, embroidered cotton stockings, trousers, shirt, and, to top it off, a white, silk dalmatic crusted with gold at the sleeves, hem, and neck.

"Lo, the bridegroom cometh," Matrona chuckled. "Let's see if he can make the bride do the same."

"You are," Maeniel said deliberately, "a nasty, salacious bitch."

"Thank you for the compliment," Matrona said. "Think she's a virgin?"

"Almost certainly," Maeniel said. "I don't believe she would trade so valuable a prize as her innocence for less than a high net profit."

"Your fortress," Matrona said.

Maeniel was combing his hair.

"I believe," Matrona continued, "you could hold it even against Charlemagne."

"You and Gavin," Maeniel said. "And neither of you knows anything about the strength of an army."

"You are the leader," Matrona said, "but watch your back. Wolves aren't treacherous . . . men are."

A few moments later, Maeniel was inspecting the dining hall. It was enormous, designed to impress a visitor with the wealth and importance of his host. Yet it had a slightly shabby, down-at-the-heels air. The elaborate wall paintings were faded and, here and there, flaking, showed white patches of plaster beneath.

The bronze lamps suspended from the ceiling were tarnished and looked as though they hadn't been polished in years. The purple velvet on the dining couches was threadbare and worn, showing the occasional bald patch. Still, Maeniel judged it would seem magnificent enough by lamplight.

A few servants were bustling around, covering the worn tables with rich damask cloths.

From the baths came the screams and shouts of Maeniel's people. Maeniel sighed because he could tell from the mixture of voices that the men and women were bathing together.

"Men and women," one of the servants muttered to another. "Filthy barbarians."

"Smile when you say that," Maeniel remarked to the man as he passed by.

The bath was warm and steamy. Maeniel's people were screaming, shouting, splashing, and dunking one another in frenzied abandon.

Matrona had hold of Gavin. She held his hair in a firm grip. Maeniel thought of letting loose with a howl, which was what he usually did when he wanted to get their attention, but decided not to. They might reply in their usual fashion and alarm the servants in the next room. He clapped his hands.

Matrona let Gavin up. He surfaced and leaned on the edge of the pool gasping. The rest came to attention.

"I have something to say to you."

"We gathered that," Matrona said. Dressed, Matrona was stocky. Naked, she was voluptuous.

Gavin eyed her longingly and edged in her direction.

"These Romans are a mannerly people, more so than the Franks, and I want proper behavior at my wedding feast," Maeniel said sternly. "The servants seeing you bathing together think you have loose morals."

Joseph, who was the size and shape of a bear and covered with soft, wet, brown hair, scratched his head and asked, "What are loose morals?"

Matrona burst out laughing, slipped, and went under. She came up blinded and sputtering. Gavin pounced. He copped as much of a feel as he could, then dunked her.

Maeniel snarled.

Gavin let go of Matrona.

"Loose morals are plenty of sex," Silvia said self-righteously. In the water, Silvia floated like a small whale.

"We can have all the sex we want," Joseph shouted indignantly at Silvia. "We're human, aren't we? They do it all the time, don't they?" He appealed to Maeniel. "You tell her!"

Gavin was sidling toward Matrona again.

Maeniel took a deep breath. He was becoming angry. "I had not wished to change," he said loudly, "because of my wedding finery. But if you irritate me, I will. Then we will see if you are so disrespectful."

Complete silence fell.

"Very well," Maeniel said. "Rules to follow: don't pick your noses or scratch your balls at the dinner table. Both habits are disgusting."

"Next you will be telling us not to get drunk," Joseph protested.

"I know better than that," Maeniel said. "However, no pissing under the table or in the corners of the room. The nights are warm here, go outside. Do the same if you wish to vomit.

"Should you ask someone, and she says 'yes,' take her to a bedroom. We have a sufficiency of those here. No rolling on the floor under the tables."

"What if she says 'yes' to more than one," Matrona purred.

"Then each will wait his turn; no fighting over who goes first," Maeniel replied sternly. "And," he continued, "last, but not least, no howling. And absolutely no skin-turning under any circumstances. I believe that covers most of the things that might happen tonight. About the rest, use your common sense."

MAENIEL WAS RIGHT. THE BIG DINING ROOM WAS much more attractive by lamplight than by daylight. The yellow flames cast a glamour of elegance over the cloth-covered tables, the fraying curtains, and the flaking paintings.

Count Otho arrived first. He was a portly man, solid and rocklike. He had thin, almost invisible lips, and a hooked upper lip and nose. His eyes were hooded and hard. He looked as though he could pronounce a death sentence not only on a man, but throw in his wife and children in the bargain, and never turn a hair.

Maeniel bowed deeply. Count Otho's eyes swept the room with a glance, then fixed on the thing of most value in it—the heavy, scrolled silver dishes on the tables.

Maeniel's people reclined on couches at the tables. They were scrubbed, slicked, sober, and on their best behavior.

Count Otho ignored the people, his eyes and mind on the silver. "Yours?" he asked, "or rented for the occasion?"

"The villa?" Maeniel asked innocently.

Count Otho met his eyes. "Please," he said, "don't pretend you're a fool."

"It's mine," Maeniel said. "I'm a wealthy man. My compliments to his majesty, Charles, king of the Franks. I am his most obedient, humble, and loyal servant."

Count Otho cleared his throat. "Hmmmm."

Maeniel plucked a heavy silver goblet from the table. The silver was so pure, it dented at the touch of a fingernail. He handed it to Otho.

Otho bit the rim lightly, weighed it in his hand. He gave it a glance of approval. "You're a generous man."

"And, if you present my compliments to the king," Maeniel said, "you'll find me even more generous in the future."

Otho tossed the cup into the air, feeling its weight. "I take it loyalty is the quality you want me to stress."

"Definitely," Maeniel said deprecatingly. "I have no army and I don't want to find a Frankish one knocking at my gate."

"A man after my own heart," Otho said. "I will be sure to mention you favorably to the king."

A stirring of servants at the gate interrupted them.

Regeane emerged from her litter. Surrounded by her personal guard, she began walking along the wide flagged path toward the triclinium.

The girl, Maeniel thought, *however calculating she is, cannot possibly know the picture she makes.*

She was beautiful. The night breeze molded her long silken gown to her virginal body. She walked not with downcast eyes, as perhaps a maiden should, but with head erect. Her young face, fair as a flower on the smooth column of her neck. Her even features softly framed by a fragile lace veil. Her midnight hair crowned with flowers. Youth, perfectly poised on the verge of womanhood. She glided toward him, her face enigmatic in the torchlight. When she reached the door to the triclinium, she extended her hand to him.

Maeniel carried its perfumed softness to his lips and kissed the fingers. "Greetings, my lady. Will you share my couch?"

Something in her eyes changed, showing she caught the double meaning in his words.

The wolf in Maeniel bristled. His hackles came up. *She's dangerous,* he told the man as plainly as if he had spoken. Then the wolf was gone, and Maeniel, the human, was telling himself not to be a fool. How could this fragile, flowerlike girl be a danger to him?

Regeane allowed herself to be taken by the arm and led to a place of honor on a high couch. She reclined next to Maeniel.

Their reclining was a signal for the rest to take their places.

Regeane and Maeniel's couch rested on a dais facing the open folding door and the torchlit garden of the villa. The rest of the guests occupied two large semi-circular couches, one on either side.

As at the Lateran, a small band of musicians trooped quietly into the center between the two tables and began to play quietly. Count Otho was examining his place setting with interest. Like the wine cup, the dishes in front of him were also heavy silver. Maeniel decided Count Otho was probably going to be a very expensive guest.

A wrinkle appeared between Maeniel's brows. In front of him, on the table gleamed silver cups and plates for each guest, interspersed with platters of late autumn fruit, pitchers of chilled white wine, and unchilled red wine. But no food was forthcoming.

Everyone looked at Maeniel and Regeane expectantly.

"How did you do it?" Regeane asked Maeniel.

"Caterers," Maeniel whispered. "I hope the waiters aren't drunk in the kitchen."

"Clap your hands," Matrona whispered sotto voce from the table next to Maeniel. Maeniel clapped his hands.

Waiters came marching out the anterooms of the triclinium carrying the gustato. Other waiters appeared to serve the wine.

Regeane looked at the appetizers. They resembled nothing she'd ever seen before, but she decided if she could eat mice, these were not so great a challenge. She found them bland with a hint of liver sausage in their ancestry.

The feast was dull. Maeniel's people on the right looked scrubbed, sober, and cowed. Lucilla, Antonius, and all the Roman party on the left looked rigid, sober, and disapproving. Only Otho looked relaxed. He appeared to be totaling up the value of Maeniel's table silver. Maeniel thought he looked like a man who feels he's on to a good thing.

Maeniel sighed.

Regeane reclined stiffly next to him. She might, as far as propriety was concerned, have been across the room.

The appetizers were cleared away. Otho appeared satisfied in his estimate of the silver's value. He then began examining Regeane, totaling up her worth.

Lucilla and Antonius reclined beside Otho.

"She's beautiful," Otho observed darkly.

A servant began serving an expensive, but almost nauseatingly sweet white wine.

Antonius smiled. "I had noticed she's easy to look at."

"I don't much care for beautiful women," Otho grumbled. "They're usually profoundly stupid, self-centered, and unspeakably vain. Someone with those character flaws is a walking recipe for trouble."

"I don't believe stupidity, vanity, or selfishness are Regeane's problems," Antonius mused. "None of those characteristics are highly developed in her nature."

"Then what's wrong with her?"

"Nothing," Lucilla said indignantly and perhaps a trifle guiltily.

"Nonsense," Otho snapped. "Something is definitely wrong with her. An attractive girl, descended from the royal house, should have been married years ago."

"I believe," Antonius said smoothly, "her family was very poor, and her mother was a devout woman who was unwilling to give up her daughter's company."

"Balls!" Otho whispered. "Her beauty will attract lovers the way a flame calls out to moths. This foolish Maeniel is in for a bad time."

"She will fob them off with sweet smiles and polite refusals. Besides, this Maeniel, as you say, looks as though he can keep order in his own house," Antonius replied softly.

"Wealthy as he is," Otho growled, "she will ruin him. Spending his substance on clothes and jewels."

"Nonsense," Lucilla snapped. "The dear girl never shows the slightest disposition to be greedy, rather the reverse. She is plain in her tastes and very temperate in her habits."

"Hmmm," Otho said. "Virtuous, discreet, temperate. What's the matter? Is she sterile?"

Lucilla reared up on the banquet couch and stared at Otho indignantly. "What! She is a fair virgin bride and well you know. Such are usually fecund as a well-watered vale in May. It's a known fact—"

Antonius kicked Lucilla in the ankle. "Shut up, Mother. You are allowing yourself to be drawn in the most outrageous fashion."

Otho began laughing.

Lucilla closed her mouth with an audible snap.

"Either something is wrong," Otho muttered, "or she is wasted on this Maeniel."

"Nothing is wrong," Antonius said blandly.

Otho chuckled. "Is she stupid?"

Lucilla sipped her wine, her cheeks burning.

Antonius snorted. "Which do you consider most dangerous— stupidity or intelligence?"

Otho sipped some of the thick, sweet wine. "My, this is disgusting."

"It has a certain snob appeal," Lucilla said.

"Definitely," Otho said. "It would be a big hit at the Frankish court. I wonder if Maeniel's generosity would extend to a couple of amphorae to take home with me to the king?"

"Absolutely," Antonius said. "If his doesn't, the fair Lady Regeane's will."

"You're her chamberlain?" Otho asked.

"Yes," Antonius replied.

"In answer to your question, I believe stupidity is the most dangerous. Stupid people are more apt to refuse to face facts, to barricade themselves behind some obscure point of law or their own silly notions of propriety. Or worse yet, refuse to make a decision until they are facing disaster. Whereas I have found the intelligent can be persuaded to deal with the world as it is on some level of reality."

"She's intelligent," Antonius said.

"Obviously," Otho said. "She was intelligent enough to pick you as a chamberlain. And you and she obviously know what you get for nothing is . . ."

"Yes," Antonius sighed and finished the sentence for him. "Nothing."

On the high couch, Regeane reclined stiffly next to Maeniel. Her wolf senses were acutely aware of his warm bulk next to her. She felt the healthy heat of his body radiating into the air. She could smell him. Pomade, that would be his hair. Soap and sun-bleached cloth, those would be his wedding garments. A faint tang of wood smoke hung about him. He must have been in the kitchens checking on the food.

They lay parallel to cach other, face to face.

"How's the food?" Regeane asked.

"How did you know?" Maeniel said.

"Charcoal," she answered.

"Ummm," Maeniel said. "Revoltingly ostentatious, but the flavor isn't bad."

"Nice," Regeane said.

"I had to restrain the cook," Maeniel said. "He wanted to pour wine into everything. He used up enough saffron and pepper to dye half of Rome yellow and burn up the stomachs of two-thirds the clergy and people. And you would be able to smell the cinnamon and cloves in Athens if the wind is right. Anything he cooked that had fur, fangs, or feathers on it, he put them back on after he finished cooking it. There's a really magnificent white peacock back there. I think it's dead, but I'm not sure. There's also a wild boar that would be rather frightening if it didn't have an apple in its mouth, a pheasant made of artichokes, and a large artichoke made of pheasant meat. Nothing looks like what it is or tastes like it's supposed to. The whole thing cost an arm and a leg, not to mention a foot and hand they had me throw in behind them. I hope your Roman friends will be happy."

Regeane began giggling helplessly. "Is the cook rented, too, like the villa?"

"Oh, yes," Maeniel said. "Thank God I don't have to take him back to the mountains with me. Up there we dine on simpler fare."

Again, the woodsmoke smell. It seemed part of his skin. She could see him standing beside a small fire at dawn, the rays of light falling through the rising smoky haze. A horse stamped nearby. The air was cool.

In her heart, Regeane knew she was dreaming again. As she

had done when Gundabald had her chained by the neck. And as she had done when she handled the cloth and the necklace. The difference was, she didn't want this dream to end.

He rested one foot on an oaken deadfall. He was wearing a simple green tunic, brown leggings, and boots. He held a leather tankard in his hand. A stirrup cup. He sipped, licked his lips appreciatively, then turned to her. "Will you ride with me, my lady?"

Regeane drifted toward him. "Yes, oh, yes," she whispered.

Men passed on his other side, only just visible in the smoky haze. They led horses, two magnificent beasts—one a blood bay, the other a steel-gray Barb—along with tall strawberry hounds, straining at their leashes.

His eyes rested on her. They possessed her, devoured her. She belonged to him. He would strike at the devil himself if ever the Lord of Hell tried to take her from him.

She paused when she was standing so close to him she could come no nearer. His breath steamed slightly in the cold air. The heat radiating from his body warmed her. She touched his hand, the one that held the cup. "Beer?" she asked.

"No, wine."

"Give me a sip."

He lifted the cup to her lips.

She drank. The taste of such a vintage alone was intoxication, slightly warm, sweet, yet with the tart bite and aroma of green apples. "Ahhh," she sighed.

His free arm stole around her waist. "We will ride higher into the mountains. I know a place just above the clouds, overlooking the whole world. We will stop there and take our ease." His head bent lower and he began kissing the droplets of wine, one by one, from her lips. Oh, so very gently.

She sighed again and slowly, her eyes closed. On the edge of sleep, one dreams of falling. Regeane plummeted and was jerked awake by the shock of fear.

Maeniel laughed. "Am I so dull that I'm putting you to sleep?"

She blushed violently. "No."

His brows lifted. "Oh."

Regeane shifted her weight uneasily on the cushions. The

dress strained against her thigh, for a moment pulling the fabric against her breast and stomach.

Maeniel took a deep breath. His nostrils distended like a nervous stallion's. He looked away abruptly. When he met her eyes again, something new was in his stare. He reached out and lifted the necklace at her throat.

Again, she saw him as he must have been in first youth, sleeping recklessly on the sun-warmed stone, the fair woman at his side combing her long hair. The vision faded and vanished as his hand dropped marginally lower in what was almost, but not quite, a public caress. Regeane remembered Gundabald's insults. "I am told," she stammered, "that I am not well endowed."

"A blatant lie," he said. "You are superb in every way. Fresh as the first wildflowers blooming through the winter snow; clean as mountain air blowing through the high passes; fragrant and delicious as new-mown hay on a hot autumn evening."

His touch still looked casual. It wasn't. His fingers were hot. They moved gently up, crossing her shoulder, then the skin at the nape of her neck. She was particularly sensitive there, she didn't know why, something from the wolf perhaps. At any rate, she quivered slightly at his touch, her knees loosened. She colored, a flush burning in her cheeks. She felt her lips and—yes—another part begin to swell. Not wanting to be embarrassed by showing passion so openly, she bowed her head.

Antonius watched intently. "He looks as though he's ready to eat her alive," he said to his mother.

"Yes," Lucilla replied, "and she looks only too happy to be the main course at his next feast. I hope to God both of them know what they're doing."

"Depend on it, Mother, they don't," he sighed.

"Beautiful," Maeniel said. His hand continued up, stroking her hair. "Simply beautiful."

Regeane realized her forehead was almost resting on his shoulder. He was closer. Trying to break the spell, she said sharply, "You're a connoisseur."

His hand stroked her cheek, reached her chin, and lifted her head. Only a few moments ago, they'd been sitting several feet apart. Now, her face was inches from his. "Beautiful maiden, exquisite maiden," he whispered, "you have absolutely no idea how good my credentials as a connoisseur are." Then he gave her a chaste, brotherly kiss on the forehead and moved away.

Regeane breathed a sigh of relief.

"Am I so importunate?" Maeniel asked.

"No," Regeane said softly. "I think my mind is corrupted by a sensual madness I have never felt before. I feel guilty and fear what others might see."

"Ah," Maeniel said. He lifted his hand in a wholly artificial gesture of profound grief and pressed the back to his forehead. "What? Is there a stain of shame in your heart?"

"No," Regeane said. "My heart is fine and so are all my other body parts. It's gossip among the Roman aristocracy I fear. You wouldn't believe how fast and far a tale can travel in the mouths of women." She mimicked, " 'Oh, you should have seen them. She couldn't wait to feel his mouth on hers. And he . . . he was no better, undressing her with his eyes before the wedding guests . . . trying to hide his stolen caresses under the guise of politeness . . . disgusting, my dear . . . and in a marriage such as theirs where decorum should be the order of the day.' "

At the tables, Lucilla and Antonius watched them. "Whatever they may or may not understand," she said, "well . . . man is paper, woman fire, and desire a mighty wind. And depend upon it, my son, that wind is blowing here."

Antonius sighed. "Did you take precautions just in case?"

"Of course." Lucilla waved one hand and almost upturned a huge silver urn decorated with grapes, purple and white.

Wax? Antonius thought and he still couldn't tell. Whatever substance composed the grapes, it was not grapes. "The mercenaries?" Antonius asked. "Where are they?"

"Surrounding the villa," Lucilla replied. "In case of . . . accident."

The music became louder and louder. When the waiter appeared and tried to refill Antonius' cup, he covered it with his palm and shook his head. The noise level in the room was increasing. A jug passed surreptitiously among the musicians. They played just slightly out of tune.

Regeane noticed with alarm that a number of people were beginning to wear glassy stares.

Maeniel noticed with alarm that Gavin had managed to cross the room and was now sharing the couch with Augusta. Next to the bride, she was undeniably the most attractive woman in the room. *Oh, no!* he thought. *Whatever men may think about the chastity of barbarians or wolves, Gavin was always on the prowl.*

"Did you buy the wine?" Regeane whispered to Maeniel.

"No, why?"

"There's no telling what they put into it," she said.

"What!" he exclaimed softly. "Put what into it? You mean they put things in it? What things?"

"Opium, wormwood, hemlock, silphum, things like that," Regeane said.

"Christ!" Maeniel said. "Where is that damned food. Maybe if we get some food into them . . ."

The guests, including Maeniel's people, were now looking exceptionally loose. Gavin was whispering into Augusta's ear. She listened with downcast eyes.

Silvia reclined next to Joseph and Gordo. She'd chosen a golden gown, an unfortunate decision. She looked a little like a miniature sun as the glittering folds cast back the lamplight.

Someone goosed Silvia. She bounced into the air with a screech. The couch where she was lying made a cracking sound, creaked, and swayed ominously. Gordo and Joseph managed to look innocent.

"I think the couch is an antique," Regeane said helpfully.

Maeniel scrubbed his face with his hand. "Where is that damned—"

As if on cue, a trumpet yelled fuzzily at the entrance to the dining room. The cooks and servers entered carrying the food.

The first was evidently a wild boar. Its tusks were gilded and the rest of its body appeared to be covered with shiny white enamel, painted with pictures of different culinary herbs.

"What is that?" Regeane asked as it passed her for the first time.

"Hell if I know," Maeniel answered.

The white boar was carried round the horseshoe-shaped table three times while the out-of-tune trumpet continued to bleat like a sick sheep.

Finally Augusta, who had fallen asleep with her head pillowed on Gavin's arm, awakened. She looked around, blinking her way back to consciousness.

The trumpet made a particularly horrible sound.

"Jesus," Augusta shouted. "Somebody kill that thing and put it out of its misery." The rest of the guests gave her suggestion their enthusiastic endorsement and the trumpet was silenced.

Maeniel managed to stop the ornate boar's progress long enough to carve it. It turned out to be a rather complex meat loaf surprise, composed of beef and pork with pockets of fennel, cheese, and liver. The guests fell on it, aided in their gluttony by a pork raisin sauce sweetened by wine lees.

The white peacock entered next, carried by not less than four servers. The trumpeter couldn't resist. The peacock reached the table just as the instrument screeched and gave vent to six, or perhaps, seven sounds that were rather like loud farts.

Augusta looked offended. The rest of the guests thought the sounds hilarious.

Augusta banged her cup on the table. "Shut that fool up," she shouted. "Stick a turd in that horn and put it to sleep. More wine all around. I am dry as the great desert of Arabia."

The wine jugs appeared and made the rounds.

Maeniel looked down at the white peacock. It rested full feathered on a heavy silver platter, its head tucked demurely under one wing.

The four cooks stood before Maeniel and beamed with pride.

"Oh, what a shame," Regeane whispered. "It's so beautiful. It can't taste very good. We would have been better off with roast chicken."

Maeniel heaved an eloquent sigh and gave the bird a tentative poke with the carving knife.

The bird jerked its head out from under its wings and fixed Maeniel with glittering eyes. It didn't look pleased.

The four cooks gawked at it, then turned on each other. "You were supposed to prepare it," they shouted with one voice as they all pointed at each other, then fell to waving their arms wildly and screaming accusations at each other in vulgar street Latin.

The peacock glared wickedly at Maeniel and drew a bead on

his left eye with its narrow beak. He ducked just in time; he felt the sharp beak part his hair.

The big bird wheeled, presenting Regeane and Maeniel with a clear view of its rear. The feather fan opened wide. It gave an absolutely unbelievable cry and hopped to the floor. It exited the triclinium at a stately pace, with all the confident air of a conqueror, the raucous applause of the guests ringing in its ears.

Maeniel looked at the still-wrangling cooks. "Silence!" His voice had the quality of one boulder striking another.

They fell silent in mid-screech.

"Get the rest of the food and serve it before the good sense and reason of my guests is totally obliterated by drink. And I want no more disgusting and undignified noises from that damned horn. And while I do thank you for a new experience, I have never had a dish I tried to fillet, attempt to carve me first. Do not serve me anything else that jumps off the plate and flees when I try to eat it."

The cooks nodded and scurried out. The rest of the food arrived. It was apparent that, except for the peacock now winding its way around the reflecting pool with its spread feathers glowing white in the gloom, the chef had done himself proud.

The giant artichoke proved to be made up of spinach seasoned with bacon, olive oil, and hard-cooked eggs. It was delicious. A hedgehog, made of real artichokes, followed. They were stuffed with bread crumbs seasoned with cheese and a mélange of fresh herbs and dark, spicy olives. They set off the chicken dishes perfectly: tender capon in shaved almonds and almond cream brushed with fresh sage; slow-smoked, pink-fleshed birds laden with bacon in a dark wine sauce, others simmered in red wine, wrapped in pink, salt-cured ham accompanied by melon slices, or breasts of chicken simmered in white wine spiced with saffron and tarragon, the broth filled with Sicilian ribbon dumplings, followed by, in case anyone was still hungry, no less than a dozen suckling pigs perfumed with sage and fennel.

The wines were the crowning event on an evening rich in splendor: there was a flowerlike white, faintly redolent of sweet cecily and lush basil; a red, old, smooth-textured, filled with the complex tastes of smoke drifting up between the vine rows as the harvesters feasted on escargot and oreletans, of long nights in dark cellars, resting while a wind that seemed to rise from the frozen Dolomites stripped the vines in the long fields bare of a last spring frost nipping the tiny green grapes, lending them just enough spice to grace the final harvest. A taste that resonates on the tongue like the orgastic final moment of lovemaking.

Regeane toasted Maeniel with the white over samples of all the chicken dishes. He toasted her with the red over suckling pig cooked in apples and spiced with the juice of Iberian sour oranges.

The guests who had imbibed too freely were slipping into the arms of Morpheus. A few, inspired by Bacchus, went after the bird.

A small group chased the peacock round and round the pool in the peristyle. The bird was slow; the pursuers even slower, being very unsteady on their legs from the wine at dinner. They took turns falling into the reflecting pool and having to be fished out by their comrades. At this juncture, they usually took a break to imbibe more liquid refreshment, just to keep off the cold, you know.

Gavin was bestowing the most elaborate compliments on Augusta. Augusta's husband, Eugenius, was present. He was sober. Every time Gavin began to plant a kiss on one creamy freckled shoulder, Eugenius began to play ostentatiously with the hilt of his dagger. Augusta was blind drunk, well past the point of speech and giggling constantly.

Antonius and Lucilla were stone cold sober, as was Matrona. All three individuals were giving Maeniel and Regeane dark looks.

Maeniel and Regeane were not—sober, that is. They'd reached that ecstatic stage of tipsiness where all women are beautiful and men handsome, where lights burn brighter, music is created by the celestial choir, and all our inhibitions are like cobwebs to a careless hand.

Deep in Regeane's soul the wolf was afraid, but Regeane's woman's mind dismissed her with contempt. The woman was drunk but only partly on wine. Desire was raging in the woman as it never had before. Ah, indeed, what she felt now was beyond mere desire. It was an overwhelming compulsion that burned not only all fear away, but reduced even common sense and reason to pale, dusty ash. She must have this man.

As he looked at her the way the big, gray predator looks at a deer, she was aware he was caught up in the same heedless, mad conflagration as she.

Near the couch where they rested was one where Silvia, Gordo, Joseph, and others rested. Most were unconscious, but Silvia, a gleaming mound in the candlelight, tried to crawl off, presumably the remains of the wine had reached her bladder. The couch gave a loud crack and settled to floor level.

Maeniel's eyes rolled heavenward.

"I hope it wasn't a valuable antique," Regeane said.

"Doesn't matter." Maeniel helped Regeane to her feet. "When the owner of the villa comes to collect damages from me, it will metamorphose into a cherished heirloom belonging to his family since the days of the Caesars, which cannot be replaced by mere precious metals in the form of coin. But, alas, he will continue, in these degenerate days base metal must compensate for beauty, antiquity, and family pride. He will content himself with something, preferably not in plebeian copper, or mercantile silver, but aristocratic gold.

"Ummm," Regeane murmured, as she realized she was being steered away from the banquet hall into an empty room. She stopped and dug in her heels for a second.

"It's all right," he said. "We're married."

The wolf looked at Regeane from her primordial darkness. She seemed concerned. How like her human side to cloud her mind with drugs or drink. Something was wrong. Wrong as it had been the night she feasted with the pope.

Maeniel eased her along, one arm over her shoulder. He was pushing. Away from the braziers in the banquet hall, she could feel the heat rising from his body. He brushed aside a curtain. The sound of rings clattered in Regeane's ears.

Regeane found herself in a room lit only by a single candle set in a sconce. Maeniel closed the curtain with one hand and pulled her to him with the other.

This kiss pulled no punches. His tongue explored her mouth. His arms and hands molded her to his body, her hips against his.

Her breasts tingled and caught fire as they moved against a chest that seemed plated with steel.

At length, he freed her and she came up for air gasping. Yet again, the prickle of uneasiness stirred in her mind.

"Not quite with me, are you?" he gasped as he clutched her against his body. "But come, drink some of this."

Regeane saw a beaker and a silver cup on the table.

"These are precious," Maeniel said, gesturing toward them, "and really old. It is said that Livia, the sister of Augustus Caesar, had them made for her favorite lover and modeled for the female figure herself."

The figures carved into the beaker in low relief showed a man disrobing a woman, kissing her breasts as he eased the tunic down over her hips.

The cup on the outside was encircled by rubies. A deep bloody fire in the darkened room. The bottom of the cup, modeled in high relief, showed the two figures caught up in love's embrace. They were fully joined, but she leaned a little back. His hands caressed her and her face showed the preoccupation of ecstacy.

Regeane and the wolf looked down at the culmination of desire. The room spun as though she were falling. The message the wolf sent was one of deep disquiet. *This will not end as you wish.*

But his arms were around her and her desire was rising again, all the stronger for being briefly quelled.

This kiss was less intense, but his searching hands sought and found places that responded to his caresses with shocks of pleasure.

When he'd drawn a few gasps from her, he released her and filled the cup from the flagon. "Drink," he whispered.

"I don't know," Regeane said. "Do you want your bride unconscious? I've had quite a lot of wine."

"No." His voice was gentle, hypnotic and intoxicating at once. "This is the wine of desire. Spring mead. In spring the bees feed on white poppies blown by March winds. The first fragrant myrtle, wildflowers that dazzle meadows still draped in snow. The wine of love. And it is bestowed on lovers alone."

Regeane drank. The mead was an inexpressibly sweet essence

of springtime. A liquid dissolving on her tongue. A tingling beginning with her heart and radiating out to the tips of her fingers. Her fears slept. Her consciousness was drenched with desire and had room for nothing else.

He kissed her again. She tasted the mead on his lips.

He lifted her chin with one finger. "Whose are you?" he asked.

"Yours."

"Take off the dress," he said.

She did, pulling it over her head and throwing it aside, thinking, *We are never going to reach the bedroom. But who cares . . .* She wore a linen shift.

He kissed her again. Parts of her body were almost numbed by pleasure and when his fingers brushed them through the shift, they felt as though they burst into flame. She wanted him in a way that was unbearable, simply unbearable. She would die if he did not possess her.

"Will you do anything I want you to do?" he teased.

"Yes."

"The shift."

In a second, the shift was on the floor. She was still clad in a sleeveless silk undershift, the strophium at her breast and linen loin cloth.

He reached up under the shift. The strip between her legs fell. His hand moved up. The shift rose with it. He looked down at the soft, curly delta of Venus. She blushed. He could feel the heat against his skin.

He pushed the shift higher and loosened the strophium at her breasts. It fluttered to the floor. Then he let the shift fall and caressed her body through the silken fabric.

"Are you drunk?" he asked.

"Yes."

"Are you virgin?"

"Yes." Her answer was an indrawn breath.

"Do you know what a man's organ is?"

She nodded and noticed he'd spread his mantle and outer tunic on the long table.

"Very well," he said. "You understand what I'm about to do with mine."

"Ohooo."

"At this juncture, I'll take that as a yes."

His hands had continued their explorations. As he spoke, Regeane felt lost in a garden of rare delights, except that he was plucking the flowers. Slowly, that part of her, the spirit that whispered of the ancient past and sometimes the dim future sent an image to her mind.

She was standing with him. They were knee-deep in a mountain lake. The lake was a place of wild beauty, bounded by pines and thickets of fern and pink roses. A narrow falls dropped from high-back rock, dotted with green-gray lichen and moss. Mist from the froth at its base dampened her lips and frosted her eyelashes.

Their bodies were joined deeply, almost painfully. She was possessed by the man whose arms were around her.

His body was wet. He wore a crown of yellow-flowering water weed. His shoulders and arms were netted with another bearing white, scented flowers. *What was he?* she wondered. She remembered the tales of maidens ravished by gods who demanded adoration as well as love, and absolute possession of spirit as well as body. Was she not one of those maidens and was he not some sort of god? How does mortal flesh bear immortal fire?

He moved and waves of mind-bending pleasure coursed through her. He moved again. Thought was wiped out. Also, memory. Everything dissolved into the power of what flesh was doing to flesh.

She returned to the darkened room. She rested quietly in his arms. That had been a memory? Dream? The future? No matter. It wasn't real, but this would be.

He pulled off the shift over her head. She was naked.

"You know what I'm about to do?" he repeated.

"Yes." Her whole body shuddered. The confining shift off, she spread her legs to receive him. "I think I'll die if you don't," she said ingenuously.

"So be it," he said, and began lifting her to the table top.

The knife glittered in the air over his shoulder.

Deep in Regeane's soul, the wolf roared a warning. Desire died. Her left hand shot out and caught the wrist of the man holding the knife. The man tried to tear her grip from his wrist. But she was, after all, not a mortal woman. He looked shocked for a split second at the pain she was inflicting. Then he jerked his arm down and, using Maeniel's shoulder as a fulcrum, he tore his arm free.

Maeniel thrust Regeane away, then turned, whipping around with the speed of a striking snake. The assassin's knife scored a gash in his shoulder.

Antonius threw back the curtain, torch in one hand, a Roman short sword in the other. Antonius drove the sword in just below and up under the man's shoulder blade, paralyzing his right arm.

But Maeniel saw the stiletto in his left hand, aimed and rising toward his heart. He stepped in boldly and, catching his attacker by the shoulder and jaw, twisted his head hard right. The killer's neck snapped.

The sound was a wet one. *Like a green twig,* Regeane thought. When Maeniel flung her away, her head had cracked against the table and, for a moment, her body was numbed. The wolf tried forcefully to take her, but the torch in Antonius' hand quelled her. She watched as the assassin fell bonelessly to the floor, dead before his skull cracked on the marble tiles.

"Goddamn it, you killed him," Antonius shouted.

"No choice," Maeniel said, pointing to the deadly stiletto.

Regeane pulled herself to her feet with one hand while feeling for a scalp wound with the other.

Lucilla ran into the room. She grasped at the curtain for support. It tore. She fell forward, but Maeniel caught her and returned her to an upright position. She stood and stared down at the assassin. "My goodness," she said, "Petrus."

"You know him," Maeniel said very, very softly. In that softness crouched almost infinite menace.

Antonius replied by thrusting his mantle at Regeane. "Woman! You're naked! Cover yourself."

Regeane snatched the mantle and wrapped it around her body. Then she hurriedly began gathering up her clothing from the floor.

The few remaining sober guests converged on the doorway.

"Mother knows a lot of people. Some of them are even

quite respectable—some are not," Antonius said trenchantly to Maeniel.

Regeane slipped into another room. It was very dark, but she could see enough to tell that it was a small storage closet. One small barred window let in the cold night air.

She remembered a story from the Bible. In Genesis, once the grace of God is withdrawn, nakedness is accompanied by shame. This was true. She had gloried in her nakedness with Maeniel. She had felt clothed, glowing with desire. Her fears and inhibitions dissolved at his touch.

The wolf was silent, gazing at the vast spill of stars through the barred window, a dusting of light across the dead black sky.

She remembered the gray one and the clean mountain wind. She remembered Maeniel's frozen features—the death's-head grin as he bared his teeth and struck his enemy down. Attractive as the thought of loving him might be to her hot and pulsing body, the night, the wolf, and her cold, incisive human reason told her it would be folly to trust him with her secret. She had just seen him kill a man with his bare hands.

He led his band of ruffians not by any right, human or divine, but because he was the strongest and could quell revolt with fist and sword. They respected him not because he was best, but because he was worst among them. Sooner or later the she-wolf would have to fight for her life.

So . . . now . . . she felt no desire. Only the cold, flesh-piercing wind through the open window and shame, deep shame and vulnerability at her nakedness. She was indeed that naked and alone.

Suddenly, beyond the door she heard a woman scream.

XXXI

REGEANE WOKE. SHE WAS LYING ON ONE OF THE couches in the triclinium, wearing a soft linen robe. Her head ached. She reached up and found a very tender spot on the left side of her head. She turned to sit up and realized the room was strewn with dead men.

One lay across the table, his throat cut. Another was lying in the doorway of the triclinium, his head in a pool of blood. Another lay across the musicians' fallen chairs, a spear through his body.

The wolf brought Regeane to her feet immediately. *How long had she been unconscious?* Not long. The first gray dawn was filling the peristyle garden outside. She had to find out what had happened before she created a disturbance.

She stumbled from the triclinium into the room where she and Maeniel had their moment of passion. It was empty.

Just ahead was another curtained doorway. She pushed through it and found herself in a narrow Roman bedroom. A mirror rested on a small vanity table near the bed. She picked up the mirror and looked into it. Her features were blurred both by the mirror's age and the dim light, but her eyes were clear. Her hair was free of blood and there remained only a small swelling on the side of her face.

As she looked, her features blurred again. It seemed as though she smelled smoke. The eyes in the mirror looked back at her through a veil of blowing flame, then smoke obscured them. The metal grew hot in her hand.

She still had the presence of mind to turn and fling the mirror facedown on the bed.

She spun around, realizing that someone was watching her.

The room had, as was the custom in most Roman homes, two doors, one leading into another room and the other to the peristyle.

Matrona was standing in the door to the garden.

"What happened?" Regeane asked.

"Many things," Matrona replied, "none of them good. Basil's men attacked right after you went into the other room to dress. Like a fool, you opened the door at the sound of Lucilla's scream. You were clubbed down. You must have a very hard head. At first, we thought you were killed, but we were too busy trying to defend ourselves to help you."

"You appear to have been successful," Regeane said.

"Even so." Matrona said. "What did you see in the mirror?" Matrona's eyes were pools of darkness. She seemed to look at Regeane out of infinite time.

"My face," Regeane said.

"Oh, no," Matrona chuckled. "You saw more than your face. I know, because that is my mirror and it once belonged to a princess of the great people who lived here long before the Romans made the Tiber stink: they of the painted tombs. Tell me, what did you see? If you tell me, I can help you."

Regeane's mouth was dry. "I saw only my face," she insisted.

"As you wish," Matrona replied with another shrug. Then she moved very close to Regeane and examined the bruise on her temple. "Nothing much," was her judgment. "The way the soldier hit you, the way you fell, I had thought you much more severely injured."

"Well," Regeane said. "I'm not. Where is Antonius?"

"Outside with my lord."

Regeane pushed past her and out to the garden.

Matrona walked over to the bed. She picked up the mirror and gazed down into it. After a few seconds, her brow furrowed and an expression of great sadness crossed her face. Then she placed the mirror face down on her toilet table.

A fine-boned and beautiful goddess decorated the back. She rested in a chair, scroll on her lap while a boy capered before her, playing the double flute. Matrona's fingers brushed the delicately etched mirror back. "Goddess, queen of the heaven they called you once," she said. "Now I can no longer remember your name."

REGEANE FOUND ANTONIUS AND MAENIEL TOgether. The clothing of both men was torn and bloodied. Antonius had a bandage on his arm. Maeniel looked surprised to see her. Antonius didn't.

"My lady," Maeniel said with a bow, "we had thought you badly injured. We were just discussing a way to find a physician for you." He looked a bit baffled and at a loss, to see her so seemingly uninjured.

A hint of dawn breeze tugged at Regeane's long gray gown. They stood near the statue of some god Regeane couldn't identify. It was beautiful, but had one missing arm. *Presumably,* Regeane thought, *the one holding his ritual insignia.* The deity's face was one of androgynous beauty. His head lifted to gaze into the brightening sky in the east.

Regeane felt a tightening in her belly muscles. They quivered. At the same time she felt a dreadful certainty. An assurance that when this now-dawning day was ended, many matters would be settled forever.

"Today is the day the synod meets, isn't it?" she asked Antonius.

"Yes," he answered.

"Why is this so crucial?" Maeniel asked.

"It is a day of decision for not only the people of Rome, but for the surrounding great magnates," Antonius explained. "Desiderius, the Lombard king, has long wished to control the papacy so that he may use it against his enemy Charlemagne. He would unseat this pope and elect a Lombard prelate, one who would do his bidding and declare Charlemagne a usurper.

"The people of Rome and the magnates, the great lords, and landholders surrounding Rome must now choose between Desiderius, the Lombard king, or Charlemagne and the Franks. What's more of a certainty is that Desiderius will destroy this narrow state that still belongs to the pope and the people of Rome. He would absorb it into the Lombard duchy and make the pope's vicars of Christ his court chaplains. Not a desirable thing from Charlemagne's point of view, or ours. Living as we do in this tiny remnant of what once was the greatest empire on earth."

He stopped speaking. They stood quietly. Antonius could be devious, he could bandy half-truths, he could tell an outright lie and confront his listener with bland innocence, but both Regeane and Maeniel were moved at this moment by his utter sincerity. And they knew this man spoke the truth as he understood it.

Then, to Regeane and Maeniel's surprise, he burst into tears. "They've taken Mother and I'm sure they're torturing her now."

"Oh, God," Regeane said as she embraced him. "Why?"

Maeniel answered. "We believe, Antonius and I, that she gave the task of . . . shall we say . . . removing your uncle to Petrus. It seems he heretofore often performed these little tasks for her. Antonius believes he was bribed into Basil and Desiderius' service by a larger sum of money."

Regeane whispered the filthiest Frankish obscenity she knew under her breath. "I knew I gave them too much money."

"No," Maeniel corrected her. "I can't think they bought him with your money. We believe your uncle must have despaired of controlling you and practicing extortion on me, and made common cause with Basil and the Lombard king. The purpose of the raid was to kidnap you and Lucilla. It seems Lucilla has already been accused of being a practitioner of the black arts. Of having put the pope in the Chair of Peter by dealing with the foul fiend, the enemy of man."

"What . . ." Regeane started to ask about the leprosy charge, but Antonius dried his eyes quickly and gave her a warning glance. She stepped away from him. Propriety didn't allow even a great lady familiarity with any man other than her husband.

Maeniel studied them both—his expression opaque. "But then, the charge doesn't matter, does it?" he asked. "Only that it be a sufficient excuse to destroy Hadrian. In fact, that's why the Frankish king sent Count Otho and his men to stiffen the resolve of the Romans, not to repudiate Hadrian."

"Yes," Antonius said, his voice filled with bitter grief. "Mother will say whatever they want, whatever is most convenient for them. And it remains to be seen if the Romans stand behind Hadrian or not."

"You are going to the synod, aren't you?" Regeane asked.

"Yes," Antonius said. "When they produce Mother, my friends and I will try to free her from Basil's clutches, whatever she may say and whatever her condition. But what I want you to do is take Regeane and flee. If you ride now, you can be at Ostia by nightfall. You have enough gold to procure a barque that will return you to Franca. You can sit safely in your mountains in a few weeks."

Regeane stepped away from the two men. The light was brighter, but a thick mist filled the garden with a pale haze and obscured the rising sun. "No," she said. "I'm not leaving. You and your mother have been friends to me. More than friends, givers of wise counsel and protection. I have been able to help before and maybe I can be of service in this extremity. I will not go."

Unspoken words hung in the air between them. She was Maeniel's wife now. The contract was signed. They had been alone together. Consummation could be argued.

Antonius spoke the words. "Use force."

Regeane didn't defy them. She answered very simply, "It won't work."

Maeniel looked down at his hands. They were the big, strong paws of a fighting man, large, thick-fingered, and muscular. Last night he'd broken a large man's neck with them. He looked up. "Force, no!" he said. "Somehow I don't think the lady would respect my force any more than she respected her uncle's and cousin's. I will not take an enemy to my bed, or stare at her across the supper table. Besides, I share the decision of my lady's mind. I pledged my loyalty to the king of Franca, Charles, so-called Charlemagne. My word is my bond. Even if it is given to an insect like Count Otho. I will support Charles' candidate for the papacy. And, as Charles' liege man, I will not desert him in time of need."

Regeane remembered her fears last night about Maeniel. Fears that he was a freebooter, an unprincipled brigand. She saw now these fears were false ones. She stretched out her hand to him. "I see my lord is a man of honor. I hope he will be so in his dealings with me."

He took her hand and saw in her eyes a look of almost mad desperation. "I hope—I believe—I am—as you describe me in all things, my lady," he said as he lifted her hand to his lips and kissed her fingers.

Antonius dried his tears with his mantle. "Mad . . . mad . . . mad barbarians," he whispered.

Matrona spoke from behind Regeane. "I will find you another dress. Go and bathe. The one you're wearing belongs to Silvia. You might as well be in a tent. Come. There are baths here for women and men. I've paid the servants. They are heating the water." She clapped her hands. "Attend me. Do as I say. The bishops and cardinal priests are now filing into the choir at the Lateran. Mass is about to begin. We must make haste. The synod is about to be convened."

Regeane and Antonius hurried away. Maeniel turned to follow.

"Wait," Matrona said. "I want to talk to you."

Maeniel raised one brow. "What?"

"Come," Matrona commanded. "Follow me. What I know now is too important to be left to chance."

She led him to the place where he had nearly been killed. The assassin was lying on the floor where he fell. The room was flooded with light now. The curtain was torn and there was a glass-covered opening in the ceiling. She bent down near the assassin and lifted the dead man's right arm. She showed Maeniel the wrist Regeane had seized to save his life. The hand flopped.

"The bones are broken," Maeniel said, astonished.

"One is, one is not," Matrona said, "but the tendons are torn. No common woman seized him. She saved your life. The reason there is not more bruising is because he died very quickly and did not bleed. Had any ordinary woman reached over your shoulder and tried to stop the killer, he would have broken her grip and possibly some of her fingers and buried his knife in your back."

Maeniel knelt facing her. "Then . . . what?" he asked.

"She is the silver one," Matrona said.

He quickly rose to his feet. "No," he said.

Matrona grunted cynically and stood. She walked toward the garden. Maeniel followed. "I hear from Gavin that you think you are old because you have seen a few Caesars," she said.

When they were outside, she sat down on a bench near the pool and gazed out over the still water. There were patches of blue in it as the haze was broken by the new sun. Turquoise sky, white clouds and gray chased themselves by in the still water.

"Before the gods that made the gods was I," Matrona said. "I cannot tell you of what an age I am because when I was born, we did not put the four seasons into a year. Every winter was a kind of death to us and we mourned the passing of life and beauty. We awaited every spring with bated breath—we were afraid it might not come—and when it did, we were mad with rejoicing at the world's rebirth.

"I sojourned long with my people. I rode the hollow ships when we came to Greece across the sunlit, wine-dark sea. I sat by the hearth in a smoky hall and heard a blind singer call the fair, blue water that. I cast oracles for the Latins at the time they freed themselves from the people of the painted tombs. Those old Romans loved and feared my skin-turning powers. In the end, fear prevailed. I was driven out with flaming brands and curses.

"I found another people in the mountains. That sword—the gladius Antonius carries—I saw its shape first when the Roman legions crossed the mountains into Gaul. I saw the troops through the blowing snow. Chased the invaders along and away from my people with my voice. And fed when the killers lost their way and perished in the cold." She smiled grimly.

"What happened to your people?"

Matrona shrugged. "They were like the rest. Men cannot accept the sovereignty of the beast. They will not believe they are our kin. They will not believe we spring from the same root, and are part of the same tree, and when that tree falls, we will both perish. My people were happy and free. I led them to high meadows, into valleys where I knew the Romans would never come. But they were not content. They dreamed of Roman gold, of Roman luxury. Dishes and drinking vessels of silver and gold. Red wine and white. Soft, fair women, clothed in velvet and silk. At first the Romans bribed, then conquered them. And again I was alone.

"I don't say these things to boast or win sympathy. Only that you be aware I know many things. The girl is one of us. None but one of us could have crushed that man's wrist. I saw her look into my mirror. I cannot say what she beheld, but she was able to do as I do. We use it to see into the world beyond. I repeat, she is one of us."

"I don't . . ." Maeniel began.

"Big, gray wolf," she said, "don't trouble me with your skepticism. Now at least you know how you appeared to Gavin. You will need carriages to ride to the Lateran. I must see to harnessing the mules." So saying, she strode off to the stables.

Maeniel stood looking after Matrona quietly. What she said explained a lot about both Regeane and herself. He had long known her for one of the strongest, most dependable of his band. If she had, in truth, seen the dawning of the world, it would explain her strength and iron will. Both she and he had endured through time.

Matrona was as good as her word. When Regeane entered the peristyle garden, a mule litter waited at the iron-barred gate. She paused beside him. Matrona had found an old, but respectable cloth-of-gold dress. She wore a silken shift under it. Her face was almost as white as the cloth. "My lord." She bowed her head slightly.

"My lady," he replied, bringing her hand to his lips. He remembered the silver one floating over the grass, her fur glowing with the icy sheen of precious metal set off by the bold, black highlights at the ruff, the belly, and the inner legs.

God, she was beautiful in both guises. After he had kissed the tips of her fingers he lingered, playing with the soft hand. He remembered the assassin's crushed wrist. If Matrona was right, she'd saved his life.

He and Matrona might age more slowly than mortal humans, but age they did. And, moreover, had the knife found his heart before he could flee into the change, he would die as quickly and as finally as any man.

She withdrew her hand gently, but firmly, from his. "I must

leave, but I thank you for everything." She hesitated. "I am of Antonius' mind. Go to your mountains. Be free."

"Life is but coin for the spending," he replied softly. "We are not gifted with breath, our faces are not turned to the beauty of the world . . . that we may cringe and hide from its pain and difficulty. We gaze upon beauty and ugliness alike and do not fault or criticize the giver. I am at your command. I, and my men, will ride with you and Antonius, as your escorts."

"Be careful," Regeane said. "I will take you at your word."

He bowed and ushered her toward the gate and her carriage.

MAENIEL LED THE FOUR WHITE MULES THAT DREW the vehicle, being careful to keep the pace comfortable for the woman inside.

Gavin rode beside him. He pelted Maeniel with accusations, entreaties, warnings, dire threats, and at last, pleas. "Are you out of your mind? Is your brain invaded by maggots? Have you taken leave of your senses? My God, think what you're doing! This Frankish girl could get you killed!" He continued to harangue Maeniel until they reached the Lateran.

Maeniel listened. He despaired of making Gavin understand. He had searched for this girl for a thousand years, and in an instant, he might lose her.

"You have never loved a human woman before," Gavin growled.

"Have I?" Maeniel said. "Have I not? If not one, a thousand, and they are dust. All . . . all dust."

There were those before I was captured as a man, he thought. *They have no names.* But the rest. My God, each was a spot of guilt on his soul. A place of pain from which his mind turned.

Morgana, ugly, but desire incarnate. Creamy freckled skin, large jutting breasts, a generous mouth always ready to laugh or kiss. Wide, giving hips. Hair of fire.

Guinevere. He still challenged men like Gavin who spoke ill of her. Maeniel shivered and looked up at the broken cloud sweeping across the sky. Sometimes the vessel of the flesh is too frail for the spirit poured into it. Her body was nothing but a fragile lamp for a fire too bright for a mortal shell. When they laid her on the pyre, stars fell from heaven, flashing against the midnight black empyrean. The heavens themselves mourned her.

"Oh, yes," he said to Gavin. "I have loved women. And paid the forfeit of my loving. Now, they are dust. And if I enumerated even a few of them, I would unman myself."

He halted the carriage on one of the side streets near the Lateran. The square was crowded. People were pushing in around the church steps. Maeniel turned to Gavin. "Are you ready to obey me?"

Gavin looked both despairing and disgusted at the same time. "Of course, and give my life for you." He dismounted.

Regeane pretended not to notice anything.

"My lady," Maeniel said as he handed her from the litter.

Gavin, standing right behind him, snarled, "My lady, my ass."

A second later, Gavin was sprawled on the cobbles, staring up at the sky and then at Maeniel's and Regeane's retreating backs. He wasn't sure quite how it had happened.

Matrona helped him to his feet. She didn't laugh at him. "May happen you're right," she said. "We may be walking into disaster." The massive Joseph and Gordo stood next to her. "But for the moment, we are one." Then they swept forward and surrounded Regeane and Maeniel as they tried to force their way to the Lateran steps. "It is the law," Matrona said. "He leads, we follow . . . into the fight."

Regeane saw Maeniel's people come up. Facing such a mass of armed men, and, she saw with some shock, women, the crowd parted easily. In a few seconds, they stood in the square in front of the church. The crowd left the open space in the center empty. The papal guard blocked entrance to the church doors. Antonius, dressed in white, waited with the pope's men-at-arms.

In his unbleached linen and wool, he looked like an ancient Roman. But he wore no toga, only a thick mantle and tunic. A heavy gold belt pulled it in at the waist and another heavy gold chain was around his neck.

At his signal, the pope's men opened the bronze doors for them. People stepped aside quickly to let them enter, crowded away from them in fact.

"The word is out," Antonius muttered. "There will be some hideous accusation against all of us before this is finished."

On the altar, mass was ending. The high wooden choir stalls running lengthwise against the church walls held the bishops and cardinal priests of the city. The great nobles filled the center of the church.

They and their wives were a rainbow of color to Regeane's eyes. She had not known so many rich fabrics existed—silk shot with brocade, cloth of gold striped with cloth of silver. The colors sang. Blues, warm as a summer sky, contrasted with the silken sheen of a winter midnight. Scarlet, rich as a rose's heart, shaded away into imperial purple, delicate spring violet, or crystalline amethyst. A feast set off by flashes of green and gold, each and all vied for the eye's attention. Jewels glittered around necks, arms, hands. Veils of silk, linen, and lace covered women's heads.

This glittering throng was the pope's supporters, judges, and friends. These were as much papal electors as the priests ringing the church. They stood to suffer most if the pope's Frankish policy failed. And had the most to gain if it succeeded.

Regeane looked up and realized the roof of the Lateran church was fitted with panels of frosted glass. She and the glowing throng were bathed in warm, blue-tinged light.

The space near the altar was clear. The white marble floor was lightly dappled with color from the stained-glass windows in the walls, and faint watery blue from the skylight.

Regeane glanced at the faces ringing the altar.

Gundabald and Hugo were there. She snorted slightly in derision. She'd told them to bathe, and it looked as if they might have. Their hair and beards were trimmed and glistened with what might be pomade. The garb they wore looked newly purchased and amazingly clean. Silve hung on Hugo's arm. She wore a clean blue velvet dress, a smirk, and a wedding ring.

Regeane let out a whoop that she tried to turn into a cough. Hugo knew she was laughing at him. He went scarlet. But Gundabald studied her with a really frightening glower of hatred. Near them stood Basil with a large contingent of fighting men. Gundabald's stare said as clearly as if he had spoken,

You'll laugh out of the other side of your mouth soon enough.
Regeane's laugh ended in a shiver of fear.

Barbara and Emilia were present with Elfgifa. When the
child saw Regeane, she tried to break away and run to her, but
Barbara and Emilia both had fast hold of her hands. At length,
she was persuaded to obey them. Near them, among the nuns,
stood the old woman from the lodging house. She held the hand
of a very scrubbed-looking small boy. Regeane recognized
Postumous and felt a thrill of surprise knowing the one she'd always thought of as the old woman must be Postumous' mother.

Even Cecelia was present, though heavily veiled. Rufus stood
with a large contingent of his men on Regeane's side of the
church. He was accompanied not only by fighting men, but by
other nobles who apparently were his liege men. Regeane had
not known he was so powerful. Near him and apparently under
his protection stood many of Lucilla's maids. Regeane recognized Fausta and Susanna among them.

On the altar the mass ended. Hadrian's acolytes removed his
vestments, leaving him wearing only the simple white that is
the prerogative of the Vicar of Christ. He stepped forward from
the candlelit sanctuary into the clear light from the cathedral
ceiling.

Basil pushed his way from among the contingent of armed
men near Gundabald and Hugo. He was as splendidly dressed
as any of the nobles, but the black and gold tunic he wore covered mail. His helmet was under his arm. His sword at his side.
He raised his arm and pointed an accusatory finger at Hadrian.
"False priest, you are pope, not by the election of good Christian men, but placed in power by the evil one himself. You are
the Devil's minion and his power seated you in most blasphe-
mous fashion in the chair of Peter."

The church was hushed.

"Where is she, Basil?" Hadrian asked.

Regeane could see Basil was taken aback. She heard a
scuffling of feet. Men of the papal guard entered the basilica at a
dead run, filling the side aisles and pushing people away from
the entrance. They shot a huge iron bolt across the immense
bronze portals.

A ripple of fear ran through the crowd of magnates that filled the church. Even the nuns huddled together more tightly. A few made the sign of the Cross, but Barbara simply sighed. Elfgifa, trying to take it all in, was bright-eyed with excitement. Not the adults, however. Almost all of them looked frightened.

"Where is she?" Hadrian repeated. The quiet fury in his voice was sufficient to quell a riot. *Only a pope or a king can sound that way,* Regeane thought. For the first time since she'd known him, Basil looked frightened.

"You are inches from death, Basil," Hadrian continued. "Where is she?"

Basil looked around wildly. He might have many more of his supporters in the square, but inside the church, they were well outnumbered by the pope's men. He had been very neatly mousetrapped by Hadrian.

On her left, Regeane felt a stirring. Antonius was moving aside his mantle ever so surreptitiously so that he could reach the sword in his belt. Maeniel on her right, was doing the same. Both men moved closer to her. All over the church Regeane could see similar stirrings among the men of the warrior class.

"She confessed," Basil shouted.

"Basil," Hadrian replied, "given sufficient inducement, almost anyone will confess to anything. I want her here now. Produce her forthwith."

Regeane heard a succession of snapping sounds and a gasp of absolute horror around her.

Maeniel seized her. He dropped to the floor and arched his body over hers. She lifted her head and looked out past his arm. The men of the papal guard had archers among them. The popping sounds had been the noise of the compound bows being drawn. Most of the men had emulated Maeniel, diving for the floor and taking their women with them.

Basil and his men were still standing.

"That's it," Hadrian said. "Stay where you are, Basil. If you drop to the floor, my men will take it as a signal to fire."

Basil beckoned to one of his men. When the soldier approached him, Basil spoke quickly into his ear. Both Basil and the soldier glanced at Hadrian.

Hadrian nodded. The soldier ran out of the church through the vestry.

Boom! Boom! Boom!

Regeane had forgotten the bishops and cardinal priests of the city. They had been sitting quietly in their choir along the walls of the basilica. Since the wooden seats were elevated, they could see over the heads of the crowd. They were not menaced by the pope's soldiers who stood in front of the choir seats with their backs to the prelates.

Boom! Boom! Boom!

Regeane twisted under Maeniel, but shifted his bulk only slightly. "What's that noise? Let me up. I'm suffocating. I can't see what's going on."

Maeniel chuckled and raised his body slightly.

Boom! Boom! Boom!

"What is it?" she asked again.

"Hush," Antonius answered. "It's one of the bishops. He's unhappy with Hadrian's high-handedness. He's pounding his crozier against the floor of the choir stalls."

"What's going to happen?" Maeniel asked.

"Nothing," Antonius said, "unless the others join him."

As quickly as Antonius spoke, they did, and the entire basilica resounded with crashing booms as the rest made their opinion felt.

Antonius said, "Shit."

"Not a good development, I take it," Maeniel said.

Hadrian lifted his left hand in signal to the archers. The bows were lowered. Their strings loosened gradually. The booming died away.

The notables in the center of the church began rising to their feet, breathing prayers of thanksgiving.

Basil's men who had been bunched into a tight group, each man competing for a spot behind someone else, relaxed, spread out, and gave each other room.

Basil's face began to show some color. "We have proof," he screamed.

"Proof!" someone shouted. "Hell, death, and damnation! I have been this day frightened out of my five senses and few wits. Proof of what, I ask you? What crime has been committed by His Holiness?" The speaker stepped forward and Regeane saw Rufus, Cecelia's Rufus. His face was scarlet with fury.

Basil beckoned to . . . Gundabald!

Gundabald walked slowly to the central space between Hadrian and Basil. He stopped and pointed a finger at Regeane. "There she stands. The daughter of the evil one himself."

His arm dropped. "It is said," he continued, "that the demon may appear as an angel of light. So did he to my poor sister, Gisela. He seduced her with his store of gold, his bodily beauty. He pretended to wed her . . . to hold her in honorable marriage." Gundabald lifted his arm again and pointed to Regeane.

"He got this hell-spawn child on her." His arm fell again and he turned to the Roman notables. "Luckily, we got my sister away from this visitor from the realms of darkness. But we found to our horror she was with child."

Regeane felt the harsh movement of air in and out of her lungs. Her lips, face, and fingers were numb. She hadn't known she could feel as much fear as she felt this moment. The church was absolutely silent. They were hanging on Gundabald's every word.

"Alas," he said, "my sister was a saint. We told her to strangle such a babe at birth. Send it hence to join the legions of the damned. But to her eternal sorrow, she didn't. Instead, she wore out her life in penances, weeping for her sins, trying to redeem . . ." His voice rose. He looked and pointed at Regeane again. ". . . this daughter of darkness. She has powers," he roared, his voice echoing under the roof. "She can walk on two feet or run on four. No lock or bolt can hold her. By night she can be as mist, joining in the airish vapors to escape through a shuttered window or under a door. She can wear the semblance of a bat and fly to and from the gates of hell. She can wear the semblance of a wolf and couple lasciviously with either man or beast. The very night her mother died, she ran four-footed and took her bestial lovers—as many as wanted her—by moonlight."

Sister Angelica stood among the nuns. She screamed an ear piercing yell that rattled the roof tiles, and then she had hysterics. "I knew it!" she bellowed. "I knew it when the girl saw Hildegard. The dead are as the living to her. The little demoness is one with the foulness of the grave. Send her hence. She belongs not with the living."

Gundabald walked over to where Regeane stood and stopped just out of arm's reach. He looked almost as if he might be sober. The whites of his eyes were yellow, but no longer a web-work of broken blood vessels. He studied her with grim satisfaction. "You're dead, my girl," he said quietly. "Dead before the sun sets this day." Then he walked back to Basil.

Basil stepped forward and joined Gundabald. "Antonius!" he shouted. "Come forth."

Antonius moved out into the center of the floor, hand on his sword hilt.

Basil eyed him fearfully. "Antonius . . . you should be . . . dead. The last time I saw you, you stank of the grave. Your face was so eaten away, you . . . must cover it, lest even strong men turn from you in horror. Your hands were claws, the bones pushed through your skin. The devil's mark was on you. All in this room know you were doomed—rotting, while yet alive." Basil turned toward the crowd of notables behind him. "All here know, I tell you." His voice rose to a shriek. "You know . . . None of you can contradict me. None of you would dare lie, not while you stand before the altar of God. You know."

No one in the crowd spoke, but none would meet his eyes, either.

Basil turned back again. This time to confront Hadrian. "Now . . . now I see him. He stands before me . . . a healthy man in the prime of life. When not a month ago, he carried the marks of God's curse . . . on you for trafficking with a harlot, a witch, and—" Basil pointed to Antonius. "—a sorcerer.

"This girl, who her own kin repudiate . . . this girl dressed in silk and cloth of gold . . . is no saint with a healing touch. What damned and damnable spawn of darkness did she summon to pull your minion back from the brink of nothingness? To wield such foul power, she must indeed stand close to the throne of hell. And you—" Basil's voice was a roar. "You must be sworn liege man to the king of devils, else he would not have sent you such a servant."

Everyone was silent as Basil stalked back to rejoin his men.

"Nonsense," Antonius said loudly. "Nonsense," he repeated more loudly. "None can look on this sweet virgin's face—" He gestured toward Regeane. "—and believe she is less than an innocent, virtuous maid."

Basil shouted, "The eternal enemy of man can appear to those he would deceive . . . as an angel of light."

Antonius shot back, "I can well believe you are an expert on the diabolic, Basil. The ancient lords of the pit are bosom friends, if not near kin to you."

"Enough," Hadrian intervened. "I can well believe something strange has happened here. These accusations are very disturbing. Some explanation must be offered . . ."

He didn't get a chance to finish his speech because three men entered through the vestry. They were half leading, half carrying someone wrapped in a black robe with a hood. Even as far away as she was, Regeane could smell blood. Old blood, thick and rotten, the raw meat stench of fresh blood and, worst of all, burned flesh.

Lucilla, Regeane thought.

Sister Angelica began wailing. She was not as loud. There was no way a mere woman could fill the gigantic church with noise, but there was a stirring among the great nobles. Men cursed and women wept.

The group carrying Lucilla stopped. The only thing keeping her upright was the grip of the men holding her. When they let go of her, she slid slowly to the floor. The robe covered her body, the hood her face. The soldiers drew away from her and joined the rest of Basil's men.

She lay in the open space before the altar, looking like a small pool of black ink against the pale marble caught in the strange, blue light from above.

Hadrian stood on the sanctuary steps gazing down at the figure before him, his fists clenching and unclenching, a man not wanting to look at what, sooner or later, he must see.

As Regeane watched, it began to struggle. One bloody hand was thrust from the robe; raw patches oozed where the nails had been. It scrabbled for purchase on the slippery marble. The dark figure seemed to be trying to turn on its side.

The crowd drew back with a collective gasp of horror, drawing away from the broken Lucilla as they might have from a dog with its back shattered by a wagon wheel, but still moving, eyes begging, needing to be killed.

Regeane felt a terrible loneliness. The wolf's memories stirred in her mind. She saw a wolf hanged on a gallows like a man. Another tethered, a bonfire built over his body, and burned alive. And yet another roped by two horsemen and torn asunder as they rode in different directions.

The cruelties humans practice on each other are echoed in the ferocity of their behavior to those—God's innocents—the beasts.

"No." Maeniel gripped her arm. "When those doors open, we're out of here. My men and I will ride for Ostia. We will kill anyone who tries to stop us. In a week, we'll be in the mountains. Once you sit in my fortress, no one will harm you."

She glanced at him, then at Gavin. He was goggling at her, his mouth open.

"Wolf," he said, "bat, fog?"

Maeniel clipped him expertly on the ear. "Shut up, Gavin."

Gavin shut up.

"Suppose there's some truth in what they say?" she asked bitterly.

"Nothing you could do would be worse than this," he replied.

Regeane shook off his grip and began hurrying toward Lucilla. Antonius followed.

Lucilla was moving. She had gotten on her side. Her left hand was more injured than her right. She used her good hand to lever herself into a sitting position.

Regeane reached her and dropped to her knees beside her. The hood fell back from Lucilla's head. One eye was closed and matted with blood. The other was open. Her mouth was pulped and oozing blood. Her face was a mass of bruises. Regeane looked down into Lucilla's robe and saw more blood soaking through her shift. Three fingernails on her left hand had been pulled out. On the right, the fingers were swollen.

"Bastards," Lucilla whispered. "Tell me, Regeane, did they put out my right eye? I can't tell. I can't see through it."

Antonius took the corner of his mantle and began wiping the blood and crust away. The eye opened. The white was scarlet, but an almost beautiful expression transfigured Lucilla's face.

"The other things they did to me don't matter. I can see. Curse them to an eternal hell," she moaned. "But then it doesn't matter. When I catch up with them, I'll send them all to God and He can do what He wants with them."

Then, to Regeane's horror, she caught Antonius' shoulder with her right hand and levered herself to her feet. "You know what to do," she whispered in Antonius' ear.

"Mother, I don't know if we have time. But when you disappeared, word went out throughout the city."

Lucilla turned to Regeane. "Buy me time," she whispered. The two good nails of her left hand bit into Regeane's arm.

"Yes," Regeane answered.

Lucilla collapsed, going limp in her son's arms. Antonius scooped her up and carried her out of the church through the vestry into the Lateran palace.

Regeane heard a child crying. She turned and saw the sound was coming from Elfgifa. Emilia held her as she sobbed against her aunt's neck.

Boom! Boom! Boom!

The church echoed with it, coming from the electors' stalls. Hadrian raised his hand and the booming died away.

A very old bishop continued standing as the others took their seats. "These are serious charges," he said to Hadrian, "and you must refute them or be removed. You cannot settle this by force of arms."

Hadrian studied Regeane for a long moment. His eyes were clear and gray. They reminded her of a storm surf on a winter sea. "Are there any other witnesses?" he asked.

Gundabald pushed Silve forward. "My son's good wife."

Silve looked absolutely paralyzed with terror.

"Well, girl, is Regeane what her uncle says?" Hadrian asked.

Regeane's chin lifted. She fixed Silve with a stare of red rage.

Silve looked up at Hadrian, down at the floor, up at the ceiling, around the crowd, anywhere and everywhere but at Regeane. Gundabald lifted his fist.

"Yes!" Silve squeaked hurriedly. "Yes! Yes! Yes!"

Regeane stepped toward her, fists clenched. "You little whore. I helped you. I saved you and you're calling me a witch. How dare you?"

Silve made a gargling noise and whined, "No, no, no . . ." She scuttled away from Regeane and found herself headed toward Gundabald. She whimpered as she saw his face twist with rage.

"Come here, girl," Hadrian said. Silve walked toward him. "Now," he pointed to Regeane. "Girl, on your soul's life, tell the truth. Is she what her uncle says she is?"

Silve turned and faced Regeane. She sniveled. Her eyes were red-rimmed and sad, but this time they met Regeane's. "I don't want to condemn you," Silve said with a sort of pitiful dignity. "And yes, she's right. I am a whore of the lowest sort. I don't know if she's a daughter of the evil one, but, yes, she can see and speak to the dead. And I, with my own eyes, saw her turn from human to animal and back again."

A huge collective sigh broke from everyone in the church and a babble of talk rose from the spectators.

Silve turned and walked away, head bowed, feet dragging. Hugo tried to catch hold of her arm. She jerked away and hissed at him like a serpent.

Regeane realized Maeniel and his men and equally formidable women were gathered in a semicircle at her back. Again, Hadrian stared at her, looking down into her face. She understood Maeniel's people were ready to fight.

No, she thought. *No.* As at the stream when she'd been dying of the cold, it wasn't the wolf, but the woman who fought, who rebelled.

The wolf was present. She trotted along the beach. Water would rise around every paw mark as her feet sank into the fine-grained sand. The shiny combers tumbled over into thick foam with a roar. The fog all around her sealed her in white silence. High above, the gulls swooped and called. Their shrill, almost angry cries a counterpoint to the thunder of the breaking seas.

"Well?" Hadrian asked, bringing her back to the church.

Boom! The ear-splitting sounds started again as the staffs and croziers of the bishops struck the floors of the choir stalls. It continued for a moment, then died away. There was silence.

The old bishop spoke into it. "Whatever the woman, Lucilla, has done, she has been punished. The girl, Regeane, must answer the charges. If you free her, Hadrian, we will believe you her accomplice." Boom! His crozier struck the boards and the other prelates signaled their agreement in the same way. The church seemed to quiver with the din.

Hadrian raised his hand. Silence fell. A silence so deep that Regeane could hear the murmur of the crowd outside in the square and the sound of the west wind buffeting the church.

Regeane was ready. "I am royal. The blood of Frankish kings runs in my veins." She paused, surprised at the loudness, the confidence ringing in her voice. Then, drawing breath, she continued, "My father was a Saxon lord, and he and his kind held the northern forests even against Roman legions. I would shame to see such a lineage brought low by foolish talk of the evil one. Foolish talk, moreover, by a drunken wastrel and a wine-sodden whore. Nor will I submit to judgment by any mere man." She raised her voice to the highest pitch she could. "I am the daughter of kings. God is my only judge, and to Him only will I submit. I invoke my right to trial by combat . . . the judgment of God."

"Very well," Hadrian answered. "There remains only for both sides to choose their champions."

Boom! The church resounded with the thudding of staffs and croziers, and, at the same time, a tremendous shout went up from the assembled notables in the church.

This, Regeane thought bitterly, *was something they could really understand.*

When the noise ended, Maeniel stepped forward. "As the lady's wedded lord, and a right ready man of my hands, I am her only proper champion."

The cheering continued. Regeane was hustled away by the pope's guard to an unfinished chapel near the entrance of the church. As she was pushed into the small marble room, she heard the giant bolt on the cathedral door being pulled back and the roar of the mob.

One of the guardsmen paused as they left the chapel. He removed his helmet and eyed her gravely. She recognized him as one of the servers at the pope's banquet, the one who had given Elfgifa her cup. "My lady," he said quietly, "I suggest you commend your soul to God, for I have seen Basil's champion, and he doesn't lose."

"Thank you," Regeane said. Her lips felt stiff.

Maeniel entered behind him. Up to now she had not realized how big he was, but he bulked large against the boy blocking the door. He put his hands on the young man's shoulders and turned him around easily. "The lady is already frightened enough," he said. "Let's not scare her anymore. I, too, have seen Basil's champion, and I believe I may just be able to handle him. Now, go out. I would have a moment's private speech with my lady." So saying, he eased the young man out into the church.

Regeane circled the room quickly. The floor was mosaic tile done in the form of a bay wreath. The green leaves were picked out, overlapping, circling the center. Golden ties at the back were formed by gilded tessarae. The walls were marble, filled with smoky, gray markings. Three high lanceolate windows showed only clear blue sky. A gray marble bench ran along both side walls.

Regeane tottered over to the bench and sat down. She wouldn't look at Maeniel, but stared down at her hands in her lap. "You should run away," she said.

"Why?" he snorted. "Because Basil's champion is an overweight monstrosity? I tell you, girl, such men are often less able to defend themselves—"

"No!" she interrupted. "Because I'm guilty."

"Indeed. Fog?" Maeniel asked softly.

Regeane laughed. It wasn't a pleasant laugh. "No! How would one become fog? That's silly," she said, raising her eyes to him at last.

"Sounds logical. Bats?" he inquired.

Regeane looked away irritated. "Nonsense. A bat is a very small creature. How would I go into a bat?"

"Not easily, I think. Wolf? The wolf is . . ." His voice trailed off. "I can understand the wolf more easily."

Tears streamed down her cheeks. He sat down beside her on the bench. Her fists were tightly clenched in her lap. He brushed her cheek lightly with the back of his hand.

"Regeane," he said softly, "my adored one, I don't mind you speaking these fancies to me or among my people. Goodness knows they have enough strange ideas of their own. But I would caution you not to speak so before strangers. They might misunderstand."

She turned and stared into his face, eyes wide in stark disbelief. "You think me mad," she gasped.

"No, no, no. Hush," he whispered. He had her in his arms and pulled her head over so it rested against his chest. "No, I do not think you mad, but I'm not willing to believe that wastrel uncle of yours. What did he want you to do?"

She was past hiding anything from him. "He wanted me to help him kill you."

"Yes," he answered, "and you were too honest. So now, when you refuse to fill his coffers with my gold, he tries to ruin you and take your life. When I am done with this Basil's champion, I will take care of him. I'll leave his carcass to rot. I would not feed his bones to my hounds or strips of his skin to my hawks. And as for the other two, your cousin and his little rental cunt, I would not care to depend on them to tell me if it were day or night. A bit too much of that wine they like to drink, and they might not know."

She sighed deeply and began laughing. "I almost believe you do not care what form I assume, so long as I am a proper wife to you."

"I believe you will be," he said, stroking her hair. "Once I have you in my mountains, in the hall of my fortress, warmed, cossetted, and fed well on our cheeses—you will be filled with delight at their variety and their richness; on our rich dark bread—Matrona has a different loaf for every day of the year; and on our amber beer, you will forget these sick and sorrowful fancies bred by your uncle's cruelty and neglect."

"Suppose I don't?" she asked in a voice choked with tears.

"Well, I have certain rules," he said. "You may not kill or even frighten our sheep, goats, cattle, or horses. We are dependent on the milk, yes, even from the horses, for cheese-making and the greater part of our wealth. And I will not want a wife who crouches on the hearth rug and cracks marrow bones with her teeth. I do not allow my dogs in my bedroom. I will not tolerate a wife who sheds, either. My rugs are Persian. The sheets are of the finest Egyptian linen. My furniture is crafted by the most skillful mountain carvers. The bed curtains are heavy brocade, and the goose-down mattress and comforter are like sleeping among clouds. I will allow no fleas."

Regeane began laughing helplessly. He turned her face up to him and kissed her. Her tears were a salty taste on his lips. "Better?" he asked.

"I've done all I could," she said.

"Yes." He rose. "Now leave Basil's champion to me."

The door opened. Barbara, Antonius, Elfgifa, and Postumous entered. Elfgifa tried to run at Regeane, but Barbara wouldn't let her. Instead, she made the child walk over to Regeane and give her a decorous kiss, but then Elfgifa lost control and hugged her. Regeane lifted the child onto her lap.

"What's going to happen?" Elfgifa asked tearfully.

"Nothing," Regeane replied. She could feel in the child's desperate clinging to her the little girl's doubts about the adults' comforting lies.

Postumous approached her like a grown-up and kissed her outstretched hand. She read the smoldering fear in his eyes.

She pulled Elfgifa away and handed her back to Barbara. The nun's face was lined with worry. "Get the children out of here, Barbara. Get the children away. Whatever happens, they shouldn't see this."

"Don't worry," Barbara said. "Emilia is leaving tomorrow for Wessex with both of them. She got a message to Elfgifa's father. He says he will welcome the little boy and foster him. His mother didn't want to let him go, but she knows he'll have a better future there than he does here, especially if the Lombards win. Basil would kill her and the boy the way he'd flick a fly off the rim of his cup, and just as quickly."

Elfgifa bucked away from Barbara and ran to Regeane again. Regeane caught her by the hands.

"My father says that we shouldn't desert our friends in time of trouble," she told Regeane.

Regeane kept the two, small hands in hers to prevent the child from clinging to her. She kissed her on the forehead. "Friends also respect each other's wishes, and I would be more unhappy than I am now if I knew you remained with me to be injured, or perhaps killed. Go now. Your duty in hospitality requires you to care for Postumous. He accompanies you to the Anglo-Saxon kingdoms of your father. Postumous doesn't know the language and has no friends. Even as he helped you in his country, you must care for him in yours."

Elfgifa stepped back, a look of almost adult sadness in her face. She turned and, taking Postumous by the hand, she and the little boy preceded Barbara through the door.

"Hail and farewell," Regeane whispered. "May God accompany you and preserve you from every evil forever."

A roar rose from the crowd outside. Regeane started. They had seen Basil's champion.

Antonius said, "Now I imagine Maeniel has put in an appearance. Regeane, have you any idea of what kind of miserable cruelty you have brought down on yourself?"

"What do you mean?" she asked.

He extended a piece of cloth to her. It was undyed linen, the coarsest of homespun. She took it from his hands.

"You must stand tied to the stake," he said, "with the faggots piled around your feet, watching your champion fight the battle. If he loses, yields himself as conquered, or is killed, they light the fire. Now, take off that gold gown and put this on. I'd keep the silk shift. This damned thing is not fit for sacking and without something under it, you will be rubbed raw. I'll leave while you change." So saying, he hurried out of the room.

Regeane quickly pulled off the golden dress and threw it on the bench. Then she dropped the penitential shift over her head. It was like a piece of sacking. It covered her from head to toe and trailed a bit on the ground. The sleeves hung to below her elbows.

Wind thundered at the building again. The bronze doors to both the cathedral and the chapel rattled and boomed. Outside, the crowd noise was only a murmur.

Regeane looked up. The three lanceolate windows showed only blue sky flocked with a few small clouds the west wind sent racing by.

She was alone. Where to find courage? She and the wolf met in her soul. The wolf rested, couchant. She looked into Regeane's eyes as if to say, "You know this isn't the end." But Regeane thought, *How will I bear it when they light the fire? And they will.* She was sure this mountain lord Maeniel thought her mad. Even with the best of intentions, how hard would he fight for a madwoman? No, she was sure she was doomed. She stood for a moment, then gave way to a violent and uncontrolled trembling all over her body. The momentary panic passed, leaving her both lucid and calm.

She straightened her back. She remembered the serpent in the haunted church. She had refused to show fear in front of Silve. In the mob out there were a thousand Silves, brutes ready to be titillated at the sight of a woman being burned alive. And she would not bring shame on the blood royal by showing fear in front of them.

The door opened. Antonius and four members of the papal guard entered. Regeane's further memories of her journey to the stake were fragmentary. They tried to get her to remove her shoes, saying that a penitent should be barefoot. She responded by stating flatly she was not a penitent. "I have done nothing for which I need do penance."

They did manage to persuade her to remove the fillet that held her hair back. Antonius took her arm. The papal guard pushed their way through the mob.

The journey wasn't as bad as she'd supposed it would be when they stepped out of the Lateran. She'd been afraid of stones and curses, but most of those gathered near the church were either indifferent or greatly amused, eyeing her the way they might have gawked at some rare bird or beast, a tiger or monkey being led by for their entertainment.

The stake itself was a stone post, six feet high and roughly a foot wide with an iron ring fixed to it waist high. Four steps led up to it.

Gundabald and Basil waited there. They were mounted on horses and they directed the way she was fastened to the post. Her wrists were lashed to the iron ring. But Basil and Gundabald added a further refinement—a chain leading from the iron ring to a bronze collar around her neck. The executioner twisted her head to one side and held her cheek against the stone post while he hammered it shut. Gundabald and Basil both loomed over her and examined the executioner's handiwork.

"That cannot be undone with a key," Gundabald commented. "It will have to be pried off."

Regeane turned her head so as not to look at them. Antonius stood at the foot of the steps looking up at her. Her mouth was bone dry. "Please," she asked him, "I'm very thirsty. Give me something to drink."

Antonius asked and someone produced a clay flagon with a bit of sour wine, mostly lees in the bottom. The taste was ghastly, but she took a mouthful.

Basil and Gundabald were laughing together. "Her mother was a damp rag, always weeping, but that father of hers . . ." Gundabald turned and glanced down at Regeane. She let the mouthful of wine fly. The stream caught him right in the eyes. The raw wine stung. He screamed and the horse bucked, nearly unseating him.

She shouted hoarsely at Basil and him, "Filth, the names of either of my parents are profaned by your lips."

The crowd around Gundabald's horse scattered, cheering Regeane even as they dodged. Basil pulled his horse's head around viciously and rode toward her, his fist lifted for a really savage blow. Regeane tried to think of a way to duck, but she was pinned by both collar and wrists. Someone rode between them. She recognized Rufus. He roared at Basil, "Away with you, sir. Your cruelty exceeds all measure."

Gundabald, no horseman, was already halfway across the square. He contented himself with bringing his horse under control. Rufus and his men surrounded the post and pushed the crowd back. They formed a protective half-circle around her, allowing her to view clearly the battleground in front of the Lateran.

Rufus spoke loudly to both Basil and the mob. "The lady will be subjected to no further insults or indignities. Her life is at hazard, that is enough. I will tolerate no further abuse from anyone. I have given fair warning. The next man to violate my orders dies."

"My lord," the executioner protested, "I must pile the faggots at her feet. It is the law."

"To be sure," Rufus sighed. "Go ahead."

The executioner, a small gray man with watery eyes, and two boys who were apparently his sons, began to unload a nearby cart filled with wood. They began dumping bundles of thin sticks on the steps to the post.

Regeane looked down at the stones at her feet. They were granite blocks, but she could see they were scorched, and thick soot was ground into the spaces between them. In fact, she could smell, even with her human senses, charcoal and stale smoke. The wind whipped her hair back. Even the heavy canvas shift fluttered and flapped around her body.

Hadrian and his people took up positions on the high steps to the Lateran church. Regeane realized they meant to be comfortable—folding stools and chairs were being carried from the palace for the assembled notables so they could watch the drama unfold without inconvenience.

Hadrian, alone, stood on the very top step of the church.

"He wanted to bless you," Rufus told Regeane, "but we refused to permit it. If he clothed you in the majesty conferred by the Vicar of Christ, how could we tell if you were guilty or not?"

Regeane nodded.

"Girl, you have chosen the one form of judgment against which there is no earthly appeal. If the very angels in heaven came to earth bearing proof of your innocence, we would still have to burn you if your champion loses."

Hadrian looked over at her. He didn't raise his hand, but he stood a tall, lonely, pale figure against the glowing robes of his flock. Sharing her discomfort, even as she was sure he would share her fate if Maeniel failed.

The crowd gave a murmur of delight, and she saw what she was sure must be Basil's champion enter the improvised arena in front of the church. He was the biggest man she had ever encountered. So large, he was almost grotesque. Everything about him was gigantic. Legs, arms, hands, feet, chest, and shoulders. He topped Maeniel by at least a foot, and his whole body was bigger by similar proportion than his opponent's.

Maeniel stood quietly on the Lateran steps. He was armed. Helmet, mail shirt, greaves on his thighs, and shin guards. He was examining several swords being proffered to him by his people.

Then, Matrona arrived with one. The sheath was old, the leather cracked and peeling, but when he drew the sword, it shimmered with the cool glow of moonlight on still water. When he lifted it into the sun, rainbows played along the glowing metal, sending red, yellow, blue, purple, and green fire dancing along the steel.

Regeane heard Rufus' indrawn breath. He'd placed his horse close to her. "What is it?" she asked.

"The sword," he replied. "I had always believed such things were legends."

Regeane shrugged as well as she could. "It's pretty, but . . ."

"Pretty?" he snorted. "But then you're a woman not a warrior. For the first time today, I begin to believe Basil will not have things all his own way. My lady, I would not have any idea where to find such a weapon, much less have the courage to wield it."

Basil's champion stood, his naked blade in his hand. It was, like everything else on him, larger than other men's, longer than Maeniel's sword by at least a foot. He studied Maeniel with mild, but brutal amusement in his heavy-lidded eyes.

"What's his name?" she asked Rufus.

"Scapthar," Rufus said. "And I might add, he has been Basil's champion for a long time. He has twenty-seven kills to his credit. He began by challenging poor farmers to fight, forcing them into duels. Then, he killed them, took their lands, and sold them. His career of successful villainy came to Basil's notice. He hired him. They have been together ever since."

As Regeane watched, Scapthar shouted something to Maeniel. Maeniel who was finishing a cup of wine ignored him.

Scapthar walked toward Maeniel, raising his sword. Maeniel watched him over the rim of the cup. Scapthar swung his sword down, but suddenly Maeniel wasn't there, though Scapthar nearly did kill a few of the innocent spectators to the match. His hard swung sword rang on the stone, sending sparks from the street.

Maeniel, only a few feet away, handed the cup to Gavin and drew his own sword. Scapthar wheeled quickly and drove another blow at Maeniel. He parried and the sword rang like a chime, giving forth a sound eerily like a cry of joy. A few in the crowd gasped, and from the corner of her eye, Regeane saw Rufus cross himself.

Neither combatant carried a shield. Scapthar apparently wanted to swing his sword with both hands. Methodically, he began to hunt Maeniel down. Every time Scapthar struck at Maeniel, Regeane's heart pounded. Sometimes he came so close, she was sure Maeniel would be bisected or lose an arm or leg to Scapthar's gigantic sword. But somehow it never happened. Maeniel, it seemed, was blessed with a quickness a viper might envy. But she was to find that, unlike a viper, he could strike while retreating.

At first, despite his inability to land blows, Scapthar seemed to have things his own way. He pursued Maeniel relentlessly. The crowd parted to let them pass. Regeane heard bets being placed as to how long it would take Scapthar to catch and kill him.

The fight swayed one way, moving away from her to the other side of the square, then toward her, and the two men fought almost at her feet. Maeniel kept making Scapthar miss. The wind was still blowing hard, the sun now high in the sky. It burned into Regeane's face, arms, and back.

Regeane's eyes fixed on Maeniel, she saw he was holding up well. Perspiration was only a light sheen on his exposed skin, whereas Scapthar was sweating so heavily it dripped from his chin and stained his shirt. Even so, Regeane wasn't sure when Maeniel began to close with Scapthar.

The sun had reached its zenith, and with a heavy heart, Regeane began to believe Maeniel was slowing. Scapthar's blows were getting closer and closer. But each time the miraculous sword turned them, sometimes when Scapthar seemed within a hair of killing or crippling his opponent. Each time Maeniel's sword would aim its sweet, ringing cry of derision at Scapthar. And each time it spoke, it struck. At first, only a shallow cut or two on Scapthar's arm. Nothing really, scratches only on a man Scapthar's size. But then Regeane realized Scapthar was leaving a trail of blood. Moreover, a trail that grew thicker as the fight progressed.

The heat was becoming intense, in part because of the sun beating down on the exposed stone surfaces and in part because of the packed bodies of the multitude watching the battle.

For a moment Regeane tore her eyes from the combatants.

The square was packed, people filled every nook and cranny of the flat, open space. Hawkers sold wine, fried bread, and filled pastries of all kinds. Spectators covered rooftops of every building, including the steep basilica. All porches and balconies were filled, and four or five viewers fought for position at every window.

"Regeane!" Antonius stood next to the stone post, as close as he could get. The bundles of faggots prevented him from getting too near.

"Where have you been?" she asked. "There weren't this many people here this morning. What's happening?"

"Mother asked you for time," he answered. "Well, you gave it to her. We are four—Hadrian, Mother, you, and I."

"Five," Regeane said, nodding toward Maeniel still coolly fencing with Scapthar.

"Five, then," he said. "And none of us may see tomorrow's sunrise, but neither, I promise, will Basil."

Regeane's attention was jerked away from Antonius by a loud shout from the crowd. Maeniel had been tripped. She saw Maeniel falling. Scapthar pounced with better speed than Regeane had seen from him all day. But Maeniel rolled into the man who'd tripped him. He fell over Maeniel's back, and Scapthar's sword cut him in half.

The crowd scattered, leaving Maeniel, Scapthar, and the corpse in the open space.

"Admit you are beaten, Scapthar," Maeniel said. "Let me go my way and take the woman. I don't want your life."

Scapthar shook his head like a wounded bull. "I don't get paid for letting men live. Or women either."

Regeane saw something harden and change in Maeniel's face. And found herself thinking, *I hope he never looks at me that way.* Then they closed again.

The sun moved from overhead. Clouds began rolling in. They were thick and dark with bright edges and didn't completely cover the sky. The wind picked up, sending everyone's clothes to flapping. Regeane's wolf nose caught the scent of rain on the wind.

Even the most ardent spirits in the crowd didn't have the

energy to cheer or scream insults any longer. They followed the fight as silently as the two combatants.

Maeniel and Scapthar went for each other in deadly earnest. Scapthar driving Maeniel before him, round and round the square, trying to exhaust him. Maeniel mercilessly inflicting a new wound on each pass. At last, they ended where they began, in front of the steps to the Lateran Basilica.

The pope stood there, and the bishops and cardinal priests of the city. They had waited as the long day wore away, a day everyone realized had reached its ending.

Scapthar was a mass of blood. Those looking at him could hardly believe he was living. His clothing was soaked with gore, his armor smeared with it. When he paused, pools of sticky red dripped from his clothing.

Yet it was only too clear his opponent was tiring also. Maeniel's face was gray with exhaustion. His tunic had been sweat-soaked and dried, then soaked again. He'd also been wounded in the leg. Nasty, but not crippling or fatal. His boot squished blood with every step. Every time he lifted his arm to parry Scapthar's blows, he moved more and more slowly.

The sun was low in the sky close to the horizon. It shone down the streets leading to the square and filled them with a last golden haze.

Regeane at her post was approaching her limits, also. Her hands were numb. No matter how vigorously she wiggled her fingers, nothing seemed to restore the circulation. Her fingers felt as though they were pierced by knives. The staple of the collar had rubbed her neck raw. She'd had no food or drink all day. Her tongue felt leathery and her lips were cracked.

Maeniel and Scapthar circled each other, both looking almost too weary to attack. A deep hush filled the square. Scapthar stepped back and gave a roar like an enraged bull. The strange light flashed on his sword and armor, turning them to flame. Then, he loosed the sword like a throwing knife, directly at Maeniel.

Maeniel stepped to the right, expertly deflecting the thrown sword.

Regeane screamed. She'd seen the point of Scapthar's attack. As Maeniel stepped away from the sword, he moved within range of Scapthar's maul-sized hands. In a second, he was going down, one of Scapthar's fists around his throat, the other holding his sword arm by the wrist.

Regeane screamed again as the two men grappled on the ground. Not wanting to see Maeniel die, she looked away and saw the executioner with a torch. *No,* she thought. *No.* But then, *Yes!* Her teeth sank into one side of her lower lip. Her mouth filled with blood. It dribbled down from one corner to her chin in a thin stream. For a second she met Rufus' eyes. He tried to turn away, but her gaze held his, her eyes two pools of blank blackness.

The executioner raised the torch.

Rufus drove the point of his sword at the man. He backed away in confusion and dropped the torch. One of Basil's men picked it up and threw it quickly into the pile of faggots. A bundle of the dry wood caught with a roar. Regeane's body bucked at the post. The ropes tore her wrists. She thrust against the collar and her neck gave, but not the brass. Then, she was still. She had only a moment of pain-free life left.

She saw Basil riding forward through a crowd that sounded like a storm surf to claim his victory. On her left, she heard Rufus say, "I will not let you feel the flames," and saw his sword rise. The setting sun was in her eyes.

She heard a sound, an unearthly yell rise from the mob. A scream of rage and triumph so terrible that even in this last extremity, it made every hair on her body rise. Through the blowing flame she saw Maeniel on his feet, his left arm red to the elbow, fingers dripping blood, something clutched in his hand. Basil was close to him. He threw whatever it was in Basil's face.

Rufus shouted, "He's won! My God, he's won. Get that fire away from her." Then, miracle of miracles, they were throwing water and raking the wood from around her feet.

And she knew she was going to live. Wonderfully, unbelievably, she knew she was going to live . . . to live. *Oh, God,* she thought. *Thank God . . . to live.*

Scapthar wasn't quite dead yet. The crowd drew back. He was lying on the cobbles, blood pumping from between his legs in spurts. He screamed, a sound that tore at her ears. He screamed . . . opened his mouth to scream again . . . and died.

Basil turned his horse away and tried to ride back to his men. Someone was pounding at the collar around Regeane's neck, trying to get it off, when she saw Basil die. Antonius appeared in the crowd near him and drove a sword into his horse's neck. The dying beast's legs folded under it. A dozen hands pulled Basil down. From the sounds she heard, she didn't think he was alive when his body reached the ground.

Basil's men tried to make a stand. Against the comparatively unarmed citizens, they might have succeeded, but Rufus, his men, and Maeniel's people joined the Romans. In short order, all that was left to do was mop up.

Someone found a flagon of halfway decent wine. She drank it mixed with water. It went directly to her head and so she made no protest when Maeniel came to claim her.

He lifted her to the saddle in front of him. She found all she wanted to do was rest her head on his shoulder and her arms around his neck. From there, she saw the last half-circle of the setting sun dip below the horizon.

The sky above them was a dome of thick, black clouds with blue edges, here and there laced with lightning.

The downpour began before they reached the villa. They stopped the horse and stood in the dark, empty street and let it pour over them, allowed the clean waters of heaven to dissolve the perspiration of terror from her skin, wash the blood of slaughter from his body. The icy water laved his wounds and began healing them. It plastered her hair to her scalp. They opened their mouths and drank from the springs of heaven.

It was still pounding down when they reached the villa. Their clothing was completely soaked. He led her to a side room where they toweled themselves dry. It was lit only by a single candle. He left and returned dry, wearing a clean tunic. He offered her a coffer. She opened it and lifted out a gown.

It was white, heavy, raw, pure silk, almost priceless, sewn with gold at the bodice, sleeves, and hem. She slipped it over her head.

I must leave, she thought. Her mind was clearing. The fabric caressed her skin, a sensual delight. He kissed her gently with an exquisite tenderness. Another sensual delight. *I'll leave in the morning,* she thought.

He led her to the triclinium. There was possibly more food on the table than there had been at the wedding feast. Hams, cheeses—white, yellow, blue—wines in flagons, clay bottles, and even amphoras chilled in a tub of snow. Scattered among this largess were whole haunches of pork, beef, tender lamb, and veal. Bread was scattered everywhere—the thick, rich, dark Roman breads made with dates, onions, herbs, olive oil, and cheese.

Maeniel's people were feasting. They were all wearing arms and armor. Some looked battered and bloodied.

There were no candles or lamps. Only torches lit the room. The couches had been replaced by benches. Two chairs were at the high table. Maeniel led her toward them. His people stood and, raising a shout, lifted their cups to Regeane.

The curtains separating the triclinium from the garden belled out, then flapped in the wind. Regeane shivered.

The wolf rose, swimming up from profound darkness. She was, as always, voiceless, but Regeane realized the woman and the creature were at odds. The narrowed, blazing gaze caught and held her.

Their chairs were so close Maeniel's arm pressed against hers.

The wolf directed her mind away. She saw the huge gray. The vision was clear. She could smell the wind of the heights, taste the purity of air blowing over a snow-covered glacier locked in eternal winter on peaks so high they thrust through the thin blanket of air covering the world.

The gray wolf climbed higher than the trees or even grass, beyond the path of the ibex who take a road over barren, wind-swept rock seemingly dancing along the edge of the sky. He ran though the air was thin and the cold so intense it struck through the triple thickness of his coat and brought him almost to agony.

Higher and higher he struggled over snow-covered ice, skirting crevasses yawning like frigid, toothless mouths breathing out inky, silent, freezing death. Up above him rose a ridgeline drenched in moonlight, glittering against a dead black sky.

Up and up the gray toiled, indifferent to the burning pain in his lungs, the stretch and return of muscles and tendons that seemed ready to simply tear free of his bones with the next step. Up and up toward what seemed, to the untutored eye of the woman, the roof of the world.

Someone touched her face. The vision faded. She realized Matrona was bending over her and Maeniel had hold of her hand.

"My lady," he spoke softly, "are you well?"

Matrona stroked her cheek. "Stop swilling, you sots! Get a plate of food together and pass it up to our younger sister here. She needs food. And wine, no, not that Campagnan red, but some of the white, chilling in the snow."

In a few seconds a plate and goblet were thrust before her. Sausage—beef and pork—roast beef, loin of wild boar, all smothered in their appropriate gravies. Some sort of greens cooked in cheese and oil, and wine, cold and thirst quenching. Every mouthful was pleasure. No, more than pleasure. Each was a different variety of ecstasy.

Sometime later, when she looked up, the food was gone. Maeniel's arm was around her shoulders.

"There, are you better now?" he asked.

"Yes." The yes was a sigh of repletion.

The arm around her shoulders tightened, the back of his free hand caressed her cheek.

In the deepest darkness of her brain the wolf gave a cry of fear and fury. *Go,* it said as clearly as if the word had been articulated.

No. The woman turned toward her dark companion. *He is lost, the gray one, lost. We are separated by the power of king and pope, law and God* . . . Then she felt a terrible uprush of sorrow because she knew the silver one spoke the truth and, sooner or later, she would leave this man's bed and seek her final freedom in the moonlight. As it was in the beginning, is now, and ever shall be, world without end. Amen. The parody of a prayer pronounced her victory and her doom.

Gundabald stepped between the curtains separating the triclinium and the garden. Six of Basil's mercenaries were with him. They all held crossbows in their hands. A look of madness was in Gundabald's eyes. His loaded crossbow was pointed directly at Maeniel's chest.

The room went utterly and absolutely still.

"What do you want, Gundabald?" Maeniel asked.

Gundabald laughed. *Perhaps it was a laugh,* Regeane thought. An ugly cackle in the silent room.

"Everything I have tried has failed," he said. "Even now, the mob hunts me. But I and my friends here don't take well to the role of outcast fugitives. Not when the table in front of us holds enough treasure to make us all wealthy men for life."

Regeane glanced at the silver and gold dishes, the ruby-studded cup near Maeniel's hand.

Maeniel shrugged. "Matrona, give it to them. After all, it's only gold and silver."

Matrona replied with a grunt and rose. She began to collect plates and cups and dump them into a sack she'd made of her mantle.

Not even Regeane noticed that as she worked, she was moving closer and closer to the semicircle of men in the doorway.

No! Regeane thought. *No!* The crossbow was pointed directly at Maeniel's chest. She remembered her father, the wound that ended his life. Pink and white roses, the petals steeping in blood. She knew what Gundabald was going to do. The wolf knew what Gundabald was going to do. The wind she remembered in the convent cell's darkness, the wind from beyond the world; she felt it start and begin to blow. Suddenly, the air in the room was thick with the smell of blood and roses.

Regeane pulled free of Maeniel's arm, kicked the chair to the floor behind her, and stood.

"Sweet niece," Gundabald said. "Sweet niece, if you are wise . . ." he repeated.

But the wind was blowing harder now, the curtain flapping wildly. Regeane understood. She had summoned it. Her life summoned it and, perhaps, her death.

"Uncle," she spoke one last warning, "go. Go! Go now or you will surely die."

The crossbow bolt swung away from Maeniel toward her. All of the glittering lethal stars swung toward her.

She was the silver wolf, for one horrible moment entangled in her dress, then she was free and coiled like a spring. A shimmer of moonlight with bared fangs, she went for Gundabald's throat. She expected to die in mid-leap . . . but she didn't.

Gundabald was brutal and coward, but he was no fool. She'd flung herself into his trap.

Something like a black cloud flew toward her. The steel meshes of the net closed around her. The wolf struggled on the floor at Gundabald's feet.

Gundabald gave a yell of pure triumph. He shouted to Maeniel, "Look! Look! Look what you have married!"

The mercenaries thrust their torches at Regeane, blinding the wolf. Then she was woman again, and all the crossbow bolts were trained on her.

"Now," Gundabald shouted, "I think you will be glad to pay me to take her away."

Regeane sighed. A simple sound, but a terrible one. Her sigh was the cry of one who has struggled long against death, but now yields to the cold embrace. The protest of one sunk in grief who realizes the full meaning of everlasting separation from one deeply loved.

Everyone in the room felt the pain in that sound, even Gundabald. "How she can feel so much is beyond me," he said, but he steadied the crossbow in his hand and pointed it at her heart.

"Gundabald!" Maeniel's voice shouted and the gray wolf stood on the table challenging him.

Gundabald's eyes dilated and his jaw dropped. Regeane thought that he looked, for all the world, like a man whose worst nightmare has come true.

The faces of the mercenaries went ashen with fear. A terrible blast of wind struck the entrance to the dining room. The torches on the walls burned blue.

Maeniel was gray as are dark storm clouds or a rock shadow on a snowy glacier. His leap held such power that it carried him all the way from the table to where Gundabald stood. Then he was man again. His left hand tore the crossbow away from Gundabald. With the right—man to man—he killed him.

The whole pack bolted over the tables at the mercenaries. They came four-legged, without weapons, clothing, or armor; furred, fanged, and enraged . . . eyes glowing in the darkness.

Wind screamed through the room. Wine bottles and crockery

shattered as the pack leaped forward, heedless of anything but the attack.

Maeniel lifted Gundabald by the neck, throttling him. Gundabald struggled violently, kicking, clawing at Maeniel's face while his own grew darker and darker.

Outside a nightmare chorus of screams and snarls rang out as the pack caught Gundabald's men and killed them.

"I swore," Maeniel roared, looking directly into Gundabald's eyes, "that I would kill her tormentor with my bare hands—" Gundabald's body went limp. He hung like a rag doll from Maeniel's fist. "—and I have," he finished as he dropped Gundabald's lifeless body to the floor.

The wind died, the torch flames flared.

Maeniel knelt down and, with trembling hands, helped Regeane free herself from the net. "My God," he whispered, "my God, why did you do that? Why didn't you let me handle it? The minute they were out the door they were dead men."

"No, he never intended to let you live. That was how he killed my father—with a crossbow bolt through the heart."

Maeniel glanced over at the sprawled, lifeless body. "Perhaps you're right. Are you hurt anywhere, in any way?"

"No," she whispered as he embraced her. She closed her eyes and rested her head on his shoulder. Then she felt the wolf, in the silence of her heart, rest her head against the same shoulder in perfect love and trust. And they were one.

His arms tightened protectively around her. It was some time before they both realized the stone floor they were kneeling on was hard and the night breeze was cold.

Maeniel rose, went to the table, and dropped his own tunic over his head. Then he wiped his hands carefully and gave Regeane her dress.

"You didn't tell me," she said, "and when I tried to make my confession to you . . ." Her voice rose. "You . . . treated me as though I were a madwoman."

"Regeane, we were the principal actors in one of the finer dramas played out in this city since the Imperial court moved to Constantinople. How many ears do you think were pressed against that door? Five, ten, two dozen, or even more. And, as for afterward, heaven help me, you'd been through so much. I was afraid for you. Afraid your mind might snap. I thought my fears were realized when you went for Gundabald. I was mercilessly slow about his death. He felt the full agony every—step—of—the—way." Maeniel spoke the last words through clenched teeth.

Then he extended his arms to her and she yielded bonelessly to his embrace. They still stood there as the wolves entered.

Gavin returned first, naked and annoyed. He saw Regeane looking at him and dove for his clothes. "He has a lot of human habits," Maeniel commented. "Shame is one of them."

Matrona followed. She seemed comfortable in her skin. "They're dead," she said. "Later we'll take the bodies and dump them. We weren't hungry. At least not that hungry." She and one of the others carried Gundabald's body away to join his companions.

The rest trailed in, dressed, and made ready to eat and drink, especially to drink, again. But before they sat down, Gavin lifted one of the amphoras that had been chilled in the snow. They all filled their cups with the slightly sweet vintage flavored with a touch of honey.

Regeane took Maeniel's hand. She was weary to the point of falling, but filled with the deepest peace she'd ever known. She stood, looking at them as they raised their cups to her.

God, they were a wild, savage crew—masters, she was sure, of their mountain fastness. She would be their lady, a fascinating and sometimes dangerous task. She wondered if she'd be equal to it.

But Maeniel spoke, "My brothers, my friends, my companions in arms, but best of all, those who run with me along the trackless paths of moonlight. I give you Regeane, your lady. The silver wolf and my wife."

A Conversation with Alice Borchardt

Question: I'm sure everyone is fascinated that you and Anne Rice are sisters; I know I am. How did you both come to be writers . . . and what led the two of you into fantasy and supernatural fiction?

Answer: Anne wrote a little about our childhood in *Violin.* I have never written about it and have no plans to. But I will say that being Irish places us among a people to whom reality is a contingent experience. We are not entirely here. Nor do we base our lives on probability but on inspiration, illumination, and even hallucination if necessary. For example, I met God—or rather, experienced him—in church when I was twelve. I have written about that experience many times, but it's like trying to explain color to someone born blind. My identity flows from that moment. Another important experience was meeting Odin the Norse God of war and poetry on a streetcar. He had one gray eye, wore a black overcoat and a black hat. I had a snake in my pocket.

Q: I don't know what to ask first: why you had a snake in your pocket or what Odin was doing riding on a streetcar!

A: I had a snake in my pocket because crawfish were free. We are now in the midst of gooey nostalgia about the fifties but most people have no memory that America had barely emerged from the Great Depression and from a war that struck almost every family in America in some way. Television of the time celebrated the upper-middle-class lifestyle: *Father Knows Best, Ozzie and Harriet.* But most of us were not upper middle class. As a family with seven people to feed, we needed all the help we could get. A short expedition to the Florida Avenue Swamp would yield anywhere from four to seven pounds of live crawfish. Two hours' work—supplemental groceries. We happened upon the snake (a beautiful salt-and-pepper king snake), and some of the men in the post office where my father worked wanted to see him before we returned him to the swamp. The rest is probably just a child's overactive imagination.

Or maybe not. (I note in passing that this type of snake is now in grave danger from his admirers. They have been hunted almost to the point of extinction by those wanting them for the trade in exotic pets.) I can't say that admiration was the reaction of my father's friends to what I saw as a thing of great beauty. Possibly that disjunction between my personal judgment and the overall dislike and intent to murder on the part of most of the men and all of the women I encountered brought on the experience with Odin. Who knows? But it would appear the world has come around more to my way of thinking since that unhappy event with this particular benign and beautiful creature, the salt-and-pepper king snake.

Q: *How do your werewolves differ from those popularized in movies?*
A: The movie werewolf is simply a projection of our worst fears about ourselves. We hope those fears are false. We hope we are better than that. But we're not. Remember Mark Twain's remark about the cat: If you could cross a man with a cat, it would improve the man but deteriorate the cat. The werewolf Regeane, for example, from *The Silver Wolf*, is a bit more ethical and compassionate than most of the people around her.

Q: *Because of her lupine nature?*
A: Yes.

Q: *Both* The Silver Wolf *and* Night of the Wolf *are*

set in times of great cultural upheaval. In the former, the last vestiges of Roman civilization are being over- whelmed by the emergent Christian world of the Middle Ages. In the latter, it is the world of the Druids, with its close ties to a vastly old yet still vibrant Celtic tradition, that is crumbling before the onslaught of Rome.

A: Historians often put me in mind of the joke about the drunk who drops his watch while coming home from a bar late one night. Instead of groping around in the dark where the watch was lost, the drunk makes his way to a street lamp and begins looking for the watch there, the logic being that under the lamppost he can at least *see*. But the most important and interest- ing events of history have a tendency to occur in the dark, during obscure and difficult periods.

Q: How do you balance the factual limitations of his- torical fiction with the creative freedom of fantasy?

A: The problem with history is not working it into fan- tasy but keeping it from turning into fantasy. For instance, at present we are being told "we won the Cold War." I have some doubts about this. Something very much like what the anthropologists call "systems collapse" occurred within the Soviet Union. Far from us causing it, we may have been herded toward the same destination. The burdens of the arms race were creating great stress in the United States as well, but for a great many reasons—some of which may never be clear to us—the Soviets went down first. Now we tell ourselves pretty fairy stories about our own prowess rather than examining the circumstances sur- rounding the rapid failure of the Soviet empire. Somehow I don't think future historians are going to give us the credit for what happened. In *Night of the Wolf*, I wrote about the Roman Empire. But the exploitation and destruction of a people's way of life practiced by the Romans have occurred again and again throughout history. For example, the economic underpinnings of the Roman Empire were strikingly similar to Hitler's Third Reich—consider the use of slave labor, to name just one area. Hitler committed genocide. So did Caesar. The only difference is that Caesar did it a long time ago. One reason the Victorians admired so-called classical civilization was that they were playing the same game in China, India, and, yes, Ireland. There is far more fantasy in some very sober statements about history than there is in many a so-called historical fantasy, and a lot more truth in fiction than is found in some history textbooks.

Q: The Silver Wolf *tells the story of a young woman named Regeane who, in the midst of a culture not exactly known for its respect for women, learns to respect herself and to command the respect of others in part by accepting the frightening sexual and violent aspects of her own powerful lupine nature. Is this a journey faced by all women?*
A: Yes! So what else is new?

Q: What about Maeniel's parallel journey from wolf to man, instinct to reason?
A: Maeniel would say reason is a dubious gift. He understands love and compassion in his wolf existence; in fact, these are the very qualities that allow Imona to draw him into the tortured complexity of human life. It's been said that reason separates human beings from animals, but does it make us better? We humans are a dangerous bunch. Hitler and Caesar are as characteristic of Western civilization as Christ or Socrates. And it is notable that of the latter two, we crucified one and poisoned the other—and would most likely do so again if the opportunity presented itself.

Q: As in Dostoyevsky's parable of the Grand Inquisitor.
A: Our species does two things well: art and war. We reward the practitioners of both with the highest accolades. We are poets and killers.

Q: Speaking of which, Dryas is a warrior but also a priestess in the Celtic culture that you so vividly describe in **Night of the Wolf.** *What can you tell us about the historical origins of the fictional Dryas?*
A: A lot is known about the Celtic people, but no two authorities can agree on what any of it means! I made Dryas up, but she came from a variety of sources. Studies by Nerys Patterson of kinship in early Celtic society. Many books on early European religion. Other studies of Indo-European society. Despite much talk of male domination, women were very important in the tribal societies formed by the prehistoric farming peoples of Europe. Though often secondary to men, they controlled a great deal of wealth and power and had a lot more control of their own lives than many historians are willing to give them credit for. For example, I often hear historians say that the Celts sacrificed criminals to their gods. I don't think so. To wear the torc, I suspect, meant that you were available for sacrifice. The torc seems to have been worn by warriors *and noblewomen.* They offered themselves up (who really knows to what gods?) as sacrifices for the lives of their people. Such men and women were not seen as victims or martyrs but as honored heroes.

Q: Critics have commented on the sensuality and visceral immediacy of your prose. Aren't these some of the same qualities that distinguish the perceptions and reactions of Maeniel and Regeane from those of the majority of "civilized" humans around them?
A: Yes! I try very hard to bring the reader to experience the same things my characters do. To me this is

the essence of the writer's art. But in a larger sense it is possibly the essence of a life well lived. All we get is now! Otherwise the aphorism that "life is something that happens to you while you're making other plans" is an unfortunate truth. "Life is a watch or a vision between a sleep and a sleep." It should be a vision and, as Rita Mae Brown says, "a feast for the senses."

Q: Have you found your metier with werewolves as your sister has done with vampires?
A: For the present.

Q: Any chance of a sisterly collaboration in the future?
A: No. But *Night of the Wolf* will be dedicated to my sister:

> To my beloved sister,
> known to the world as Anne Rice.

> *Out of darkness smile on me faces I may never see.*
> *Out of sleep are reaching still arms*
> *that I may never fill.*

> At every important junction in my career,
> you have always been there for me.

> *Ad memoriam.*

In the deepest place of sorrow, there is no time.

Q: Will there be a third book to this series?
A: Yes, but writing is not a wholly conscious process. It's best not to tamper with it before you begin. I won't know what the third book is about until I finish writing it!

In NIGHT OF THE WOLF, Alice Borchardt moves from the fall of the Roman Empire even deeper into the mists of history—to ancient Druidic Gaul—to tell the enthralling, seductive tale of the uncanny wolf Manael.

As a wolf, he fought for the survival of his pack. As a man, he surrendered to the desires of his own unfamiliar flesh. But in both forms, this hunter would soon become the prey. For even as the conquering forces of Rome swept across the land, the stage was being set for a battle between the shapeshifting Manael and Dryas, the powerful Druid priestess summoned to destroy him . . .

NIGHT OF THE WOLF
by Alice Borchardt

A Del Rey hardcover.
Available in bookstores August 1999.

Join us online to find out more
about the stunning sequel to
THE SILVER WOLF!

NIGHT OF
THE WOLF
by Alice Borchardt

Visit us at

www.randomhouse.com/delrey/

for sample chapters, reviews, a quiz,
and much, much more!